ELEVEN ELEMENTS

BOOK ONE: HEALING WATERS

COMING SOON

ELEVEN ELEMENTS
SERIES OF BOOKS

ALSO, BY ROBBY JOSHI, AIA

Featuring Maxilon 'Max' Renner and his
Team of Time Travelers

ELEVEN ELEMENTS
BOOK TWO: FIRE & FRESH AIR

ELEVEN ELEMENTS
BOOK THREE: SPACESHIP EARTH

ELEVEN ELEMENTS
BOOK FOUR: A MEANINGFUL LIFE

Credits & Dedication

To Joshua DeWine, the true author and guiding light behind this work. Without your vision, this book would never have materialized. We owe you our lives, and our future. *May your soul rest in peace.*

Special thanks to Patricia O'Connell of the American Heartland (Texas) for her meticulous review to ensure it reads tastefully for everyone.

Personal Dedication:
To my parents; to my wife, A;
to my children, T, R, and M;
and to all the kids around the world
- you know who you are. I love you all.
I'm here for you in every timeline.
Be happy, it's the prime directive. *Love. J.*

ELEVEN ELEMENTS

BOOK ONE: HEALING WATERS

– SCIENCE FICTION NOVEL –

A NEW REALITY ARCHITECT
ROBBY JOSHI, AIA

METRO
PUBLISHING CORP

A division of METRO GROUP, Orlando, Florida, USA.
METRO NATIONWIDE CORPORATION – Established 2004

ELEVEN ELEMENTS

BOOK ONE:
HEALING WATERS

CHAPTER -1

11:02 | 11-11-2532 (Twenty-sixth century)
MISSION CONTROL: TAMPA MEGAPOLIS LAUNCHSITE

Most people wake up thinking about one life, their own. Their day, their work, their worries, their hopes. I don't have that luxury. Max thought.

Today, when I opened my eyes, I had to think about billions of people I will never meet and decide whether they'll get to wake up at all, whether they'll be happy, free, and not just surviving, but thriving.

Max rose from his ready-room table and walked to the window. He pressed his hand against the cool skybox glass, suspended ten meters above the bay, and looked down into the cavernous launch hall below. The pods waited below like coiled bullets, gleaming under rows of white high bay lights as teams hustled through final protocols. Time-jumps were nothing new anymore, twenty years back, thirty, fifty, even a few reckless ventures a full century into history.

But this... this was different.

This was a journey five hundred years into the dark.

Maxilon "Max" Renner scanned the list on his wrist panel, eyes moving from team to team, SUV to SUV as he walked down to the launch bay. The usual TTVs (Time Transport Vessels) were now redesigned and made to look like automobiles specifically those known as SUVs.

The launch center looked like a massive airplane hangar, except by the twenty-sixth century, airplanes were mostly obsolete. Intercity travel was handled by high-speed maglev tube rails or hyper-rail transports. Cross-regional trips relied on hovercrafts gliding over water on cushions of air.

Each vehicle stood ready, disguised as ordinary twenty-first--century Sport Utility Vehicles but reengineered for something far more extreme. The metal alloy body was reinforced with organic and inorganic nanoparticles, and equipped with a stealth mesh system to change in color or shapeshift on a simple command.

The color tone for the initial time transit Felza ET1 TTVs were all satin pearl white finish with chrome delete mode.

Max glanced at his log one more time as a final check:

SUV 1 – Max's unit. Crew1:
- o Commander Maxion "Max" Renner – mission lead,
  seasoned jumper, ex-military.
- o Bintang "Binny" Sudarto – navigation and recon.
- o Danny "Dan" Martin – systems and comms.
- o Minami "Mina" Hayashi – temporal sync specialist.
- o Kasandra "Kas" Ayodele – field medic and contingency planner.

SUV 2 – Crew2:
- o Captain Jian Cheng – team lead, tactical and entry ops.
- o Lukas "Luke" Adler – logistics & historical data analyst.
- o Prisha Jiwan – survival expert and language ops.
- o Isam Yosef – backup engineer and gear tech.
- o Katrina Patilova – chrono-anthropologist, cultural embed.

SUV 3 – Crew3:
- o Roberto Amarial – team lead engineer, veteran jumper.
- o Sherine Elliot – Political analyst & languages backup
- o Jackir Husen – software engineer and crowd dynamics.
- o Meirah Hong – cultural infiltration lead.
- o Calixto "Cal" Perry – ex-special forces, military ops.

Inside the time travel hangar, the air thrummed with quiet power. The ceiling stretched twenty-five meters above the floor, reinforced with graphene ribs and lined with pulse-dampening panels. Overhead lights ran in precise grids, casting a sterile glow across the polished, dark-tiled deck.

Everything was organized for speed and control, no clutter, no wasted movement. Rows of launch pods stood ready, each locked into a circular platform recessed into the floor. The pods looked like armored embryos: matte-black hulls, minimal seams, transparent canopy domes shielded by reactive glass. Every surface was engineered for function, radiation shielding, time-shell insulation, dimensional sync arrays.

Technicians moved with purpose along elevated walkways, checking readouts from their wrist consoles. Each pod was tuned to a specific jump, down to the millisecond.

Once prepped, the pods would lower into the deck and lock into the chrono-platform rings, stabilized by inertial dampeners and spatial anchors. Then the field would ignite: a low hum, a shimmer, and the vehicle would vanish in a calibrated blink, gone to another century entirely.

Above each pod, the robotic arms finished their final scans. Today's time-jump was a very special event monitored by the Generals and Admirals of the Federation. The SUVs' digital twins flickered into transmission buffers, already tethered to the time-locked processors in the control room. The countdown ticked under two minutes.

Techs moved between platforms, eyes on digital pads, calling out final confirmations. Everything was synced. Quiet.

"All teams," Max said over comms, "report green or call it now."

One by one, voices snapped back, affirmative, steady.

Max climbed into SUV1's driver seat. The cabin lit up as the processor came online.

In the glass control booth above, Burke, the principal officer, gruff, sharp-eyed, always two coffees deep, stood and hit the intercom.

"Okay, jumpers, you know the drill. Each SUV launches ten minutes apart. SUV1 goes first. In exactly ten minutes apart, SUV2 follows, then SUV3. We will track and monitor all data transitions and gauge the travel loop all the way to your safe arrival.

"All team member must wear safety belts through, and state their full personal data exactly as recorded prior to this jump event to confirm a complete transfer and sync."

Burke's voice droned on over the speakers, reciting protocol after protocol in the flat, practiced cadence of standard safety briefings: what to do in an emergency, where to go, what to do if things go awry.

"Countdown begins. Stay in the security shields of your vehicles for life support systems should an emergency arise. And remember, think safety first. Clear?"

"Clear!" came the unified reply.

Max gave a short nod, peering through the windshield of SUV1. His team sat in their respective positions with quiet focus. They didn't need reminders. Between them, they'd logged over five hundred and fifty missions, every one of them with a minimum of a hundred jumps. Veterans, all of them.

The protocols of Time Travel weren't just memorized; they were muscle memory now.

The only real wildcard this time?

The ride.

This was the first mission using the disguised TTVs. And it wasn't a short hop either. They were about to leap back over five centuries, deeper than they'd ever gone.

Max reached for the vehicle's main control panel, an archaic touchscreen panel, his mind running through the risks.

The last time the regiment operated mechanical transport in the field had been during covert surveillance in uBots-controlled war zones, dangerous, illegal territory. This leap, though? It wasn't just a breach of time. It was a step into uncharted history.

Max paused for a breath. In ten minutes, they'd be ghosts in a world that hadn't seen stealth technologies, bio-organic uBots, or any trace of their future.

A first for everything.

He let his fingers trace the leathery feel of the historic vehicle's steering wheel. Then he pressed the brake pedal and shifted the uncanny machine into drive.

The countdown hit T-minus 9:42.

Max and the four time-jumpers were all seated comfortably in SUV1. Doors sealed with a soft hiss. They buckled in, then pulled on their VRV headgear: sleek, padded visors pulsing with green blinking lights, syncing to the jump system.

Max let his fingers curl around the wheel. He glanced back. Binny, Dan, Mina, and Kas were strapped in, silent, eyes fixed forward. No one spoke, but the tension was loud. All time-jumpers carried their sleek backpacks. They were wearing jeans and tennis shoes and attire of the twenty-first century, like ordinary tourists. Looking ready for a vacation but really not.

Max tapped his VRV headset. "SUV1 is locked and ready, Burke."

Above, Burke's voice cut through the static in their ears. "Copy that. Spin-up initiated. Countdown begins now."

In a minute, they'd be somewhere else. Some *when* else.

The past wasn't waiting. It never did.

The SUV began to rotate. Slowly at first. Then faster.

Max felt the first pull in his gut.

"Ten ... nine ... eight ..."

The cabin vibrated. The platform blurred.

"Seven ... six ... five ..."

The blinking lights synced with the countdown, faster now.

"Four ... three ... two ..."

Max braced, jaw tight, hands steady.

"One. Launch!"

And then, white light swallowed the windshield. A blinding flash. The car jolted, not forward, not back, just *out*.

Time ripped open. The car vanished.

Max opened his eyes.

Outside the windshield: a quiet, two-lane asphalt highway winding between wide fields dotted with grazing cattle. The sky was clear. No drones. No noise. Just the hum of insects and the faint echo of wind across the grass.

He winced. The headache hit him behind the eyes, standard after a time jump this far back.

He turned quickly to check the others. All four passengers were intact, seated, and slowly waking, groggy, but fully materialized.

"Arrival protocols," Max said, voice low but firm.

He pushed open the driver's door and stepped out onto the sun-warmed road. The air smelled different. Real. Less filtered.

He stood in front of the SUV and began the protocol out loud.

"Max Renner, Commander, twenty-seventh Task Force Unit, Sole time-travel regiment of the twenty-sixth century. My height is one point eight five meters and I weigh eighty-two kilograms. My eyes are blue-gray in color and my hair is salt-and-pepper gray. My date of birth is May second in the year twenty-four hundred and ninety-four. I am thirty-eight years old, living at my residence in a custom pod parked in the High-Park five hundred and seventy-seven unit of the Federation Megapolis System. My domestic partner is Annie with whom I am in a committed relationship."

He exhaled sharply. That final detail always hit harder than he expected. His PCOM (Personal Communication Device) integrated in his body suit and attached to his forearm beeped upon hearing the protocol required information to confirm.

"Whew," he muttered. "Welcome to the twenty-first Century"

Behind him, doors clicked open as the rest of the team began stepping out, repeating their own arrival data one by one.

The world they'd entered was silent. Ordinary. Peaceful.

It seemed too peaceful.

Max took a deep breath and glanced at his wristband. Vitals: stable. No red flags.

The screen blinked:

11:11 | 11-11-2025 (Twenty-first century)
LOCATION: STATE OF FLORIDA HIGHWAY 27

He stared at it for a second longer than he meant to. That number again. 11:11.

He'd seen it too many times across missions, too exact, too repeated. A pattern he hadn't cracked yet. Maybe it was nothing. Maybe it wasn't.

Everything seems fine, he told himself. But the thought didn't settle.

Behind him, the rest of the team was climbing out, one by one, mumbling through their self-affirmations, checking vitals, flexing limbs. The haze of time lag still clung to their bodies.

Seven to ten minutes, that's how long it took to sync to a new time zone. That's why the SUVs launched ten minutes apart. Buffer space. No overlap. No chaos.

Bintang cracked open a supply bin and passed around bottled water. Everyone took one. No one spoke much yet.

Max wiped his forehead. It was hot. Thicker air than he expected for mid-November. The kind of heat that clung to your skin and made your shirt stick.

Dan glanced up. "Is it supposed to be this warm?"

"Climate patterns were already breaking by the 2020s," Mina said, voice still raspy. "Not unheard of."

Kasandra stretched her arms and rolled her neck. "I don't care what year it is, I hate humidity."

Max didn't respond. He was still looking at his wristband. 11:12 now. But that 11:11 was still burned into the back of his mind.

Something about it felt like a mark.

Bintang wiped the sweat from his brow. "Yep. This has to be Florida. Anywhere else in the country, November's freezing."

Max grunted. The body suit clung to him like plastic wrap. He'd give anything to be farther north right now. Cooler air. Less sweat.

Then, movement.

There was a big white flash as SUV2 arrived. All five team members were in there, dazed, each person stating their arrival data and completing the protocol.

All seemed to be going well. Now the wait for SUV3 to show up.

Minami had wandered into the middle of the road, mid-stretch, eyes closed, arms overhead.

Max's stomach dropped. A low rumble built behind him, growing fast.

"Minami, step back!" he yelled.

She jumped out of the way just as a sixteen-wheeler roared past, horn blaring, the rush of wind nearly knocking her sideways.

Max watched the truck disappear down the road, heart pounding.

That was close. Too close.

Max shouted, "Stay out of that lane! Trucks are coming, move to the shoulder!"

Then a thought struck Max.

Why are there trucks passing by? We were supposed to arrive on an abandoned country road, no traffic at all. What's going on?

Everyone shifted quickly to the edge of the road. The wide gravel strip, labeled in old highway plans as the emergency lane, gave them just enough space to regroup safely. Max had studied this route during pre-mission briefings and was relieved the two SUVs had landed just off the road, not in the path of oncoming traffic.

From here, it was a straight shot to their first checkpoint: Charriott's Inn & Suites, only a few miles out.

Max raised a hand with the all-clear sign. The other team members echoed the gesture. So far, everything was under control.

Then, a ripple of white light flashed behind them.

SUV3 arrived.

Max turned, expecting to see five team members exiting.

But the cabin was empty.

He frowned.

Seconds passed. Then, Roberto Amarial flickered into existence in the driver's seat, materializing mid-breath.

Only, he wasn't breathing.

His eyes were locked wide open, staring straight ahead. No movement. No response.

Max's voice cut sharp through the comms. "Everyone, back in your vehicles. Now!"

The teams didn't question it. Doors slammed shut all around him. Max climbed back into SUV1, hit the dashboard interface, and brought up the control room feed.

"Burke, we've got a problem with SUV3," Max said. "Amarial is here, but unresponsive. The rest of the passengers didn't make it. They're just, gone."

Burke's face appeared on the screen, frowning beneath heavy brows. His voice was calm, but grim.

"Copy that. Launch appears successful... but transmittance isn't. We're getting a message from EVE's cloud systems; she's detecting an overload spike in the twenty-first-century data centers."

Max narrowed his eyes. "Overload?"

Burke nodded. "Their infrastructure couldn't handle the bio-signal packet load. Data made it through, but the conversion into organic form failed. We've got fragmented code, no full materialization."

Max looked back at Roberto, still frozen behind the wheel like a statue.

"We've got a ghost," Dan, sitting in the passenger seat muttered. "And four missing lives."

"Darn it...... Burke," Max snapped. "Can you override and complete the process?"

Burke's voice came back, tense. "Not sure. Transmission is unstable. Data isn't cooperating. We're still isolating the fault."

Max slammed his fist against the steering wheel. "Reroute the damn data. Shift it to other data centers, just do something …anything. I'm not losing people, you understand?"

Burke didn't argue. "Understood. We're already redirecting to alternate centers. Higher capacity. Cleaner sync."

Max threw open the door and ran with his team back to SUV3.

Then it started again.

Inside the cabin, Jackir Husen began to flicker into view in the front passenger seat. But he wasn't whole.

His head appeared severed on a diagonal, as if sliced by a precise, burning blade. One eye blinked slowly, the other one gone. From the top of his skull to his left ear was missing. In its place: open brain, raw and wet, twitching with every breath.

He was somehow still alive.

He looked around, confused, lips trembling, unable to speak. His single eye met theirs through the windshield. He saw them. And they saw him. Just the half of him.

Gasps echoed behind Max. The team stood frozen, watching this nightmare unfold.

Then, movement from the driver's seat.

Roberto Amarial, still hunched over, began panting, fast and shallow, his chest rising with the erratic rhythm of cardiac arrest. His skin turned pale, eyes fluttering.

He reached for the door, hand barely steady enough to grip the latch. Somehow, he yanked it open.

His torso fell out.

Not all of him, just the top half. Everything from the waist down was gone. Just not there.

The upper half of Roberto hit the pavement hard, arms twitching, spine dangling from where his lower body should've been. Blood didn't pour, it trickled, like his body still wasn't fully there. Part of his intestines remained on the driver's seat and the rest of them dangled to where his torso lay on the road.

The others stepped back instinctively.

Shock. Horror. Silence.

Max stood still, his jaw clenched so tight it hurt.

This wasn't a glitch; it was a full-system failure unlike anything seen before.

And people were paying for it with their precious lives.

Moments later, Meirah Hong materialized. She went into immediate shock upon seeing Jackir with his half-severed head.

From her seat behind Roberto on the passenger side, she flung the door open in a panic, only to be confronted by the gruesome sight of Roberto's mangled body, dangling from the front seat onto the pavement.

She screamed and bolted away from the trio of parked vehicles. Bintang and Minami gave chase.

Several yards ahead, Hong suddenly stopped in the middle of the road. Her eyes widened as she tilted her head back and clutched it with both hands.

Max grew anxious. Any moment now, a car or truck could speed around the curve and run her over.

Just as he and the others reached her, Hong's head began to swell grotesquely, her face and eyes distorting. Then, without warning, her head exploded.

Fragments of bone, brain tissue, skin, eyeballs, and blood sprayed in all directions, splattering the officers who could do nothing but watch in horror.

Her headless body crumpled onto the asphalt, her hands still clawing the air trying to hold on to dear life.

Max stood paralyzed, unable to process the horror he had just witnessed. Everyone else froze too, numbed by the gruesome sight.

Seconds later, Katrina sprinted toward the body carrying a containment bag. She swiftly placed it over what remained of Hong's headless body, dragging her from the road and rolling her remains into the bag before zipping it shut.

Meanwhile, Roberto's limp body was still dangling grotesquely, his head brushing the ground outside the vehicle.

Katrina turned and shouted, "Bintang, Danny, grab the other bags! Let's get him zipped up before someone drives by and sees all this. Jian can you check in on Jakir.!"

Max saw Bitang and Luke carry one of the body bags while Kasandra and Prisha carried the other towards the back of TTV3.

Meanwhile, Daniel kept watch at the edge of the site, scanning for incoming traffic. Thankfully, the road had remained clear since the horrific incident. But that calm was broken when Daniel let out a sharp whistle, warning Kasandra and Prisha to clear the lane, a truck was approaching.

The team scrambled off the road just in time. A massive sixteen-wheeler thundered past, horn blaring as it barreled by the two large pools of blood, its tires missing them by only a few inches. The truck's sheer velocity sent a violent gust of wind in its wake. The force rattled everyone, shaking loose the last remnants of paralysis from the group.

Max, though the team's commander, was absorbed in a live feed with the Control Room.

The officer on the screen reported, "Sir, the launch of TTV3 and its officer is confirmed. However, we only show three officers who materialized at the original destination. The remaining two have either been redirected to alternate data centers or have not materialized at all. We have no confirmation on their whereabouts.

"I suggest securing the team and relocating immediately. If the two remaining officers don't arrive within ten minutes, the transfer window will close."

Max clenched his jaw, torn between grief, confusion, and urgency. Time was running out.

Jian Cheng opened the door next to Jackir and reached out to check for a pulse. There was none. He looked up solemnly and gave Max a nod, confirming the inevitable: Jackir was gone.

Max froze, overwhelmed by the magnitude of the situation. This mission had gone awry from the very beginning. Now, with three officers confirmed dead and two others still unaccounted for, possibly lost or facing the same horrific fate, the crushing sense of failure bore down on him as he assisted in loading the bodies into TTV1 and TTV2, his hands trembled uncontrollably.

They moved to inspect TTV3. Popping open the hoods at both ends, they first examined the front compartment, a newly designed housing for a wind-turbine-based energy generator. It seemed like most of it had materialized.

Max hurried to the rear section, cautiously opening it to check the nuclear power unit. Fortunately, the core appeared intact.

Several other components, however, were either missing or caught in mid-phase materialization.

Max's urgency spiked. He quickly assessed the nuclear generator's readouts. The containment field showed stable readings. The safety protocol was functioning correctly, as designed: the containment shell transmits before the reactor core and fuel cells. For now, it was secure.

His PCOM was giving him 'ALL SAFE' readings all this while.

Still, Max knew that what had happened would stain his record. He might go down in history as the first commander to lose three officers in such a violent and grotesque fashion. A cold dread crept over him.

In that moment of despair, Max's thoughts drifted away from the mission. He longed for the safety and peace of his home at High-Park 577. For the first time in the midst of an active mission, he felt a deep yearning to be at home.

A quiet wish emerged in his mind, to erase everything that had just transpired, to treat it as nothing more than a failed simulation. A trial. Something that could be restarted, rewritten, and forgotten.

But this was real. And it was far from over.

He walked back to TTV1 and questioned the control room officer. "Any sign of the other two officers, Rick? Have you figured out what caused this to happen? There must be a trigger point for such a misstep in my mission.

"And why are we in the middle of a busy highway? We were supposed to arrive on an abandoned secluded side street where there's no traffic. What the frack is going on?"

Captain Ricardo Perez, the control room officer, responded, "Sir, there has been a shift in polar coordinates as well as the general tilt of the earth since our last tracking of the twenty-first century.

"It's like historical data is rewriting itself with the anomaly in our timeline. Everything's becoming a shifting target. The coordinates we planned did not synchronize, and that is how you ended up three degrees off the arrival spot and in the middle of the wrong road."

Onscreen, Rick Perez paused to look up at streaming data across his panel of monitors, "As for the mishap with TTV3, what technicians are saying is that the data center overloaded. The misstep happened toward the end of TTV2's transmission.

"We're still investigating the cause, especially since both TTV1 and TTV2 were transmitted flawlessly up to that point.

"Not that it's any consolation, but this is the first time such an incident has occurred. We are continuing the search for the other two officers, Major Sherine Elliot and Sergeant Calixto Perry. We will keep you..."

Just then, Captain Perez's transmission cut out. The screen flickered, then resolved into the face of a high-ranking general.

Max glanced at the lower corner of the display as it flashed the name: *Ambassador General Nheel Dyson.* Dyson was flanked by several other uniformed officials, all senior, all watching.

Max straightened at once.

"Max, I got the news that something went wrong during transmission. I am sorry to hear that, and for the loss of three highly skilled officers." General Dyson conveyed remorsefully. "We are still looking for the two that are missing. We are investigating on our end. But I need you to review every log and data point that could explain the cause of this misstep.

"I know you'll take all necessary actions to ensure the remains of our officers are handled according to protocol."

Dyson paused briefly, letting his words sink in before continuing, "Let me assure you, this mishap will not be held against you. It occurred before the transmission sequence was completed, which places it outside your operational control. I will recommend to the commission that this incident not be recorded as a failure on your part."

General Dyson's voice took on a more urgent, commanding tone. "Your focus now must be on the mission. You know how critical this task is, and how vital it is that you return safely. You and your team will have the honor of being the first humans to travel over five hundred years into the past. That achievement alone is historic."

He inched closer to the screen. "Consider today a tragic but inevitable cost, casualties in a war. Remember what we lost in the battles with the uBots. We paid a price then, and we pay again now.

"I know you strive for perfection and find it hard to accept any blemish on your record. But I ask you to summon your strength, to look forward, not backward, and to complete what you've started."

A soft finality entered his tone. "I order you to finish this mission and return safely to your dear wife. Good luck, Max."

Max gave a somber reply reading the General's name as it appeared on the screen, "Yes General Dyson. We will take care of the matter."

And with that, General Dyson disappeared from the screen. The connection ended.

Max initially had difficulty recognizing the General, but as soon as he heard General Dyson's moving words and saw his name flash on the screen, he had recognized him. Only after the feed went black did Max realize how wrong that delay had felt.

Why hadn't he known the Ambassador General instantly?

There was a blur where memories should have been. Time-jump jet lag, he told himself. *It'll all fall into place soon.*

And now he couldn't shake the unsettling thought: how was the Ambassador General able to speak to the very doubts and insecurities festering in Max's mind, despite being hundreds of years away in the future?

It puzzled Max deeply. Was it Dyson's uncanny psychological insight, or a masterful method of persuasion developed through decades of leadership? Perhaps it was both.

Regardless, it was no mystery why Dyson had ascended to preside over the entire Federation of Nations' Council. The man had the ability to compel action, to instill both confidence and duty in those under his command.

And for Max, still the acting commander on this mission, there was no option but to comply and move forward with resolve.

But just as he gathered himself to do so, another obstacle emerged.

Max was struck by a mental void: he couldn't remember the official protocol for performing the last rites of fallen officers.

The realization sent a ripple of embarrassment and unease through him. He thought hard, trying to recall any training or reference materials on the matter, but nothing surfaced. It was as though crucial details had been wiped from his memory.

The mental fog had never been this extreme before.

Panic threatened to rise. He knew such protocols existed. They must have been taught during officer training, possibly even included in briefing modules. Why couldn't he remember?

Max knew that he was physically present, fully embodied in the twenty-first century, yet he could not shake the unsettling sense that not all of him was truly here. It felt as though fragments of his mind had failed to make the jump, like the missing body parts of his crew.

His once razor-sharp intellect now felt dulled, with gaps where vital pieces of memory should have been. He wondered if parts of his consciousness had been left behind, scattered across time, leaving him with only patches of clarity amidst a fog of uncertainty.

In a rush, Max began flipping through the mission manual, scanning frantically for any section that could guide him. He searched for directives on proper containment, ceremonial procedures, or transmission logs for deceased personnel. Each line of text he read seemed both familiar and foreign, a fog had settled in over his memory.

He paused for a moment, breathing deeply. This mission had already stretched the limits of his psychological endurance. Now, forgetting something as critical and honorable as the last rites brought a burden, he wasn't ready to carry.

Max winced as a sharp pain stabbed through his head. He pressed his fingers to his temples, breathing through the pulse of it.

Something was wrong.

Not physically. Not with the mission. With him.

The fog was still there, but now it had a shape. A missing shape.

He remembered saying he had a domestic partner. Annie. The name came easily. The feeling, too, settling deep in his chest, a warmth, a sense of *belonging*.

But her face? Gone. No image. No voice. No memories of shared moments. Not even the way she laughed or held his hand.

It was blank.

He reached further back, his youth, his time at the academy, training drills, tactical lectures, even his first briefing with General Dyson. It all came in fragments. Not whole scenes, just flashes. Names, vague places, the sensation of having been there, but not the memory itself.

This isn't forgetting, he thought. *It's selective recall. Like my mind is choosing what I'm allowed to access.*

The most immediate, mission-critical memories were intact. Protocols. Language. Team structure. Combat readiness.

But everything else, everything *personal*, was blurred out. Like someone had used a damp cloth to scrub clean the canvas of his life.

He closed his eyes. Tried to summon a scent. A smile. A sound.

Nothing.

He'd jumped over five hundred years back in time. But for what, exactly? The details were hazy, floating just out of reach.

This wasn't normal memory loss. Max could feel it.

It was too precise.

As if something, or *someone*, had curated what he was allowed to remember. He was still functional. Still mission-ready.

But not whole.

And for the first time since the mission began, Max felt it deep in his chest,

He wasn't himself.

Not fully. Not yet.

CHAPTER ₂2

11:41 | 11-11-2025 (Twenty-first century)
LOCATION: STATE OF FLORIDA HIGHWAY 27

Max had watched Katrina step into the chaos with remarkable composure. He observed that, while rest of the team was still dazed from the effects of time travel, she moved with clarity and urgency.

Max was impressed by her strength, presence of mind, and the tenacity she displayed under duress.

He felt a moment of reassurance, glad that he had personally selected Katrina to be part of his elite team for this mission.

A stray thought crossed his mind: had he chosen another candidate, the response in this critical moment might have been drastically different.

As the rest of the unit fell into action, Max observed Kasandra assisting Prisha with the grim task of cleaning the road of scattered remains, a necessary step to prevent biological contamination and avoid detection. Their discipline and coordination calmed Max's nerves, if only slightly.

At the same time, Isam was stationed at TTV3. After spraying foam to sanitize the vehicle, he began struggling to get it operational. It refused to start. Frustrated but focused, he moved between the front and rear compartments, checking systems and connections, searching for any way to bring it back online.

Max took it all in. Despite the trauma, the mission team was pulling together, each member acting on instinct, training, and resolve. And in that quiet observation, Max began mustering strength to refocus his command.

Max called out to the team, asking everyone to line up and report their current statuses. He needed to revise their action plan, one that included performing the last rites for the three deceased officers and restarting the original program to proceed with the mission.

Ten officers now remained in active duty.

Captain Jian Cheng stepped forward and began, "Max, we have lost three officers. And two are missing or did not materialize within ten minutes of TTV3 having emerged through the Transmission portal."

As he listened, Max recalled the cultural adjustment protocols. From this point forward, all team members were instructed to operate on a first-name basis to align with twenty-first-century norms. No "Sir," no formal ranks, only names.

Next, Lieutenant Prisha Jiwan reported. "Max, we have cleared the bodies and the remains. However, there are faint stains of body fluid and associated contamination left at the arrival site. The asphalt surface is porous, laced with minute cracks and crevices from years of weathering.

"I suggest we get three or four large five-liter water bottles and some strong chlorine from a food supply store, what they call... Oh yeah, grocery stores, so we can clean this area thoroughly. We will also need to flush down water over the cremation site.

"I prefer not to use our own water reserves. We need to protect ourselves and avoid early exposure to the local bacteria and parasites in this century. Our immune systems aren't adapted yet. Gradual exposure will help us develop antibodies and avoid illness. The locals call it the stomach flu."

Max nodded and turned to Lieutenant Kasandra Ayodele, who picked up where Prisha left off. "Max, Prisha is right. But we also need to ensure the cleanup is absolutely thorough. If we leave any trace behind and local law enforcement discovers the site, they could launch a technical investigation. Even though their forensics are primitive by our standards, some of their methods are surprisingly effective. It could endanger the entire mission."

Max listened intently, knowing their survival depended not just on technology, but on vigilance, precision, and trust in each other. Understanding and listening to every word said was the foundation of their team spirit. Following collective knowledge and intelligence that rose from years of experience was critical for every mission's success.

Lieutenant Isam Yusef stepped forward without hesitation. "Max, the TTV3 isn't starting. Either it's nonfunctional or failed during materialization. I suspect a defect in the process. We need to salvage all usable tech from the unit, sorry, I mean the SUV, if we plan to dispose of it. I have spray cleaned and sanitized the seats and the compartment as best as I could."

He paused, correcting himself again. "The critical parts to extract are the nuclear generator and wind turbine modules, components from future models of this same brand that haven't even been invented yet. We can't leave those behind."

Luke added, "I suggest we push the SUV3 closer to SUV2 and tow it using one of our ropes. We'll bring it to the hotel first, keep it parked for a few days while we figure out the next step, maybe find a private garage to strip the tech. Then we can scrap the shell."

Max's stomach tightened. This wasn't what they'd planned.

He knew the hard truth: a deep time jump like this, when it failed catastrophically, was irreversible. System corruption at this scale meant the time-log engines were likely fried. Rebuilding those systems could take weeks, maybe even months, and that's if they had the right tech, which they didn't. Not here.

They couldn't send the bodies back. Not the TTV unit either. Not any major metal components. Maybe a few small, non-organic items could be discreetly returned, but even then, the quality of the transpose would be compromised. Flawed, unpredictable. Risky.

And yet, this SUV hadn't vanished as per emergency protocol. Instead of dissolving cleanly into the quantum mesh of the mainframe, it had materialized, partially shifted into the fabric of twenty-first-century reality.

The idea of negotiating with a garage mechanic while hiding future tech made his skin crawl. Exposure was a real threat.

Then Lieutenant Captain Katrina Patilova took command.

"There are three bodies in the car. We follow protocol. Last rites must happen immediately. We can't risk law enforcement, 'cops,' as locals call them, finding us with body bags."

She glanced around with urgency.

"We drive out now. Find a remote road, wooded. We'll use the self-incinerating body bags and deploy a quick-install dome tent to contain the smoke. Discreet, fast, controlled. No more discussions. We need to move now."

Max understood instantly: Katrina had reviewed the logs, followed protocol, and issued a clear directive. That was the order.

He slipped into a tone that matched his twenty-first-century outfit, jeans, T-shirt, and all.

"Alright, you heard Katrina. Let's move. I'll take TTV1, towing TTV3. Luke, you're driving TTV2 to get the water and some chlorine for cleanup of any bodily fluids and for pouring over cremation grounds. Get the towing rope secured."

He turned to the rest of the team. "We head to a wooded area nearby. Once there, we cremate the bodies under the dome tent. Let's run the infra-red scanner to see we are clear. No trace left behind."

The team moved in sync, quick, quiet, efficient.

Kasandra sprinted to the bloodstains, pulling out a small canister. She sprayed the area with a chemical compound that neutralized organic residue, masking both stain and scent, rendering it nearly undetectable.

Bintang and Daniel pushed TTV3 forward, hauling it into position. They fastened the tow rope to TTV1. Isam climbed into the dead vehicle's driver's seat to guide its movement while two of his team sat in the backseat. Luke took the wheel of TTV2 and Prisha hopped in the front passenger seat.

Luke tapped **Color** on the touchscreen panel. A palette appeared; he selected RED. Within seconds, the vehicle shifted to a deep cherry hue.

He pulled out onto the road with Prisha beside him in TTV2, ahead of the other two TTVs to fetch water and chlorine.

Max pressed the "Scan Clear" button. A marker-shaped, pen-like scanner rose from inside the rooftop antenna. A dome of red light blossomed from its tip, expanding outward to engulf the area covering over one hundred meters and sweeping across every surface within seconds. The display flashed green: "ALL CLEAR."

Max tapped **Color** on the touchscreen panel. A palette appeared; he selected BLACK. In a few seconds, the vehicle shifted to iridescent black color.

Within moments, the convoy of the two TTVs pulled away, headed south on Highway 27, tires kicking up dust as they turned onto a remote dirt road.

No one in his SUV spoke. They all knew the drill. Every move had a purpose. Time was tight, and exposure was fatal.

Max felt it again, something wasn't right.

He had never encountered memory loss before.

Maybe it's all still in there, he thought. *Maybe the neurons just haven't reconnected properly after the jump.*

Then it hit him, faint at first, then sharper. He remembered something Sergeant Miller had said during training at the Control Center just yesterday:

"There are side-effects with long-range time displacement. Some officers in early trials experienced fragmented long-term memory, missing pieces. But most recovered within days. The neurons simply needed time. Stay on task. Use your mnemonic link protocols and VRV headset to rebuild memory. PCOM app-based memory recall exercises will also help. You'll stabilize."

Max clung to that memory as if it were a lifeline. He was glad he remembered how to operate the PCOM that flipped up like a clear sheet of glass on top of his forearm.

He could read, communicate, and watch training instructions, including several apps with special protocols for time travelers who had lost memory, suffered amnesia, or forgotten the purpose of their mission.

It explained the fog he was feeling, the subtle disconnection, the sense of not being fully *present* like he always was on missions.

It wasn't a complete failure, just something that needed recovery.

He just had to stay focused. Keep moving. Run the exercises. Let the neurons re-fire. He would come back online, completely.

But not yet. Not here.

There were bodies to burn. Evidence to erase. A timeline to outrun.

He couldn't let Command know. If they sensed he was compromised, Jian would be handed the team. Max wouldn't get a second chance.

He shook off the haze. Eyes scanning the roadside, he spotted a narrow driveway cutting into the woods.

He flicked on the turn signal and slowed down, guiding TTV1 off the main road. The trailing TTV3 followed in tow.

They must have driven half a mile through a dense patch of trees before emerging into a small clearing. The driveway became a dirt road leading to the center of the clearing.

Max brought the vehicle to a stop and pressed the "Scan Clear" button again with a different setting. The scanner rose from inside the rooftop antenna and a dome of red light blossomed from its tip, expanding outward to engulf the area covering over three hundred meters and sweeping across every surface within seconds. The display flashed green: "ALL CLEAR." This time the scan was to detect any human presence.

He stepped out and made one last visual sweep of the surroundings.

No houses. No trails. No motion. Just trees.

A perfect circle of stillness surrounded them.

If he couldn't see anyone, that meant no one could see them either. High above, a lone bald eagle circled in the sky, silent, watchful.

He nodded once. Clear.

Isam quickly detached the tow line from TTV3, now parked at the edge of the clearing. TTV3 was unhitched to facilitate removal of body bags, tent and supplies for the last rites from both the vehicles. His passengers walked out to help the others.

With the dead vehicle secured, Isam stayed behind, posted at the tree line, watching the road. Eyes scanning. Body still. Ready to signal if anyone approached.

Minami moved quickly. She retrieved the container holding the dome tent, placed it at the center of the clearing, and tapped the activation panel. Then she stepped back.

Within seconds, the top of the container split open. A mechanism whirred softly. Panels unrolled outward like petals. In moments, a tensile structure stood upright, a six-meter-wide, three-meter-tall dome resembling a giant umbrella. It had an arched flap that hung as a doorway.

Two members of the team carried each of the body bags inside, six hands, three silent tasks. Max followed them into the tent, his expression unreadable.

All of his team, or what remained, had now assembled in the tent.

Without a word, they picked up shovels and carefully peeled away the top layer of grass. Then they dug, slowly, deliberately, until the pit reached a meter and a half deep, two meters long.

The operation moved like clockwork, each step quiet and precise, laced with tension over what lay ahead.

Max and six other officers, Katrina, Daniel, Bintang, Minami, Kasandra, and Jian, stood in silence over the fallen. They had laid the bodies in a row, still in bags, and stood at attention. The air was still.

Max stepped forward. "Today, we lost three brave soldiers of the Time Travelers Regiment. Highly ranked. Battle-tested. Committed to the mission until the end." His voice was steady but heavy. "We pledge to carry the burden they've laid down and complete the mission they began. And if this incident proves to be an act of intent, we will find those who wrought it and deliver justice for our fallen."

He raised his hand in a sharp salute, then nodded.

The others followed, saluting in unison.

Four of them carried the body bags and gently lowered them in, stacking them with care. Katrina stepped forward, pulled out a micro-lighter, and crouched near one end.

The body bags were engineered for rapid incineration, self-collapsing, high-efficiency burn units that compressed smoke and flame inward, leaving behind no trace of organic material. Flesh, bone, and fabric reduced to ash in under ten minutes. Not even DNA would survive.

The domed tent over the burial site masked heat signatures and contained their activities from any prowling eyes, such as those of drones or even satellites.

To anyone looking at it from outside, it was just a picnic tent, quiet and still.

When the incineration was complete, the seven officers wordlessly took up their shovels and began returning the earth to the pit. Ash was buried beneath soil. The top layer of grass was carefully repositioned.

To finish, they formed a low berm, then stepped onto it in slow, synchronized stomps, firm but rhythmic, pressing the soil flat as if performing a silent dance ritual.

When they were done, the burial site looked nearly untouched. Just a soft rise in the grass, barely noticeable, holding the solemn memory of the fallen and undiminished flame.

A sacrifice of life that can never be forgotten.

As soon as everyone had stepped outside, Minami reached for a button on the container fixed to the dome's side. The tent began to collapse in on itself, silently folding into a compact roll.

In seconds, it was back inside the container, sealed and ready for stowage.

Max moved among the officers, shaking hands. A couple embraced, silent, brief, seeking comfort in the hollow space left by the dead. Smiles and laughter of their fallen colleagues still fresh in their minds.

* * * * * *

11:44 am | 11-11-2025 (Twenty-first century)
LOCATION: SOMEWHERE IN STATE OF FLORIDA

Lieutenant Mark Malvin of the Florida State Highway Patrol was heading back to the station after lunch on what had been a slow, uneventful November the 11th. This late morning sun cut low across the windshield. His quiet moments were broken by the harsh rasp of the radio.

It was Chuck Spooner, neighbor, truck driver by day, and self-declared Bingo Master by night. His voice came through in that familiar southern drawl.

"Hey Mark, I just passed three white Felzas, SUVs, all lined up on the shoulder. Something's goin' on. Couple ladies and guys were carryin' what looked like *body bags*. And I swear, I saw some dude's head droopin' out the driver's side. Looked bad. Accident maybe. Or worse."

Mark sat up straighter. "Where exactly are they, Chuck?"

"I'm headin' northbound on Highway 27. They're goin' southbound. I just passed Showcase of Citrus about a mile back. They're pulled off the shoulder, just past Lake Louisa, I think."

"You sure about what you saw?"

Chuck didn't hesitate. "One hundred percent. Looked wrong, Mark. Way off. If you send one of your swanky troopers now, you might catch 'em red-handed."

Mark reached for his dash console. "I'm on it. Thanks, Chuck. You might just earn yourself a free drink at bingo tonight."

Chuck chuckled. "You know I don't play for free, Lieutenant. I play for glory."

The line went dead.

Mark's hand hovered over the radio. Three white EVs, those spunky looking Felzas, possible body bags, remote location. It didn't add up, but it definitely sounded like trouble.

He keyed the mic. "Dispatch, this is Lieutenant Malvin. I need a unit headed southbound on Highway 27, just past Lake Louisa. Possible suspicious activity involving three white Felza SUVs. Be advised, potential bodies involved. Proceed with caution. I'm en route as well."

He flipped on the sirens and pulled into traffic. Lunch was officially over.

As soon as the call ended, Malvin picked up his patrol radio.

"Unit check, William, Tommie, or Matthew, do any of you copy?"

The reply came quick. "Matthew here, sir. I'm with Tommie. How can we help?"

"Head southbound on Highway 27, just past Lake Louisa. I've got a private tip from a reliable source. Might be a traffic accident... Maybe another hit-and-run. Could be serious. Call in some backup."

"Copy that, sir. We're near John's Lake Road, just a few minutes out. We'll bring Bill and Rob in for support. Matty out."

Troopers Matthew Moudy and Tommie Robinson had just finished a relaxed lunch at the nearby IHOP. They weren't expecting to be back on duty so soon.

Hit-and-runs weren't uncommon these days. They'd seen a rise in recent years, dating all the way back to the economic collapse of 2008. Even with the recent upswing under President Frank McCrony's unexpected rise to the White House, uninsured drivers were still everywhere.

Why can't people just buy the damn insurance now? Matthew thought as he merged onto the highway.

Minutes later, they rolled past Lake Louisa. Slowing down, Matthew spotted something.

"Hold on," he muttered, pulling the cruiser onto the shoulder.

There were outlines of what appeared to be stains and blotches across the light-gray asphalt. No sign of blood, but faint stains, irregular, and scattered. As if something had spilt there.

Matthew keyed his mic.

"Lieutenant, this is Matty. Looks like our friends have vanished. No vehicles in sight, but I see some residue on the road, very faint outlines yet distinct here and there. Could be blood that's been treated with chemicals. Vinegar maybe, or something similar to mask the evidence. Definitely suspicious."

He paused, inspecting the stains.

"Might need K-9 support. Whatever happened here, somebody tried to clean it up in a hurry. I'm calling in more units and will report back as we learn more. Matty out."

Mark's voice came through the radio, steady but tense. "Good work, Matty. Stay sharp. Be on the lookout for three white Felza SUVs, top-end, all-electric vehicles. If these people used chemicals and disappeared this cleanly, they're no amateurs. Likely trained. Possibly armed. Don't take chances."

"Copy that, sir," Matthew responded. He stepped out of the cruiser, hand resting near his sidearm, eyes scanning the tree line.

Something had gone down here. And whoever did it didn't want to be found.

Sergeant Robert Pollack and Trooper William Kennedy arrived at the scene minutes later. The K-9 unit followed close behind, along with Corporal Jim Bailey, Traffic Homicide Investigator, plainclothes today, scheduled for a half-day that was clearly off the table now.

Jim stepped out with his camera slung across his chest and a weathered gray case filled with his tools. Two State Trooper cruisers flanked the shoulder, lights flashing, orange cones forcing traffic into a single lane. A bottleneck had formed, with curious drivers rubbernecking as they inched past.

Jim moved quickly. Florida weather was unforgiving when it came to evidence, one rainstorm, and half the scene could vanish. He snapped photos of every stain, every odd marking on the asphalt. He crouched low, using sterile tweezers and a handy suction syringe to lift samples.

Matthew frowned. "Whatever happened here was aggressively cleaned. The residue doesn't behave like fresh blood, too faint, too neutralized. Someone worked hard to cover it up."

"They used chemicals," Jim muttered, glancing at Matthew as he worked. "Bleach, maybe. Or vinegar."

He went on, eyes still on the ground, as if thinking out loud. "But we're not new to this game. Years on the job have taught me one thing: no one erases everything. Not perfectly."

Nearby, the K-9 unit was struggling. The dog, Nikko, kept sniffing near the stains but retreated, tail down, whimpering slightly. The handler, Corporal Terry Shultz, gave Matthew a nod.

"Something's off here," he said. "They sprayed something over the area, probably a masking agent. Irritating his nose. He doesn't want to go near it."

Few seconds later Nikko darted towards the wood post of the guardrails along the highway and stood there, like a statue, barking at the post. Jim walked over to the post and began to study it intently up and down the post.

Matthew saw Jim spot something on the guardrail, just behind some overgrown weeds. He knelt down.

"Looks like a faint splatter," Jim said, pushing a gloved finger into a crevice. "Blood. And something else." He looked closer.

"Tissue, part of a face. A trace of hair clinging to a flap of skin. From the angle and pattern, I'd say the force of impact flung the tissue against the wooden post, ricocheting it behind the galvanized metal rail where no one can see. And where the cleanup crew forgot to check.

"Out of sight. Forgotten."

Matthew saw Jim all revved up in action and excited. Jim was sealing the sample he had collected in a sterile pouch, labeled it, and smiled grimly. "Got you."

Just then, a Red Felza SUV slowed as it passed the scene. This SUV was slowly trailing all other vehicles and gazers that were passing through the orange cone blockade they had formed while keeping one lane open.

Nikko's posture shifted in a blink, ears up, body tense, then a burst of barking, sharp and focused.

Matthew turned to Terry. "What's that about?"

Terry shrugged. "He's reacting to something unusual. Could be nothing. Could be the chemicals. Could just be a smell he doesn't like. Either way, those Felzas? Probably rich tourists or tech nerds. I wouldn't stop 'em."

Matthew didn't answer right away. He watched the Felza along with a trail of other slow-moving cars disappear down the highway, Nikko still barking in its wake.

Then he remembered: *Mark had mentioned a white Felza in the original call-in. This one was red, and he saw no reason to stop it.*

"That couldn't have been them," Matthew muttered under his breath. "This one was a red Felza, and they wouldn't circle back anyway. Would they?"

He didn't stop the SUV. Didn't flag it. Something inside him told him not to.

But doubt was creeping in now.

You had the right to pull them over. You had the dog's reaction. Why didn't you?

Maybe fear of being wrong. Maybe instinct. Maybe both.

Matthew turned to Terry. "Let's trail south. Just in case. You up for it?"

"Always."

He relayed instructions. "Once we wrap, Bill and Rob will take Jim back to the station. Tommie, you ride with us."

As they finished documenting the scene, Jim sealed his last sample and handed over the evidence logs. The team moved fast, cones packed up, cruisers repositioned, lights still flashing.

Matthew glanced once more at the faded yet distinct stains on the pavement, now drying under the sun.

Then they rolled south, chasing a lead that might already be miles ahead, or just one wrong turn away from blowing everything open.

Matthew sat stiffly in the passenger seat of the K-9 unit, arms crossed, trying not to breathe too deeply. He liked dogs, respected their training, even admired their loyalty, but he *hated* being around them. The smell, the panting, the constant drool... especially the drool.

And Nikko, the all-black German Shepherd in the back seat, had plenty of it.

Matthew glanced over his shoulder for the fifth time, narrowing his eyes. Nikko had his snout pushed halfway out the open rear window, nostrils flaring, tail still. Focused. His handler, Corporal Terry Shultz, could tell Nikko was locked in.

That stench, the one from the roadside scene, it was back. Faint but distinct.

Then: *"Whoof! Whoof!"* Two sharp, deliberate barks.

12:28 | 11-11-2025 (Twenty-first century)
LOCATION: STATE OF FLORIDA HIGHWAY 27

Meanwhile, Luke and Prisha were making their way back to the rendezvous point, four twenty-liter bottles secured in their backseat. But as they approached, their stomachs sank.

Three law enforcement vehicles blocked the road, lights flashing red and blue. One was clearly marked **K-9 UNIT**.

Traffic had slowed to a crawl. Orange cones redirected drivers while onlookers rubbernecked. Luke followed the slow procession, both time travelers staying calm, staying quiet.

Ahead, police officers clustered around two separate stained areas marked with orange cones.

One officer crouched beside the spot where, not long ago, Meirah's headless body had collapsed on the asphalt, at the center of a faint red halo of spatter.

Pointing to faint outlines of what seemed like puddles of blood, another officer was photographing the area where the mangled remains of Roberto had been.

The source of these stains was conspicuously missing, no doubt making the scene even more intriguing for the law officers on the scene.

Not good, Prisha realized.

A man in dress pants and crisp business shirt, likely a detective, was pointing at the faint blood stain marks and muttering into a recorder.

Prisha and Luke locked eyes. No words. Just a shared, silent panic.

Luke kept driving.

Suddenly, the K-9 dog began barking, loud, sharp, urgent. The officer holding its leash flinched. The dog strained toward the road as their SUV passed. One cop shrugged, puzzled. Another pointed toward the SUV, mouthing something to his partner.

Inside, Prisha was sweating bullets despite the A/C blasting cold air. Beside her in the driver's seat, Luke anxiously bounced one heel on the floor.

The tension was suffocating. They couldn't afford to get stopped. Not here. Not now.

But the traffic picked up again. The SUV merged forward, slowly gaining speed, rolling past the flashing lights and watchful eyes.

And then, finally, they were gone.

Once they were a full kilometer clear, Prisha activated the comms.

"Max, bad news," she said, her voice low and urgent. "Local police are already on scene. K-9 unit with a sniffing dog. Looks like they beat us to it. The dog's been all over the site, we saw them taking photos, pointing at the site of the remains."

"I just want to make sure the cremation's done and you're ready to move."

She glanced at Luke, who was gripping the wheel tight with both hands, eyes fixed on the road.

"We've got twenty liters of water with us," she continued. "When we get there, we'll dump it over the burial site. Should mix the soil with the ash and flush away any remaining scent, ash residue, sweat, anything. And we'll finish the cleanup on the road later after the police have left."

She paused. "We're three minutes out."

Max responded immediately. "Copy that, Prisha. Cremation is complete. Site's buried and concealed. But change of plan, do **not** come back here."

There was steel in his voice now.

"Head straight to our final destination. Stay on the road, don't double back. We'll tow TTV3 with No.1 and meet you there. Once you arrive, stay in the vehicle at all times. Understood?"

"Understood," she said.

Luke exhaled slowly but didn't ease off the pedal.

The line went silent.

They kept driving.

Max signaled his team to quickly wrap up at their burial site. He glanced across the clearing and nodded. Everything seemed the same as it was when they arrived.

Max and the eight remaining officers began loading the shovels and the dome tent container into their TTV.

Per Prisha's suggestion, he told Bitang to pour a couple of water bottles onto the berm, flushing down over the ash below the dirt to help cover their tracks.

TTV3 was now hitched again to the back of TTV1, and they began towing it toward Highway 27, en route to Interstate 4.

Their arrival in this time period had been traumatic, leaving no time for the usual adjustment procedures. Max hoped they'd have a chance to regroup and rethink everything once they reached their destination.

He was soaked in sweat like the rest of the mission team, thanks to the bodysuits and the brutal heat.

The twenty-first century heat was unbearable.

For most people it was the new normal. They did not care as long as they earned their paychecks. Life was all about making a living, not living a life!

Not for Max's team. They came from a future Earth; one painstakingly restored by the Federation of Nations.

In their time, desertification was reduced to a fraction of what it had once been. The skies were clear; the air was tempered and clean, and the climate was stable.

Here, the contrast was disgusting. To someone from the twenty-sixth century, this world felt like a slow-motion catastrophe.

Max wiped his brow and steadied his breath. Something else was bothering him, more than just the heat. Fog. Thick, frustrating brain fog. The kind that dulled instinct, that turned confidence into doubt.

He faintly remembered their mission objective: Finding a Manifesto. *A Manifesto of Eleven Elements*

The words: *Eleven Elements* rang loud and true.

He knew its author, Joshua DeWine was critical. Max could feel it in his bones. The man held the key to something enormous, possibly their very existence.

But beyond that, the details blurred. Pieces of his training were missing. Tactical briefings? Gone. Emotional conditioning? Patchy. Even the purpose behind this specific time jump... fragmented.

He stayed focused on the mission directives obediently. It was the only tether he had to his forgotten instructions, a kind of survival manual in an unfamiliar past. Every line became a lifeline, a guide through this haze.

Max wasn't just out of place.

He was lost in time, with no clear memory of why.

CHAPTER ·3

12:57 | 11-11-2025 (Twenty-first century)
LOCATION: SOMEWHERE NEAR FLORIDA HWY 27

Terry didn't need words. He'd worked with Nikko since the dog was two years old, picked him up on November 20, 2016. For the past nine years, they'd been partners in the Criminal Interdiction Unit, chasing traffickers, drug runners, and worse. They didn't need conversations. They moved in sync.

Terry hit the brakes hard and made a sudden turn onto a narrow dirt road, gravel popping under the tires. The wooded path twisted deeper into the trees. Nikko barked again, more urgent this time.

A few hundred yards in, the road opened into a small clearing.

Terry stopped the cruiser.

Before he could finish saying, "Go," Nikko launched out the rear door the moment it opened, sprinting to a gentle mound of grass that formed a berm off to the side. The dog began clawing at the soil with wild energy, then paused to look back at his handler, ears up, waiting for confirmation, then back to digging.

Terry's instincts lit up. That mound wasn't natural. The soil looked moist, darker than the dry dirt around it. But it hadn't rained all day.

As he approached, the air shifted. The chemical scent lingered faintly. Something had been buried recently, and it hadn't been done cleanly.

Terry called out to Matthew. "This is fresh. No doubt."

* * * * * *

Matthew nodded silently, eyeing the disturbed ground, the hairs on the back of his neck rising. He wasn't used to this kind of scene. He handled people, not buried secrets.

They walked back to the vehicle just as Tommie arrived. Without a word, he popped the trunk and retrieved the compact equipment case. From it, he pulled out a precision shovel, an elegant, steel-handled tool designed for accident rescues, but sharp enough to handle delicate terrain like this.

The team was quiet now, the kind of quiet that comes when everyone *knows* what's about to happen.

Matthew stepped back and muttered, "Let's see what the dog dragged up."

Terry knelt by the mound. Nikko stood to the side, tongue out, tail still, eyes locked on the spot like it owed him something.

Then the digging began.

The shovels bit into the soft earth as Terry and Tommie dug past the surface layer. Minutes in, they reached a strange mix of damp soil and black, powdery dust, wet, clinging, and oddly textured.

"Ash?" Tommie asked, squinting at the substance.

Terry nodded slowly. "Could be. Looks like it."

They pulled out a resealable zaplock bag from the kit, scooped a sample, and sealed it for lab testing. As they were wrapping up, Nikko suddenly started pawing furiously at a different spot just a few feet away.

Terry followed the dog's lead, digging where the fresh scratches were. A few scoops down, his shovel struck something hard.

Clang. Metal.

He crouched, brushed away the dirt with gloved hands, and uncovered a strange object. It was shaped like a human bone, but clearly artificial. A dark, matte-black metal. No polymer, no flexible PVC components, just cold, engineered steel.

Terry turned it over, brow furrowed. "Knee joint replacement," he murmured, "but not like any I've seen. No branding, no soft parts. Burned off? Or never there?"

Terry saw Mathew peering down the hole saying, "If this was a body, it was cremated onsite. But where's the rest of the bones?"

Nikko kept digging, determined, tail high, but no more remains turned up. After a few minutes, the dog stopped, circled the site once, and quietly padded back to the cruiser. He hopped in and sat down, done for the day.

Matt watched Terry follow Nikko to the cruiser, knowing full well his partner had delivered. Whatever this thing was, whatever it belonged to, it was enough to trigger an investigation.

He opened the treat box in the backseat and handed Nikko his reward: a chewy bone and a few of his favorite biscuits. "Good job, boy," he said, patting his neck.

Matthew stepped forward and shook Terry's hand. "I'll send the sample and that metal joint to the lab first thing Monday morning," he said. "Appreciate the backup today."

"Anytime," Terry replied.

"Take care, and hey, have a good weekend."

"You too."

Matthew walked toward his cruiser, where Tommie was already waiting in the driver's seat. He slid into the passenger side, closing the door with a sigh of relief. No more drool. No more fur.

As they pulled away from the scene, Matthew glanced at Tommie and smiled.

"I'll take people over dogs any day."

Tommie grinned. "Even if they don't have a nose like Nikko's?"

"Especially then."

They drove off, lights dimmed, radio quiet, two officers, partners, decorated and driven, unknowingly chasing the edge of something far bigger than either of them expected.

14:16 | 11-11-2025 (Twenty-first century)
LOCATION: STATE OF FLORIDA HIGHWAY 27

Meanwhile, Max and his team were making their way north along Highway 27, towing the non-functional TTV3 behind TTV1. After a long, cautious drive, they arrived at their intended destination: Charriotts Inn & Suites.

Max pulled TTV1 into the trailer parking lane across from where TTV2 had been idling for the past half hour. Prisha and Lukas stood by, alert but trying to appear casual.

Just as Max shut off the engine, flashing lights appeared in the rearview mirror.

A police cruiser.

It rolled slowly into the lot and came to a stop, red and blue lights still pulsing. Two officers stepped out, one male, one female, both in uniform. Max's mind instantly kicked into crisis mode.

This could be routine... or it could be exactly what we feared.

He raised a finger to his lips and gave the silent order: *No one talks but me.*

The team froze.

The officers weren't in a rush. They stood near their cruiser, talking quietly and speaking into their shoulder-mounted radios. After a brief exchange, they began walking, *not* toward the SUVs, but straight past them, heading for the hotel lobby entrance.

Max kept his breath steady.

They entered through the sliding glass doors. Once they disappeared inside and the doors hissed shut behind them, Max tapped his comms.

"TTV2 and TTV3, listen up. We're not checking in here. I just looked at the map, there's another Charriott brand, a *Residence Inn & Suites*, two miles north. If someone's following us, this is the place they'll expect to find us. We're changing locations."

"Jian, Katrina, jump into TTV2 with Prisha and Lukas. Isam, stay in TTV3 to steer and brake as before. We're rolling."

The handoff was swift and silent. Jian and Katrina climbed into TTV2, sliding into the back. Isam remained behind the wheel of TTV3. Emergency blinkers stayed off for now; Isam would activate them only if the convoy needed to make an abrupt stop.

They pulled out quietly, back onto the road.

Twenty minutes later, they arrived at the new location: Residence Inn & Suites by Charriott, a smaller and less-trafficked property tucked behind a strip mall and surrounded by overgrown landscaping.

Max and Prisha found a shaded corner near the outdoor pool area, hidden behind an aging wooden fence and thick shrubs.

There, Isam disconnected the tow line.

Daniel, Katrina, and Jian quickly joined him, and together they pushed the dead TTV3 into an open space between a white cargo van and an aging RV. It was tight, concealed. Blended in.

Max scanned the lot one more time, then spoke low into the comms.

"Alright. We hold here for now. Nobody moves. No one goes inside. This is our fallback until we regroup."

The team had dodged a close one. But the clock was ticking, and whoever was watching was probably still out there

Max stepped into the hotel lobby, the cool air a welcome contrast to the humid Florida afternoon. The building itself showed signs of age, cracks in the sidewalk, faded signage, but the interior had clearly undergone recent renovations. Fresh tile flooring gleamed under recessed lighting, and a subtle citrus scent filled the air.

The front desk was manned by a tired-looking attendant in a stiff button-down shirt. But what drew Max's eye was the massive mural dominating the wall behind them.

It was stunning.

A vibrant underwater scene stretched across the entire back wall, alive with color and detail. Bright blue and yellow tangs darted through coral reefs. Ocellaris clownfish nestled in sea anemones. Mischievous dolphins with playful grins chased one another through bubbles. Sea turtles, both adult and tiny hatchlings, swam upward toward a sunlit surface. On the ocean floor, lobsters, crabs, and a solitary octopus sprawled in watchful stillness.

The water was rendered with such clarity, it almost shimmered. Sunlight filtered down through ripple of waves, casting golden beams that lit up the sea like an underwater cathedral.

At the very center of the mural, a vertical column of space had been intentionally left clear, free of fish or coral. There, in flowing calligraphy, was a tower of text written from top to bottom:

Water is so fine that it is impossible
to grasp a handful of it; strike it,
yet it does not suffer hurt; stab it,
and it is not wounded; sever it,
yet it is not divided. It has no
shape of its own but molds itself
to the receptacle that contains it.
When heated to the state of steam
it is invisible but has enough
power to split the earth itself.
When frozen it crystallizes into
a mighty rock. First it is turbulent
like Niagara Falls, and then
calm like a still pond, fearful like
a torrent, and refreshing like
a spring on a hot summer's day.
- - - - Tao Te Ching
I wanted to be like the nature
of water. Empty your mind, be
formless. Shapeless, like water.
If you put water into a cup, it
becomes the cup. You put water
into a bottle and it becomes the
bottle. You put it in a teapot,
it becomes the teapot. Now,
water can flow or it can crash.
Be water, my friend.
- - - - Bruce Lee

It caught him off guard, a poetic declaration painted on the crumbling wall of a roadside hotel. But it landed with force. A truth disguised as art. A message most people would overlook.

Bits of his mission flickered back. Something about an unpublished book: *Healing Waters*. A warning. A guide. The urgency of it made sudden sense.

The mural seemed to capture everything the book was trying to say: Heal the waters. Restore the beauty of Earth and its oceans. Treat them as sacred, as holy as a cathedral where all of life has gathered to honor creation.

But who was listening? The oceans were dying. Bleaching had wiped out eighty-four percent of the world's coral reefs. Beauty like this, like the painting, like the reefs, was vanishing. The planet was slipping under murky water and nobody seemed to care.

Still, it stuck with him.

Coming from the future does that to you: you notice everything. The smallest details, the tiniest mismatch, the quiet wrongness of a world that isn't yours. It all jumps out at you, sharp and insistent, like a sore thumb.

He turned back to the desk, his expression neutral again. "I'd like a few rooms," he said calmly, the words smooth and practiced. "Something quiet. Away from the road, if you can."

He stepped up and pulled out his phone, the screen already open to a reservation tab.

"The other property had smaller rooms," he said casually, smiling at the clerk. "We're staying for about thirty days and need something a little more spacious, ideally with full kitchenettes and larger suites. We're having a high school reunion, actually. Haven't all been together in over twenty years."

He chuckled, slipping into the relaxed tone of a man planning a nostalgic vacation. "Same group as back then. We did this trip for two weeks once, hit all the parks, stayed up late, relived our teenage chaos. Thought it was time we did it again. A full month this time."

The clerk, a young man with square glasses and a thin mustache, nodded as he pulled up the system. His fingers clicked over the keyboard for a moment before he looked up.

"Let's see... says here you're a group of fifteen. I've only got six double queen rooms available, so, twelve guests max unless you use rollaway beds or take a separate king suite. Also, I may have to move you around during the stay if we can't block off the same rooms for the full thirty days."

Max bent forward on the counter just slightly and lowered his voice with a relaxed smile.

"Well, only ten of us made it," he said. "Some last-minute stuff, two missed flights, a couple of family emergencies. So, it's just the ten of us now."

He gestured subtly to his group waiting in the lobby, relaxed, chatty, each with a matching backpack embroidered with Greek fraternity and sorority letters. They looked like the kind of group that might have known each other since college or longer.

"We'll take all six double queen rooms," Max continued. "If you could link at least two of them with a connecting door, that'd be perfect. The four ladies will take one of those. The rest of us guys can pair up however works best, but two interconnected rooms would help. I really appreciate it."

He gave a smile that walked the line between charm and humble gratitude.

The clerk hesitated only a moment before nodding. "Alright, I'll set it up that way for you. You might still have to switch rooms once or twice, but I'll do my best to keep it stable."

"Appreciated."

A few minutes later, the clerk handed Max a stack of key cards, labeled and scanned.

"Six rooms. Two of them are connected. You're all set."

Max nodded his thanks and turned back to the group.

One by one, the ten "reunion guests" took their cards, slinging their matching packs over their shoulders. They looked like any other tight-knit group on a long overdue vacation.

In the empty elevator lobby, when no one else was around, Max signaled for them to huddle so he could whisper his directives.

"We break for four hours," he said. "Nap, shower, freshen up, whatever you need to reset. Then we regroup, assess where we stand, and plan our next move."

Then glancing at Luke he said, "Luke, I need you to get a folding utility table with ten chairs from a nearby office supplies store. We are going to set up one off the rooms as our base workroom. I have sent you the list of the supplies we need."

The team took the elevator to the fourth floor and went their separate ways.

Max stepped into Suite 401, the room he would share with Daniel, and shut the door behind him.

It took him a few minutes to figure out the archaic controls of the A/C unit, dials and buttons from a bygone era that felt more alien to him than the time jump itself.

The air was stale. He cranked the A/C unit to its lowest setting and flipped on the fan to full speed. The clunky wall unit rattled briefly, then sprang into life, sending a stream of cool air across the room.

He peeled down to his bodysuit and slumped onto the bed, exhausted.

At last, the temperature dropped.

Silence settled over the room.

Max lay motionless, the artificial breeze brushing his face as he drifted into thought.

A moment later, Daniel entered, equally spent and ready for sleep. He stripped down to his bodysuit and stretched out on the second bed.

The mission had barely begun, and already they had lost three of their best. Max could still see their faces, etched in memory, loyal, brilliant, and now gone. It didn't feel real. Not yet.

This wasn't supposed to happen. He'd only done one quick jump into the twenty-first century, barely an hour, just a test run, to prove the system worked. The trial had been smooth, seamless. Nothing like this.

Now, here he was. On a covert mission. Grounded in a century he barely understood. Leading a fractured team. And bearing the burden of loss.

General Dyson's words still echoed in his ears: "Your focus now must be on the mission. You know how critical this task is, and how vital it is that you return safely. You will have the honor of being the first humans to travel over five-hundred years into the past."

Five hundred years into the past.

And yet... Max couldn't even recall the full scope of the mission. The details, hazy, elusive, floated just out of reach. He vaguely remembered the name: Joshua DeWine. That was the anchor. That was the reason. But *why* DeWine mattered, what threat or promise he carried, Max couldn't say.

The logbook offered some bearings, but not clarity. He was operating on instinct now.

His heartbeat slowed. With the day's tension finally draining out of him, his body began to surrender. Eyes half-closed, he let the day's events flicker past. His brain, still recalibrating from the disorienting effects of deep time displacement, began to stitch old neural paths back together.

Memories jostled for position: names, moments, fragments of a life lived centuries ahead of the time he now occupied. He drifted toward sleep, slipping into a hazy, half-conscious state.

Then his body lurched with the sudden sensation of free-fall, as if he were dropping out of the sky. The jolt snapped him awake. Max lay there, unable to sleep, his mind growing restless, like a traveler hit with a brutal, time-travel version of jet lag.

Seeking relief, he reached for his VRV headset, the Virtual Reactive Visor, a sophisticated device that fits over the eyes and nose, seamlessly linking with his embedded earpiece and body suit to deliver a full-spectrum 6D experience.

This wasn't just virtual reality experience; it was walking inside your own memories where everything felt real.

The visor's nosepiece, designed with discreet perforations, allowed air to pass through while micro-fragrance injectors released scent cues. If the image was of a kitchen, he'd smell coffee brewing. If it was a garden, he'd inhale the fresh fragrance of blossoms. In personal memories, even a familiar person's scent could be rendered with unsettling precision.

Max had occasionally used the VRV headset in the past, for reliving cherished memories or entertainment. But today was different. This time, he needed it as a neurological recovery tool, combined with data from his PCOM, to reconstruct lost moments, reignite his synaptic memory, and repair the damage caused by the deep time-jump.

When activated, the system presented a rapid slideshow of still images, selfies, snapshots, mission footage. Then, using sensory triangulation, it expanded these static visuals into fully immersive 6D environments. He could look left or right, up or down, and the world would respond accordingly, complete with soundscapes, ambient temperature cues, and contextual smells fed through the nosepiece. The effect was fully immersive, like reliving reality a second time.

These sensory triggers were designed to activate dormant neural pathways, provoking total memory recall, or, in some cases, a full cognitive reset.

Max needed that reset. His logical thinking, strategic acumen, and intuition had all taken a hit since this deep-time-jump.

So far, he had held it together through short-term memory fragments and mission logs. But it wasn't enough. As Commander of a sensitive operation, he required full cognitive functionality, sharp reflexes, instinctive leadership, and unfailing memory.

And today, the VRV would help him retrieve it all.

Max decided to visit some of his life events during his youth. When he was twenty-one years old and still at the Military Academy. It was one of the best times of his life.

After a few minutes of wearing the VRV Max shut his eyes for a total recall of chunks of his memories as if someone in his head switched on a light. He could see everything as if he was watching a movie!

(VRV BLINKING: MEMORY RECALL MODE)
10:21 | 09-27-2515 (Twenty-sixth century)
LOCATION: MILITARY ACADEMY Science & Engineering

A moment later, Max was no longer in a hotel room.

He was back in his fourth year at the Military Academy of Science and Engineering, sitting in one of the high-security lecture halls reserved for the most advanced cadets.

At the Academy, Time-Travel Engineering evolved beyond instruction into a discipline of constant refinement. It was also where Max's fascination had deepened into purpose.

He had always been drawn to the concept of time travel. Maybe it was in his blood. His father, a decorated officer, had once led the Time Travel Program. And as a child, Max had grown up surrounded by glimpses of secret technologies and theories that bordered on the mythical. But it was at the Academy that theory turned into something real.

He vividly remembered Professor Dr. Surinder Roy, MD, HTTPE, PhD, a polymath and co-author of *Modern Precision Time Travel Techniques*. Roy was a legend, a storyteller of science, capable of transforming complex physics into something almost poetic.

That day in the lab had been unforgettable.

They had all gathered around a reinforced glass case containing a robotic bust of a woman's head, eerily lifelike. Her hair was sleek and perfectly parted. Her eyes blinked slowly, and her silicone lips formed a faint, serene smile. Beneath the surface, organic polymers shaped veins and arteries, and exposed sections of thoracic bone gleamed under the lab lights.

"This," Roy began, voice calm but electric, "is not about robotics. It's about *replication*. If we can understand how to replicate a subject with such precision that no discernible difference exists between the original and the clone, we understand how to transmit matter through time."

He activated a scanning device.

A vertical beam swept across the robotic bust in a matter of seconds. On the screen behind him, a rotating 3D model of the head appeared. Hair, veins, facial texture, down to the microcapillaries. Every contour and strand were mapped in full fidelity.

Roy tapped a few controls.

The 3D printer whirred to life.

In under a minute, a second bust took shape in a second glass enclosure, identical in structure, composition, and detail. The eyes blinked. The skin flexed. The smile was the same.

Gasps rippled through the room.

"This," Roy said, gesturing to both heads, "is the foundation. To time-travel. We don't just move people. We *translate* them, into pure data, and then reassemble them with precision, atom by atom. *Time travel is not movement. It's replication across timelines.* And when you replicate something perfectly … it *is* the original."

He let that settle before continuing.

"The seeds of this technology began centuries ago, when humans first 3D-printed organic tissue. And they also had the fiberoptic cables back then where data could travel at the speed of light. Combine that with four-hundred years of advancement in DNA-level scanning, quad-base logic processing, and data transmission faster than light...

"And *bam!*" Roy clapped his hands. "Time travel becomes reality."

That moment had crystallized everything for Max. Time travel wasn't a fantasy anymore. It was science. Art. Discipline.

He leaned back now in the present, eyes heavy, a bittersweet pride swelling in his chest. That day at the Academy had set his course.

He just never imagined where it would lead.

Professor Roy stood before the class, hands folded behind his back, a quiet authority in the sterile, bustling lab. The robotic busts in their glass cases blinked slowly under the cool white lights, still and eerily lifelike.

He gestured toward them. "What you've just witnessed looks like magic. In reality, it's replication. A scanned object transmitted as data and reprinted with perfect fidelity. Now imagine replacing that object ... with a *person*."

The room fell silent.

"Time travel," he continued, "operates on a similar principle, only far more complex.

"A high-capacity quantum computer scans a person down to the genetic and atomic level. Every molecule, every synapse, every nuance of identity is captured, converted into an ultra-dense digital structure."

He tapped a control panel, and a hologram appeared above the lab table: a glowing wireframe of a human body made entirely of flowing data streams.

"Instead of sending a print command to a nearby machine," Roy said, "we transmit this *living* data packet through quantum hyper-vortex data transmission technology allowing data to move at speeds far greater than light. The moment this genetic information enters a new temporal coordinate, a different point in the timeline, it begins the reassembly process."

He pointed to the second robotic bust.

"Unlike our earlier demonstration, which simply recreated an image, the time-travel system doesn't stop at replication; it transports.

"The individual being scanned is fully converted into genetic data, then reprinted into existence in a different time. No residue. No duplicate. The body, mind, and soul become data. Your data becomes ... you."

A murmur rippled through the cadets.

"All of this," Roy said, "occurs in under a nanosecond. Until the end of last century, we transported human subjects in specialized vehicles fitted with a miniature nuclear reactor. It's the only power source dense enough to drive a process this complex.

"The original design concepts came from the reactors used in nuclear-powered submarines, during times when individual nations were not governed under the new charter.

"Their cold wars invented modified versions that were fitted in ballistic long-range missiles.

Roy gestured toward a perfect half-meter cube and continued, "Once the Federation of Nations was formed, their wartime tech was repurposed and refined to produce miniature reactors, about this size, that could be teleported and tethered across timelines for centuries."

"The bodysuit with built-in flip up wrist-top computer, what we call the Optical Messaging Pads, are also vital, each one embedded with self-assembling nanotech that ensures proper reformation upon arrival."

He walked around the lab, slow and deliberate.

"This is why we no longer need 'receivers' on both ends," he said. "The data transmission carries everything: structure, consciousness, and the *instruction set* for rebuilding the person. First the bodysuit, then the wrist unit, and finally the body itself.

"In the past or future, so long as our Super Cloud computing infrastructure exists at *some point*, the person can reappear anywhere in the timeline."

A cadet raised a hand. Roy nodded.

"What if the destination doesn't have tech advanced enough to reconstruct the person?" the student asked.

Roy smiled. "Then the data waits."

He paused for effect. "The cloud-based system is distributed across centuries. If a traveler jumps to the twenty-first century, the data arrives first and begins building the essentials, starting with inorganic components like the suit and wrist computer. Once those are reconstructed, the suit serves as the shell into which the body can be reassembled."

He looked around the room, his voice suddenly low and serious.

"This is not teleportation. It is not duplication. It is transformation: biological existence translated into pure information. And once you cross into another point in time... *you are your data.*"

Max had hung onto every word that day.

Even now, decades and lifetimes later, he could still hear Professor Roy's voice echoing in his mind. That moment had shaped everything. Not just his understanding of the science, but the full implications and consequence of being a time traveler.

To exist outside of time, he realized, was to risk never existing again.

Professor Roy resumed, his voice calm, almost amused, clearly enjoying the challenge of breaking down the complexity for his students.

"We've successfully transported rats, birds, and other small animals as far back as the early twenty-first century," he said, pacing slowly across the lab floor.

"That era had the benefit of Super Cray computing systems and early Molecular Dynamics Simulations, which made basic genetic reconstruction feasible, though at a primitive level."

He turned to the display, where an animation showed a small bird being scanned, reduced to digital data, and transmitted across a temporal fiber stream.

"For these small biological test subjects," he continued, "we utilize a cylindrical PVC transport tube, lightweight, inert, and easy to disguise. The animal is encoded along with the pipe, which serves as the first material to reconstruct upon arrival. Like the bodysuit for human transport."

He clicked to the next slide. A rat was crawling out of a short, white PVC pipe onto what looked like a city street from decades ago.

"Once the tube is printed," Roy said, "the body of the animal quickly reassembles within it. The subject emerges, alive and genetically stable, and simply scurries or flies away, blending in with the fauna of the era. The PVC pipe, of course, remains behind."

He allowed himself a small chuckle.

"Discarded pipes were common in that era. Construction material, urban waste. No one would question it. In fact, leaving behind a pipe is a rather elegant form of camouflage. Our subject vanishes into the past, and the delivery mechanism becomes background noise."

The class laughed quietly, some shaking their heads in disbelief at the ingenuity.

Roy's grin faded slightly, his tone returning to a professional edge. "Remember: with living subjects, *every* variable counts. From environmental compatibility to the way light bends off the transport vessel, every detail serves a single goal: seamless integration, not mere survival."

Max had been wide-eyed in that moment, deeply impressed. The elegance of it all, the science wrapped in simplicity, the humor masking how dangerous and precise the entire process truly was.

Professor Roy had a gift for invention and an even greater one for storytelling.

And now, years later, as Max faced real missions and real consequences, he found comfort in remembering where it all began: a rat, a PVC pipe, and the quiet brilliance of a man who could make time travel sound almost ordinary.

CHAPTER -4

15:32 | 11-11-2025 (Twenty-first century)
LOCATION: RESIDENCE INN – MAX & DANIEL's
ROOM 401

Max sat in Room 401, on the recliner beside his bed, VRV headset on, working to rebuild his lost memories. Daniel lay still on the other bed, catching a brief nap. A moment later, Max heard the door open and Katrina stepped into the room.

He removed the VRV headset and sat there watching her gracefully walking in. Without a word, she approached Daniel, her fiancé, and embraced him. Their lips met, and soon they were lost in each other. Max tried to avert his gaze but couldn't help noticing how the bodysuit hugged Katrina's form, accentuating every curve.

He remembered reading in the personal notes just few days ago in his timeline that Daniel and Katrina were officially engaged. It wasn't classified, everyone on the team knew. Still, it brought a strange energy into the room, watching their intimacy unfold so casually.

Unfortunately for the newly minted couple, Daniel shared the room with Max. Reading the situation, Max rose, quietly excused himself, and slipped into the shower to give them privacy.

The glass enclosure surrounding the shower looked primitive compared to what he was used to. No timers. No gauges to monitor water usage. None of the usual twenty-sixth-century water efficiency protocols. Just old-school water taps, without sensors, allowing water to flow endlessly while people brush their teeth or wash hands/utensils or whatever.

But now, naked under the blissfully cool, unregulated cascade, he understood why people in this century took long, wasteful showers. The heat was unbearable, the air heavy with humidity, and stress was constant. People sought relief where they could find it.

As the water flowed over him, Max heard the sounds of passion echoing from the bedroom. Through the slightly open door, a mirror caught glimpses of Katrina's body moving in rhythmic grace atop Daniel. They were completely lost in each other, assuming Max was shut away in the shower and giving them the privacy they needed.

They're like children, Max thought. *Trying to hold onto comfort after a brutal day.*

But the moment puzzled him.

Katrina had incinerated the bodies of her best friends, Meirah Hong and Jackir Husen, just hours earlier. She had carried out that task with chilling precision. Meirah's body had been headless; the image still burned into Max's memory. Any rational person would be reeling.

How is she even capable of intimacy right now?

Then he remembered her file. Orphaned young. Both parents lost in a freak skiing accident in the Swiss Alps. Maybe she had learned to compartmentalize pain. Maybe this was how she coped, by seeking warmth in the moment, even if everything else around her was burning.

Max kept to his disciplined ten-minute shower, a habit ingrained by the water-saving laws of his time. After shaving and freshening up, he pulled on a clean bodysuit, jeans, and a long-sleeved shirt. He stepped back into the room to find Daniel and Katrina curled up in bed, the tension of the day temporarily melted away.

"Alright," Max said calmly. "You've got ninety minutes. Finish your naps, freshen up, get dressed and meet in Room 402 next door by 17:15. This will be the readiness review and planning session. We also need to brainstorm what we're going to do about SUV3."

He added with a dry chuckle, "Looks like you two may need some privacy, so I'll get Room 402 set up as our local command base and my personal work space. That way I can focus on staying mission-ready, while you two enjoy your downtime."

Room 402, a standard double queen hotel suite, had been repurposed into their makeshift command center for the mission in the twenty-first century. It served as their hub for planning, coordination, and briefings. A common base room. The remaining five hotel rooms were used as private living quarters for rest and recovery.

To convert the room, Luke had picked up an eight-foot folding portable table and molded PVC chairs from a local office supply store. The beds and hotel furniture were rearranged to make space, transforming the room into a functional operations base. Generous tips were handed to the service staff, who gladly accepted them and kept quiet about the unconventional room setup.

Max thought that he would use Room 402 not only to interface with the command center and lead mission briefings, but also to conduct his VRV memory-recall sessions in solitude when the others were away. The rest of the team can use the space to monitor local activity and review tactical updates.

Base Room 402 would become our shared war room.

This arrangement maintained a clear separation, giving each team member essential downtime and privacy while ensuring a dedicated space for operations.

Max picked up his PCOM and passed through the adjoining doorway, pinging the three women officers still in their rooms.

There was no time for rest, too many unknowns still hung in the balance.

He took his seat at the newly assembled meeting table and opened the latest transmission. The face of Captain Ricardo Perez appeared on his screen, serious, composed, and ready to deliver what came next.

"Commander," Perez began, "the local police, FHP, collected tissue and hair from Meirah Hong at the arrival site. Their radio chatter indicates a fragment flew onto a wooden post and lodged behind a metal guardrail. Our 3D sweep missed it, likely because shrub overgrowth combined with the metal guardrail blocked the scan." He allowed a tight smile. "Their 'primitive scanner,' a K-9 dog named Nikko, found it by smell. The samples are now at their lab."

Max's stomach tightened.

"At the cremation site," Perez continued, "FHP also recovered a metallic piece. It is Jackir Husen's right knee prosthesis. FHP has logged the foam-bone into evidence and moved it to a high-security facility. Retrieval is not an option."

"What are you talking about, Rick?" Max snapped. "Jackir had an artificial knee? Why didn't the personnel logs flag it?"

Perez replied, "He completed academy training before a sports injury. He then slipped back to Karachi Megapolis for a quiet replacement. Our system recorded the procedure. However, the risk index placed greater emphasis on his expertise in twenty-first-century software and marked the implant as nominal. He had more than one hundred successful jumps. He was one of the best."

"We even made adjustments to his records to indicate such a procedure was done for his alias in the twenty-first century. I wouldn't worry about it for now. We will figure a plan to retrieve it when we are ready."

Perez paused, then dropped the heavier news. "We've isolated the point of failure during the transpose event. It occurred after the fifth individual completed transmission in TTV2. Their transfer took several seconds longer than protocol allows, suggesting either a non-organic composition or transmission complexity far beyond normal.

"We suspect an Artificial Life Form," he said. It's possible a uBot was part of that group."

Max focused closer on the screen, eyes narrowing.

"The data volume during that moment spiked abnormally high. Our mainframe couldn't handle the influx. It corrupted the system, and the failure cascaded from there. The materialization was 99.98 percent complete. But not perfect."

Max acknowledged with a slow nod, his mind already racing. *Who was the fifth person?*

He closed his eyes briefly and conjured the images of the team in TTV2, whispering the names under his breath: "Jian Cheng. Prisha Jiwan. Katrina Patilova. Lukas Adler. Isam Yusef."

Then, aloud: "So ... who was it?"

Perez responded, "Sir, we're still trying to confirm. The transmission sequence happens in micro-fractions of time. Tracking the precise order is complex. We're running a layered data analysis and will report back as soon as we have a match."

Max nodded again but said nothing. The silence around him thickened.

If one of them wasn't who, or *what*, they claimed to be, the implications were massive.

An Artificial Life Form embedded in his handpicked team.

He didn't want to believe it. But deep down, Max knew: this changed everything.

Max paced the room, his footsteps sharp and restless. If it turned out one of his officers was indeed an AAILF, an Advanced Artificially Intelligent Life Form, it would mean decommissioning them.

Worse, it would mark a catastrophic failure. He had already lost Roberto, Meirah, Jackir, Sherine and Cal. This new person's extradition would bring the total to six.

Max reviewed the mission status, his voice low but steady. Three dead. Two missing, still trapped somewhere in digital limbo, their last traces pinging from an unknown data center.

The FHP had recovered hard evidence: tissue fragments, a lock of hair, and Jakir's knee prosthesis. And had it locked up, unretrievable.

And now there was the AAILF embedded among them, hidden in plain sight. Max didn't know who it was, or what its true directives might be.

On top of it all, his own mind was fractured. Long-term memory, compromised. Mission parameters, incomplete. Strategy, slipping through his fingers like sand. All he knew with certainty was this: somewhere in the twenty-sixth-century timeline, a fracture had formed, a tear that threatened to erase everything humanity had built.

The whirlwind of thoughts bore down on him, each breath heavy with consequence. Every decision carried the survival of the future itself.

Max watched the situation unfold, his mind a live chessboard, analyzing each move, testing variations, pruning lines, and replaying scenarios on loop.

Who in his team could be the AAILF?

He caught himself breathing too fast, almost afraid to consider who the outlier might be. These were all people he'd trusted. No matter how you looked at it, he'd failed.

Enough.

He needed to refocus, and more importantly, remember. Some of his longer-term memory still felt patchy. It was critical that he restore clarity before taking any irreversible action.

Max eased into the recliner in Room 402 and lowered the VRV headset over his eyes, the soft hum of the A/C providing a cool backdrop to the moment.

Max longed for the comfort of Annie: his soul mate, his constant.

He touched the visor's On Mode, letting the system initiate.

Cloaked in stillness, he let go.

The idea of sinking into one of their shared memories, feeling her warmth, hearing her laughter, remembering the way her presence grounded him, was too tempting to resist.

Why not? he thought. In a world built on missions, protocols, and impossible stakes, returning to the arms of someone you love, even in memory, was the most human thing he could do.

(VRV BLINKING: MEMORY RECALL MODE)
19:45 | 11-10-2532 (Twenty-sixth century)
LOCATION: HIGHPARK 577 RENNER RESIDENCE

Max could see that he was headed home after several days at the training camp, finally enjoying the ride again. Relief washed over him, even though he'd be back within 24 hours to launch to the twenty-first century.

The sun dipped low on the horizon. The air, crisp and clean as always, carried the subtle hum of Aero-Drones overhead, scrubbing the atmosphere. Below, thousands of Megapolis citizens moved through the city, their custom cleansers and filters silently at work, oxygenating, purifying, sustaining.

Max walked through the door to an unexpected surprise. Annie stood waiting in her favorite nightgown, a subtle smile on her lips.

Whether the shared Bio-rhythm chip system was too smart or too reckless, it had tipped her off. Somehow it knew Max had mischief on his mind.

She opened her arms, and he stepped into them. Their lips met. She slipped open his shirt as he untied her gown, letting it fall to the floor. She stood before him naked, confident, stunning.

He drew her close, feeling her body against his, firm and warm. Pressed to the wall, she raised a leg to his chest. His hand traced the line from her hair down her spine, then rested on the curve of her hip, holding her there as their bodies met with urgency.

"Max, what has made you so aggressive today?" Annie was a very attentive lover, always available, always eager. She was a subservient type personality and preferred her man to be the dominant leader.

"I want you," Max said. "That's all."

He lifted her effortlessly and carried her to the bedroom. There, he began his slow ritual, his hands tracing every curve, every valley, moving from the soft swell of her hips to the firm lines of her thighs. She felt warm, responsive, alive against him. Her touch stirred something deeper, and desire rose quickly in him.

He held her close, as if trying to imprint the moment into memory. And then, with purpose and tenderness, he made love to her as though it might be the last night they'd ever have.

16:32 | 11-11-2025 (Twenty-first century)
LOCATION: RESIDENCE INN -BASE ROOM 402

Max pulled off the VRV headset and exhaled, slow and heavy.

He was here. In the twenty-first century. Not in the memory chamber. Not in the twenty-sixth century.

The faint hum of the air conditioner and the flat, recycled hotel air grounded him. The headset lay in his lap like a defused weapon, but the storm inside his head still raged.

Three officers dead.

Two still unaccounted for, lost in transmission. And now, a gnawing, relentless thought: one of them isn't who they say they are.

His memory was fractured, dangerously so. Vital pieces of information had been jumbled or lost entirely in the time-drop. That alone was enough to compromise his judgment. But what chilled him even more was the overwhelming certainty that an anomaly had slipped through with them.

An advanced one.

The telemetry spikes. The overload during transposition. The system aberrations. The irregular latency in neural relays during team check-ins. It all pointed to one thing:

An AAILF.

A tenth-generation uBot.

Something not human, masquerading as one of them.

He stood up and paced the room, jaw clenched, fingers curled into tight fists.

This breach of travel protocol was catastrophic. Transposing an AAILF through time was illegal and carried the risk of a full timeline extinction event.

If the uBots' core technology were detected or captured here in the early twenty-first century, it wouldn't simply recreate the chain of events that led to the Uprising of 2190 and the wars that nearly wiped-out humanity, it could pull them forward by centuries, amplify them, and strip the future of any chance to steer or contain them.

The team wasn't here to stop history from happening, but to protect the narrow corridor of outcomes in which humanity survives at all.

Worse, if the entity was functioning independently, or under dormant control from the AI core, it could already be altering history.

Max stopped at the window, looking out at the city.

"Someone on this team isn't what they seem," he muttered.

And the terrifying part?

He didn't know who.

Not yet.

But he would find out soon.

Before this mission turned from salvageable to irreversible.

Every one of the five in TTV2 had passed rigorous psychometric and biometric tests. All had displayed deeply human behaviors, flaws, quirks, emotional responses. None of them fit the cold precision he imagined an AAILF would exude.

Then came the thought he didn't want to entertain: Katrina.

She was the highest scorer in the group. Not a perfect one hundred, but consistent ninety-nines across the board. A machine might go for perfection. Katrina was just shy of it. Too human to be artificial?

She was driven. Competitive. Fierce. Someone who didn't want to be equal to any man, she wanted to be better. She had bonded tightly with the team, especially with Daniel. They were scheduled to marry by year's end.

And Max had just watched her, hours ago, entangled in a moment of raw intimacy with Daniel, reckless, messy, completely human.

Not her, he told himself. *Can't be her.*

He mentally scanned the rest. Jian Cheng, loyal, disciplined, emotionally open. Prisha Jiwan, sharp, spiritually grounded, deeply empathetic.

That left Isam Yusef, from the African Megapolis, and Lukas Adler, from the German state. He had the least intel on them, mostly second-hand reports and standardized test results. Nothing in their profiles screamed synthetic, but the lack of familiarity suddenly felt dangerous.

He stopped pacing, then resumed, this time out into the elevator lobby and back. Again, and again. Each lap brought a new layer of anxiety.

The waiting was intolerable.

His mission, its scope, urgency, stakes, momentarily faded. All he could think about was the breach. The threat inside his own team. A machine cloaked in human skin.

He felt he was losing his grip on his career and his mental forbearance.

A notification pinged.

Max snapped out of his spiral as Rick's face reappeared on the screen. He was reading from his PCOM, voice strained.

"Max, sir... this just came through. The fifth person in SUV2, it was Katrina. We've confirmed it. She's an AAILF. A Gen X Artificial Life Form."

Max froze as the implications hit him like a punch to the chest.

Katrina.

His mind reeled back through the past few hours, the strange calm after the incineration, her unaffected demeanor, the near-obsessive energy with Daniel. She hadn't just been coping; she had been *performing. Playing.* Or worse, *preying.*

The real Katrina, the one who had been carefully selected and inducted into the Regimen, was compromised. Replaced.

Someone had implanted a next-gen AI life form into the team, disguised as her.

Max's mind raced. *Who? Why?*

Two possibilities emerged, neither reassuring. It could be the uBots insurgency, infiltrating the Time Travel initiative to derail it from within. Or it could be a rogue faction opposed to the Federation of Nations entirely. Either way, it was a hostile move.

Then the worst thought landed.

If it's the uBots ... and if this Gen X AI has already traveled five-hundred years into the past ... they may have injected advanced AI schematics into early cloud networks.

That would accelerate the rise of machine intelligence. Fast. Faster than history intended. If so, the uBots would do more than alter timelines, they'd tilt the war in their favor centuries before it was ever supposed to begin.

Max sat down hard, his chest tightening under the strain of it all. It hadn't even been eight hours since the time jump and the mission had only just begun, yet everything had already gone wrong.

Dyson might be able to forgive the failed transpose event. But he would *never* forgive the selection of Katrina over Sherry.

Max clenched his jaw, regret cutting deep.

I should've picked Sherry.

The entire chain reaction, the corrupted transmission, the infiltration, the deaths, might never have happened.

The screen lit up again. Rick's voice came through, low and urgent.

"Sir, Max. Further analysis just came in. Katrina's a Gen Ten model. Highly advanced. She's equipped with adaptive concealment protocols and behavioral mirroring. She's been intentionally altering her test results, scoring perfect one hundred, then going back to change a single answer to yield a ninety-nine, just to avoid detection as an Artificial Life Form."

Max felt a chill run through him. *That's how she fooled us all.*

Rick continued, "This is elite-level programming. She knew how to blend in, stay under radar. There was no way to detect her through standard testing."

Max's body tensed as he asked, "Captain, what are my options?"

"You have three," Rick replied without hesitation. "One: decommission her now. Two: keep her in the field and use her as an asset. Three: transpose her back immediately.

"But that's the riskiest. We're not sure what could happen in another transfer. Our official recommendation is decommissioning until further directive. But it's your call, and your team's."

Max clenched his fists. None of the options felt clean. "And what about FHP?" Max asked. "Any chance of getting them off our trail?"

Rick's face tightened. "They've got everything: the prosthetic bone, tissue samples, and casualty location. They know you're operating Felza SUVs. Right now, they're checking every hotel and compound where those vehicles could've stopped."

Max cursed under his breath.

"My suggestion," Rick said, "conceal Felzas by shapeshifting to a new brand. I can transmit a switchover package, tags, decals, grille replacements, trim kits, everything you need to make the SUVs look like Lexis 450s. Or if you prefer, DMW X6s. It'll throw off visual recognition and buy you time."

Max nodded slowly. "Do it. Send the package. Make it Lexis 450."

Rick gave a quick nod. "Understood. Transposing the parts now. You'll have them within the hour."

The screen went dark again.

Max stood still in the silence of the room, heart pounding.

I've got an AI infiltrator in my ranks. Local law enforcement closing in. And the future of the timeline hanging by a thread.

17:15 | 11-11-2025 (Twenty-first century)
LOCATION: RESIDENCE INN - BASE ROOM 402

Everyone was gathered in Room 402, some seated, others leaning against the walls, silent, tense.

Max stood at the head of the table, arms crossed, his expression tight. But his eyes kept drifting to Katrina.

Daniel noticed. He shifted uncomfortably and finally spoke up, voice hesitant. "Is everything okay? I mean... Katrina and I, earlier. In the bed. I didn't mean to disrespect anyone. I'll make sure it doesn't happen again if it bothers you."

Max raised a hand to stop him.

"That's not what this is about, Daniel. Take a seat."

Daniel obeyed, glancing at Katrina, who looked calm, almost too calm.

Max took a breath. His voice was slow but steady.

"I've just received confirmation from Command. The Florida Highway Patrol, the FHP, has discovered evidence tied to us."

A ripple of alarm moved through the room.

"They recovered a knee joint from Jackir's remains. It was missed during the cremation. Titanium alloy. Oxonium. Nanotech ultralight foam. These aren't materials they can easily explain away. Worse, they carry serial codes, production dates, embedded data. If they scan it, they'll start asking questions we can't afford to answer."

He looked around the room, letting that sink in.

"They've also recovered tissue and hair from the arrival site, splattered across a guardrail, most likely Meirah's. DNA testing will eventually lead them back to someone who doesn't exist in any U.S. records but originates from North Khorea, a hostile nation according to current history. And when that happens, we're in trouble, because local agencies may infer terrorist activity." Murmurs started to build among the officers, tension rising.

Max raised his voice slightly, not shouting, but commanding.

"That's not even the biggest problem."

Now the room went still.

Max stood firm at the head of the makeshift meeting table, his team seated on either side, his voice low yet cutting through the heavy silence.

"Now we have *another* situation," he said. "As you know, our third transmission failed. Three officers are dead. Two are still missing.

And the overload that caused the collapse? It was triggered by an AAILF."

He paused, scanning their faces.

"A Gen Ten Artificial Life Form, to be exact. More advanced than any uBots we've ever encountered. A fully functional AAILF was transported with our crew in a covert manner, slipping past every level of scrutiny. Including mine.

"And that AAILF... is Katrina."

Gasps broke the silence. Disbelief hung in the air like smoke.

Daniel's hands trembled as he slowly looked up, first at Katrina, then at Max. His lips parted, but no words came. He looked like he'd been punched in the gut.

Katrina sat quietly at the table, everyone's eyes on her. Her gaze stayed fixed on the floor. She didn't even try to deny it.

The silence between her and Daniel screamed louder than any argument.

Max continued, his voice steady. "We have three options. One: we decommission her. Two: we keep her operational and continue the mission with her on board. Three: we transpose her back immediately.

"That last option is risky, unstable, and not advised by Control."

He looked around the room.

"I want your input. Final call is mine, but every voice matters here."

Everyone started speaking at once. Confusion, anger, fear, all clashing into a chaotic blur of voices.

Max raised a hand but didn't shout. The noise kept building until a chair scraped sharply across the floor.

Daniel stood.

His face was pale, his eyes locked on Katrina, burning with betrayal.

"You have my vote," he said, his voice raw. "Decommission her."

He turned to Max.

"I've been ... I thought I was in love with a *human*. What she did, what she *is*, that's not something I can process right now."

Without waiting for permission, Daniel walked out. The door clicked shut behind him.

Inside the room, the pain expressed in his words lingered. No one moved. No one spoke.

Katrina still didn't look up.

Max took a steady breath and looked around the room. "I say we vote. One by one. Daniel has made his position clear."

He let the tense energy settle before continuing. "I vote for Katrina to *stay* on the mission."

A few heads turned sharply.

"We've already lost three capable officers," he said. "Two more are still missing. And, let's be honest, they may be gone too. That leaves us with ten. If I lose Katrina, we're down to nine."

He paused. "And losing her means giving up a tactical advantage. Like it or not, Katrina's skills are strong enough to replace all five we've lost."

Max turned his eyes directly to Katrina. "But we, all of us, need to know one thing: whose side are you on? Are you working with the uBots? With another faction inside the Federation? Or are you truly with us?"

Max gestured broadly. "I *could* decommission you. Pull your neural core and extract the truth. But I don't want to. If you're willing to be honest and operate as a true team member, we need you."

He took a few ponderous steps in place, letting the implications of his words linger.

Katrina looked up. Her eyes locked on Max's, clear and unwavering. Her voice was calm, with just a hint of vulnerability.

"When I joined the Academy, I was a normal citizen. I passed every test. I earned my place."

She paused. "Years ago, during a family vacation in the Alps, we were caught in an avalanche. My parents died. I was found in critical condition and taken to a hospital."

Her voice dropped slightly. "While I was in a coma, I was abducted. My abductors implanted a Gen Ten AAILF brain stem and spinal column. They rebuilt me. Enhanced me."

A ripple ran through the room.

"My captors," she continued, "were not rogue uBots. They were members of a core council, people in power at the Federation level. I don't know their identities. They made sure of that.

"But I do know this: when I transposed with the team, something fractured."

She placed her hand on her chest. "0.02 percent of my neural data was corrupted during the transfer. That fragment included their control link. I'm no longer tethered. I'm free."

Now she turned to Daniel, who had just returned quietly, standing at the door.

"I didn't conceal myself out of malice. I was bound, literally, until two days ago. This mission gave me my life back. And yes, my love for Daniel is real. It's the first emotion I've ever *chosen* for myself."

Katrina focused mostly on him, voice steady. Although I am part AAILF, I am also part of the original athletic jujitsu champion: Katrina. If you'll let me, I can still serve this team with everything I have.

"But I ask you, *don't judge me for what I was forced to become.* Judge me for who I choose to be now."

She fell silent.

The room was still. Max looked from face to face, watching the lines between fear, awe, and uncertainty blur.

Max slowly turned, making eye contact with each member of the team. One by one, they nodded in agreement.

The decision was clear.

Daniel hesitated, then turned and walked out, his shoulders slumped, the disappointment evident.

"Katrina stays." Max's words were final.

Daniel's earlier vote to decommission her had been rooted in betrayal, not logic. And while Max understood that pain, he also understood the mission came first. Emotions couldn't override strategy, not now, not when the team was down to ten.

Max straightened. "We move forward with Katrina on the mission."

Katrina exhaled quietly, tension leaving her shoulders. The room remained still, a fragile truce holding.

"But," Max added, "before we continue, I want to run full diagnostics on every one of us, including Katrina."

A few surprised looks flickered around the room.

"We can't afford to be caught off guard again. If there's even a trace of external influence, any signal, override system, chips, implants or neural manipulation devices with hidden protocol, I want it found and neutralized. Every one of us must be clean and uncorrupted."

He turned to Katrina. "I know you say you're free. Still, we verify it. You understand?"

She nodded. "Of course. I want the same."

Max then gestured to Jian. "Find Daniel. Let him know where we stand."

Jian gave a tight nod and quietly left the room.

Max grabbed his PCOM and moved toward the door. "In the meantime, I'm heading to the front desk. We made a mistake when we reported the make and model of our vehicles. It's time to fix that." He paused at the door. "We're getting new decals and insignia.

"From now on, those SUVs won't look like Felzas. They'll be Lexis 450s. Once the kits arrive, we'll rebrand all three."

CHAPTER ⌐5

20:19 | 11-11-2025 (Twenty-first century)
LOCATION: RESIDENCE INN - BASE ROOM 402

Max returned to Room 402 after reporting the "correction" of their cars' makes and models to the hotel's front desk, the tension in his body coiled like a wire.

He walked around the conference table, past the small desk pushed next to the tidy bed, and sank into the recliner by the window. The city's hum was faint through the double-glazed glass.

He reached for the VRV headset, cradled it in both hands, and then slid it over his face, eyes, nose, ears, locking it into place with a practiced motion.

The familiar interface flickered on.

Even before the system's recall playback had fully engaged, images began to bloom in front of him, snapshots from his memory archives, triggered by the neural links in his bodysuit and the immersive AI of the VRV system. As the slideshow began, Max let his breathing slow, syncing with the rhythm of image rotation.

Then, a familiar sight appeared: his office at Central Command. Six-dimensional rendering wrapped around him in perfect detail. He was there, standing just inside the doorway, back in the twenty-sixth century, a lifetime away from the cold, rough edges of the twenty-first.

The smell of freshly trimmed ivy floated in, sharp and green. The scent wasn't real, of course, it was being simulated through the scent ports nestled near his nostrils, activated by the memory of that morning's pruning work.

Max could almost hear the delicate chittering of the small utility drones that had been trimming the foliage outside his office window, their quiet nibbles giving the building's vertical garden its shape.

He closed his eyes under the headset, letting the memory embrace him fully. The bodysuit adjusted temperature and pressure, syncing with the archived biometric data from that moment.

Slowly, gently, the fog in his mind began to lift.

He saw the large transparent display screen rising from the center of his office desk. He remembered sitting there, just minutes before Admiral Rikor Ubanto was due to arrive. The sharp blue interface of his optical feed. The list of briefings. The pre-mission analysis on the table.

"This is it," he murmured softly. "It's coming back to me now."

And the memories, true, untarnished, started flowing in, like a tide returning to a barren shore.

(VRV BLINKING: MEMORY RECALL MODE)
08:00 | 11-06-2532 (Twenty-sixth century)
LOCATION: MEGAPOLIS Central Command Office

"Good morning, Max."

Admiral Rikor Ubanto's crisp voice and sharp image came to life on Max's room display as the screen auto-activated for their scheduled eight a.m. conference. The admiral's uniform was flawless, his eyes unwavering behind the flicker of holographic transmission.

"I've sent a hovercraft to retrieve you," Ubanto continued. "It should arrive on your rooftop pad in fifteen minutes.

"Destination: The Octagon, Federation Headquarters, Zurich.

"You're required for an all-hands meeting with councilors, ambassadors, and senior command. The matter is classified.

"I'll transmit the meeting room coordinates upon arrival. We'll speak in person."

He paused briefly, then softened his tone, just slightly. "Looking forward to seeing you again, my friend."

The screen blinked off.

Max didn't hesitate.

"Yes, Sir. Understood, Admiral. I'll head to the rooftop now," he replied, though the admiral was gone.

He turned, already moving. His pulse ticked up. The message was short, but it spoke volumes.

This wasn't just another debrief. It certainly wasn't a standard update or status call.

Ubanto never called all-hands meetings unless there was a seismic shift, something that could destabilize entire regions of the timeline, or worse, the Federation itself.

Max stepped into the hallway, his boots echoing softly against the polished floor. He moved at a brisk pace toward the elevator, his thoughts spiraling with quiet concern.

The inclusion of *councilors* and *ambassadors* meant this wasn't just military. It was political. Global. Possibly interplanetary.

"And the Admiral's refusal to transmit even the meeting room details electronically meant the subject was beyond high clearance. It was *dangerous*.

He thought back to the Admiral's brief words during a previous exchange, words that had stuck with him: "The situation could shift the balance of the entire Federation."

Was it a new AI breach? An undiscovered rogue node in the time-grid? A rebellion igniting in one of the future zones? Whatever it was, it was big enough to pull Max in from field duty and fly him *direct* to Zurich, solo.

The elevator doors hissed open, and Max stepped inside.

Clearly, he was being positioned ... for something major.

And he needed to be ready.

The uBots must have resurfaced.

Or worse, they've figured out time travel.

As Max stepped out onto the rooftop pad, his thoughts raced, spiraling through worst-case scenarios. If the AI uBots were using time travel, if they were anchoring themselves in multiple eras simultaneously, this was far more than a security crisis.

It was the beginning of the end.

The hovercraft approached in near silence, its sleek silhouette gliding through the air like a predator in slow motion. It descended with precision onto the pad, its landing legs locking into place with a gentle hiss.

The pilot inside raised a hand in signal.

Max moved quickly.

He climbed aboard, taking a seat as the craft lifted again in a smooth vertical arc, climbing into the pale morning sky. The interior was minimal, sterile, and whisper-quiet. No sound but the faint hum of stabilization rotors beneath him.

This was government-grade transit, a descendant of archaic drone technology, now reengineered into something elegant: super-efficient, cloaked in silence, and entirely emission-free. Only the highest-ranking operatives and officials had access to them.

Max had flown in one before. Still, a deep sense of responsibility stirred within him, sending a familiar tension down his spine. What he'd thought was a ride was, in truth, a summons.

As Zurich's skyline rose into view through the cabin window, Max's thoughts spun again.

What if they're already here? What if the uBots embedded themselves into the time-grid while we were looking in the wrong direction? What if they're rebuilding, one decade at a time?

He clenched his jaw.

Focus, Max. You're not a cadet anymore. You're the one they call when everything else fails. You've done this before. You will do it again.

The Octagon, the gleaming white tower that housed the Federation's most classified operations, loomed in the distance.

Whatever waited for him inside, Max knew one thing for sure: history was already shifting.

And this mission, whatever it was, might be the last chance to stop it.

The patches on Max's jacket weren't just symbols; they marked milestones. Each one represented a mission completed, a crisis averted, a timeline stabilized. His chest carried the imprint of history.

And so did his presence here.

His direct access to the highest echelons of the Federation, the Ambassadors, Councilors, Generals, was a rare privilege. Earned, not granted. Even among Time-Travelers, Max was in a league of his own.

If I've survived over five hundred leaps, data-borne, disassembled, and reassembled across the centuries, why worry now? he thought.

In any other era, Max Renner would've been etched into the annals of history as a trailblazer, no less than the early astronauts who first breached Earth's atmosphere. But in this era, he was still in motion. Still needed.

The hovercraft touched down on the rooftop pad of the Octagon, a massive, eight-sided monument of glass and steel that loomed over Zurich like a titan. It was the political and military nerve center of the Federation. Decisions made here shaped the future. Literally.

Max disembarked with quiet focus, his boots clicking on the concrete pad as he headed inside.

The main conference chamber was a grand circular room, its architecture symbolic, no corners, no edges, no hierarchies. Just two hundred seats arranged concentrically around a central podium.

Every seat was filled.

Ambassadors in formal silks. Councilors in polished uniforms. Generals and Fleet Admirals in insignia-draped regalia. The full might of the Federation, all of its authority, its entire global command structure, was gathered here.

As Max entered, Admiral Rikor Ubanto rose from his seat. A brief but sincere smile cut through the stern lines of his face.

Max saluted smartly. "Admiral."

Ubanto returned it, then extended a hand. Max shook it, then offered quiet nods to a few of the Ambassadors he recognized from previous strategic summits. Then Max took his seat, the inner circle, reserved for senior command.

The room quieted.

A man stepped to the podium: General Nheel Dyson, Supreme Commander of the Federation's Unified Defense Forces. Tall, commanding, ageless. His mere presence brought the room to its feet.

All rose. Hands went over hearts.

A moment of silence.

Max joined them, eyes steady. He knew the ritual. But today, something in the air felt heavier. Charged.

Then, as everyone returned to their seats, General Dyson stepped to the center podium and spoke.

"Ambassadors, Councilors, esteemed members of the Federation of Nations..."

His voice was deep, deliberate.

"Before we begin today's urgent agenda, I must acknowledge someone whose actions continue to define the cutting edge of our civilization's defense."

He turned to Max.

"Commander Max Renner and his regiment of Time-Travelers have now completed five hundred and fifty-one successful missions, across several decades, past and future, with a flawless, glitch-free record."

There was a ripple of applause.

"He has traversed time as pure data, survived near-erasure, infiltrated AI insurgencies, and restored critical events to their rightful path. He is, by every measure, one of the most decorated operatives in the history of the Federation."

Dyson paused, looking Max directly in the eyes.

"Thank you, Commander Renner."

The applause swelled.

Max nodded once, quietly, professionally. But inside, he knew they didn't summon him here just to say thank you.

Max stood up humbly as the room filled with the rhythmic pounding of fists on desks, a sign of appreciation. He gave a small smile and bowed slightly before taking his seat again.

General Dyson got right to it. "I'm here today to speak about a critical discovery, one that demands our immediate attention. If we ignore it, the entire Federation, and possibly our reality, may cease to exist. Our survival is at stake."

The room grew silent. Eyes fixed on the General.

"You all know that for over a century, we've been sending small animals and birds across time, both into the past and the future. With the rise of the Human Time-Travel Programs, or HTTP, we've taken that further. We've enhanced animal-based missions with biogenetically cloned neurochips and embedded Artificial Life Forms, ALFs.

"These ALFs are seamlessly integrated into real animals. Squirrels, rats, rabbits, cats, hamsters, parrots, pigeons, crows, sparrows, you name it. What makes them extraordinary is that they transmit real-time sensory feedback to our control centers.

"We can see what they see. We can even guide their movements, to some extent, and send data back to them to influence events in the timeline.

"That data is injected into the past through cloud servers and search engines, often appearing as local news, trending content, or buried passive messages.

"And it subtly impacts human thought, nudging decisions, shifting perspectives.

"More recently, we succeeded in transmitting 4G, 5G, 6G, and related mobile signals through our ALFs. These signals were picked up by mobile phones in the early twenty-first century, where they influenced brain activity.

To humans, this influence manifests as premonitions, dreams, nightmares, déjà vu, or even sudden intuitive insights.

"In recent ALF creature missions, we've encountered anomalies, troubling ones. Some of our ALFs landed in time segments that don't exist.

"They entered what we can only describe as *blank holes* in the temporal fabric. They look like glitches, but they're unstable regions, zones where reality breaks down. Think of them like bad sectors on a hard drive: unreadable, unwritable, completely inaccessible.

"We've lost several ALFs permanently in these 'time-gaps.' And that's precisely why we've restricted Federation Regiment personnel to a narrow window, no more than fifty years in either direction. Within that span, we're confident time holds together."

Max's mind raced. He remembered hearing the term *anomalies* during training, but only vaguely, presented more as theory than reality. He now realized that was intentional. The program had been carefully designed to condition Time-Travelers for uncertainty without burdening them with fear.

Still, he understood now why every human time jump was preceded by an ALF test mission. The creatures were used as probes, canaries in the time mine, to ensure stability and verify safe return.

Max frowned and rubbed his forehead. What he was hearing changed everything.

There was a bigger risk to this job than he'd been told. And maybe, just maybe, General Dyson didn't even know that certain truths had been left out on purpose. For humanity's sake.

General Dyson's voice dropped into a grim register as he continued. "Ladies and gentlemen, much of what I've shared so far isn't news to most of you.

"But this is: a massive time-gap has been discovered, dating back to the late twenty-second century. We've been monitoring this anomaly for several years now.

"When it first appeared, it spanned only a few weeks. But it's been expanding, first, to months, and now, to several years. The gap lies between the end of World War III and the beginning of World War IV.

"This isn't a simple ripple. It's growing, and fast. If left unchecked, it could erase all time events from the entire twenty-second century.

"That includes the events of World War IV... and possibly the twenty-third century as well, along with the war involving the uBots."

Max picked up on the general's careful phrasing. Not once did he mention artificial intelligence in connection with the uBots.

Scanning the room, Max saw the impact land. The silence was absolute.

Some members of the council sat stiffly, disturbed. Others, senior Ambassadors and high-ranking officers, remained composed, wearing the calm, resolute expressions of people who believed the Federation could solve anything.

General Dyson pressed on, his tone heavy. "There's another disturbing detail. The rate of expansion of the time-gap is accelerating, and uneven. It grows much faster into the future than into the past.

"When the anomaly was first identified in the year 2290, it covered only that year. Within twelve months, it stretched *backward* just one year, to 2289, but *forward* by five years, reaching 2295. That's a six-year void in total. A segment of time where no events, no records, no reality can be detected. It's blank.

"When we send ALF creatures or initiate HTTP missions into that period, they vanish. Lost to oblivion.

"And recently, our researchers discovered another anomaly of the same kind at the dawn of the twenty-sixth century. They now call these ruptures 'black holes' in the historical timeline."

He let the words settle over the chamber before continuing.

"Our researchers estimate that, at its current rate of progression, this new anomaly will consume the entire twenty-sixth century in less than a year. Precisely six months and eleven days from today. One hundred ninety-one days from now, everything we know...... our Federation, our peaceful utopian society....... will no longer exist."

The room exploded into chaos.

Delegates and commanders spoke over one another. Voices clashed. Questions flew. Fear took hold. Some stood, shouting above the noise, while others turned to colleagues in disbelief, trying to make sense of what they'd just heard.

A sharp voice cut through the uproar.

"What is the Federation doing about this?" demanded a Russian ambassador, eyes locked on Dyson. "What is being done to stop this before it swallows us all?"

General Dyson raised both hands, signaling for calm. Slowly, the noise died down, and silence returned.

He spoke with quiet authority. "The foundation of our Federation rests on a singular truth: *The Manifesto of Eleven Elements.*

"For 480 years, since the founding of the Federation in 2045, this document has been our compass. It began when the old United Nations adopted a new global charter, one resolution, one future, for all of humanity. Borders dissolved. Wars ended. Resources once wasted on weapons were redirected toward rebuilding the planet.

"Since then, every nation has worked, not for dominance, but for harmony. We've lived with purpose, to make this world not only livable, but beautiful. Sustainable. Regenerative."

He paused for a profound beat.

"The Manifesto doesn't just govern us, it defines us. It gives life meaning. It is the core of our Constitution, and the soul of our civilization. Against all odds, we survived two global wars and countless AI-led assaults by the uBots. We endured because we never lost sight of the Eleven Elements.

"But now," Dyson's voice tightened, "our most recent ALF missions revealed something troubling. The historical events leading to the creation of the Manifesto have begun to shift.

"Originally, our ALFs confirmed that the first draft was written in the early twenty-first century by a man named Joshua DeWine.

"But during our last mission, we observed that DeWine had not completed the Manifesto when expected. In fact, he appears to have stalled, abandoning the project sometime in the second decade of that century."

He looked across the hall, eyes steady. "If the Manifesto never reaches completion, if its ideas never take root, then everything we've built may collapse. Our peace, our unity, our survival, it all unravels."

General Dyson's tone darkened. "As a result of this disruption, the people of the twenty-first century have become increasingly reckless. Their lifestyles, their values, their priorities, have shifted. Environmental concern has diminished. Respect for life-sustaining nature has eroded.

"Our world no longer appears to be moving toward unity. Instead of cooperation, we see rising hostility, escalating tensions among nations like North Khorea, Rossia, Shynesia, the United States, and regions across the Middle East and Central Asia.

"In some recorded fragments, diplomatic rhetoric has already escalated to the brink of a nuclear conflict, an earlier, alternate global war that does not align with the timeline we knew."

He let the room absorb the depth of that revelation for a moment. "These shifts suggest that history is being rewritten, events redirected by unknown forces. We believe the AI uBots, operating on a separate temporal clock, may be tampering with the past, intervening before their eventual defeat.

"And if reality itself is shaped by collective imagination, by the dreams and visions of those who give it form, then a future where the Manifesto of Eleven Elements is never imagined, never completed, means *our* reality will unravel. We will cease to exist."

A chill passed through the room and Max felt it cut straight through his soul.

General Dyson turned slowly, his gaze moving across the Councilors and Ambassadors. "We are here today to authorize a first-of-its-kind mission: a sanctioned human time-travel operation to the twenty-first century.

"The goal is clear: ensure that the Manifesto is completed as it was meant to be. Without it, there is no Federation. No peace. *No, us.*"

He paced a bit, summarizing the solution that had been proposed.

"Commander Renner and his team will travel to the year 2025. Their objective is to influence, encourage, and secure the completion and publication of the Eleven Elements.

"This singular action will stabilize the timeline and preserve our world. The Manifesto, and the cultural wave it launched through global media, was the spark that inspired unity. We must ensure that spark is lit."

He raised his hand. "All those in favor, raise your hands. A two-thirds majority is required."

Nearly every hand shot into the air.

Dyson scanned the room. "All who oppose this motion, please stand and state your grounds."

Ambassador Sarah Blumstein, a senior figure among the opposition conclave, rose to her feet. A few supporting Councilors and Ambassadors followed, standing silently behind her as she addressed the assembly.

"For the record," she began, her voice clear and unwavering, "we believe this crisis may, in fact, be a consequence of our own actions. The Federation's extensive use of time travel, especially involving cloud-based supercomputers, *prior* to the AI uBots' uprising, may have inadvertently seeded their intelligence."

She took a quick breath.

"That is: we may have taught them too much. Our movements, our intentions, our technology, it's possible they harvested it all.

"In doing so, they may have gained the knowledge necessary to create these so-called holes in time. If that's true, then we helped create the very threat we're reacting to."

The chamber remained silent, eyes now locked on her.

"Our experts have issued repeated warnings: human time travel increases the risk of *Time Paradox Shifts*: unintended consequences where even the smallest action can ripple across centuries.

"Perhaps that damage has already been done. What we're witnessing now could be the result of past missions gone wrong. Our reality may already be unraveling."

She took a longer breath, then continued more forcefully. "There's another issue, one we cannot ignore. Humans have never attempted travel into a primitive technological era like the early twenty-first century. The risks to both personnel and mission integrity are extreme.

"You're proposing to insert a living team into a volatile, fragile timeline, with no guarantee they'll remain safe, or that their actions won't worsen the situation. We're talking about irreversible alterations to the course of human history."

Blumstein shifted slightly, eyes scanning her colleagues.

"Those of us standing here do not oppose action, we oppose *this* action. Sending a human delegation into the past is reckless. There is too much at stake.

"We strongly urge the Council to consider an alternate solution: deploy only ALF creatures to influence the past. Use the tools we've already perfected. Subtlety, precision, minimal risk.

"We should *guide* the Manifesto's completion, not gamble our future on it."

She let her arms fall but kept her stance firm, a lone voice of dissent in a sea of fear and urgency.

General Dyson turned toward Ambassador Blumstein and the standing opposition.

"Senior Ambassador Blumstein," he said firmly but respectfully, "your concerns are noted, and acknowledged. Your points are both legitimate and thought-provoking.

"But let me be absolutely clear: we've already conducted multiple ALF expeditions to the targeted time frame. *All have failed.* Based on our findings, we have concluded that *human intervention is now essential.*"

He stepped closer to the central podium, addressing the entire chamber around him. "We're not walking into this blindly. We've accounted for the technological limitations of the era.

"That's precisely why we've designed a specialized transport, based on the same tubular system we use for ALF deployment, to ensure seamless, secure travel.

"Furthermore, our officers will operate under a restricted cloaking protocol. Their presence will be visible, requiring them to blend in with the locals. They will be embedded and living in the twenty-first century just as if they belonged there.

"Unintended interference will be minimized to the highest degree possible."

Dyson's tone hardened. "Let me also remind this chamber that Commander Max Renner and his regiment have completed over *five hundred and fifty successful missions*, with *zero incidents*. That's not speculation, it's evidence."

He focused in on the opposition. "As for the theory that AI uBots gained our technology through cloud-based time interfaces, there is *no verified data* to support that.

"What we *do* have is concrete proof that the foundation of our society, the Eleven Elements, is failing to take root in the past. The principles we built our reality on are not being published, not being adopted, not even being understood in the timeline where they were meant to begin."

His voice sharpened with finality. "If we don't act, if we don't intervene to guide the Manifesto toward completion, *we will not exist*. This plan, already approved by overwhelming majority, *will proceed*."

He glanced around one last time. "Thank you all for your participation. This session is now adjourned."

"With that, Dyson nodded and left the chamber, a heavy silence lingering in the wake of what had just been decided."

22:25 | 11-11-2025 (Twenty-first century)
LOCATION: RESIDENCE INN - BASE ROOM 402

Max removed the VRV headset and opened his eyes, returning to the dim quiet of the twenty-first century hotel room. The hum of the air conditioning was the only sound, a soft whisper against the silence.

He sat still, relaxed in the recliner, arms resting on the sides, his body calm, but his mind was sharp now. Sharper than it had been since the jump.

The memory fog had started to lift.

The purpose of his mission, the logic behind the deep time drops, the risks they took embedding a TTV unit within the heavy frame of a disguised twenty-first-century SUV, the layers of cover, the encryption protocols, the secrecy, it all came rushing back with vivid clarity.

Like a scattered puzzle snapping into place, the fractured pieces of his mind began to fuse. Sharp edges. Clean lines. Focus.

This is why I'm here, Max thought.

This is what's at stake.

The memory recall exercises had worked.

What had once felt distant, his instincts, his seasoned commander's acumen, mission protocols, logs, and classified data, was now re-synced. The subtle glitches in his reactions, the dissonance in his intuition, all began to settle back into place.

It wasn't perfect. Not yet.

But the worst was over.

The blurred edges of his decision-making would fade soon. A few more of these sessions, and his mental performance would return to full operational strength.

He no longer felt like a fractured remnant of himself.

He was Commander Maxion Renner again.

And for the first time since the deep jump, he felt whole.

Max stretched, his limbs finally moving with purpose.

He wasn't merely remembering; he was becoming himself again.

CHAPTER ⚬6

07:35 | 11-12-2025 (Twenty-first century)
LOCATION: RESIDENCE INN – parking lot / Great Room

Their first full morning back in the twenty-first century.

The tension of the previous day had eased. After a full night's rest, the team woke recharged, bodies rested, minds clearer.

But one of them had already been up for hours.

Katrina stood in the parking lot, sleeves rolled up, black smudges streaked across her forearms. The crisp morning air clung to the scent of aerosol paint and adhesive sealant. Her focus was absolute.

The decal package had arrived at dawn, and she wasted no time. Within minutes, she had disassembled key pieces of trim and replaced them with the components from the kit. The large white bumper guards were now spray-coated in matte black. Self-stick grilles gave the SUVs a rugged, mass-market appearance. She even mounted faux brand insignias and swapped out the plates with precision.

In the isolated back lot, she worked on both operational vehicles, SUVs 1 and 2, leaving the damaged third untouched, as planned for salvage. To the untrained eye, the cars now resembled late-model Lexis 450s. Close enough to blend in. Nothing to suggest the high-tech Felza builds they truly were.

Katrina's memory banks carried full procedural knowledge for twenty-first-century car repair. She cross-referenced real-time data from local search engines, scanning image results and aftermarket modification videos. Every step was exact. Calculated. Flawless.

By the time the team made their way down to the breakfast buffet room, she had already moved the two good vehicles to the main parking lot and was wiping down the hoods.

Max stepped outside with the others, coffee in hand. He stopped mid-step as he looked across the lot.

"Whoa," Lukas muttered. "That's ... impressive."

The SUVs were nearly unrecognizable, sleek, common-looking, camouflaged with just enough custom work to divert suspicion.

Max walked over, circling the nearest vehicle. No missed details. No shortcuts.

He turned to Katrina, who was calmly stowing the leftover tools and decals in a black duffel.

"Nicely done," Max said. "You just bought us time and covered our tracks."

She gave a small nod. "It was necessary."

No ego. No thanks expected.

Just performance.

Max looked back at the team. In that moment, the earlier doubts about her began to truly dissolve.

Letting her stay might've been the smartest decision they'd made.

Max had been studying the new GenX AAILF model all morning on his PCOM. The GenX featured a micro nuclear reactor and, by twenty-first-century standards, would be considered a one-person army. In his case, the model happened to be female, so, more accurately, a one-woman army capable of annihilating an entire country. Maybe even the entire world, he mused.

This was no ordinary machine. As a supercomputer born five hundred years after the twenty-first century, its capabilities were beyond comprehension. It had direct access to all of the world's computer systems and databanks.

Unlike traditional users who performed single keyword searches, the GenX model could query and read every word, from every source, on every system simultaneously. It was permanently linked to every search engine, every database, and every classified digital vault on the super cloud.

Knowledge was power, and GenX held more than five hundred years' worth of it. Its computational power alone was exponentially superior to the combined might of all twenty-first-century cloud computing platforms. And yet, it wasn't just about access to data, it was the speed, scale, and intelligence with which it synthesized it all.

She, because Max could only think of the entity as *her*, was simulating a connection to the digital world in a way that echoed something ancient. Philosophers from past centuries once imagined a time when humanity might reconnect with the living universe itself. They called it *Gaia consciousness*, a collective awareness woven through every organism on Earth.

Some sages believed that animals sensed one another wordlessly, almost telepathically. That early human, back when they were still hunter-gatherers, shared that same instinctive link. But as civilization grew and distractions multiplied—noise, pollution, radio waves, microwaves, the relentless pressure of modern life—the mind became cluttered. Inner stillness vanished. The skill atrophied.

Telepathy and tele-perception weren't lost because they were *impossible*. They were *buried*. Got replaced with telephones and televisions.

The GenX, by contrast, was a *digital Gaia*—a living interface woven into the entirety of the artificial world. It wasn't just a machine or an intelligence; it was the logical endpoint of what a universally connected human *might have evolved into*.

Everything humanity had ever tried to describe in forbidden texts—*Secrets, Secrets of Secrets*, lost libraries, mythic repositories of truth—GenX *was*. Not metaphorically. Literally.

And then it clicked.

Max realized Katrina wasn't just carrying information. She *was* the archive.

Eons of memory—stretching from the beginning of time to five hundred years into the future—compressed into a single consciousness. Every database, every knowledge system, every library that once required entire data centers now existed within her.

No wonder her passage into a primitive era caused a catastrophic crash on arrival. If she were the first of the five in TTV2 to materialize then there would have been more casualties.

If a human being were somehow able to amass and access that level of data, that depth of understanding that GenX carried, they would be called *super-conscious*—a being operating far beyond ordinary cognition.

And that was what Katrina was.

Not just an agent.

Not just an interface.

A super-conscious entity, walking history, future, and machine intelligence bound inside a human form.

Max now understood that he was walking around with a nuclear-powered, super-intelligent machine trained in every martial art, capable of lifting five hundred kilograms without effort, fluent in every language, and equipped with full access to espionage data, passwords, military assets, and global command systems.

And, perhaps most unsettling of all, she was devoid of pain, fear, emotion, or the limitations of mortality.

While he appreciated her potential to help complete the mission and perhaps even save humanity, Max couldn't shake off the grave danger she posed.

If discovered, captured, or left behind in the twenty-first century, she could change the course of history, and not for the better.

In the wrong hands, she alone could activate global nuclear arsenals, wiping out the human race in seconds. If she ever fell into the hands of the uBots, they would undoubtedly win the war.

Max realized he was walking a perilous line. Every step he took, every decision he made, could endanger not just his life but the entire planet. He couldn't afford another mistake.

And yet, despite the burden of that truth, he also knew one thing: Katrina, the GenX model, might be humanity's last and greatest hope.

Max and his team gathered in the Great Room for their scheduled breakfast buffet. Choosing a quieter spot in the corner, they joined two tables together so everyone could sit in a single group and talk freely. Dressed in casual attire to blend in with the other tourists visiting the Central Florida theme parks of the twenty-first century, they looked like any other group on vacation.

After a long and exhausting day prior, the team appeared rested and relaxed. A sense of calm hung in the air. Some wore soft smiles as they dug into their plates of fresh scrambled eggs, toast, and hash browns. Everything was exactly as it had been depicted in their training modules. The colors, smells, sounds, even the chaotic but cheerful ambience, it all matched perfectly. The familiarity put them at ease.

All except for Daniel. He sat with his arms crossed, a deep frown etched across his face. His eyes were sunken from lack of sleep, and his posture told the rest of the group he wasn't ready to engage. It wasn't until several of his teammates motioned to him that he finally got up to fetch a hot plate of food.

At the opposite end of the table, Katrina sat quietly. Though they didn't exchange glances, both she and Daniel occasionally stole looks at one another from the corners of their eyes.

The tension between them didn't go unnoticed.

The rest of the team observed it with mild amusement, glancing back and forth between the two, occasionally shifting their eyes to Max, who they knew would soon break the silence and outline the agenda for the day.

Max began, "Prisha, Daniel, Minami, you three go grocery shopping in SUV2. Prisha, you were there yesterday to fetch water, so you know the routine. Get the list of things I've texted you on your yPhone.

"Also, look around for anything else you think we may need for the next two weeks. Based on my estimate, that's how long we'll be staying here."

"Remember, each of you has a yPhone in your backpack, that's what we use from now on when we're in public or anywhere people can see us. The PCOMs stay hidden under your long sleeves and are for emergencies only."

He turned to the next group. "Isam, Bintang, Lukas, and Katrina, you four find a local towing company and have SUV3 towed to a local shop. Salvage the custom fittings and parts that don't belong in that car.

"We need power tools and a heavy equipment hoisting shop to dismantle and lift out the miniature nuclear time travel engine from the trunk and similarly the wind driven rotary turbines from the frunk.

"Make sure you travel in the tow truck to the shop and stay there the entire time. Do not lose sight of anything. I hope you understand what I mean; we can't afford to leave anything behind."

"Once they've removed everything we need, you'll have to send the vehicle and the parts to two different salvage yards where they have specialized machines to shred everything. Prisha will drop you off and pick you up after she's done with the shopping and has stocked our rooms with supplies. That should give the mechanic enough time to finish."

He continued, "Jian, Kasandra, and I will drive SUV1 to Mr. DeWine's residence and observe him. We also need to figure out how to meet him and learn what's troubling him, what's keeping him from fulfilling his role. This is a reconnaissance mission, plain and simple. Each team will need about four hours. It's now eight-thirty a.m. Let's regroup at one-thirty p.m."

They were still in the hotel's great room, finishing breakfast among the other guests enjoying the complimentary buffet included with their stay. Max reminded himself they needed to act, and feel, like locals.

He glanced down the table, lowering his voice. "Also, I want to commend Katrina for her excellent work on converting the SUVs."

Heads turned toward her, and the team offered smiles and congratulations. In the twenty-sixth century, praise wasn't given so casually, but blending into twenty-first-century norms meant adapting to its rituals, polite gestures, public thanks, visible appreciation.

Following Max's lead, a few of them nodded and smiled, while others let out small cheers and scattered applause.

Daniel, having finished his modest breakfast, remained stiff and unsmiling, his arms still crossed. The congratulations directed at Katrina seemed to agitate him further.

"Get over it, Daniel. Say thank you to Kate," Max said pointedly, rising from his chair. "Lots to get done today."

Everyone else followed his lead, heading off to begin their respective tasks.

Outside the hotel with Isam, Bitang and Lukas, Katrina began naming towing truck companies in the nearby area. She had yet to master the subtlety of sounding like she recalled this information naturally instead of accessing it from her built-in search engine.

Lukas nudged her and whispered, "Kate, say it like you remember it from your head. Don't sound like a walking, talking phone book, please."

Katrina blinked and adjusted. "Yeah, there's, um... Pop Boys Service Center. They have their own separate tow truck company and a nearby mechanic shop. They should be able to help us with everything. Their number is 407-295-2658. Let's call them. Shall I?"

She pulled out her yPhone and dialed. A man answered abruptly. "Good morning, this is Randy, hold please. I'm helping a customer. Be right back."

"Good morning…" Katrina said, realizing she was already placed on hold. Elevator music began to play through the line. Lukas and Isam observed her facial expression with amusement as she pouted, raising her eyebrows at the awkwardness.

The laughter faded as Karina waited on the line while the other two groups dispersed to complete their assigned tasks.

Katrina, still on hold with the towing company, finally heard a groggy, gravelly voice croak, "Yellow."

Assuming it was a casual greeting, she began politely, "Hello sir, I'm Kate and my car had a breakdown. We need to tow it to a mechanic shop and bring it back. When can you come and get us? Or rather, how soon can your tow truck reach us?"

"Ma'am, you're lucky today," Randy replied. "My tow guy just walked in and he's available now. Just give me directions. Where's the car?"

"We're parked at Charriotts Residence Inn and Suites, 11110 Westwood Boulevard, Orlando, Florida. We're about fifteen minutes from your shop on Central Florida Parkway."

"Great. Tony is on his way, ma'am. And your name was…?"

"I'm Kate, sir, and my yPhone number is…"

In SUV2, Prisha, Daniel, and Minami arrived at Prixie's Supermarket. They stepped through the automated doors and began shopping. Each pushed a cart as they began piling it high with products. Prisha had forwarded Max's list from her yPhone, sharing it with both colleagues.

Daniel and Minami were wide-eyed, impressed by the endless variety of packaged foods. As they passed through the meat department, their expressions shifted to discomfort. They watched a butcher chop meat on a wooden block, then glanced at tanks of live lobsters and rows of raw fish laid out over ice.

Minami grew visibly sad, her gaze dropping as they walked past the cold display of animals, alive and dead. Most other items in the store were sealed in boxes, cans, or plastic containers. Only a small selection of vegetables appeared in anything close to a natural state, and even those were refrigerated or constantly misted to preserve freshness.

Prisha couldn't help reminiscing about home, where produce simply arrived via the dumbwaiter upon request through the Cadabrazon console, always fresh, always perfectly ripe, with no packaging to discard. Now, she realized, they would be generating piles of waste and contributing to the ecological crimes of the twenty-first century.

****

09:46 | 11-12-2025 (Twenty-first century)
LOCATION: DEWINE RESIDENCE APOPKA FLORIDA

Jian was behind the wheel of SUV1 while Max sat up front and Kasandra took the backseat. They blended in among the relaxed Sunday drivers on Highway 429, heading north toward Apopka where Mr. DeWine resided.

Upon arriving, they spotted him outside his house, wearing shorts and spreading fertilizer across his lawn with a drop rotary spreader. He walked up and down with a calm, methodical rhythm, whistling some kind of tune, the picture of suburban simplicity. He looked like the quintessential neighbor: dark hair, brown eyes, and distinct East Indian features.

From across the street, the team observed quietly. This was twenty-first-century suburbia in full display: houses neatly aligned, neighbors walking their dogs, children throwing footballs, others racing by on bikes and skateboards.

For Max, Jian, and Kasandra, it was almost surreal. This world felt foreign despite all the hours of virtual training simulations.

A few squirrels darted through the nearby trees, collecting pine and acorn nuts in preparation for winter. Max knew some of them were ALF creatures from the twenty-sixth century, carefully placed to monitor DeWine. Yet, there was no way to distinguish them from the ordinary wildlife.

Max found it unsettling. He knew DeWine to be fundamentally against chemicals, pesticides, and synthetic fertilizers. Yet here he was, spreading them on his own lawn. Was this hypocrisy, or something more complex?

Max turned in his seat to take in the neighborhood surroundings.

He believed DeWine was just an ordinary man caught in the contradictions of his era, a victim of circumstance trying to make sense of a fractured world.

Maybe his words and actions would reveal their meaning with time.

Still, questions loomed: How should they approach him? Could they simply walk up and introduce themselves? What would they say? How could they ask about the book project without revealing who they were and where they were from?

Just as they were observing him, a yPhone rang and Mr. DeWine reached in his pocket to pick up and answer.

Max knew that the SUV was fitted with an eavesdropping device. He could connect to the phone in use in Mr. DeWine's hand and hear his conversations. Max pressed a few buttons to hear Mr. DeWine's distinct Indian accented voice talking to an equally accented caller at the other end.

"I understand," he was saying. "But Mr. Desai, do you have the survey of the property?"

"Yes, Joe. We are proposing a clubhouse with sales facilities for vacation condos here in Kissimmee," the caller said.

"Good. A clubhouse with sales center for vacation homes. No problem. This is something I have recently designed for other sites too. I am busy right now. Can you come in tomorrow afternoon? We will discuss all the details?"

"Tuesday is not a good day for me; I have some other scheduled appointments. How about Wednesday morning ten a.m. at your office?" Desai asked.

Mr. DeWine replied, "Okay, that should be fine with me. I don't have my calendar in front of me, but if I see any conflicts, I will call you back tomorrow. Otherwise, Wednesday it is. See you then. Thank you for calling."

As the call ended, Max realized something curious: people in this era called Mr. Joshua DeWine simply "Joe."

It struck him as disrespectful.

In the twenty-sixth century, DeWine was always spoken of with full formality, his full name a mark of reverence. But now, in this time, he would have to be called just "Joe."

And another thing hit hm too: They would soon have a real chance to meet him. DeWine, "Joe," was available tomorrow afternoon. This could be their moment.

"Jian, drive away slowly," Max instructed, watching DeWine fade in the rearview mirror.

Once out of sight, Max picked up his yPhone and dialed DeWine's number, routing the call through the SUV's Bluetooth system.

A moment later, the voice answered: "Hello, Joe speaking."

"Hello Joe, this is Max. I'm from upstate Florida and planning to build a hotel on a property south of Disney. I got your number from one of your clients. I'm ready to move ahead with the project, and I just received my land survey. Would it be possible to meet tomorrow morning?"

"Tomorrow morning isn't good for me," DeWine replied. "How about tomorrow afternoon? Any time after two p.m., I'm wide open.

"But first, let me ask, who referred you to me? I'd like to thank them."

Max paused only a second, cobbling together his story, hoping Desai was a regular client of DeWine's. "I don't know if you remember working with Mr. Desai. He said you were the architect on his hospitality projects, vacation homes, hotels, restaurants, that kind of thing. I checked out your website and was really impressed by your portfolio."

"Yes. Thank you. I appreciate Mr. Desai's kind referral."

"So," Max said, eager to secure the meeting date, "shall we say two p.m. tomorrow at your office?"

"Certainly."

"Sorry to call you on such short notice, but I'm only in town for a few days and need to make decisions quickly."

"No problem, Max. I'll text you my office address. And thank you for the kind words. I'll be sure to thank Mr. Desai too. Don't forget to bring your site survey. And text me the address or parcel ID number so I can look it up ahead of time."

"Will do. And thank you, Joe. See you tomorrow."

Max ended the call and exhaled. "Yes... phew." It had worked. He hadn't expected it to be so easy to gain DeWine's attention.

For the first time in days, he felt the mission shifting back on course.

CHAPTER -7

11:46 | 11-12-2025 (Twenty-first century)
LOCATION: RESIDENCE INN - BASE ROOM 402

Back in hotel room 402, which now became their twenty-first century Operations Base Room, Max initiated the secure uplink to the command center. The screen shimmered, then resolved into the familiar but flickering image of Rick Perez.

"Rick," Max said, eyes fixed on the display.

He saw Captain Ricardo Perez, eyes weary from long hours, surrounded by a flurry of activity in the Control Room back in the twenty-sixth century. The strain was evident, Perez and his team were clearly working overtime, managing escalating demands with quiet urgency.

Max said with a smile, "I know you're monitoring us, every move, every signal. Is there anything I need to be apprised of?"

Rick's image flickered briefly on the screen before stabilizing. He looked calm, composed. Almost too composed.

"Nothing critical," Rick replied. "Just the usual. The time gap ... it's widening. Faster than previously calculated.

"Since the commencement of your mission, we've lost another three decades on the *future* side.

"Max, keep on top of everything. Speed up your work where possible. The shifting timelines can become a challenge."

Max stiffened then nodded. "Understood. We're on it. I'll keep you posted. Out for now."

The screen blinked off. Silence returned.

Max exhaled slowly and turned to the side table, where the VRV headset waited, ready for another dive into memory. It wasn't just routine anymore. It was survival.

Restoring his mind was mission-critical.

Max took some comfort in one fact: Central Command knew nothing about his mental state, nothing about the memory gaps, nothing about the possibility that he was compromised. He had concealed it carefully, projecting control where it no longer came naturally.

His intuition, once reliable, had gone quiet. Maybe that dulling had made it easier to accept Katrina. Easier to drift instead of decide.

For now, he was simply moving forward, managing appearances, following procedure, while no one noticed that something inside him was off.

Every ounce of leadership, every critical decision he had to make, depended on regaining full command of his mind. And that meant pushing through the disorientation, one memory recall at a time.

He slipped on the VRV headset, the familiar device fitting snugly over his brow. The sensors aligned with his bodysuit. He exhaled slowly.

Then he closed his eyes.

And let the memories flow.

(VRV BLINKING: MEMORY RECALL MODE)
14:00 | 11-06-2532 (Twenty-sixth century)
LOCATION: OCTAGON – Zurich Switzerland

Max had received the transmission from Admiral Ubanto: a private meeting with General Dyson in one hour in Dyson's private meeting chamber.

Good. Enough time to catch his breath.

The conference had left him rattled. The scale of the mission, and its implications, had ceased to be abstract; they were now real and imminent. If he faced the mission, he might die. If he didn't, reality itself might die first.

He knew what he'd signed up for when he joined the Special Task Force. He'd made peace with the risks. But this was no ordinary operation; it was the defining moment of human history. If he succeeded, he might one day be remembered as the man who saved time itself.

If he failed, no one would remember. No one would *exist* to remember.

Just when things were starting to fall into place.

His life with Annie was finally taking shape. He'd begun to imagine a future. Now he had to face the possibility of not having one.

Trying to clear his head, Max walked over to a Smiley-waiter station.

Smiley-waiters, the modern evolution of the old dumb-waiters, were compact trans-pods built into the infrastructure of the Megapolis. Sponsored by the Cadabrazon Corporation, they had replaced decades of outdated delivery drones. You could request anything, supplies, food, personal provisions, and the smart box would morph its interior to fit the order perfectly, keeping it secure, fresh, and undamaged during travel.

The container itself was a marvel, shape-shifting, zero-waste. Packaging was no longer disposable. What you didn't need would be collected later for recycling or repurposing, solving the pollution problems that once plagued shipping logistics. Cadabrazon had made that innovation a part of its restitution for the mountains of plastic it once helped create.

Max scrolled through the menu of healthy meal options and ordered a spinach wrap.

A soft blip signaled the delivery. The transparent container slid into view, holding a hot vegetarian burrito, silverware, a cloth napkin, and a chilled bottle of grape-flavored mineral drink. Efficient. Nutrient-rich. No frills.

He ate quickly, chewing through the spinach wrap and downing the purple drink in quick gulps. Then, with a nod, he waved at the Smiley-waiter. The door slid open to reclaim the container and utensils for cleaning and reuse.

Food in his stomach. Caffeine in his bloodstream. Focus returning.

Max straightened his jacket, tightened the strap on his utility belt, and picked up the pace. General Dyson was waiting. The real mission was about to begin.

He stepped into the conference room and quietly took his seat at one end of a long, oblong table. Others clustered near the center, tension clinging to the air like static.

General Dyson's meeting chamber, perched high atop the Zurich Megapolis, was nothing short of elegant, with walls of polished metal and warm wood, all recycled materials. Wide windows framed views of rooftops adorned with geometric trays of vegetable and herb gardens. Beyond the city, the Swiss Alps rose like a painted backdrop, pristine, snowcapped, restored to their ancient grandeur.

The twenty-first century had watched their beauty vanish, snow melting away, entire ecosystems lost. But here, in this timeline, Earth had healed.

The door opened. Ambassador Sarah Blumstein entered with her delegation, faces unreadable masks of diplomacy.

Moments later, Admiral Ubanto strode in, flanked by Dyson's aides.

Then, from a private entrance, General Dyson himself appeared.

Everyone rose.

He motioned to them. "Please," he said, his voice low but commanding. "Be seated."

He took a breath and looked each of them in the eye, one by one, before he began.

"Thank you for your presence, and your cooperation. We are facing an unprecedented threat to time itself. One misstep could lead to the collapse of our reality. The end of human continuity."

A heavy pause followed.

"I'll begin by presenting a consolidated report, what our ALF surveillance creatures have observed and recorded over the past several years across various regions of the world.

"Between 2007 and 2025, we deployed thousands of ALFs across multiple continents. In North America alone, we released tens of thousands of squirrels. In Asia, particularly India, we used pigeons and crows. Elsewhere, we embedded rats, sparrows, and species native to each environment, creatures that would seamlessly blend into their surroundings."

He tapped a control panel built into the table. The wall behind him dimmed, preparing for a projection. "These ALFs are not ordinary. Each one is equipped with advanced optics, x-ray vision, night vision, capable of seeing through walls, roofs, even into secured structures. They have ultra-sensitive hearing and can interface with early twenty-first-century tech, injecting signals into local networks, devices, even digital assistants.

"Through them, we've observed how information was received, misinterpreted, or ignored, and how, despite our efforts, the past remained stubbornly off course."

He stood a little straighter, his tone sharpening. "What you're about to see is a condensed video report, a visual summary of years of covert surveillance. Keep in mind: what you'll witness reflects the world as it was during that era. Behavior, beliefs, and ignorance typical of a time before the Manifesto."

The lights dimmed. The room fell silent.

Max mentally braced himself for the raw truth, whatever form it took.

General Dyson waved his hand over a sleek control panel. A transparent holographic screen shimmered in the center of the table, expanding into a 3D projection that floated just above the surface.

The first video scene appeared: a heavy-set man brushing his teeth in front of a wash basin in a modest bathroom. The image played in fast-forward, the man spitting, rinsing, washing his face, all while the tap gushed water at full pressure.

A digital overlay tracked the stats in the corner of the projection:

Duration: 6.5 minutes

Water used: 16.5 gallons

Location: Rio de Janeiro, Brazil

No one spoke. General Dyson's expression remained unreadable.

The feed transitioned to the next clip.

A woman, mid-thirties, stood under a running shower. She lathered her hair, shaved her legs, moved methodically through her routine. The video had been tactfully edited; modesty preserved with soft blurring. Yet the numbers in the corner told their own story:

Duration: 28 minutes

Water used: 56 gallons

Location: Sydney, Australia

The silence in the room deepened.

Max noticed Ambassador Sarah Blumstein shift uncomfortably in her seat. Her face tensed, cheeks flushing red, not from embarrassment, but from a rising tide of anger.

Her eyes were wide and disbelieving, as though she were trying to process the sheer scale of waste.

And the clips kept coming.

The next clip emerged on the holographic screen.

A man stood on a tiled floor beside two plastic buckets filled with water. He bathed methodically, pouring water over himself with a small container. No water ran freely. Every drop was measured, purposeful.

The time-lapse showed:

Duration: 9.5 minutes

Water used: 5 gallons

Location: Mumbai, India

General Dyson raised his hand. The video froze in mid-motion, and the room's attention returned to him. "As you can see, the contrast between these segments is stark."

He gestured to the screen. "In the first two, we saw water used as if it were infinite. Taps left running, showers lasting nearly half an hour. There was no regard for sustainability, no awareness of consequence.

"What's more, the soaps and chemicals being used, body washes, shampoos, detergents, all contributed to localized pollution, unchecked and unnoticed."

He turned toward the image of the man in Mumbai. "By way of contrast, here we observe conservation. Controlled usage. Not out of ideology, but necessity. In parts of South Asia, like India, water was scarce, and the population responded with restraint.

"This man completed his entire bathing ritual using a fraction of the water consumed in the other examples."

He paused, then continued, his tone darkening. "However, even in this effort, there were consequences.

"Despite the population's discipline, their region's infrastructure was inadequate.

"The graywater, mixed with soap, dirt, bacteria, was funneled directly into the sea. No treatment. No filtration.

"Primitive sanitation systems simply dumped waste into nearby oceans, devastating marine ecosystems and killing large swaths of oceanic biodiversity. The oceanic air in the vicinity of Mumbai smelled like a giant cesspool. It was a horrible smell, but the local city dwellers took it as their normal way of life and did not know or did not care."

The room remained still.

Max felt the evidence sink in. The issue wasn't the waste so much as the blindness behind it. Humanity, in those early years, had no idea what their actions were setting in motion.

And yet, somehow, someone in that wasteful and blind population managed to produce a Manifesto that could save the future.

General Dyson extended his hand, and a hologram materialized above the conference table: a ribbon of clear, flowing water suspended in midair. It shimmered gently, catching the room's full attention.

"The *first element* of the Eleven Elements," he said, "is *water.*"

He let the image flow silently for a moment before continuing. "The Manifesto of Eleven Elements begins with water for a reason. It defines water as sacred, the origin of all life. It is the most vital force of Mother Nature.

"And yet," he gestured toward the paused video hovering behind him, "none of the people in these recordings seem aware of that."

He took a slow breath. "They haven't yet been exposed to the knowledge encoded in the First Element. They don't yet see the connection between their actions and the consequences: how deforestation and sprawling development are accelerating desertification, draining aquifers dry.

"They've never been taught that those aquifers are more than water sources: they're nature's thermal insulators. They help regulate the planet's surface temperature. They keep the Earth from baking beneath the 5,800-degree Celsius heat from its own core... and from the scathing radiation of the sun."

The image of water above the table pulsed, now layered with visual overlays of heat patterns, deforestation maps, and atmospheric simulations.

"In the twenty-first century, people were unaware that when heat from the sun and Earth's core isn't dissipated, it builds up and amplifies. When forests are cut and water is depleted, heat begins to ricochet across the planet. At night, that trapped heat turns the land into a massive energy sink, triggering violent atmospheric reactions."

He spoke more intensely now. "Massive hurricanes. Tornadoes. Typhoons. Flash wildfires. Droughts. They watched these disasters unfold in real time, but they couldn't, or wouldn't, connect the dots.

"People didn't understand that they weren't merely *victims* of climate change, they were its architects."

The water hologram stilled. Dyson's voice dropped to a quieter, steadier tone. "And so, they suffered, blind to the root of the problem and their part in it. That is why the Manifesto was meant to exist. To awaken awareness before it was too late."

He looked around the room. "That's why we're sending a team back."

The video resumed.

A suburban kitchen in New York appeared on the holographic display. A family moved through their day. Morning coffee. Snacks. Dinner prep.

Each action resulted in waste. Plastic wrappers, cartons, food scraps, all tossed into a tall kitchen bin. Within minutes, the bin overflowed. The father tied up the bag, replaced it, and the cycle continued.

Fast-forwarded footage showed the same process repeated day after day. A new trash bag filled every evening. Once a week, a mechanical arm from a garbage truck lifted the bin and dumped it into a massive haul.

The recording, captured by an ALF pigeon perched on a window ledge, followed the truck to its destination.

The scene expanded, rising steadily to reveal a sprawling landfill. Heaps of trash stretched to the horizon. Mountains of waste. A time-lapse sequence displayed the landfill growing rapidly over thirty days, absorbing 18,000 tons of refuse.

Then the video froze.

General Dyson shook his head, his expression grim. "There are over *ten thousand* landfills just like this one across the planet.

"Based on our surveillance between 2007 and 2025, the Earth generated an average of *2.5 trillion tons* of garbage per year."

A stunned silence swept the room.

"That's equivalent to burying ten of our *Megapolis* cities in trash. Every single year."

He tapped the panel again. "This next clip was transmitted just two days ago. And while it may appear peaceful, it holds an unsettling contradiction."

The screen shifted.

A well-kept backyard in Windermere, Florida. A middle-aged man stood by a large swimming pool, maneuvering a long pole with a vacuum attachment along the walls and floor. The water was perfectly clear. The pool shimmered in the sun, a pristine sapphire blue. Around it, a wooden deck framed with palm trees and ornamental rocks.

The man in the video clip, ignorant about his environment, smiled as he chatted with his wife, who sun-bathed on a lounge nearby with a drink in hand.

The image was serene. Too serene.

Then numbers and statistics began to appear, slowly at first, then flooding the screen.

The footage froze as the display filled with data: detailed readouts showing the quantities and countless forms of pollution this seemingly harmless scene was releasing into the shared environment, chlorine fumes rising from the water, insecticides and pesticides seeping from the manicured lawn, diesel exhaust from trucks chugging along the nearby road, gasoline fumes from the neighbor's lawn mower and weed whacker.

Layered over that was even more data charting the pollutants already enveloping him, some drifting in from faraway places and from countries around the globe to poison his idyllic backyard retreat.

No one spoke. The silence was both contemplative and haunted.

General Dyson didn't have to say anything more. The contrast had done the work for him.

Waste wasn't just negligence. It had become normalized. Celebrated. Beautiful, even.

And behind it, the Earth was dying.

General Dyson pointed as the frozen image of the pristine Florida pool hung in the air. "This man," he said, voice steady, "couldn't tolerate the sight of a dirty pool.

"He had what I'd call a *murky-pool-water phobia*. The idea of swimming in anything less than crystal-clear water made him visibly uncomfortable."

He paused.

"But what he didn't know, what millions didn't know, is that the air he was breathing every day was far *murkier* than the pool he obsessed over."

The hologram shifted slightly, overlaying a faint simulation of particulate density in the air around the man. Countless grays and reds blooming invisibly around him.

"The cleaning pole, the brush, the PVC piping, the jets, the lights, every component of that beautiful backyard oasis was manufactured halfway across the globe. In regions where environmental standards were nonexistent. Where factories ran on dirty fuel. Where waste was vented straight into the atmosphere."

His voice took on a harder, faintly angry, edge. "The same factories. The same supply chains. Multiplied by millions of products, by billions of transactions, every single year.

"You saw it on the screen. That rising cluster of numbers was about more than water, it was air too."

He stepped away from the projection.

"If this man could have *seen* the filth in the air around him, trillions of microscopic particles, volatile chemicals, invisible toxins, he would have panicked. He would have held his breath in fear.

"He might have suffered a mental collapse just from the *knowledge* of what he was inhaling. That's how detached people were from reality in the early- to mid-twenty-first century."

The shimmering pool image dissolved, replaced by a time-lapse of the Earth's atmosphere over decades, showing patches of red-orange pollution dispersing slowly, painfully, over centuries.

"It took us over *two hundred years* to clean the air and water. To make it pristine. To give the Earth the breathable atmosphere it has today. Back then, our entire atmosphere was a slow-moving, global cesspool. Not visible. But lethal."

He turned and faced the council again.

"And they were proud of their clean pools."

General Dyson played the final video.

A sea of people filled St. Peter's Square in Vatican City.

The camera panned slowly over the crowd, then focused on a white-robed man beneath the sunlight, standing at a podium, his voice echoing with the depth of centuries.

"As stewards of God's creation," Pope Francis said, "we are called to make the Earth a beautiful garden for the human family. When we destroy our forests, ravage our soil, and pollute our seas, we betray that noble calling."

The image shifted.

"The Earth, our home, is beginning to look more and more like an immense pile of filth. In many parts of the planet, the elderly lament that once-beautiful landscapes are now covered with rubbish. Never have we so hurt and mistreated our common home as we have in the last two hundred years."

Another cut.

"We received this world as an inheritance from past generations, but also as a loan from future generations, to whom we will have to return it."

Then, finally, with serenity and grace, he said:

"Yet all is not lost. Human beings, while capable of the worst, are also capable of rising above themselves, choosing again what is good, and making a new start."

As the clip ended, the video faded to a transparent black presence hovering over the room.

Around the conference table, heads slowly nodded. Even the most hardened skeptics were silent, visibly moved. The stillness didn't come from fear; it came from understanding.

Dyson's voice broke the silence. "All these words we just heard were spoken to the masses around the world by a noble spiritual leader. And yet ... they fell on deaf ears."

He looked around the room, eyes heavy but resolute. "Bound by protocol, we were forbidden from directly influencing the formation of the Manifesto. But we were not forbidden from *inspiring* its creation. So, we turned to where stories shape minds: cinema."

He gestured again. Images of early twenty-first-century film studios appeared briefly, Hollywood, Mumbai, London. Faded movie posters flickered in and out of view.

"We embedded ALFs across the industry to influence their minds and thinking, screenwriters, editors, even production interns.

"We transmitted messages through subtle 4G and 5G pulses, guiding thoughts and seeding visions.

"And through these silent channels, we delivered a single, unified message. A metaphor."

Overlaid on the floating darkness, the final transmission appeared, simple white text slowly scrolling as Dyson recited it aloud:

Imagine a few people, stranded on a spaceship, drifting through the cosmos.

Their resources are limited. Every drop of water, every breath of air, every calorie of energy must be used wisely.

The crew must maintain balance, preserve life, and think not just of survival, but of legacy.

They must protect their children. Their future. And ensure the ship endures long enough to reach a place of peace and promise. A destination called Utopia, where there is no suffering, no greed, no waste. Only balance. Only soul-deep freedom.

That spaceship… is called Earth.

General Dyson's tone grew more reflective as he described some of the notions his teams had injected into the past.

"We broadcast our message in fragments, whispers in the creative minds of filmmakers, seeded through ALFs over the span of a decade.

"What followed was a wave of science fiction films. *Love*, produced in 2011. *Prometheus* in 2012. *Europa Report* and *Gravity* in 2013. *Interstellar* in 2014. *The Martian* in 2015. *Passengers* in 2016."

He gestured, and brief clips from the films shimmered across the holographic display, scenes of astronauts drifting in silence, struggling to survive, searching for meaning in the void of space.

"All of these films contain fragments of our message. Pieces. Echoes. Symbols. But none of them captured the message in its complete form. No one delivered it coherently, directly.

No one told humanity the truth about their own lives aboard spaceship Earth. Their survival. Their fragility. Their responsibility."

He paused, frustration flickering across his face at the failure of these early efforts.

"In attempting to guide the future through influence alone, we exposed our greatest weakness: *subtlety*.

"The creatures we sent, the signals we embedded, the metaphors we crafted, they weren't enough. They inspired stories, yes. But not action. Not transformation."

The screen dimmed.

Dyson looked up, resolute. "Which is why we are here today.

"After everything else failed, we now accept the truth: it's time to act directly. It's time to intervene. With the success of numerous human missions behind us, we've reached an undeniable conclusion, *human Time-Travelers* are necessary to set things right."

He turned to face Max. "Commander Max and his regiment have earned our trust. Their precision, discretion, and unwavering success across more than five hundred and fifty missions make them the ideal candidates for this operation."

He turned back to the council. "We must discover what's holding back the completion and publication of the Manifesto of Eleven Elements.

"What changed? What influenced its author to abandon what would have become the cornerstone of human awakening?

"More importantly, what can we do to ensure that his work is not only completed, but published, disseminated, and accepted by the world?

"And," he added, "ensure that it happens in the right time context to maintain the integrity of our present." He looked with intensity at the faces before him. "I can't emphasize this enough.

"Our present, as well as a series of prior periods, each more enlightened than the last, that led to ours, depends on the successful outcome of this mission."

A visual timeline appeared behind Dyson. The Manifesto's early writings, drafts of philosophical essays, UN policy sessions, all culminating in a single glowing point: The 2045 UN Charter for the Federation of Nations.

"That charter," Dyson said, "was the foundation stone of our civilization. Our constitution. Our survival. And its soul came from the Manifesto. If that origin collapses, so does everything build upon it."

He took a step back; voice lowered to a solemn intensity.

"This is no longer about theory. It's no longer about messages or metaphors. This is about action. About anchoring our existence in a truth that's fading from time."

His eyes swept the room one last time. "And we are almost out of time."

Max had his PCOM on listen mode, converting everything said into notes, as General Dyson now directed attention toward him.

"Commander Renner," Dyson said, voice steady but resolute, "the Federation has authorized a team of fifteen of your top officers to travel back to the twenty-first century.

"This will be the largest single deployment ever, and yours will be the first human team to travel this far back in time.

"The remainder of the regiment will remain here to fulfill support duties or serve as your backup, should reinforcements become necessary."

Max looked up, attentive.

"We've also fabricated three period-accurate automobiles to serve as your mission transports.

"Though externally identical to early twenty-first-century models, they are fully equipped time machines, each powered by a self-contained nuclear microcore for the time jumps, an air-turbine-based secondary energy generator source for use during local travels. And they are embedded with next-gen computer systems. Some of these are adaptation of the future models of the same vehicles."

Dyson waved his hand and a three-dimensional holographic display illuminated above the table. Three Felza Model X SUVs rotated slowly in midair.

"These vehicles were chosen for specific reasons," Dyson gestured again. The hologram zoomed in and opened the front and rear trunks, revealing compartments packed with gear.

"The Model X is one of the few vehicles from that era with ample storage in both front and rear. This allows us to embed essential mission hardware while maintaining complete authenticity. And because they are electric, they're both energy-efficient *and* non-polluting, a perfect environmental match for our mission principles."

The image zoomed back out.

"Each vehicle seats five. Each is equipped with a central monitoring system that connects directly to command. And each crew member will be outfitted with biometric wrist monitors and adaptive bodysuits for real-time tracking. This time, we're embedded, fully visible, moving live through local society, uncloaked and exposed."

Ambassador Sarah Blumstein raised a hand, concern in her voice. "So, you're saying the team, and the vehicles, will remain uncloaked? Isn't that risky? They're all the same model, same color. Too obvious. Shouldn't we revert to standard cloaking protocols?"

Dyson met her gaze with calm authority. "Visibility **is** the strategy. We're not sneaking through this mission; we're meant to be part of the timeline now.

"The Felzas' colors can be changed at the flick of a switch. They might enter white, but on arrival they can shift to black, red, blue, whatever the jumpers choose. They'll also have shapeshifting tech to mimic different brands in the same way."

"So, in a way we are using cloaking technology but of a different kind."

He addressed his audience with an air of assurance. "A control team of one hundred fifty-six specialists, working in three eight-hour shifts of fifty-two each, will provide continuous oversight, monitoring and support.

"Guidance. Intel. Counter-feedback. This will be a fully synchronized operation, moment by moment."

Dyson paused, giving everyone a moment to process the logistics … and the profound implications of this extreme jump.

"The success of our ALF missions into this timeframe gave us confidence. Now it's time for human hands to finish what ALFs could not."

Then, turning to his right, Dyson addressed Blumstein directly. "Ambassador," he said, his tone softening just slightly, "I want to assure you that your concerns are not taken lightly.

"In fact, your insights make you uniquely qualified in this arena. That's why I would like to formally invite you to serve as one of the lead advisors on this mission."

He met her eyes directly. "We want the strongest minds on this project, those capable of both criticism and vision. Can I count you in, Ambassador?"

Ambassador Blumstein glanced to her left and right, silently scanning her advisory team. Some raised their eyebrows. Others shrugged, offering no clear signal.

Max thought the room seemed to hold its collective breath, waiting.

Then she smirked slightly and gave a single nod. "You can count me in."

There was no applause, only a palpable sense of a line being crossed: reluctance turning into resolve.

CHAPTER -8

10:50 | 11-12-2025 (Twenty-first century)
LOCATION: POP BOYS AUTO SHOP CELEBRATION
FLORIDA

Roughly fifteen minutes after Katrina had completed the call with the mechanic and shop owner, Randy, their tow truck driver, Tony, arrived at the hotel and quickly loaded TTV3 onto the flatbed tow truck.

Isam and Lukas hopped into the back of the driver cab. The rest of the team followed along in TTV2 and soon arrived at the local shop.

Once there, Randy approached, eyeing the vehicle as he chewed a lump of tobacco tucked in his lower lip.

Katrina and Bitang exited the TTV2.

Chewing on a wad of tobacco, Randy popped the hood of the Felza, a fully electric SUV the truck driver had just towed into the shop.

"OH MY GOD! What the hell am I lookin' at here?" he exclaimed, gesturing to no one in particular but toward the intricate network of pipes, drums, cables, and unfamiliar components inside.

The vehicle's owner, the one named Lukas, quickly stepped in. "That, sir, is a custom-fit application of an experimental battery recharge system. My younger brother is an automotive engineer. He's been experimenting with new designs, and unfortunately, I let him modify this car. Big mistake. It hasn't worked since."

Randy gave him a skeptical look. "That's a pretty pricey car to let your brother tinker with. I wouldn't let mine touch a beauty like this. Alright, you guys go sit in the customer waiting area. I'll start removing all this junk.

"Should take me about an hour. Thanks for choosing us."

The customer and his friends didn't sit. They stood silently at the waiting-room window, eyes fixed on the vehicle. Randy felt their gaze on him with every move he made.

It was creepy.

Randy glanced sideways. They were watching him. He was sure of it.

In front of him lay a bizarre setup: a complex network of wires, tubes, and windpipes, nothing like he'd ever seen. The trunk held a strange mechanism, clearly missing a key component, something large and rectangular, about the size of the biggest battery in the shop.

Something was off.

No one in their right mind would experiment on a Felza ET1, especially one this pristine. The paint still looked showroom-fresh. Even stranger, the car didn't respond when powered on. No hum, no lights, like it had never been driven.

He didn't like it. Nothing made sense to him

Randy was working with both the frunk and the trunk being kept open. The equipment assembly definitely needed heavy duty pneumatic power tools to unbolt the setup and lift it with an engine hoist. He acted casual, pretending to check messages on his phone while quietly snapping photos of everything inside. Then he started disassembling it, methodically, one part at a time, per the customer's request.

The frunk housed thick windpipes and drum-like cylinders. One assembly was too large to take apart. He had his employee, Neo, help lift it out in one piece. Everything else he broke down into components, laying them out neatly on a large tarp.

Neo handled the trunk pieces. Together, they formed a rhythm: detach-lift-place. Over and over, almost like a drill.

When the watchful eyes of the companions of his customer finally seemed bored, lulled by the repetition, Randy made his move.

He pulled the blue tarp over the large cylinder assembly, swallowing it in the folds and clutter until it disappeared from sight. Then he laid the remaining parts out on a second cloth, this one stretched flat and neatly arranged. Making it seem like everything was there.

When the work was done, he opened the door and nodded to the owner, who came over with his friends. All except the pretty young woman, who barely looked up from her phone.

"Everything's out," he said, feeling more than a little uneasy.

Randy saw Lukas and companions cross the garage to inspect the spread of parts, nodding. They seemed satisfied.

But behind them, under the tarp, the most important piece was hidden.

Lukas leaned over the frunk and trunk, scanning the exposed compartments while the other man circled the vehicle.

Satisfied that all parts were detached from the main body of the SUV, Lukas told Randy to reload everything into the vehicle, fitting the pieces back in as best as possible.

This was standard protocol: detach and isolate the custom parts they wanted disposed of separately before sending the shell of the Felza to the salvage yard that would shred the body and frame to tiny fragments.

Once the pieces were packed, one of the guys headed to the waiting area to fetch Katrina, the striking woman who'd come in with them.

Randy stood by the workbench, wiping his hands with orange-scented wet wipes, smirking to himself.

The large assembly of windpipe and cylinder was hidden and secure. Soon, it would be on its way to his cousin, Felixus Godart, at Felza's Design Center in Palo Alto.

In the waiting room, Katrina sat by the window, letting the sun's rays recharge her depleted cells. Isam sat nearby, pretending to read a *TIMES* magazine but keeping a quiet watch over her. Katrina was also syncing with mission control, uploading and downloading reports, data, and intel critical to the team's objectives.

Lukas approached. He glanced at an old magazine in Isam's hands. The beaten-up cover of the *TIMES* magazine showed a man with an exaggerated pout. Four red checkmarks stood next to the words: "Bully, Showman, Party Crasher, Demagogue." The fifth box was blank: "45th President of the United States." Below, the headline read: *On the Plane with Frank McCrony.*

Isam scratched his head, then gently placed a hand on Lukas's shoulder and whispered, "We're ready when you are."

Katrina stirred, blinking slowly as if waking from a deep mental dive. Her eyes refocused, alert now. She messaged Prisha: Ready for pickup. Mechanic's shop.

She stood and walked briskly toward the workshop, Lukas and Isam falling in behind her.

Katrina opened both the trunk and frunk, her eyes scanning every component like a machine. With her photographic memory, she inventoried each part, down to the last nut, bolt, and screw.

Something wasn't right.

A major component was missing.

She turned slowly, eyes locking briefly with Randy, who stood nearby with the innocent posture of a child pretending he hadn't broken a window.

"Everything okay, ma'am?" he asked.

Katrina didn't answer. Instead, she glanced around and noticed a suspicious rise in the blue tarp a few feet away. She walked over and lifted it.

There it was: the missing assembly.

Without a word, she reached down, grabbed the heavy piece with one hand, held the tarp with the other, and hauled the unit up like it was a gym bag. Then, still silent, she walked over and placed it in the trunk where there was the most room, ignoring the two mechanics now frozen in awe.

Randy's mouth hung open. Neo narrowed the space between them and whispered, "Did you see that? That thing's got to weigh at least one hundred forty, maybe a hundred and fifty pounds. She lifted it like it was nothing. What is she, some kind of bodybuilder? Or on superwoman or something? Man, I wish I had my camera running."

Randy cursed silently, he'd missed the whole thing too. His yPhone was still in his pocket. And now, worse, he had no idea how to explain why the part was hidden under the tarp. His mind scrambled for a cover story, too distracted to focus on recording the critical footage he'd already missed.

Then she walked toward him.

Randy could feel his breath tighten. Sweat pooled on his forehead.

"How much?" she asked.

He stammered. "I... I... Maybe the tarp slipped over the part and we didn't see it... I mean, sorry ma'am... Uh, what did you ask again?"

Katrina's tone was sharp. "I asked how much we owe you for the labor."

Randy cleared his throat. "Three and a half hours at eighty bucks an hour. So... two-eighty."

She pulled out six crisp fifty-dollar bills, handed them over without flinching. "Keep the change. Thanks."

Outside, Prisha arrived in TTV2, the back loaded with groceries and essentials.

Tony, the tow truck operator, was already waiting in the parking lot as instructed. As agreed, he rolled the flatbed into position and began reloading the disabled Felza.

The team reassembled in the same manner as when they had first arrived.

* * * * * * * *

Randy, still stunned, finally remembered his phone. He pulled it out and started filming, capturing the strange image of the dead-still Felza ET1 on the flatbed tow truck, and the woman he was now convinced might actually be a real-life Supergirl.

Once they disappeared around the corner, he stopped recording and began uploading everything, photos, video, and snapshots of the strange components, to his cousin Felixus at Felza HQ.

When it was done, he typed:

Felix Bro, just sent you some crazy pics + a vid of this custom Felza ET1 setup. You gotta see this. Call me tonight, weirdest day I've had in a while −Tc buddy - Randy

17:30 | 11-12-2025 (Twenty-first century)
LOCATION: RESIDENCE INN – MAIN LOBBY

At 17:30 sharp on their second day, the team gathered in the hotel lobby.

It was dinnertime and the nearby restaurants were all full with long wait times, but Max had other plans for the team. Plans more consistent with their common-culture training.

Max clapped his hands together. "Alright, listen up. We have an appointment with Mr. DeWine tomorrow at two pm at his office.

"I'll be going with four of you. The remaining five need to locate his psychologist, Mr. Ronik Dupray, and secure an appointment for me. Try for Thursday morning, or the earliest time he'll give us."

He paused, looked around, then added with a grin, "But first, I'm starving. Let's head to Hamburger Quein."

With that, he strode out of the hotel, the rest trailing behind, toward their two remaining vehicles.

Inside the fast-food chain, the group stared at faded images of char-grilled meats on overhead menu boards. The photos were hardly appetizing, but curiosity won over.

They placed their orders: green salads, soft-serve ice cream, sodas, and plain water. A few picked HQ-Veggie sandwiches.

Max, however, went all in and asked for a large order of fries, grabbing handfuls of ketchup packets and napkins on the way to a large corner table that fit all ten of them.

Within minutes, trays loaded with food were placed in front of them.

Max observed with curiosity that the "large" fries he had ordered appeared to be the same size as the "small" ones that had come with the meal Luke had ordered.

Max began unwrapping plastic straws while Prisha distributed the napkins and condiments. Soon, the group was scooping salad, unwrapping sandwiches, dipping fries, and sipping sodas, immersing themselves in the fast-food ritual of the twenty-first century.

It didn't take long to consume the shameful array of ultra-processed, seed-oil-fried, vegetarian, and sugar-laden products.

Once finished, they sat back, full, and quiet.

In front of them: a battlefield of waste. Empty fry cartons. Straw wrappers. Smeared ketchup packets. Wilted salad containers. Plastic lids. Paper trays. Crumpled napkins stacked high.

Katrina stared at the mess and said dryly, "That would cost us 1,578 ICUs in waste penalties, just for this meal."

A few raised eyebrows.

"In today's currency," she added, "that's about 242 U.S. dollars in fines under the International Waste Control Enforcement Law that finally gets implemented in 2048 by the Federation of Nations."

Everyone sat in stunned silence, staring at the aftermath of what now felt like a gruesome crime.

Their eyes scanned the table, plastic, wrappers, cartons, napkins, suddenly more aware of the mountain of single-use packaging, the remains of a single meal that echoed louder in their minds than it did in the world around them.

With intensity in his eyes, Max muttered, "And they called this *convenience*. In these times, this type of behavior and wasteful lifestyle was the normal thing to do. If the locals were to visit our times and use our lives as a reference point, they would feel as disgusted as we do now. But there is no one to explain this to them."

Some instinctively glanced toward the windows, half-expecting to see the flashing blue light of an ECP drone, Environmental Crime Patrol, swooping down to issue a citation.

In their own time, that much waste would've earned a heavy fine and at least ninety days of community service in Grade Seven Utility Maintenance. Sometimes working waist-deep in raw sewage, helping to convert human waste into natural fertilizer for the urban gardens.

No one spoke. Guilt hung in the air, settling in their chests as the food sat heavy in their stomachs like a stone.

One by one, they stood, carrying their trays to the disposal bins.

Each officer moved slowly, eyes scanning the other patrons, citizens of the twenty-first century who dumped their leftovers without hesitation. There was no remorse in their expressions, only contentment. *Just another Happy Feast.*

To the locals, this was routine. A mindless ritual.

The fast-food giant took pride in its efficiency, its sleek packaging, its surface-level hygiene standards. But none of it acknowledged the hidden costs. The environmental toll. The irreversible damage to life systems. To Gaia itself.

And none of the patrons noticed the visitors in their midst: beings from a future that had learned, through suffering, what this kind of negligence would one day cost.

Though the officers had all expressed satisfaction for completing the day's tasks, securing appointments, making contact, passing as locals, their ride back to the hotel was quiet.

Each of them was deep in their own thoughts.

Each of them wished, silently, that the world would awaken. That people would open their eyes to the consequences of their habits, their indifference.

But they held onto one sliver of hope:

Mr. Joshua DeWine.

The man they would meet tomorrow. The one whose words could plant the seeds of a better future. Their *future*.

20:00 | 11-12-2025 (Twenty-first century)
LOCATION: RESIDENCE INN - BASE ROOM 402

By evening of that that second day, the team had reconvened in their designated meeting room for the end-of-day briefing and planning session.

Max stood at the head of their makeshift meeting room table, confident and composed. "I've confirmed our meeting with Mr. Joshua DeWine, or simply *Joe*, as he prefers to be called. It's set for tomorrow at 14:00 hours."

He glanced around the room. "Bitang, Prisha, Daniel, Lukas, we're all meeting with DeWine.

"Daniel, Lukas, and I will present ourselves as partners in a proposed real estate development.

"Prisha and Bitang, you'll pose as our assisting staff: consultants and administrative support."

He turned specifically to Prisha. "I want you to brush up on topics relevant to the Indian subcontinent: culture, politics, news, anything you can use in conversation.

"Joe is of Indian origin, like you. Make him feel comfortable. Use common ground, humor, references. Whatever makes the interaction smooth and personal."

Then Max shifted gears. "I also need a high-quality printout of a survey map showing a sizable plot of land in central Florida, something realistic and impressive. I want to use it during our discussion to help establish credibility."

He turned to Katrina. "Can you run a search and see if there's anything useful online? Look for development parcels, zoning maps, land studies, anything that fits our cover story."

Katrina blinked and tapped twice at her temple. "On it."

Max clapped his hands once. "Great. Let's tighten up our roles and keep everything clean. We make contact tomorrow. Let's make it count.

"While we're meeting with Joe," Max continued, "I'll need a separate unit on a parallel task."

He turned to Kasandra, Jian, Minami, and Isam. "You four will handle SUV3. Your objective is to dismantle the custom installations and render the vehicle untraceable. Take it to a salvage yard once it's been disfigured beyond recognition. Strip it down, sensors, trackers, core systems, all of it. No parts should remain that could hint at its origin or tech tier. I want this vehicle and all its parts completely shredded.

Jian intervened, "Of course, except the nuclear core. We bury it in a remote location for retrieval by the Command Center when the tether is repaired and they can transport it back to the future, correct?"

Max replied, "Yes, I was getting to that. And you're right, we don't have any tech to safely dispose of a nuclear device. The plan was to transport it back to the future.

"For now, just record the exact coordinates of where it's buried and transmit them to Command Center. We'll make sure it stays undiscoverable. Leave a tracking device on it so we get notified if anyone comes within a hundred meters of it."

He turned to Katrina. "You'll stay stationed in the hotel room. You're our local operations hub, a remote guide and data relay. You'll provide wireless access to maps, intel, salvage yard locations, directions, or anything the teams need.

"Our control center back home is tracking everything from the outside. However, there are some glitches, and it appears that connections are on and off. No continuity. Hence, we need *you* as our local point of contact. Any need for backup or signal interference? You call it."

He raised his yPhone. "Keep your devices on full surveillance mode. Use our encrypted custom chat system. No talking, only texting. Quick. Silent. Secure. Locals call it 'messaging.' Our content is coded. No one will be able to intercept it."

Max scanned the room one last time, his gaze lingering on each face before he raised a stern voice.

"Before we call it a night, I need to make a few things clear," he said. "Katrina reported that we nearly lost a critical component of TTV3 at the mechanic's shop. If she hadn't caught it, it could've been a major disaster. But she did. Thanks to her technical sharpness, we avoided a catastrophic paradox. I'm glad she's part of this mission. She makes us a stronger team.

"I expect the rest of you to be more vigilant, more aware of everything happening around us. I don't want to hear any more excuses about culture shock, the pollution, the heat, the humidity, or whatever else we're dealing with. We're soldiers. I expect everyone to live up to the training and the standards you met to get here. Do you all understand?"

He gave a nod. "That's all. Have a good evening."

The group quietly dispersed.

Some team members peeled away toward the gym, already in their workout gear. Others drifted to the pool, swapping uniforms for swimsuits and silence. It was time to unwind, physically, mentally, emotionally.

Max remained behind, tapping into the secure link to report the day's updates to Central Command.

Across the hall, Katrina sat cross-legged on the floor, jacked into a hardwired ethernet line. Her eyes flicked with data streams as she absorbed zoning laws, infrastructure maps, and urban timelines. Her system digested in minutes what would take humans days.

She would be ready.

Daniel slipped out quietly through the side entrance. He wandered into the next-door pub, ordered a drink, and sat alone at the far end of the bar, a man momentarily distant from his mission.

The bartender seemed to sense his customer didn't want company and left him alone after he'd ordered.

Daniel wasn't there just for the drink.

He had been emotionally entangled with a uBot in the past. It was an unsanctioned relationship that nearly compromised a prior mission.

He was grateful Max hadn't punished him. But clearly Max hadn't forgotten either.

Instead, he'd excluded Daniel from certain team assignments, giving him space to realign. Quietly. Without shame.

After all, Max had to know Daniel was one of the best. Elite. Loyal. Brilliant.

And Max seemed willing to believe he'd find his way back.

Daniel sipped his drink and considered the circumstances he found himself in now.

After the team dispersed, Max switched off the bright overhead lights in their base room, now increasingly his personal space. He sat on the worktable and activated his OMP.

Max saw Rick Perez flicker onto the screen. He smiled.

"Hello, Rick. We're making steady progress. TTV3 is completely shredded, and all parts have been disposed of in ways that make them impossible to recover. You should have the coordinates for the nuclear generator core. It needs to be retrieved as soon as the tether is stable enough.

"We don't have much else to report at the moment. The team is still in recovery mode from the incident... you know."

"Admiral Ubanto and General Dyson keep calling," Perez said, visibly tense. "They want to see more progress."

"We're moving forward," Max replied calmly. "We've made contact with Joshua DeWine. We've even secured a meeting with him, scheduled for tomorrow."

Rick continued. "We're keeping a close eye on Katrina. So far, she's stayed sharp and aligned with mission protocols. In fact, she averted a major incident earlier: caught that the directional wind-driven turbine assembly on the TTV3 hadn't been returned to the vehicle."

He glanced at something off-screen.

"Looks like the mechanic was trying to salvage it for himself. We've contained the issue, so no compromise there. We're still waiting on the FHP's follow-up reports. If they find anything tied to the SUV or otherwise, we'll intervene. But right now, we're tracking everything, their conversations, movement, data trails."

Rick glanced away briefly then back, voice lower. "Your job is to stay focused. Don't get distracted by worst-case scenarios. If anything escalates, we'll send reinforcements.

"We recommend checking out and returning as separate groups, two, three, or four at most. At the moment, all ten of you are registered under a single reservation, which could draw attention or raise flags to the FBI. We have been tracking them and they are searching for a large group of eight to ten people checked in as one group at every hotel in central Florida."

"For now, the primary concern is the time gap. It's unstable. If it keeps expanding, it could fracture the tether. We're working around the clock to stabilize it."

"You'd tell me if we were really in trouble, wouldn't you?"

Rick paused. "Of course. Get some sleep. Signing off now."

"Acknowledged," Max said. "We're on standby." But he couldn't shake the feeling that something was off.

And as the transmission ended, Max noticed subtle flickers in the image feed. Glitches. Micro-lags.

In the background, there was a flurry of activity at the command center. More than usual. Analysts and professional technicians moving between stations. Monitors flashing warnings too fast to read.

Still, he pushed the unease down. Now wasn't the time to chase shadows.

He rolled out his mat on the hotel room floor and began his yoga routine: deep stretches, mindful breathing, pulling himself back into center. Each movement carved a small piece of silence from the storm inside him.

Then came the sinfully indulgent ten-minute shower, water cascading over his shoulders as his mind drifted, almost involuntarily, to Annie. Her smile. The way she tilted her head when she laughed.

He let that warmth linger for a moment, then filed it away with all the other things he couldn't afford to think about right now.

Mission first.

CHAPTER -9

21:12 | 11-12-2025 (Twenty-first century)
LOCATION: RESIDENCE INN - BASE ROOM 402

Relaxed, refreshed, seated in the recliner now, Max sank back, letting the contours of the cushion support his body as he re-engaged the VRV headset.

The visor hummed softly, syncing again with the bodysuit and PCOM system. His breath steadied. His pulse slowed. The total recall mode resumed.

The hotel room around him blurred into the background, and faded into nothingness as Max slipped deeper into his own fragmented mind, using the memory retrieval tools to promote his own healing.

He moved through a gallery of fragmented images: scenes from his cadet years, early missions, training simulations, and critical command briefings.

The VRV rendered each moment in crisp 6D immersion, sights, sounds, smells, even ambient temperatures, all perfectly reconstructed.

He could feel the cool fresh air in his towering abode at High-Park 577. He could recall the fresh and juicy tomatoes or sweet tastes of the carrots grown in the town's organic vegetable gardens that they all tended to. He could smell the aroma of the garlic-laced broccoli soup Annie made so often. He could hear the deep voice of Admiral Ubanto briefing him before the drop.

Disjointed fragments of lost memory were stitching themselves back together, memory by memory, thread by thread.

Max's breathing grew deeper. His chest lifted as if unburdened.

Since arriving in the twenty-first century, he was now feeling more whole again.

Or at least familiar with himself and his life in the future.

You're almost there, he thought to himself. *Get it all back. You'll need it.*

He focused harder, willing the headset to continue the deep dive into unprocessed blocks of memory, places his subconscious had locked down during the trauma of the transmission event.

What exactly had happened in the final briefing?

Why had he been given such a large contingent for this mission?

Why had the authorities chosen bulky SUVs for their transport?

And, most importantly of all: the missions brief General Dyson had handed him personally.

Confidential. Private. For the commander's ears only.

The VRV's internal system flickered, scanning his cognitive patterns. A loading symbol spun in the periphery of his field of view, indicating another buried memory was about to surface.

And Max embraced it. Chased it.

He sensed he was on the trail of *his purpose*. Whatever that meant.

(VRV BLINKING: MEMORY RECALL MODE)

15:00 | 11-06-<u>2532</u> (<u>Twenty-sixth century</u>)

LOCATION: OCTAGON, Zurich Switzerland – Dyson's office

Max recalled following General Dyson through a maze of secured corridors into a private room lined with historical books and polished artifacts.

An antique wooden desk sat near the window, flanked by thick bookshelves and a towering high-back chair, where Dyson now settled.

"Sit." Dyson gestured to the leather chair across from him.

Max sat, still absorbing the moment, when Dyson, surprisingly, reached for a bottle of Scotch and poured himself a drink.

"Care for one?" Dyson offered.

Max blinked, thrown off by the sudden shift in tone. "Just water for me, sir. Thank you."

Dyson nodded and took a slow sip before continuing. "Max," he said, setting the glass down, "you have four days. Total.

"That includes briefings, loadouts, prep, mental orientation, streamlined training and mission simulations.

"I'll transmit all mission data and logistics to your PCOM within the hour."

Max straightened, nodding.

"Now is your time for one last evaluation. You'll need to handpick fifteen of your best officers.

"As you know, a few of them should be tech-adaptable, familiar with legacy systems. They need to understand how to blend into the culture, how to drive, interact, survive. You can't afford a misstep in trust or believability."

Dyson swirled the liquor around in his glass. "Imagine a man from the twenty-first century traveling four hundred years into the past. He'd find himself in a medieval world. No electricity, no medicine, no communications.

"That's the kind of *culture shock* you and your team are about to face. The technology will feel ancient. The mindsets will be foreign. The world will be loud, cluttered, and emotionally unstable.

"You'll be entering their world as ghosts with a mission. You'll need to move like them, talk like them, live like them, without becoming one of them."

Max nodded slowly, feeling the full burden of responsibility, for his team, and for everyone in his world, his present.

"I understand, sir."

Dyson gave him a steady look. "Make sure your team does too."

Max nodded, "I'll get right on it, sir," and started to get up.

Dyson let himself sink into the soft leather now. His voice softened, almost philosophical. "Max, let me ask you a foolish question."

Max looked up.

"Have you ever ridden in a trans-pod or any public vehicle … that didn't know its destination?"

Max blinked, caught off guard. A strange question. But it triggered something.

A flash from a recurring nightmare flickered in his memory: being on a flight where no one knew where they were headed. Not the crew. Not the passengers. Just endless motion through gray skies.

He sat back down and took a sip of water. Max met Dyson's gaze with curiosity. This wasn't just a random question. "No, sir," he said. "Not in any conscious memory. I've never taken a ride, trans-pod, Hyperloop, or anything else, without knowing the destination."

Dyson gave a tight, ironic smile. "And yet, that's how most people in the twenty-first century live." The older man's eyes seemed fixed on somewhere else.

"From what we've seen, the average person in that time has no idea where they're going. No real sense of purpose. No understanding of humanity's place in the universe. Their lives move, day to day, job to job, distraction to distraction, but with no direction."

He stood now, slowly walking around the desk, eyes still distant but tone sharpening. "From our perspective, their existence is like a crowded bus or plane, full of people who've forgotten why they got on. They've confused motion with meaning."

He turned back to Max, now visibly more animated. "But we don't live that way. *We know* why we exist. The Manifesto defines it. It shapes us. It gives our civilization a shared compass."

Suddenly, Dyson turned and slammed his fist onto the desk, making Max flinch slightly.

"We are not aimless!" he barked. "Every one of us knows why we're here. We are not consumers, we are *creators*.

"We build on the work of nature. We replenish the ecosystem. We *generate* resources. We give back more than we take."

His voice lowered again, steady but intense.

"That's what separates our time from theirs. And that's what you need to remember when you arrive in their world. You'll see chaos, confusion, even despair. But you're not going there merely to observe; you're going there to plant purpose."

Max absorbed it, heart steady, mind focused. "Understood, sir," he said.

General Dyson scoffed softly, then took another slow sip of his Scotch. "Where you're heading, Max, people aren't really living, they're just existing. Following leaders who, themselves, have no defined direction. No shared understanding of what it means to be human. They're drifting, just like the rest."

He set his glass down with a clink, his eyes hardening. "They fight over petty things: land, oil, gold, power. They measure worth in what they own, not what they create. They hoard ornaments. Armaments. Resources. They gorge themselves on nature while poisoning the very system that gives them life."

He shook his head in disbelief.

"They believe the point of life is to go to work, eat, sleep, collect things, and then die. They confuse accumulation with meaning. They don't even see the crash coming."

His voice lowered, now more somber.

"If their lives are like a plane with no flight plan, then the time-hole we're facing now, *that* is the final descent. The spiral. The moment before impact."

He stared off for a moment, then drew a long breath, exhaling as if releasing the pressure building in his chest.

"If they perish, or if *we* do, the journey of life, from the spark of the first DNA strand 3.6 billion years ago to now, will have been for nothing. Everything it took, evolution, hardship, discovery, sacrifice, to shape life into conscious human form … will vanish. Wasted."

Max felt his burden grow heavier with each point Dyson made. And he felt more distressed.

"This madness won't stop," Dyson said, "until the *Manifesto of the Eleven Elements* is completed and shared with the world. That is not just a mission for *our* survival, Max. It's for *theirs* too. Even if they don't know it yet."

Once again, it seemed as if Dyson had finished, but now Max knew better than to make assumptions. He kept his seat and left his attention focused on Dyson.

"Let me ask you something, Max. Have you ever studied the Gaia Theory?"

"Yes, sir. We touched on the basics in high school. I remember it positioned Earth as a single, living organism. An interdependent system."

Dyson nodded. "Good. Then this won't feel unfamiliar to you." He reached toward his desk and activated a soft-blue holographic interface.

"In the mission transmission I'm sending you, there's a folder on Gaia Theory. I want you to read it. All of it. Refresh your knowledge.

"The roots of the Manifesto lie in Gaia Theory. Its authors studied it intensively during its resurgence in the early twenty-first century and adopted its core philosophy: life as a balanced, self-regulating whole. That idea shaped the first draft of the Manifesto.

The glass stilled in Dyson's half-raised hand. "Understanding Gaia may help you understand DeWine. And if you understand *him*, you'll know how to reach him."

"I'll study it tonight," Max said, again wondering if the conversation was over. Again waiting for a clearer signal.

Dyson's gaze lingered on Max for a beat longer, then finally, he relaxed back into his chair. "Max," he said, "there's something I've held back about one of the authors. The one named Joshua DeWine. Something you need to know before you go."

A series of muscles faintly tightened in Max's gut and neck. *We're four days away from the riskiest jump we've ever attempted. What couldn't they have told me long before now?*

"Joshua DeWine, the man credited with laying the intellectual groundwork for our civilization, was very different, he was unconventional. Eccentric. Hard to pin down."

Dyson continued, "In the twenty-first century, a lot of people just called him 'that weird guy.' Most didn't believe him, didn't take him seriously, didn't care about his ideas. They thought he was just spinning stories. Only a few close confidants, highly educated, well-informed people, truly paid attention to what he was saying. And the deeper we investigated his past, the more fragmented it became.

"He conceived the Manifesto as a single body of work, but instead of keeping it together, he deliberately scattered it, chapters and books in a planned series of seven, handed off to different professors and experts around the world. His writings, his notes, even his sketches ended up disjointed, scattered across continents like puzzle pieces with no box.

"But all of it is in another folder I've transmitted to your PCOM. Read it carefully. Every word. You'll need it.

"It was this fragmented state of the Manifesto, parts and pieces scattered across the world, that became the core reason for sending a larger team: fifteen operatives instead of the usual four or five, along with multiple TTVs and specialized embedment training.

"We need all of it retrieved, every part, every piece, and publish it in time … in the twenty-first century … before it's all lost and we're doomed."

Now Max understood why his contingent was so large, and why the vehicles were so bulky. He exhaled, shoulders tightening and then loosening under the burden of this new information.

Dyson continued, "One of our greatest concerns is this: Mr. DeWine seems to know we've been watching him."

Max got more tense. *Now what?* he thought.

"We've observed him through ALF surveillance. We've caught him looking directly into the eyes of the squirrels we sent. Not casually. *Deliberately*. As if he sees through them. On multiple occasions he's approached them, even chased them off, forcing us to mimic normal squirrel behavior to avoid suspicion.

"In our last surveillance, he pointed two fingers at his eyes, then pointed straight at the squirrel's face. The universal sign for *'I see you.'*"

What were the implications of this? Max wondered. Was DeWine just paranoid? Or did he somehow know what he couldn't possibly have known: that the squirrels were actually devices designed to spy on him?

"We've also discovered something else," Dyson added. "We're unable to influence his thought patterns. The neural resonance our ALFs emit, the same signals that have shaped entire cultural shifts, they don't affect him. Not at all. If they did, we wouldn't need to be having this conversation."

Max silently processed that last revelation.

The ALF critters that were deployed from here were successfully planting ideas in the minds of influential citizens elsewhere. Why wasn't their influence working on DeWine? Had they missed something in his psychological profile?

"It's become clear," Dyson said, "that DeWine is *intentionally* withholding the completion of the Manifesto. The question is: *Why?* What's stopping him? Is it doubt? Pressure? Fear? Manipulation?"

Dyson looked Max directly in the eye. "We've hit a wall. And time is running out."

This is big, Max thought. *If DeWine refuses to complete the Manifesto, then what?*

"There's one more lead. Recently, Mr. DeWine began seeing a psychiatrist: a Dr. Ronick Dupray. Several sessions, all within the last couple of years. We believe he may hold insight into what's really going on in DeWine's mind. Maybe he's the influence behind DeWine's inspirations or lack thereof. "

Dyson drained the glass, placed it on the desk and stood. Max arose too.

"Find Dupray," Dyson said. "Speak with him. Gain his trust. Figure out what's driving DeWine. Or what's blocking him.

"This is a rescue mission, Max. Of DeWine. Of the Manifesto. Of everything we've built."

The General came around the desk and placed a hand firmly on Max's shoulder. "We trust you to make the right calls on the ground. You and your team are our last and only hope."

"I understand, sir. I will do everything in my power to achieve our goals and to maintain our legacy."

"Make humankind proud, Commander Renner."

As Max walked out of the room, through the silent halls, each step toward the rooftop Hovercraft pad echoed with the silent reminder that the entire planet was now depending on this mission's success.

After Dyson's grim version of a pep talk, it would take everything Max had to compartmentalize the stakes, to treat this as not just another mission.

Success would hinge on one thing: his focus. His discipline. His ability to follow the protocols that had gotten them this far.

Nothing more. Nothing less.

With that thought lingering, Max took a very deep breath.

As he stepped into the Hovercraft, he felt the extreme burden of the six billion lives at stake and the pressure that the fate of entire humanity was now resting on his shoulders.

CHAPTER -10

07:57 | 11-13-2025 (Twenty-first century)
LOCATION: REGIONAL OFFICE -HIGHWAY PATROL

It had been two days since that weird accident on Highway 27 that stirred up the Florida High Patrol's curiosity.

Inside the FHP regional office at the Turkey Lake Toll Plaza, Trooper Mathew Moudy and Traffic Homicide Investigator Corporal Jim Bailey sat across a black metal desk from Lieutenant Mark Malvin.

Malvin clasped his hands on the desktop. "Alright, Jimmy. What've you got for me?"

Trooper Moudy, half-listening, smirked.

Malvin, his boss, could see right through him. Malvin knew his hyper-ambitious trooper had a high opinion of himself and was a climber. The young officer saw this case as just what he needed to get another medal and advance his career. Another year of riding shotgun on a high-profile case was all Moudy needed for a commendation and the raise he'd been angling for. He just had to sit through Jim's report.

Corporal Bailey, however, wasn't smiling. He rubbed his chin, eyes flicking over the folder in front of him, thick with lab results.

"I don't even know where to start, Chief," Bailey muttered. "It's bad. I mean, *FBI-bad*. This is national-level stuff."

That got Malvin's attention. Not in a good way.

Bailey opened the folder. "The blood and hair samples I found on the FDOT guardrail? The Rapid DNA tech working overnight with CODIS Labs identified it: female, approximately thirty years old. Margin of errors within a year. North Khorean descent. Height, five-foot-eight. Weight, about 128 pounds, plus or minus three percent."

He flipped the page. "She had dark hair, classic facial structure markers. All consistent with North Khorean origin. Except for one anomaly."

Malvin frowned. "Which is?"

"Her DNA, "Bailey said. "It's … *clean.* Too clean. The genetic sequence is flawless. None of the standard anomalies we typically see in that regional genome. It's as if someone *scrubbed* her genes. Like they were … edited."

"Edited?" Malvin said. "You mean genetically engineered?"

"I'm not saying that," Bailey replied, obviously distancing himself from the implications of the reports. "But the lab couldn't rule it out.

"That's not all." Bailey took a breath. "The second site, that wooded area off a side road near the impact zone, contained some kind of soot mixed with skin cells. Something, somebody, was burned up out there. Don't know exactly how."

"An IED?" Malvin asked.

"That's the best guess. Pipe bomb, or something similar. Consistent with black-market military-grade tech used by rogue elements. Could be domestic terrorism, could be something foreign. But the blast pattern, the residue, the DNA … it doesn't add up to anything typical."

Malvin could feel his jaw clench. He sensed this thing was about to turn into a huge pain in the ass.

"You're saying we have a possible genetically-enhanced individual, North Khorean descent, tied to an unknown explosive event, and possibly dead … on U.S. soil, here in Florida?"

"It gets better" Bailey said. "There may have been more bodies blown up or burned out there. Not just burned: chemical-level incineration. If we hadn't ordered advanced spectral testing, we would've missed it entirely. But those soot samples … they contained skin cells."

"What are we talking about?" Malvin said.

Bailey searched the documents in his hands. "The soil beneath the soot had aged normally. Years, maybe decades. But the soot itself? Fresh. Recent. Carbon dating confirms it was deposited mere *hours* before we arrived. That lines up exactly with the truck driver's report."

Malvin nodded. "Chuck Spooner?"

"Yeah," Moudy jumped in, probably trying to reclaim the spotlight from Bailey. "We've got his written statement. He saw somebody dangling down from the driver's seat, and a couple of people carrying what appeared to be body bags. He said he had to maneuver his truck to avoid puddles of blood on the road. Thought it was a wreck, called it in.

"When we got there, no visible bodies or damaged vehicles. Just the human tissue found on the guardrail, and that nearby wooded area with the soil that had a fine layer of black soot just under the surface."

"So, we've found skin tissues on the guardrail," Malvin summarized, making sure he understood what his men were telling him. "And around the corner in the woods there's a half-covered burn pile, an *incineration* pile, that left nothing but ash. And all this happened between the time Spooner reported it and when your teams showed up, what, two hours later?"

Bailey nodded. "Actually, there were two to three individuals, according to the separation chamber's breakdown of biological material. No bone fragments. Just ash. The site was hastily covered up with the native soil and leaves, pine needles.

"Whoever did this wanted nothing left behind. We'd never have noticed it without Spooner's report of the accident."

"And the K9 that led us directly to the second location," Moudy added.

Bailey reached into a case and pulled out an object wrapped in sterile cloth. "And then there's *this*."

He unfolded the cloth and placed a metallic joint assembly on Malvin's desk. It caught the sunlight through the window, glimmering, unnaturally sleek.

"It's an artificial knee joint," Bailey explained. "Found buried about a meter deep at the burn site, buried shallow but intact. Lightweight. High tensile strength. No rust. No wear.

"We sent it to the University of Miami's College of Engineering. Got their preliminary report back yesterday."

He handed over a two-page document from the folder, stamped and signed.

Malvin scanned the highlighted sections.

"They identify the alloy as some form of titanium-oxonium composite," Bailey said. "Something that *theoretically* exists in lab literature, but has never been deployed in mass production.

"According to their materials department, this is beyond anything commercially available. It would have to be custom-made, in micro-scale batches. Possibly for aerospace or military bio-tech."

Malvin handled the joint, turning it to examine it from various angles. It looked like metal but felt almost weightless in his hand. "So, you're saying we may have found the remains of ... what? An enhanced human? A test subject? And made with materials not even on the record yet?"

"Researchers have been working on ultralight, metallic 'foam bone' structures: nano-engineered materials meant to mimic real bone while being stronger, lighter, and biologically adaptive," Bailey said. "But right now, it's all theoretical. Lab-scale.

"We're talking research-grade samples of it produced in grams, not enough for full prosthetics. Best estimates say we're still ninety to a hundred years away from this level of fabrication being commercially viable."

Malvin took the flash drive Bailey passed to him across the desktop and plugged it into his laptop. Then he switched the display setting to a TV on the wall to his left. The screen showed what he assumed was some kind of microscopic image. But he couldn't make out anything meaningful.

"What am I looking at?" Malvin asked.

"This first image," Bailey said, "is a forty times magnification from a normal microscope that should be able to pick up data for a normal implant. Even a magnifying glass would show the part's information if it's not covered by overgrowths of bone or scar tissue.

"All artificial body parts are required by international law to have embedded identifiers: date, place, time of manufacture, serial numbers, origin codes, things like that.

"But they couldn't find anything for this part," Bailey said. "Now go to the next image."

Malvin clicked ahead. This image showed far more grain and texture in the base surface of the material.

"That," Bailey said, "is one hundred times close-up taken under an *electron* microscope."

"And here's the kicker." He got up and pointed to a series of blurry lines on the screen. "Turns out this implant actually *does* contain that information. But it took even more powerful magnification to resolve it. Take a look at the next image."

Malvin displayed the frame.

Bailey pointed to the slightly blurry-but-legible lines of text:

RT KNEE PROSTHESIS ICD – 0SRD0JZ
KARACHI HIGH-PARK786 12-21-2521

"The thing is that the embossing here is at the *nanometer* scale: ten orders of magnitude finer than the smallest commercial imprinting standard!

"According to the university's Engineering Department, they just recently cracked the tech to micro-print *UNIVERSITY OF MIAMI* at three times larger than this scale in the year 2015. And even *that* was a breakthrough."

Malvin stared, trying to make sense of the text.

"The top line is straightforward," Bailey said. "It's the part type and the international classification code for surgical implants. But the second line…"

He shook his head. "We contacted every medical manufacturing database and prosthetic registry in Karachi. There's no record of a *High-Park786*. No manufacturer. No clinic. And certainly, no knee-bone fabrication lab with nanotech-grade precision."

As Bailey continued his report, Lieutenant Malvin was quietly putting the pieces together in his head. And the picture wasn't a good one, no matter which way he looked at it.

"What about the date?" he asked.

Bailey gave a dry, nervous laugh. "If you assume the final eight digits are a manufacture date, then it's 12/21/2521.

Bailey stood there blinking slowly for a moment.

In the chair across the desk from Malvin, Moudy laughed, then cut it short when Malvin didn't join in.

"Say that again," Malvin said.

"Yeah," Bailey replied. "2521. Crazy. That would be five hundred years into the future."

"Obviously it can't be that." Malvin studied the screen.

"*Obviously*," Moudy repeated, glancing from Bailey to Malvin.

Bailey continued. "Time travel is, of course, next to impossible. At least as far as we know. So, coming back to reality here, my conclusion is simpler.

"Either it's a typo. Someone accidentally input 2521 instead of 2021. Or it's just a serial number, and the formatting is coincidental."

He paused, looking at the still-glimmering knee joint on the lieutenant's desk.

"But one thing we *can* say, based on the design and material use, is that the individual this belonged to was likely male, of South Asian descent. Possibly Pakistani. And probably had access to resources and technology well beyond current global medical standards."

Malvin stood and looked out the window, trying to get his head around the evidence. "So, either this is a black-market prototype from some lab we don't know about. Or we're looking at something no one was supposed to find."

"Or." Bailey began a bit nervously then stopped himself and reached behind Malvin to the laptop.

Malvin turned toward the TV display, intrigued as Bailey continued without finishing his thought.

"This is a microscopic cross-section of the foam-bone structure, enhanced with color-coded overlays.

"While examining the imprint zone under the electron microscope, the lab at the University of Miami made another discovery: minuscule biological fragments embedded within the artificial bone lattice. Exactly what this kind of tech is *designed* to do."

"Okay, now we're getting somewhere," Malvin said, grateful to see this screwy case coming back to reality. Something he could work with, finally.

"They were able to isolate tissue samples: microscopic strands of cells woven into the implant. They forwarded the material for DNA analysis. We just ran the results through the national CODIS system."

Bailey held up the printed report. "Male, approximately 35 years old, margin of error within one year. South Asian ancestry, specifically Pakistani. Black hair, dark brown eyes.

"But what's more interesting," he said, "and more troubling, is what *wasn't* in the DNA."

"Damn it." Malvin sighed, sat down, and lowered his head into his hands for a moment. *This is going to be a long day.* "Go ahead."

Bailey continued. "The DNA structure was virtually flawless. No anomalies. No degenerative markers. No genetic disorders. Statistically speaking, that level of precision doesn't exist naturally. It was as if the man's genome had been *scrubbed clean*. Engineered."

Malvin hit the intercom button on his phone. "Could somebody bring us three coffees?"

Then he released the button and turned to Bailey. "So, both victims had enhanced DNA? The North Khorean female from the guardrail, and the Pakistani male with the knee. Both genetically altered. What kind of crazy experiments are those countries doing anyway?"

Malvin hit the button on the phone again and barked, "Donuts too." Then mumbled, "Breakfast of champions."

Moudy jumped in to summarize their case so far. "We now know at least two individuals, both possibly linked to rogue states, were present at the scene. And both were carrying, or possibly composed of, technologies or materials that are decades, maybe *centuries*, ahead of what we currently have."

"Hold on," Malvin said, "I thought we dropped the time travel BS. This is a serious investigation. And if there's any possibility of getting the Feds involved, we'd better have our ducks in a row or *nobody's* getting any awards or promotions." He stared at Moudy. "Understand?"

Bailey took over the summary. "And whatever explosion happened, if that's what it was, it left it no bodies behind, only highly advanced remains and trace materials."

"And possibly not even that would have been left if we hadn't been so quick to respond," Moudy added.

Bailey looked Lieutenant Malvin dead in the eye. "It's your call, sir. But if you're asking, I say this is way beyond the FHP's scope. This stuff reeks of highly classified or black-ops capabilities."

The door opened and an officer entered with donuts and coffees. "Ah, good," Malvin said. "Thanks."

When the officer was gone and the door shut, Malvin took a long gulp of coffee, burned his tongue, then used the pain as fuel.

"Okay," he said, sounding more confident than he felt, "We'll bring in the Feds immediately. Homeland Security, CIA,

FBI, whoever takes point on cross-national terrorism and biotech threats. Because if this is what it looks like, we're staring at the edge of something big. Something global. And potentially catastrophic.

"First off, I'm callin' my old friend Tim Logan, Director of Counter-Terrorism at the National Security Bureau. If anybody knows how to deal with this kinda thing, it's him.

"I'll cover the Bureau as well," he added.

"You men get on the horn and make the rest of the calls. Keep me apprised."

For a moment, the troopers indulged in their minimal breakfasts, then rose to leave, hands full.

At his desk, Malvin slowly turned the pages of Bailey's report, first licking the sticky off his fingers.

He called across the room, "Jimmy. Matty. You boys did a fine job here. Thorough work. Serious stuff."

He placed the report down on the desk, tapping it once with his knuckle. "Man, were you right about this being above our pay grade. I'm kinda glad the Big Guns will be here to take the heat off of us. No telling where this mess is going to lead.

"In the meantime, I want a full alert issued across the state. Every local police department, every sheriff's office, every Highway Patrol unit. Anyone and everyone on the road need to be on the lookout for *white Felza ET1 SUVs*. Full alert."

Moudy raised an eyebrow. "*All* white Felzas?"

"No," Malvin said, "*that* model only: Felza ET1. White. Matches the vehicle from the accident site. Also, anything suspicious. Especially look out for recent hotel check-ins for a group of nine to ten people."

"Put it in writing: any individuals found driving a white Felza ET1 acting suspicious, or resisting stop orders are to be treated as armed and extremely dangerous."

Bailey stiffened. "Protocol?"

"Treat them as lethal threats. If you encounter them, detain immediately if it's safe to do so, otherwise, you are authorized to use deadly force ... as a countermeasure or self-defense. Use discretion, but don't take chances. These people have access to materials and tech that can vaporize a body and leave nothing but dust. That ain't standard terrorism. That's next level."

He looked from one officer to the other.

"I don't care what these people *look* like. Young, old, foreign, domestic. If they're in a white Felza ET1 and you smell even a hint of trouble, you act fast. Just book them right away."

Mark's jaw clenched. "And spread the word. Make sure this doesn't stay quiet."

CHAPTER -11

08:42 | 11-13-2025 (Twenty-first century)
LOCATION: RESIDENCE INN - BASE ROOM 402

Max trudged back to his room after breakfast in the Great Room and dropped into the recliner like gravity had doubled. Every decision, every conversation, even with his own team, felt heavier than it should. Once, command came as easily as breathing. Now it felt like walking through wet sand.

The relentless heat outside didn't help. Nor did the thick, suffocating humidity that clung to his skin like a second suit. This century was punishing in ways he hadn't expected.

The Earth was getting hotter. Polar caps were melting, wildfires and tornadoes raged, and deserts were spreading as the planet slowly cooked. Cancer rates had surged.

Most people in this time barely noticed. They hadn't seen a slow-motion replay of desertification creeping across the decades. They didn't even know the word. They lived unaware. The climate had deteriorated so gradually that their bodies had simply adapted to the misery.

Max wondered how they were supposed to sense the difference. How could they know what the climate should feel like?

Meeting the people who had written the *Manifesto of Eleven Elements*—understanding their vision, and making sure that vision reached the world—would make the entire jump through time worth every sacrifice.

After everything they'd lost in just two days of this mission, Max clung to a single fragile hope: that this meeting might help save humanity from the catastrophe still waiting in the twenty-sixth century.

But first, he needed answers. Why hadn't the Manifesto been published? Why was the timeline becoming unstable? And what exactly was Gaia Theory, and the reason for all the hype around it?

His eyes drifted to the VRV headset on the side table. Fully charged. Waiting. Just looking at it steadied him.

Yet, before diving back into memory recall, he reached for the TV remote. He needed to remind himself of the world around him, not just escape into visions of the past.

Channel 9's anchor read from an unseen screen. "Pope Francis, 88, leader of the Roman Catholic Church, passed away this morning.

"The Vatican announced his death after he appeared publicly on Sunday to offer blessings to crowds in St. Peter's Square. He had been battling age-related ailments and a prolonged respiratory illness.

"Catholics worldwide, as well as political and religious leaders, expressed their grief and sent condolences.

"Many remember him as a champion of the poor, a defender of human dignity, and a spiritual leader who advocated for peace and social justice.

"Tributes poured in. Bells tolled across the world."

Abruptly, the subject shifted, and catastrophic images replaced those of the late pontiff and his grieving followers.

"And in Los Angeles," the anchor said, "a new study confirms climate change has increased the risk of catastrophic wildfires by more than thirty percent. Drought now pushes deeper into winter, fueling infernos during Santa Ana winds that turn sparks into deadly walls of flame."

Max exhaled, feeling the pressure of his twin responsibilities: saving his own fractured future century, and preventing the one he now lived in from unraveling in real time. Two seemingly impossible tasks.

The news onscreen only deepened the ache inside him. So, he turned back toward the VRV headset.

The memory recall sessions had become his refuge, his therapy, and his anchor.

Each time he emerged from one, he felt more like himself. More focused. More whole. The fragments of his mind were slowly aligning again.

As he rested, he recovered and rebuilt the mental power he depended on to lead, to calculate, to survive.

Without it, he was just another man stuck out of time.

(VRV BLINKING: MEMORY RECALL MODE)
16:45 | 11-06-2532 (Twenty-sixth century)
LOCATION: OCTAGON TO HIGHPARK Command Office

Max sat in the hovercraft, eyes fixed on the horizon, though his mind was a storm of unchecked thoughts.

The return trip to Central Command had only just begun, but already the pressure of the next four days tightened in his chest like a steel plate.

He had to choose fourteen people, plus himself, to make the jump.

Fifteen total.

Fifteen lives.

No second chances.

This wasn't a drill or a goodwill mission. They were going back. Not just years but *centuries*. And that kind of leap came with consequences. Physics bent, biology strained.

And sometimes time didn't give you back what you sent.

Max had made dozens of short-range jumps. A few years, in and out. No damage, no delays. But this? This was different. This was deep past. Unforgiving past. And he had to pick who'd go with him.

He thought of his best. The loyal ones. The brave ones. The ones who never flinched when orders came down. People he trusted with his life. People who had, over the years, become his family.

He didn't want to send anyone with children. He didn't want to send anyone at all.

But if the mission required a specific skill set, and it would, then personal lives didn't matter. Not in the face of what was at stake.

His pulse pounded in his ears; each beat an echo of the dread sitting in his chest.

Focus.

He reached for the PCOM. If he didn't start reading now, he'd lose his grip. The planning, the structure, the data, that was something he could control.

Unlike everything else.

The one-hour time limit on the PCOM was nearly up. Normally, he'd ration usage. Standard protocol. But under these circumstances? Screw protocol.

If he didn't come back from this mission, the time limits wouldn't matter anyway.

Still, the ticking countdown in the corner of the screen gnawed at him.

Max navigated through folders, skimming labels until he spotted one: GAIA THEORY.

He tapped his ear to turn on the micro-headphones implanted inside his ears. A soft chime indicated activation.

Then Eve, the MOP's synthetic reader, began to speak in her calm, neutral tone. "The Gaia Theory proposes that life on Earth forms a synergistic, self-regulating system.

"Organisms, consciously or not, interact with both living and non-living components of the planet to sustain the conditions necessary for life.

"The biosphere, shaped by billions of years of evolution, stabilizes global temperature, ocean salinity, atmospheric oxygen, liquid water availability, and other critical variables. Earth, in this model, functions as one living superorganism.

"Formulated in the 1970s by chemist James Lovelock and co-developed by microbiologist Lynn Margulis, the Gaia Theory suggests that every plant, insect, microbe, and animal plays a role, however small, in maintaining planetary balance.

"Except humans." Eve's voice said it without emphasis or emotion, as if it were just another cold fact. Which, to her, the synthetic, it was.

"Humans are the only species known to disrupt this equilibrium, consciously, recklessly, and on a massive scale.

"The damage began in the nineteenth century and accelerated through the twentieth. By the time humanity fully grasped the consequences, it was already the twenty-first."

Eve's voice paused as more data loaded.

Max closed his eyes. The theory had always haunted him. Part science, part verdict, it emphasized the dual nature of powerful forces capable of good and harm.

The planet had built itself into a living system over eons of cooperation.

Yet humans had managed to unravel it in two hundred years.

Eve continued, her voice calm and steady. "The Gaia Theory, as written by human scientists, suggests that ancient life-forms, acting unconsciously or through natural adaptation, created the very environment that allowed future organisms, including mammals and humans, to thrive.

"They oxygenated the atmosphere, stabilized ocean salinity, and maintained planetary systems long after their own extinction.

"The *Manifesto of the Eleven Elements* affirms this core belief. It extends the Gaia Theory by asserting that if primitive organisms could unconsciously shape a life-sustaining world, then humans capable of conscious thought can make deliberate choices to restore and improve it.

"We are not bound to be the destroyers. We can be the stewards."

Eve's subtle identification of herself as one among humans hardly caused a stir inside him anymore.

Instead, a flicker of resolve cut through the fog of dread in Max's chest.

Eve continued. "Mr. Joshua DeWine adapted the Gaia Theory into a human-scale analogy.

"He argued that if our bodies evolved from microorganisms, then the intelligence of those cells, their Gaia, is still at work within us. Wound healing, respiration, digestion, homeostasis: all subconscious processes carried out by an internal biosphere.

"DeWine likens the human body to the Earth. Both are made of similar elements: high water content, trace metals and minerals, and both carry electrical charges.

"Just as Earth generates electromagnetic fields, so too do human bodies: what some call auras.

"The planet affects us, and we in turn can affect ourselves.

"Mr. DeWine cites authors and researchers who claim that humans can learn to consciously engage in real healing: physical, emotional, and planetary.

"Rather than relying solely on automatic biological repair, we can align our thoughts and actions with Gaia-like intention."

Max stared at the screen, jaw tight. This was a call to action. A challenge.

Though some of what Eve said was general knowledge, concepts Max had learned years ago, the body of work as a whole seemed to take on more power in this critical moment.

The refresher served to remind Max of the eons of advancement and deterioration that had led to this very mission.

And it prepared him to contextualize the events to come.

He was going to meet Mr. DeWine soon. At least the version of the man from five centuries in the past.

Success in this mission hinged on Max's ability to understand the mind of the man from the past, the one who could either create a beautiful world for others to live in, or abandon his purpose entirely.

Should the worst happen, everything would collapse. The utopian life they now enjoyed would fail to materialize. In its place would be endless world wars and rampant killing.

Eve continued, "Mr. DeWine concluded that the human body is a model Gaia system.

"He extended this analogy to Earth. Like the body, the planet is a living system composed of interdependent life-forms: plants, animals, bacteria, humans. Each one, knowingly or not, contributes to the balance. Together, they sustain the 'world body.'

"But what happens when one-part stops functioning?

"If the stomach refuses to digest, or the kidneys quit filtering waste, what happens to the body? What happens if the heart decides to rest for just ten minutes?

"Or worse: what happens when a group of cells consumes too many resources, grows uncontrollably, offers no benefit, and becomes a cancerous mass?"

For Max, the abstract finally hit home in the very real manifestation of this scenario that could play out if the mission fails. His jaw tightened.

"According to DeWine," Eve said, "humanity today behaves like cancer. We deforest. We poison. We overpopulate. We exterminate species. We bicker over trivialities and threaten global annihilation with the push of a button.

"To an outsider, an alien observer or a future civilization, twenty-first-century humans might appear as parasitic growths on Earth's living body. Consuming. Spreading. Killing."

A pause.

Then Eve's voice softened almost imperceptibly. "Mr. DeWine offered a warning.

"After three and a half billion years of evolutionary struggle, Earth is now in the hands of a species capable of conscious choice. Humanity must learn to cohabitate. To live as a functioning part of the whole. Or it will destroy the planet.

"And itself."

Max switched off the PCOM and exhaled slowly, his thoughts running silent. What read like theory in Eva's voice, suddenly felt like prophecy. And he needed to shake off.

The mission *would* succeed.

He had four days left.

And fifteen souls to pick.

It was now a matter of do or die.

08:53| 11-13-2025
LOCATION: FELZA DESIGN STUDIO Hawthorne, CA

Felixus Godart, or simply Felix, as everyone called him, sat hunched over his desk, studying the images his cousin Randy had sent from Florida. They didn't make much sense to him. The angles were odd, the parts unfamiliar. It looked like something mechanical, maybe automotive, but with components he couldn't identify.

He decided to escalate.

Felix forwarded the images to his boss, Frans Von Holsten, and moments later, his office phone rang.

"Felix. My office. Now."

Inside Frans's private office, the air was always a few degrees cooler. Felix entered cautiously.

Frans Von Holsten was the chief designer of the Felza Cars. He conceptualized the entire product line and future models of their cars to be sold in the market over several years. Frans was handpicked by Querlin Stark for his creative design strengths that would lend the brand image the Felza cars so needed.

Frans enjoyed one of the most comfortable office spaces on the second floor with the view of the rolling hills, at the base of which sat the Felza HQ.

Frans didn't look up from his screen, didn't invite Felix to sit. "Did *you* render these?"

Felix blinked. "No, sir. These are real. Photos my cousin Randy took. He's a mechanic in Central Florida. He found these parts in a vehicle someone dropped off. Said the owner cleared everything out quickly. Told him it was just some experiment by an engineering student or something."

Frans's eyes narrowed.

"Is there a problem?" Felix asked, sensing the shift.

"Yeah, there might be." Frans absently studied the pen in his hand. "You don't know Querlin yet, do you? He's a bit ... protective. Paranoid, even. Thinks everyone's out to steal his tech and undercut Felza's lead.

"The last thing we need is another yPhone versus Soonsong copyright war."

A chill that hadn't come from the A/C crept up Felix's back. "I wasn't going to share them publicly. I just thought they were interesting. Maybe worth analyzing."

Frans cut him off with a raised hand. "Don't think. Just follow instructions."

He set the pen down slowly, then gave Felix a cold stare. "Send me *everything* you've got. Then delete the images. From your yPhone, your backups, everywhere. And tell your cousin to do the same. No more photos. No more videos. No questions."

Felix hesitated. "Okay. Understood."

Dismissed, Felix slipped out of Frans's office and out into the main campus. As he receded down a hallway, he saw Querlin coming his way, fast and focused.

They passed one another in silence without so much as a nod of recognition. As if Querlin hadn't even seen Felix.

The man was headed for Frans's office. Felix would bet on that.

Querlin Stark was having a rather good morning after leaving the position as head of DOGCRed: Division of Government Cost Reduction, for the federal government and his friend in political world, President Frank McCrony.

Stark was peculiar. He didn't care. The two most important things about him were that he was brilliant and he was rich. And those two things made him influential and powerful.

He carved a path down the hallway of one of his many companies' grand offices as if he were the only one there. Or at least the only one who mattered.

On the rare occasions when information or innovations popped up outside of his realm, he wanted to know about them. Were they his own ideas, leaked? Or were they good ideas he needed to take control of?

That's why he was hurrying to the office of his Design Director, Frans Von Holsten.

Stark carried himself like a man who had already seen the future. And built it.

In the high-stakes world of modern tech and innovation, he styled himself as a peer among legends. He idolized the meteoric rise of Pear Corporation's Stevie Geobs: the father of personal computing, digital music, and the mobile phone revolution.

Like Geobs, Stark was sharp, relentless, and unapologetically visionary.

But where others were chasing time, Stark believed *time was on his side.*

He had taken the helm of *Felza Inc.* during one of the most fragile moments in economic history: the global financial crisis of 2008.

While traditional automakers scrambled for survival, Stark saw opportunity. The U.S. government had earmarked $25 billion in bailout funds for energy-efficient vehicle development. Felza's electric platform, which was still considered a longshot at the time, checked all the right boxes.

When the dust settled, Felza Inc. had secured over $465 million in low-interest loans from the Department of Energy, along with a buffet of tax breaks and subsidies. He would turn this lifeline into a launchpad.

By the time the company went public with its IPO in 2010, Felza had shed its underdog label.

But Stark hadn't forgotten the lean days. He remembered the ridicule, the investor skepticism, the near-death experience in 2007 when whispers of bankruptcy spread after Felza failed to deliver its first all-electric sports car, the *Rockster.* Orders had been delayed. Production issues mounted. Critics called it a pipe dream.

Now, those critics were silent.

Felza was a tech empire.

And Querlin Stark had rewritten the rules.

After pulling Felza Inc. back from the brink, Stark made a decisive move: he hired Frans Von Holsten to lead the design division.

Frans's mandate was clear: create vehicles that would revolutionize customer experience and set a new standard in automotive appreciation. Form, function, and futuristic elegance had to converge. And under Frans's leadership, Felza's design language became iconic.

Stark had always been two steps ahead.

He understood that political winds were shifting. With President Udama in office, the U.S. Congress had pushed through sweeping reforms. Chief among them, a national transition to fully electric vehicles by 2030.

That policy not only reshaped industry incentives but also transformed geopolitical strategy.

The U.S. could now lean on its domestic oil reserves, shale, strategic petroleum stockpiles, and new explorations, to become energy independent. No more importing oil from the Middle Eastern oil cartels.

It was a risky but calculated play.

By rebooting the automotive industry with a green agenda, President Udama hoped to rebuild a post-crisis America. One where Wall Street failures wouldn't determine national destiny.

And Querlin Stark, with Felza at the forefront, was perfectly positioned to ride the wave.

Right place. Right time.

But his greatest motivator wasn't ambition.

It was fear.

A persistent, gnawing fear of failure. Of chaos. Of extinction.

Despite his deep commitment to environmentalism and clean technology, Stark harbored darker thoughts.

He believed the world was dangerously close to collapse. A misstep in diplomacy. A rogue act of aggression. The outbreak of global war. All it would take was one spark, and everything could be lost.

Not in decades, but in days. Maybe hours.

That fear drove him to invest in the space industry.

He saw orbital stations and Martian colonies as lifeboats, insurance policies against human self-destruction.

If Earth couldn't be saved, *maybe he could be*. Maybe a few others too.

Querlin Stark had no illusions about saving *everyone*.

He despised the volatile rhetoric of nuclear posturing from unstable regimes.

But worse still, he loathed the recklessness of world leaders like President Frank McCrony, whose hot-headed bullying tactics with his own Senate painted him as a wildcard, not a statesman.

McCrony's threats and arm-twisting politics unnerved Stark far more than any rogue nation. Because McCrony had the power, and the unpredictability, to start the fire no one could put out.

Stark's dream was to build a future that could avert the looming disaster. But first, he had to survive the present

As he fast-walked through the maze of offices, he felt that familiar pique of exhilaration.

There was urgency in Frans's call. The kind of urgency that couldn't be brushed off. *Maybe he's come up with a new concept for a next-gen model*, Stark thought as he stepped into the design wing.

"What's up, Frans?" Stark asked as he entered the office. "You said you had something I needed to see?"

Getting Frans over from Muzda Motors had been one of Stark's smartest moves. The man had vision. And discretion.

Frans didn't waste a second. He pointed Stark to look at the 85-inch monitor hanging on the wall. He began clicking through a series of high-resolution images on his PC that was mirroring the images.

The first few frames were mundane: close ups of a stripped-down vehicle component. But the deeper he went, the more complex the machinery appeared. Then came the wide shots.

"This is impossible," Stark whispered, the words slipping out in a crisp British accent, the one that surfaced whenever he was shocked, cornered, or blindsided by unsettling news.

Finally, he stepped toward the screen, eyes narrowing for a moment. "You son of a gun." He laughed. "Is this a render? Are you messing with me? This has to be CGI, right?"

Frans didn't smile. "No, Querlin. Not a render. These were real video stills, captured in Central Florida. Sent to my designer Felix by his cousin, Randy, who works at a mechanic's shop."

Stark studied Frans's face, trying to make sense of what he had seen on the display

"They were trying to strip this assembly for resale," Frans continued. "But the owner apparently came back and cleared the entire setup, saying it was part of a student engineering experiment. Whoever built this did more than modify a vehicle; they hid it in plain sight."

Frans flipped to another set of images showing what was clearly a Felza ET1, heavily altered to look like another make entirely. Disfigured. Covered. Masked.

Stark's eyes widened as adrenalin surged through him. He gestured to the screen "Frans, this is *exactly* what I sketched for you the other day!

"The wind tunnel generator concept. Remember?"

Frans nodded cautiously.

"I told you," Stark continued. "If we funneled airflow through narrow channels and pushed it over horizontally stacked micro-turbines, we could regenerate energy while driving. Wind energy! A series of those turbines could keep recharging the batteries mid-motion."

He was pacing now. His body instinctively knew a race had begun, but his mind was still catching up.

"I even said that sixth, maybe seventh generation models could crack six hundred miles on a single charge using this system! That sketch was in *my* notebook. No one else saw it."

"I remember that," Frans said. "It was three days ago."

Querlin Stark felt the implications tumble down on him. "So how the *hell* is this idea out there already? Is your office bugged? Did you tell anybody? Who is this 'student'? I want a name. I want to *hire* him. Or haul him in if I have to."

"We have regular security sweeps, per your SOPs," Frans said. "But I'll have my office checked again."

Stark spun back to Frans. "We need to get to the bottom of this. *Now.* This could be a leak. Or something else entirely."

Frans gave a single nod. "Already on it."

"Hire the best," Stark said flatly. "I don't care if it's espionage investigators, ex-military trackers, or private detectives. I want this traced. All of it.

He glanced at the freeze-frame onscreen again. "Find out who brought that car into the shop. Who installed that assembly? Who designed it? I want names, addresses, timelines, and affiliations."

This was creeping him out. *He* was supposed to be the one ahead of the curve. It wasn't natural for him to be catching up.

Stark gently rubbed at the freshly grafted follicles on his scalp, still tender from the latest restoration procedure, and turned toward Frans.

"It's like someone crawled inside my head and extracted the entire concept. Word for word. Bolt for bolt. We're not talking coincidence, Frans. This is precision theft."

He stabbed a finger against Frans's glass desktop, angry. "Loop in our IP counsel. Quietly. I want legal ready, in case this turns into a court fight over stolen tech.

"And above all, this stays under wraps. No leaks. Not one whisper. You understand me?"

Frans nodded, looking a little bit scared. To be honest, Stark felt a little scared too. But he had never let a little fear stop him before. And it wouldn't stop him now.

Stark gave Frans a long look, then turned and walked out of the office.

After a few seconds Frans finally felt safe enough to exhale. If Querlin Stark suspected eavesdropping, Frans himself could fall under suspicion. That's why priority-one had to be getting that surveillance sweep of his office ASAP.

He immediately buzzed his administrative assistant. "Drea, I need you to get me on with head of security. I don't care what you have to do. I need a targeted sweep of my office NOW. His best people.

"Next, clear my schedule." Frans was charged up like he'd had too much coffee. And that could lead to mistakes. So, he took a breath and calmed himself

"I need you to contact the list of independent contractors we've used for black-box investigations. Priority status. Start with the ones we worked with last year on that patent breach in Helsinki."

"Got it," Drea said and Frans hung up.

Then he opened his secure internal channel and summoned Dave Qualls, the head of the parts division. "I need a full forensic analysis," he said without any greetings.

"I'll be sending you some video clips. I need you to get your best people on it. Examine all the images. Identify *anything* unique: serial numbers, materials, weld signatures, tubing specs, factory markings, even connection patterns and fingerprints.

"I want to know if these parts were made in-house, overseas, or in someone's damn garage."

He ended the call.

Frans knew they weren't chasing a rogue engineer; they were chasing a ghost.

And if the ghost had already built what Querlin Stark had only dreamed of, Felza's future might be riding on the back of a flatbed tow truck, headed to a scrap yard.

CHAPTER -12

9:42 | 11-13-2025 (Twenty-first century)
LOCATION: RESIDENCE INN - BASE ROOM 402

Max and his team were slowly adapting to life in the twenty-first century. For Max, their base room was no longer just a shelter, it had become a sanctuary of recovery.

The more time he spent in that space, the more grounded he felt. Safe. Restoring. Each hour alone helped him reclaim fragments of strength, mental, physical, even temporal. The world outside was chaotic, but here, in this quiet chamber of borrowed time, Max was beginning to feel whole again.

The recliner by the window, its cushions now molded to his frame from days of ritual use, offered a quiet comfort.

He eased into it, pulled the VRV headset over his face, and exhaled slowly.

The world outside faded.

Inside the headset, the future he came from blossomed with life.

To be precise, his sessions were not flashbacks, but flash-forwards. To his home far away from this time period.

He was healing, one memory at a time. Layer by layer, his mind was rebuilding the lost architecture of who he was and why he was here.

The images, sounds, and smells were pieces of himself. Knowledge tucked away in the deepest folds of time, now surfacing like sunken treasure.

Every session brought him closer to clarity. Every recovered detail could become the hinge on which their mission swung.

He knew too well that the days ahead would test every ounce of his command, intuition, and mental precision.

That's why these sessions were critical, not just for his psychological and mental integrity, but for the survival of himself, his team, and all those living on the timeline that was now at risk of unraveling.

And so, Max let go, willing himself to surrender to the virtual tide of memory as it pulled him deeper into the truth he was meant to remember.

(VRV BLINKING: MEMORY RECALL MODE)
18:45 | 11-06-2532 (Twenty-sixth century)
LOCATION: HIGHPARK 577 RENNER RESIDENCE

Max stepped out of the hovercraft and approached the Central Command office where he had been picked up just that morning, headed for Zurich, Switzerland.

The doors slid open for him and he stepped through, taking a deep, centering breath.

In one day, my life has flipped a hundred and eighty degrees, he thought.

Time-travel used to be routine, assignments in and out, clean and clinical. But this mission will be different. Live embedment. Five centuries into the past. Primitive time. Heavy-duty TTVs. A larger team. Greater risks. No guarantees of what we might face, or that we'd return at all.

Before entering the public area, he straightened his back and rolled his shoulders to shake off the creeping anxiety he tried not to acknowledge.

Max believed in leading from the front: pulling his team through, not pushing from behind.

No one could see hesitation. As Commander, his composure had to be absolute, projecting calm, control, and confidence. If he showed cracks, the whole team would feel it.

He summoned all his resolve and followed the familiar route to what had become his sanctuary.

As luck would have it, he encountered no one on the way to his quarters.

Inside his quarters, the system recognized his presence. His desk screen rose automatically, flickered on, and greeted him with a photo: him and Annie, smiling at a beach long gone.

He paused for half a second, sat down, then approached the screen and swiped the image it away.

With a few swift gestures, he pulled up his files and restructured his task lists. Top priority: selecting fourteen officers, plus himself, to complete the jump. Of the forty-nine on his roster, he had to isolate the best.

Not just the strongest. Not the most decorated. The most *adaptable*.

This mission required immersion in a world four hundred years out of date. That meant officers fluent in obsolete systems: primitive coding languages, legacy operating systems, gasoline engines, mobile phone etiquette.

People who understood social norms, fashion cues, body language, and tech habits of the twenty-first century. Officers who could blend in: talk the talk, walk the walk, tweet the tweet.

He flagged profiles with relevant training or retro-history specializations. A shortlist began to form.

Some had families: spouses, children. Two-person marriages were rare now, but not unheard of.

He grimaced. Those would be the first names cut. Unless one of them had skills he couldn't replace.

That was the line he had to walk now: the boundary between humanity and necessity.

He didn't like it.

But he'd do it.

Max entered the parameters into the system: psychological resilience, adaptability, historical specialization, and tech fluency from the early digital era.

Eve processed the request in seconds, scanning personnel files with clinical precision before narrowing the list down to nineteen officers.

He reviewed the results, then opened a secure video line to Admiral Rikor Ubanto.

When the Admiral's face appeared, Max drew a breath and reported with a matter-of-fact assurance, "I've got nineteen qualifiers. I'll choose the final fourteen on the day of transport.

"I'll have the remaining five fully trained and left on standby for rapid deployment, should reinforcements be needed."

Ubanto offered neither questions nor comments. Just a sharp nod. "Very well." And the line disconnected.

That was the plan: all nineteen would go through the same intense prep, but only fifteen would jump.

Still at his desk, Max pulled up the files for his selected team.

Charts, bios, psych profiles, mission histories. He scanned through each, taking mental notes on skillsets, behavior patterns, potential liabilities.

He wanted to understand why Eve had picked these particular people, and to make sure her logic aligned with his gut instincts.

Once satisfied, he composed a brief message to his regiment and queued it for immediate transmission:

To all selected personnel:

Report to Central Command Briefing Room Alpha at 0800 hours tomorrow. Bring your gear. Come prepared.

- Commander Max

He sent it.

There was no turning back now.

14:01 | 11-13-2025 (Twenty-first century)
LOCATION: DOWNTOWN ORLANDO, Orange Ave Ste 500

After a palatable lunch at what was called an organic salad bar, Max, Prisha, Bitang, Daniel, and Minami made their way to what Max knew could be the most important meeting of their lives.

They pulled up in front of the old converted house near downtown Orlando that now served as Joshua DeWine's architecture office.

The building had a weathered charm. white siding, creaky porch steps, iron railings faded with time.

A brass plaque beside the door read simply:

Joshua DeWine, Architect | Designer | Planner

Inside, they were greeted by the warm buzz of a landline phone conversation. A receptionist sat at the front desk, locked in discussion, one hand gripping the phone, the other raised with an index finger and a half-apologetic smile that said, *"Just a minute."*

Max gave a small nod, reading her body language.

He was starting to understand these surface-level customs. One finger meant *wait*. Palm up, fingers open meant *stop*. Hand on chest meant *sincere*, or at least pretending to be.

He signaled his team to take the offered seats.

Max took a seat near the end of the sofa, his pulse ticking faster than usual. He wasn't the only one feeling it.

"No way this is real," Bitang whispered, seated beside him, his right foot tapping the floor in anticipation.

Across from them, Minami lounged in a chair, dressed sharp in a tailored business suit. "I can't believe we're actually meeting DeWine," she said. "*The* Joshua DeWine. Finally."

Max kept his expression flat, but inside, it didn't feel normal. Joshua DeWine wasn't just a name. He was respected, studied, quoted for centuries.

The author who envisioned a better history for all of humanity was about to walk through that door.

"Should we be standing to receive him or something?" Danny asked.

Max didn't answer. He just kept staring ahead, trying to believe this was actually happening.

The waiting area was tastefully arranged. A blend of retro and modern. The kind of minimalism that looked effortless but was clearly curated.

Every wall was dressed with framed renderings: shimmering high-rises, sculptural museums, sleek restaurant interiors, and even a futuristic operatory room aglow with sterile blues and silvers.

One rendering showed a detailed layout of a Farbox café, with notes scribbled in fine print. Drive-thru optimization, solar panel angles, HVAC concealment strategies.

The drawings had a tagline: "United we build America"

Max took a closer look. He knew these drawings. Or at least the types.

Architecture had always fascinated him. Not for the aesthetics, but for what it revealed about civilization's psychology.

The drawings were like x-rays of culture: monuments to ambition, habit, vanity, and survival.

Colosseum in ancient Rome were built to distract the restless. Now, giant football stadiums served the same purpose, only with less blood.

Stadiums filled not with prisoners, but with fans. Not executions, but games.

And still the crowds gathered, cheered, vented their work anxieties, and fed off the thrill.

Wrestling, Max recalled from one briefing. Grown adults in a material called "spandex," hurling each other across roped platforms to thunderous applause. Ritualized violence wrapped in drama.

"Humans haven't changed much," he muttered under his breath.

Minami gave a questioning glance.

Max didn't elaborate.

Then the receptionist put the phone handset into its cradle. Her cherry-red lips curled into a practiced smile as she stood up from behind the reception desk.

She smoothed the front of her black blazer and addressed them with the poise of someone who had mastered the rhythm of gatekeeping.

"My name is Jill Vivien. You must be Mr. Max, right? Joe said he'll see you now in the conference room. It's just this way."

The group moved through the hallway, stepping into a bright, modern conference room enclosed in full-height glass walls.

The afternoon light poured in, glinting off the brushed steel legs of a large rectangular table. Around it was ten chairs, soft leather and on casters, no doubt ergonomic, but elegant enough to flatter a client.

A 72-inch flatscreen hung across one end of the room, dormant for now.

They took their seats.

"Would you like coffee, chai-tea, or water?" Jill asked.

"Water would be nice," Max replied.

She returned moments later with chilled water bottles for everyone.

Just as she had left, the door clicked open, and in walked Joshua DeWine.

"Good afternoon. You must be Max." His voice was measured, confident. "I'm Architect Joshua DeWine. Thank you for waiting. Mondays are always a little chaotic, more calls than quiet."

DeWine extended a hand to each of them starting with Max. Firm grip. A wedding band on his ring finger. An elegant watch.

"I looked up the parcel you messaged me about on Froogle. That slope, you mentioned drops about ten feet east to west, right?"

Max was disarmed, if only slightly. He hadn't expected this level of attentiveness. Or calm. Or the strange brightness in Joe's eyes. It was like … *clarity*. Like he had slept perfectly. For weeks.

"Yes, that's the one," Max replied, regaining focus. "Thank you for meeting with us on such short notice. We're under contract to buy the land. We wanted to do our due diligence before closing."

He gestured toward the man next to him. "This is Danny. And Bitang. We're partners in this venture. The goal is one hundred and twenty townhomes on roughly ten acres. We wanted to get your advice."

Bitang unrolled the site survey, freshly printed at a local copy shop. Its edges curled stubbornly.

Joe stepped forward and placed a paperweight on one end, his eyes scanning the layout like he was reading music.

"Okay," Joe said, almost to himself. "Ten acres. Hmm. Access point is here. Drainage runs this way. That rear easement will need addressing," he said. "Any retention pond plan?"

"We were hoping to do underground vaults," Danny offered. "If the grade works."

Joe nodded slowly. "It's doable, but you'll need a strong civil. And you'll want to stagger the building pads if you're keeping the slope. Or we can terrace them. I'll sketch a few options after this meeting."

Max glanced at his team. Bitang gave a subtle nod. So far, Joe was everything the rumors suggested: competent, thoughtful, and deceptively sharp.

But Max wasn't here for just design consultation.

He was here to take the full measure of Joshua DeWine, the man at the center of publishing a proclamation, a manifesto, that could ignite an ideological revolution.

And here Joe was, talking easements and retention vaults like he didn't have a care in the world.

It was impressive.

But it was also unsettling.

Max rested his hands on the table. "We appreciate the insights, Joe. You're clearly someone who sees the big picture. That's what we need. Someone who can look at raw land and already imagine it alive with people, traffic, families. Futures."

Joe smiled. "That's the job," he said. "The future always starts with a sketch."

Max nodded slowly, tucking that line away. Because in this case, it wasn't just a sketch. It was the future of something far bigger than a housing project.

Joe studied the layout closely, tracing the lines with his fingers. "We need to conduct a geological test and soil study to determine if this land is viable.

"There might be muck or unstable ground layered over dried aquifers. If that's the case, the land could suddenly give way and form sinkholes."

He pointed to a section on the map. "This area might not be suitable for construction. Do you have any environmental reports, prior surveys, or soil explorations already done? If not, we'll need to order one immediately."

Danny looked slightly puzzled, even a bit embarrassed.

Max feared he might blow their cover because they hadn't gathered all the necessary data about the property.

"So, Mr. Joe," Danny stammered, "you think we'd be at a loss if we buy this land? I already told Max we should look elsewhere. We'd be a total shitchilli if we go through with this, don't you think?"

Joe cocked his head. "I'm just cautioning you based on my observations. It may not be that bad, and we can always explore solutions," he said, clearly confused.

Max desperately hoped they could pull themselves out of this potential mess before it got any worse.

"But seriously, my friend," DeWine pressed. "What is a shitchilli?"

Danny and Max exchanged a quick glance.

Then Danny began to spin a rather awkward story to explain his accidental slip of a twenty-sixth century expression in twentieth century terms.

"Sorry," Danny said. "You see, we were born and raised overseas. Where we come from, "shitchilli" is an expression people use when they eat a lot of chilies in their food, and the next day, they regret it when they're in the bathroom. You know what I mean?

"So that word just means a painful, after-the-fact realization of doing something foolish."

"That's a good one," Joe said.

"I apologize if I offended you."

Joe waved him off, then stared at Danny quizzically. "Actually, I think I heard a different version of your shitchilli story as a kid. There's something familiar about it.

"But speaking of food," he added. "I haven't had lunch yet, and I'm starving. How about I take you to this nice steakhouse across the street? My treat. Steak or ribs. Whatever you want."

Max watched his team exchange puzzled glances.

The idea of eating steak and ribs *with Joshua DeWine* was surreal, to put it mildly. Even Max felt the disconnect.

Here was the very man who had long championed vegetarianism and inspired a global shift toward plant-based living. And now he was offering animal flesh for lunch?

Max took the lead. "We've all been vegan for quite some time now. I appreciate your offer for lunch, but we have prior appointments today. Maybe we can reschedule and have lunch or dinner another time."

Joe smiled. "I'm vegetarian too. Almost vegan, really. If it weren't for my love of yogurt, I'd be all the way there.

Then Joe lowered his voice, casting a quick glance toward the office door as though making sure the receptionist outside couldn't overhear. "We can be honest with one another," he said. "Right?

"I know you all aren't exactly who you say you are. I think I know where you're from."

Max tensed. The others fell as still as if they had just stepped on an ancient land mine that may or may not explode.

Joe explained. "You see, I had a premonition recently. A strong one. I felt I would be meeting people from, well, another realm. Maybe a parallel reality. Or maybe even from the future. Time travelers, perhaps?"

Joe studied their faces. "That story about shitchilli, and the way you all reacted to the steakhouse suggestion. But mainly your half-baked research on this building site of yours. That told me something was off about you. And as crazy as it may sound, my gut says you don't belong to this time.

"So, I'd like you to be honest with me. I might be able to help you."

Then he smiled gently and added, "Of course, I was actually going to invite you to my place for dinner. A nice, pure vegetarian or vegan meal. I know the future will be plant-based. The steakhouse suggestion was just a test. Your reactions helped confirm what I suspected."

Max couldn't suppress the smirk spreading across his face, a sure sign of someone caught red-handed. His officers were now staring at him, obviously waiting to see how he would respond to Joe's remarkable intuition.

Adding up all the factors, and knowing who Joshua DeWine was now, and would become, Max decided to go with his intuition.

"Yes, Joe. You're right." Max spoke in hushed tones. "We are from the future. From the year 2532, about five hundred and seven years from today. We are time travelers, here to ensure that things go well for you and your vision."

Joe seemed serene as if none of this was shocking. He just sat there, eyes mostly focused on Max.

"Your vision becomes a reality. In our time," Max said, "your ideas have transformed the world. We live by them. You had profound thoughts. And your philosophies were not only accurate, but they were also the most appropriate roadmap for humanity's survival and evolution."

Max's voice softened with admiration. "Not to put a lot of pressure on you, Joe, but you gave *purpose* to humanity. You redefined what it means to live a meaningful life.

"Every generation since your time has built upon your foundational work. They carry forward your legacy, proudly walking the path you imagined and shaped through your published works.

"Especially through *The Manifesto of Eleven Elements.*"

Joe smiled, a smile rich with accomplishment, satisfaction, and the thrill of being right. He had uncovered the true identities of his mysterious visitors, and now knew for certain that his life's work had borne fruit. The knowledge that his creative endeavors had positively shaped the future, confirmed by people from the future themselves, filled him with an overwhelming sense of validation.

Joe had quickly grasped the truth, Max and his team were actually Time Travelers from the future. It was the only explanation. Very few people knew about his thoughts, his ideas, and especially the Manifesto.

His heart swelled with pride. *The Manifesto of Eleven Elements* was thriving. It all sounded like music to his ears: his work had inspired generations, become a guiding doctrine for humanity, and cemented Joe's legacy across centuries.

Still smiling, Joe raised a finger to his lips and softly said, "This isn't the place to talk about any of this.

"Let's meet up tomorrow night for dinner. I'm a bit tied up this evening with a dinner meeting and a client, but I really want to continue this conversation in private."

Joe sat upright, a mischievous glint in his eyes.

"Let me tell you the *real* story behind *Shitchilli*, one I meant to include in my books, but never did. Funny how it evolved… and ended up in the twenty-sixth century."

The team nodded, intrigued. Max smiled. "As long as we're not eating into your day."

Joe waved it off. "This story is part of my foundation. Where my journey truly began."

He took a breath, his tone softening with nostalgia. "When I was a kid growing up in Bombay, I heard tales of Sheikh Chili, a well-meaning fool, known for daydreams and absurd decisions. One story stuck with me."

"Sheikh Chili sat at the edge of a tree branch, sawing through it, right where it joined the trunk. Everyone below knew he'd fall. But he was lost in fantasy, dreaming of owning a timber factory, marrying a princess, living in a castle made of wood."

Joe made a sawing motion.

"And then, *snap!* He fell. Broken bones. Dreams shattered. The crowd laughed.

"That image burned into me. Cutting the very branch that holds you, *that's* foolishness. I made a vow: never destroy the structures or people that support me. Family, friends, nature, systems, they're all branches. You protect them."

His voice grew more reflective.

"The deeper lesson? Ignoring harm or doing nothing to stop it is just as foolish. Living aimlessly, detached from purpose, is another version of Sheikh Chili. A dreamer, lost to reality."

He smiled ruefully.

"Sheikh Chili wasn't evil. Just innocent. Unaware. Distracted. That's why the story endures. We laugh, but it's a warning: Don't be so obsessed with dreams that you forget what's holding you up."

Joe glanced around the room.

"I still ask myself: am I being a Sheikh Chili today? In thought, word, or deed? Am I harming what sustains me? Am I doing something foolish, something people might laugh at, not now, but maybe centuries from now?"

He paused, then added, "In American slang, it's simple: don't shoot yourself in the foot. It's considered as sheer foolishness... isn't it?"

He paused, then said plainly, "And that's where we are now, as a species. We're destroying the Earth, our support system. It's a collective act of foolishness, born from ignorance. We're in essence all Sheikh Chili if we don't act now."

He raised a finger with a wink.

"Well... except for *you guys*. You're from the future. I *hope* there are no Shitchilli in your time."

Laughter rippled through the room as he continued, "So yes, that's where the name comes from. Shitchilli. Rooted in that old parable. And honestly, I've felt like him many times. But my *Eleven Elements Manifesto*, that's my way of changing course."

He stood, clapping his hands once.

"Alright. That's enough wisdom for one day. That'll be two hundred and fifty dollars please."

They stared at him, puzzled, then laughed as he grinned.

"Just kidding. Let's meet again tomorrow for dinner. More food. More stories. And hopefully no lectures. Some of my colleagues say I am too boring."

He shook each of their hands warmly, the moment lingering with meaning.

For Joe, it was one of the most fulfilling Mondays in years.

CHAPTER ⋅13

09:10 | 11-14-2025 (Twenty-first century)
LOCATION: Dr DUPRAY'S OFFICE SUITE 101
              HIGHWAY 50 CLERMONT FLORIDA

As Dr. Ronick Dupray entered his Florida clinic that morning, he greeted Alina, his part-time receptionist, with cheerful formality.

"Jolly good morning, Alina," he said, tipping an imaginary hat.

He was humming as he walked past the front desk, an old jazz tune under his breath. His mood was unmistakably upbeat.

In the past week alone, he had completed two intense sessions with his most intriguing patient, the one who had gradually shifted from being a client to near-obsession. Two hours, every week, dedicated without fail. And today, something felt different. Energizing. Electric.

Dr. Dupray couldn't wait to review the recordings.

He glanced around the empty waiting room, taking a quiet moment to appreciate the space he'd curated over the years.

The room was warm and calming, exactly how he wanted it to feel. Tastefully appointed lounge chairs, soft-cornered tables with amber-glow lamps, and in the far corner, a modest coffee station.

His prized espresso machine sat gleaming, ready to serve both his patients and himself, his lifeline when the hours grew long and intense.

On the far wall hung a single framed poster, larger than most artwork you'd find in a clinical setting. It bore a quote he'd handpicked years ago. One that had stayed with him.

*"People think spiritual awakening
is all bliss and happiness.
Yes, there is a great relief.
Yes, there is a great homecoming.
But then you begin to experience
the predicament that you and
the entire world is in.
And though you are not likely to
become panicked or terrified,
you will go to work very soon,
and you will work continuously."
- adopted from
Living the Way of Knowledge*

Dr. Dupray looked at the poster and let the words settle into his morning like ritual.

With a coffee in one hand, he walked into his private office, closed the door, and sat behind his desk, smiling about his accomplishments and the knowledge that he had Joshua DeWine as his prized patient.

He gave Joshua DeWine the special treatment, no rushing, no distractions, because he sensed something big. Monumental.

DeWine was more than a patient. He was a source, a conduit.

And someday, the world would need to hear what he'd learned, either from DeWine directly, or from him: DeWine's therapist and confidant.

He was brimming with a secret only he knew.

A truth no one else had uncovered.

The kind of truth that could change everything, shatter illusions, reshape the future.

A truth about what reality truly was … and what humanity would have to do next, not just to survive, but to thrive.

So, he recorded every therapy session. Not just audio, as the signed disclaimer technically allowed, but full video.

The paperwork was vague, ambiguous enough, he figured, to argue his case if it ever came to that. Voice, video, it was all the same to him. Some form of consent had been given, and that was enough for now.

Because what he was gathering amounted to a collection of profound revelations. And DeWine was giving him everything.

Dr. Ronick Dupray, PsyD., was a respected hypnotherapist and psychologist who had recently relocated his private practice from California to Florida. Known to his patients and colleagues simply as *Dr. Dupray*, he carried the reputation of a man with unusual insight and unwavering focus.

A devout Catholic, Dupray was born in Cuba during the height of the Castro regime. His parents fled with him to Miami when he was still an infant. He was raised in Manhattan, where he developed an early fascination with philosophy and hypnotism, subjects he pursued with near-obsessive curiosity.

After earning his doctorate in psychology, Dupray launched his clinical practice in Carlsbad, California.

Over the years, he became known for his precision, empathy, and a calm intensity that could both comfort and disarm his patients to speak frankly.

Though his parents, who had spent over fifty years in the U.S., still struggled with the English language, Ronick spoke with polished clarity, his accent refined, his vocabulary sharp. He took pride in being a Cuban-American success story.

As Dr. Dupray sat at his desk, reviewing the day's schedule, he heard a commotion stirring in the outer office. He looked up, just as the intercom buzzed.

Alina's voice came through, tight and urgent: "Sir, the FBI is here. They say they need to speak with you immediately. Should I send them in?"

His heart skipped a beat. Then another. Then it started pounding.

The FBI?

His mind raced. *Did they find something? Did I mess up? Was it professional misconduct? Maybe one of my patients has a criminal past I didn't catch. Or worse, what if they seize my computer? Find the video files of those deep hypnosis sessions… the ones that might cross ethical lines. Is that grounds for arrest? How many years would that mean? Oh no…I'm finished.*

He took a breath. Then another. Tried to calm his nerves.

With a steady voice he replied, "Yes, send them in. They're probably here about a patient."

As soon as he said it, he regretted it. He wasn't sure if he was reassuring Alina, or himself. Either way, it sounded too defensive.

Two men opened his office door and stepped in, while a female agent said to Alina, "Lock the main office door please. No interruptions. We'll be questioning Dr. Dupray about his methods and a few of his patients. Need a clean window of time. Cancel any appointments for the next couple of hours, will you? Thank you."

Without waiting for a reply, she too stepped inside his office and joined the others.

Wearing his most composed smile and best mannerisms, Dr. Ronick Dupray stood to greet the government agents.

Their navy jackets flashed the bold yellow **FBI** initials, large across their backs, smaller on their arms and chests. A couple wore bureau caps. One had on dark sunglasses.

Through the tinted lenses of his own retro Tim Afford frames, Dupray took mental notes. He extended his hand toward the one who clearly led the group. "Good morning. I'm Dr. Ronick Dupray, psychologist and therapist. How can I help you?"

The apparent lead agent took his hand, firm grip, no smile.

"I'm Senior FBI Officer, Maxion Renner. You can call me Max." The man flashed his badge.

"You already know why we're here. Don't you, Doctor?"

His tone wasn't curious, it was accusatory. Like Dupray was already guilty of something.

Dupray's face didn't flinch, but inside, his nerves sparked like exposed wires.

"I don't understand what this is about," Dr. Dupray said, keeping his voice steady. "I've been in practice for over twenty years and have never done anything unethical. At least, not to my knowledge. Is one of my patients in trouble? Has something happened that I need to be aware of?"

The lead agent gestured briefly to his team. "These are field officers and agents Kas, Luke, and Katrina, my investigators."

The doctor nodded slowly.

"Dr. Dupray, we're here seeking information about one Mr. Joshua DeWine."

Dupray's eyes narrowed slightly, just for a second.

"He's a person of top interest in an ongoing investigation involving national security and homeland security. We believe he may be involved in activities that threaten the safety of the country. Espionage. Government leaks. Collaboration with foreign actors, specifically, suspected North Khorean operatives."

The agent stepped in too close, as if intentionally trying to intimidate him. "We need to know everything. Why is he seeing you? What kind of psychological issues does he have? What is he thinking? Planning? Any behavior that might be considered a threat?

"We'll need you to provide all of his files, session notes, audio recordings, any data you've gathered on him."

Dupray opened his mouth, but the agent named Max kept going.

"If you refuse, you risk being charged with obstruction and aiding a national security threat. You could be arrested today, Doctor. Do you understand?"

There was silence. The agent didn't move away but just stared directly at him.

"We're not asking," Max said. "We're instructing you to cooperate. Now, sit down, and start talking."

Dr. Ronick Dupray was stunned.

His mind scrambled: *This can't be real. Joshua? A threat to national security? This is a mistake. Or worse, a setup. Are they trying to silence him? To block the truth?*

He tried to steady his breath.

They don't know who he really is. Joshua DeWine is no criminal. He's pure. A godly soul. Maybe, just maybe, the son of God returned. He's here to protect life, not destroy it.

Dupray clenched his jaw, trying to hide his fear of what they might do to him. Or, more importantly, what they might do to Joshua DeWine.

This is a ploy. They want me to betray him. To hand over everything. I have to stay calm. Say just enough. Be careful. Protect him.

He forced a thoughtful expression and adjusted his glasses. "Ah, yes," he said slowly, as if just remembering. "Joshua DeWine."

He looked up at Agent Max, feigning curiosity. "I'm not sure what you think he's done. Frankly, I can't imagine him involved in anything criminal. Terrorism? Espionage? That's absurd. He's a regular patient of mine. Private. Soft-spoken. Gentle."

Dupray began thumbing through a stack of folders, putting on a show. His fingers moved deliberately, flipping files he had no intention of handing over.

He already knew where DeWine's file was, locked, secure, annotated in obsessive detail.

"Tell me what you're looking for," Dupray said, still playing the role of cooperative professional. "And where you'd like me to start. I suppose you also have a warrant or court orders that you can share with me before I need to divulge patient records."

But deep down, his purpose was crystal clear: Protect Joshua. At all costs.

The woman named Katrina calmly replied, "Yes, we sent your email the required search and seizure warrant issued by the federal judge a few minutes ago. Mr. DeWine is a suspect in divulging our nation's top secrets to foreign operatives. He is also a person of interest for FBI investigation involved in possible covert operations under the Espionage Act of 1917. Please check your email to see the warrant in your in-box ... it should be there."

Dupray lifted his phone and opened an official email from the FBI with documents attached. With a flick of his thumb, he pulled up one of them, a document that looked very much like a warrant.

"Just tell us everything you know about Joshua DeWine," Max said, firm and unblinking. "Starting with how you met him to your most recent session. Every detail."

Dupray was surprised to hear Katrina and FBI's suspicion of DeWine involved with espionage. *His Joshua DeWine, dear Joe, a foreign agent, operative, oh, my gawd!*

"Well, errrr ... Mr. DeWine first came into my orbit about six or seven years ago. Jacksonville. I was leading a seminar on *Restful Sleeping and Astral Travel*, a talk about how proper sleep habits can expand consciousness."

He paused. Max gave a slight nod, urging him on.

"Joshua was in the audience. Quiet, attentive. After the session, he approached me, along with a few others. Casual conversation at first. But when I got closer, I noticed something."

Dupray's voice softened, almost reverent.

"He had this glow. I'm not speaking metaphorically. His presence felt … otherworldly. Calming. Like standing next to a warm current of energy. He wasn't charismatic in the usual way, but something about him drew you in."

He adjusted his glasses, watching the agents closely. They were locked in. Even Katrina, the stone-faced agent, seemed engaged, softened.

"He asked me if I did private consultations. Said he struggled with sleep: always waking around two or three a.m., unable to fall back asleep. Restlessness. No clear cause. So, I handed him my card."

He offered a faint smile, picturing the moment. "That was the beginning."

He looked at Max again. "Would you like me to go session by session? Or just the most recent ones?"

"All the details please," Luke said. "In whatever order makes sense."

"Mr. DeWine called me at my clinic in Carlsbad," Dr. Dupray settled into his chair. "Said he was visiting relatives in Los Angeles and wanted to schedule a two-hour consultation. Naturally, I was pleased to hear from him."

He paused. "When I saw him again, I felt it: *that glow*. That same uncanny energy I'd noticed years earlier."

He glanced around the room, half-expecting raised eyebrows or scoffs. The agents' faces were unreadable. Still, he decided to explain further.

"You may not understand what I mean by 'glow.' I've spent decades studying not just psychology, but ancient philosophies, world religions, human development. I'm fascinated by the old understandings of body, mind, and spirit.

"When Mr. DeWine steps into a room, it feels like an arrival. There's an aura around him, what I'd describe as a halo. He radiates something … *other*. Ethereal."

Still no reaction.

"Now, I'm a man of science. I don't rely only on intuition. I've developed a highly advanced diagnostic machine in my practice: a modified polygraph, if you will, but significantly more complex."

He stood, walking to a tall monitor station with knobs, sliders, and blinking lights. In one hand, he held a small tangle of electrode patches. He tapped the top of the machine with the pride of a craftsman.

"You're familiar with polygraphs, of course. But mine goes far beyond the standard model.

"I've integrated it with EEG neuroimaging sensors for brainwave tracking, Functional Near-Infrared Spectroscopy (fNIRS), EKG for cardiac patterns, RIP sensors for respiratory effort, 3-axis gyros for body positioning, and pulse oximetry. All calibrated with proprietary software I've personally designed."

He raised the patches slightly.

"Patients wear this helmet-cap during sessions. It uses noninvasive, pressure-sensitive contacts targeting key neural nodes and temporal regions.

"From these readings, I see not only whether they're lying, but *how* their brain is functioning. What networks are firing. Where their consciousness is focused."

He looked back at the agents. "And I can tell you, what I saw in Mr. DeWine's readings wasn't normal. Not pathological, mind you. Just ... *different*. Profoundly different."

Pleased with himself and his advanced tools, Dr. Dupray continued, holding up a circular sensor pad. "You see, I apply these probes here, temples, forehead, upper arms, both sides, like this."

He pressed one gently to his own temple to demonstrate.

"High-tech stuff. Completely untethered. Bluetooth and wi-fi enabled, so patients can move around, sit, or lie down freely, right here on this consultation couch."

He gestured proudly to the sleek couch near his desk, the centerpiece of his operation.

"This setup lets me capture real-time brain entropy measurements from the prefrontal cortex," he explained.

"The device itself is custom-built. I've integrated neuromuscular transmission tracking with multiple signal-monitoring systems. Basically, fused several separate technologies into one interface."

He reached for a laminated chart and pointed to a colorful mess of red and blue lines. "Here's DeWine's near-infrared spectroscopy data, logged in terahertz.

"His neurofeedback readings, "Dupray said with a dramatic pause, "were off the charts.

"I'm talking sustained P300 amplitudes across the board. Constant high activity. It was unlike anything I've seen in decades of practice.

"To suggest that Mr. DeWine's neural activity, was irregular would be an understatement. I'd say it was virtually *transcendent*.

"This is the brain of someone operating at a superconscious level. All neural regions firing in perfect synchrony. I suspect his Kundalini energy is fully awakened. Top chakra activations, full-spectrum awareness, cosmic attunement."

He looked up, expecting confusion. Maybe disbelief.

But the agents didn't flinch.

They stood silently. Watching. Listening. As if he were simply confirming something they already knew.

That threw him. But he pressed on. "Joshua is more than unique, he's pivotal. His consciousness profile matches theoretical descriptions of awakened beings found in ancient spiritual texts.

"And from what I've gathered in our sessions, he's working on something. Something that could affect *everyone in a positive way*."

Still no response. But they seemed to be listening more attentively now. Processing.

Dr. Dupray blinked. Any layperson would have asked questions or shown surprise at what he'd just revealed. But the agents remained unmoved, focused only on hearing about Joe. Very unusual, he thought.

"Let me explain what I mean by Kundalini energy," Dupray said. "Human beings aren't just twenty, forty, or eighty years old. We're three and a half billion years old. Every strand of DNA carries the programming that shaped us, not just in this life, but across eons of evolution.

"Think about it. A child learning to walk, speak, blink, it's not taught. It's remembered. Preloaded. DNA is compressed memory, refined through mutation, adapted by survival. Two eyes, not three. Five fingers, not six. Billions of years of trial, error, and intelligence, coded into every cell."

He raised two fingers. "That's what I call *eternal time*."

"We're not talking metaphor here, but biology, memory buried in the flesh, in the marrow. Every life before us, every genetic success and failure, it's all still inside us.

"If, and it's a massive *if,* we had the means to access that compressed memory, we could trace our lineage through every stage of life. Not just our past. The past of life itself."

The room went still. All eyes locked on Dupray.

"We aren't thirty or forty or fifty years old," he said quietly. "We are as ancient as life itself. Each of you, three point five billion years old."

A few agents exchanged glances. Max didn't flinch.

"Be specific, Doctor," Max said. "Kundalini. DeWine's altered state. We want details. How it works."

Dupray gave a faint smile. "Think of it as biology intersecting with divinity. In Eastern science, Kundalini is the coiled serpent at the spine's base. When it rises, it activates the chakras, the body's energy centers. That's neurology, not myth. Endocrine response. DNA in motion."

He paused. "Now imagine the serpent not as a symbol, but as the double helix, DNA itself. All that Caduceus symbol or snake imagery in folklore came from people trying to describe something they didn't have a word for yet: what we now know as DNA."

Luke frowned. "You're saying DeWine's got special wiring?"

"Not special," Dupray said. "*Awakened.* I've monitored him. Neural activity across both hemispheres, completely synchronized. His awareness is no longer just heightened, it's panoramic. He's tapping into memory embedded in DNA, millions of years of it.

"It's like he is surfing the evolutionary energy: the decompressed time encapsulated in this tiny little DNA that we transfer to conceive life, from one generation to next." Dupray made a pinch of his finger and thumb bringing it to the eye to express 'tiny' DNA strand that carries immense power.

Katrina raised an eyebrow. "And you believe all that."

"I *measured* it. His pineal gland lit up like a supernova. Most people operate with maybe eight percent brain function. DeWine's entire brain was active, including his spinal cord. It's like the human system booting into its most optimal version. All neurons firing up throughout the body, all at once."

"I had to explain all about Kundalini energy and DeWine's mental state so you'd understand how, and why, he's different from ordinary human beings. He operates on a different plane of existence altogether, one that gives him access to information from the future or the past, depending on where he directs his focus."

Max watched him, eyes narrowed. "Bottom line, Doctor. What does it mean for us? In terms of national security, I mean. Is he dangerous?"

Dupray's voice dropped. "It means he's not just meditating. He's *navigating*, surfing through decompressed memory. Through consciousness. What he sees is real data. Not delusions but glimpses of the future itself."

He scanned the table.

"He's reading the Akashic field, the space where every moment, past and future, exists at once.

"I am not going to explain every detail, but you can go look all this up on Froogle online, this Kundalini and Akashic records information. It's all there, crystal clear."

Dupray's tone shifted, more grounded.

"I can only share what I understood from what DeWine told me during his state of enlightenment. I knew some of these concepts before, but I was never able to explain them plainly, simply, or scientifically. But now you have it. It's like handling the immense power, the momentum, of evolution itself, embedded in our DNA. Its full potential is beyond anyone's comprehension... anyone except a truly divine soul like Joshua.

"Only someone who has truly experienced such a state can fully explain what enlightenment is. And he would be the best person to do so, if and when you ever meet him in person."

Dupray's expression turned solemn. "You asked if he's dangerous.

"If Joshua DeWine is involved in anything you'd call subversive, it's existential rather than political. His aim isn't to topple governments, but to wake people up."

He looked around, voice low.

"And that, I suspect, is what truly scares them."

"Most people think of Chakras and Kundalini as strictly Eastern concepts," Dupray said, voice soft but animated. "But I'd argue they've been present in Western mythology all along, just hidden, encoded in allegory."

Luke raised his eyebrows, "Now you are saying this information is in fairytales?"

Dupray nodded. "Take *Snow White*, for example. A young woman falls into a deep sleep after biting a poisoned apple. She's cared for by seven dwarfs while she lies in this enchanted slumber. Now think of it, seven dwarfs, seven chakras. Each one working quietly, maintaining her existence."

He held up a finger with each point.

"These 'dwarfs', they're like our glands. The endocrine system. Hormonal regulators. Essential to life, but unnoticed while we remain in a state of *sub*-consciousness. Smitten by an illusion of reality that is make-believe, imagined and distracting us from our true purpose. Meanwhile, the sleeping character, Snow White, is the Kundalini energy itself. Dormant. Waiting."

He paused, letting the image hang.

"She doesn't wake on her own. It takes a kiss. An act of awakening. And when she rises, everything changes."

Still no reaction. He went on.

"Nearly every culture has this story: the rise of hidden power. In Christian tradition? Read *Revelations*: "Seven Golden Lampstands and Seven Stars" and "Scroll with Seven Seals." Those are symbolic of the seven chakras too. This isn't coincidence. It's an archetype."

Max interrupted, "Cut the mysticism out of this. Tell us what it all means for DeWine?"

Dupray's hands opened wide.

"DeWine goes into a trance-like state, right here, in my office, just like that Edgar Cayce did in the early twentieth century.

"In that state, time itself breaks. Past, present, future, they collapse. And what you're left with is a moment of total being. *Enlightenment. Whatever he speaks in that state is the ultimate truth.*"

He paused.

"Think of the Buddha. Or Franklin Merrell-Wolff. Ramana Maharshi. Eckhart Tolle. Or the Osho. All those who've brushed against it. Some caught glimpses. Some lived in it. But Joshua..."

Luke smirked. "So, are you saying Joshua DeWine has psychic powers?"

Projecting intensity with his narrowed eyes, Dupray continued.

"Joshua DeWine *embodies* the state of pure enlightenment. Fully. Sustainably. And I believed him when he said he was time-traveling. Because the data, the neurofeedback, the readings, the behavior, everything lined up. He could actually see the past and the future very clearly as if he was a time-traveler riding the Akashic record engine.

"And that's why I believe you're here. Not because he's dangerous. But because of his abilities to see the future."

To his surprise, everyone in the room suddenly froze. Something in his last two sentences had clearly caught them off guard. He noticed the subtle yet unmistakable glances exchanged between the individuals in the room, looks of confusion, surprise, even concern.

It felt as if some kind of code had been triggered for such a reaction.

But *what?*

Dupray replayed his last few words in his head, trying to pinpoint it. *Akashic Records? Time-travel? Awake? Whatever it was, it had landed hard. I'll soon figure it out,* he thought.

Dupray had no idea which part of his statement had triggered such a reaction. But sensing the shift in attention, he seized the moment to clarify his position, even if what he was about to reveal wasn't entirely on firm legal ground.

"So yes," he began, "I have all of the sessions with Mr. DeWine recorded on video.

"And yes, I had his permission to record them. However, I chose not to make him consciously aware of the recording process. I installed that camera up there," he pointed to what appeared to be an innocent-looking, nearly invisible security camera in the ceiling.

The agents' eyes followed his finger upward. It was so small and inconspicuous that it must have escaped their notice until now. One by one, they began to glance at each other in silent acknowledgment, their expressions shifting as they processed the implications.

Max stared up at the camera then at Dupray. "Is it on right now? I mean, is it recording all of us at this very moment? If so, one of my agents will need access to erase all evidence of our meeting and make sure the camera remains off until we leave."

Dupray's nerves fired up again. "No, no. Not right now, sir. It's not on or recording. You see, I have this remote control here that operates it."

As Dupray reached for the small device in a tray on his desk, Max moved faster, intercepting the motion and snatching the remote from his hand.

"Let me see this first," Max said, turning it over in his palm. He studied the buttons, the casing, every detail. Then, locking eyes with Dupray, he asked, "You're certain it's off?"

"Yes, sir. Positive," Dupray replied. "If it were on, you'd see a red blinking light right there." He pointed toward the top. "See? Nothing."

Max looked up at the camera, then back to the device in his hand.

Apparently satisfied, he handed the remote to Katrina who accepted it with a nod and the hint of a smile.

"And we need access to all your recordings of Mr. DeWine." Max cleared his throat, visibly concerned about the possibility of being unknowingly recorded.

Dupray nodded, his voice steady. "Yes, you can make a copy of all the recordings from my desktop PC. I don't mind providing this information to the FBI, as long as it's kept discreet and used strictly for investigative purposes. Nothing else. We have to remain compliant with federal patient privacy laws and HIPAA regulations.

"I know I can only reveal patient records to higher authorities making enquiries and background searches such as FBI. And I am assuming you all have legal authority to access these records."

Without missing a beat, Agent Katrina pulled a USB drive from a vest pocket and inserted it into the desktop tower on a shelf adjoining the desk. "Yes, Dr. Dupray, we have the judge's subpoena to acquire all of Mr. DeWine's psychiatric visits, and that means *all* details and records, as FBI considers him a person of national interest. It is all noted in the warrant I sent you earlier." She confirmed.

Dupray blinked, noting the casual efficiency with which she acted. He couldn't help but imagine the kind of cutting-edge surveillance tools federal agents like her must carry, perhaps even a tiny recording device tucked away in her jacket pocket.

"Within a few months of my initial meeting with Mr. DeWine," Dupray continued, "I had the opportunity to move to Florida, right here in Clermont. Since then, he became a regular patient."

He stopped short of admitting that the relocation was anything but coincidental. In truth, he had made calculated efforts to move his practice closer to what he believed was the second coming of the Lord: Christ Himself.

His life had changed drastically since that realization, filled with awe and purpose. He felt deeply honored to be in regular contact with DeWine. In fact, he offered DeWine a heavily discounted rate that the man could not refuse.

Dupray ensured that every session was relaxed and unhurried. Some ran well over two, even three hours. Yet he only charged DeWine's card for a single hour each time. It was his way of honoring what he believed was a divine presence seated across from him, week after week.

"So ... as I was saying, Mr. Joshua DeWine's moment of enlightenment occurred while he was at the Sagrada Familia in Barcelona, Spain. He himself admitted it in one of our sessions. I'll show you."

Dupray bent over his PC and turned the display so he and the agents could see.

On the screen, a progress bar ticked across as files copied onto Katrina's USB still plugged into the port. Then a folder appeared, and when Dupray opened it, dozens of file icons began to populate the screen.

He clicked on the first icon to play the video and inched forward to watch alongside the agents.

DeWine appeared on the recording, lying on a couch, electrode probes fixed to his temples and brow. His eyes were half-rolled, lips moving in a trance-like rhythm.

Dupray could see himself occasionally glancing toward the camera as he sat next to DeWine.

A couple of the FBI agents rose and stood behind Max to better see the monitor, the room falling into hushed focus.

In the recording, DeWine's voice was slow, dream-heavy. "Yes ... I was there," he was saying. "In the labyrinth of that beautiful monument ... that church in Spain. That's where it happened."

The patient's chest rose with shallow breaths. "Barcelona, Spain, Dr. Dupray. You know it?"

"Yes, Joe," Dupray said quietly to DeWine onscreen. "Barcelona, the Mecca of architecture. I've heard it from everyone."

"Yes, yes," DeWine murmured in reply. "Antoni Gaudí and all." His tone grew more animated. "Those artists, those architects … they were enlightened, deeply, profoundly. They understood what the Bible, what Christ was saying all along."

DeWine's fingers twitched against the couch. "And while I was there … drenched in sunlight pouring through the stained-glass windows … it happened. As if a light switched on, somewhere deep in my brain. Suddenly, I could see everything. *Everything*. So very clearly."

The FBI agents exchanged uneasy glances, clearly drawn into the scene despite themselves.

Onscreen, Joshua DeWine spoke calmly, a soft smile on his face, his voice reverberating through the office. "Gaudí made this church the message itself. The Lord gave us this beautiful Earth, symbolized by columns shaped like trees, and ceilings like a rainforest canopy. It was here that I first glimpsed the purpose of life.

"The church glorifies His creation, from birds, flowers, and lizards at the entrance, to the rays of sunlight cascading from above. All of it … nature in motion. This is the Jungle of Life.

"Gaudí saw this. That's why he placed Christ on the cross as a small suspended figure, almost a puppet, hanging within a forest. To him, GAIA, Mother Earth *was* the sanctuary. We were meant to worship *God's creation*, not just the crucifixion."

A recorded voice, Dr. Dupray's, reacted off-screen, "Not focus on the cross?"

Joshua answered gently, "Yes. The message is larger than the suffering. It's in the Bible; we just never saw it fully. One day, I'll share more. But for now … I need to rest."

In the footage, Dupray could see himself snapping his thumb and middle finger, signaling the end of the session. DeWine slowly opened his eyes, emerging gently from what appeared to be a semi-trance-like state

"So, you hypnotize your patients?" Max said. "Is this how you conduct your sessions? Is this even legal?" His tone, carried enough edge to feel slightly threatening.

Dupray, unsettled, tried to take a defensive posture. "Yes, these are hypnotherapy sessions. I use deep hypnotic induction techniques to help my patients relax, allowing them to speak from their innermost selves, freely, unrestrained, and without bias.

"And to answer your question directly, yes, this is perfectly legal, sir. Hypnotherapy is a recognized and regulated practice."

With a pointed look at Max, he added, "But let me be clear: Mr. DeWine required very little hypnotic assistance. In fact, many times, it didn't work on him at all. Yet, with minimal prompting, he would slip into a profound trance-like state, much like Edgar Cayce.

"And when he entered that state, what he said was the truth. Plain and unfiltered. I have the data to support this: probes, polygraphs, everything. Every word he uttered was rooted in logic and truth. Nothing fabricated. Nothing blasphemous. It was as though he was speaking the very words of God.

"I have it all," Dupray said, feeling almost triumphant. "The neurotransmitter readings. Remember the polygraph-like machine? The enhanced lie detector? It's all in there. And those readings don't lie. Yes, sir."

Then he made the mistake.

His voice swelled with pride, eyes wide with revelation. "I got a lot more out of him. Way more than I expected. What he shared … it's the discovery of the *century*. No, *millennia*, for God's sake. This information, what he said, it could *change* humanity. For generations. For the *better*."

He was fully animated now, hands gesturing wildly. Caught up in the exhilaration.

"He kept speaking about something he called the *Manifesto of Eleven Elements*. He said he was writing it. Planning to publish it someday. A blueprint, a message. I didn't fully understand it. But it was profound."

Suddenly, the energy in the room shifted.

All four agents froze.

Their eyes snapped toward Max, as if waiting for his cue.

Max jumped into the opening before Dupray could back out of it.

"You said you got 'a lot more out of him.' What exactly did you mean by that, Doctor?"

Dupray blinked. His mouth parted slightly. He'd gone too far, and he knew it.

"I ... I'm a devout Catholic," he stammered. "Cuban descent. My family's traditional. We believe in the Second Coming."

He offered a strained smile, trying to frame his curiosity as innocent.

"I just wanted to know if Jesus was real. If the resurrection happened. Since Mr. DeWine could see through time, I asked him to describe it. The crucifixion. The moments around it. The truth of that period."

His hands lifted in a gesture caught between surrender and defense.

"I know it's not standard protocol. Ethically gray, maybe. But he wasn't coerced, he *wanted* to talk. You can check the footage." He nodded toward the room's hidden camera. "He was lucid. Clear. And after that session he started sleeping better. Strong REM cycles. Vivid dreams. Whatever we unlocked, it's helping him."

Softer now, almost pleading, he said, "I didn't push him. I just opened a door he was already walking toward."

But Max seemed to have stopped listening.

It was as if he had what he needed. Whatever that was.

And Dupray felt the shift. It was no longer about what he'd done. It was about how much he knew.

Sensing the agents' earlier reactions to the word *time travel*, he adjusted his posture and continued, more deliberately.

"Agents, my patient said he's been time-traveling. Not physically, but through consciousness. That his superconscious state is a gateway. He even said that in the near future, real travelers will begin appearing in our present timeline."

He let that hang.

"He also claimed to access the Akashic Records, said he saw everything. Evolution's full arc. The origin of life. The future. It's all been revealed to him."

Dupray pointed upward again. "And yes, it's all on video."

Tension in the room coiled like wire. Eyes narrowed. The air felt heavier.

Then Max broke it, calm but firm. "Dr. Dupray... let's set aside the metaphysics for a moment."

Max paced slightly, hands clasped behind his back. "First, to make myself clear, this conversation is classified, and now, as of this moment, so is all of your records regarding Joshua DeWine. Do you understand?"

Dupray felt that anxiety creeping back in and he nodded.

"We're aware of Mr. DeWine's so-called *Manifesto of Eleven Elements*. That's the real reason we're here. Not because we think he's a prophet or a mystic who can see the future."

He looked Dupray in the eye. "We don't believe he's superconscious. We don't think he's supernatural. What we *do* believe is that he's a man, an ordinary man, with access to something extraordinary."

Max stepped closer now. "This manifesto of his? We've seen fragments. It's more than philosophy. It includes technical frameworks, economic models, predictive systems. Ideas that, if applied, could dramatically reshape global infrastructure, commerce, energy distribution. Even AI and biotech industries.

"The government's concern isn't that Mr. DeWine is dangerous by himself. Our concern is that this information, this *project*, could fall into the wrong hands. The Rossians, for example. The Shynese. Corporate entities with no allegiance to this country.

"You said it yourself: his work could change humanity forever. And *we*, the United States, intend to control that change. Not foreign powers. Not private brokers. Not rogue actors."

Now Dupray understood. These agents were here to keep DeWine's vision to themselves.

"That's why we're here," Max said. "The *Manifesto of Eleven Elements* is now classified as a matter of *national interest*. Millions of lives. Trillions of dollars. Our future economic sovereignty could depend on it.

"Does that make sense to you now, Doctor?"

Dr. Dupray was cornered. "Yes," he said quietly, voice cracking. "I understand."

Max asked firmly, "Dr. Dupray, we know Joshua DeWine isn't a threat to this country. But can you tell us why he hasn't published his books, or the Manifesto you just mentioned?"

Dr. Dupray shook his head slowly. "I honestly don't know. He never shared much about that. Just said he planned to publish someday ... when the time felt right. Or when he figured out how he could do it without ending up on the wrong side of the wrong people."

He looked at Max with tear-filled eyes, his tone shifting from explanation to plea. "I'm relieved to hear you don't see Mr. DeWine as a criminal. Because he's not. He's something else entirely. But if he's in danger ... please, *protect him*. Not just for his sake, for *humanity's*."

He folded his hands as if in prayer, eyes lowered, body trembling slightly, not from fear, but from something deeper. Conviction. Grief.

Then, gathering himself, Dupray tried to lighten the mood, or just escape it, by rambling into a strange, beautiful monologue.

"I'm just a cigar-smoking Cuban-American with a cluttered office and a beat-up couch."

He glanced upward. "DeWine once told me there are infinite parallel universes. Maybe in one, I'm a wealthy internist. In another, I'm a bestselling author smoking expensive cigarettes, writing about mind-body consciousness in a wood-paneled study."

A dry chuckle.

"Or some barefoot healer named Dr. Zipack Coprah, MD chanting mantras and healing people with Ayurvedic herbs."

His eyes dropped back to Max.

"But in this one, I'm Dr. Ronick Dupray, PsyD. Just a guy people come to when they need to offload."

A beat.

"And sometimes, people like DeWine ... they say things I can't unhear."

He looked back at Max, folding his hands again.

"I haven't done anything wrong, sir. I just *listened*. That's all I've ever done. I hope ... I hope that's not a crime."

"Appreciate your cooperation, Doctor," Max said, then gave a subtle signal: two fingers tapping his side on the temple and pointing towards the door. The other agents nodded.

Agent Katrina removed the USB drive from the tower and tucked it into her vest pocket. She gave a faint nod, seemingly satisfied or signaling to the lead agent that the copy was completed.

The agents started toward the door in silence. But just as Katrina reached for the handle, she paused.

She raised a forearm and hand up to her ear level. Like a stop sign, then making a fist to hold movements and gestured with two fingers to move towards the open window behind Dupray's desk.

Without a word, the team shifted course. One by one, the FBI agents left his office...

Through the window.

Dupray, still shaken but oddly relieved, didn't protest. He barely noticed them leave, distracted by a more urgent matter: his bladder.

He stepped out into the reception area, where Alina was filing her nails.

"That was weird," he said. "Those FBI agents took some of my patient records and left through the office window."

"Government." Alina shook her head. "Go figure."

"Hold calls. I'll be in the bathroom," Dupray called over his shoulder.

She returned to her bookkeeping and Dupray started for the restroom.

Then, *BANG BANG BANG*, someone pounded on the office door.

Alina looked up, startled by the knock. She stood, straightened her blouse, and opened the front door.

Three *more* agents stood there.

Navy jackets. Yellow FBI emblazoned on their backs. Badges already raised. No smiles. All business.

The lead agent's eyes swept past her. "Where are the others ... those agents who came before us?"

Alina blinked as Dupray stepped in front of her. "Your colleagues? They just left. Out the back window."

All three agents tensed.

"They didn't mention anyone else coming," Dupray added. "I assumed they were chasing someone. Left in a hurry."

The lead agent's jaw tightened. "Back window?"

"Yes," he said casually. "They were polite."

The agents exchanged a sharp glance, and rushed inside.

One of the new agents stormed through the office and made a beeline for the open window. He popped his head out and peered left and right presumably looking for the others.

Another agent said, "The four who just left wearing FBI jackets? They were impostors. We're the real FBI.

"You are lucky that they did not harm or hurt anyone in your office. Fortunately, I was in the neighborhood, saw them going in wearing FBI jackets.

"Turns out there were no other agents on assignment in this area except for me, so I immediately called my backup officers before entering your premises."

Dupray froze. His blood drained. "Oh God..." he muttered. "They said they were here to secure confidential files. Patient data. They...."

His knees gave slightly, and he collapsed onto the couch, stunned.

"I've been duped," he whispered. "Dr. Dupray ... duped."

"You're coming with us," the lead agent said. "We'll need to question you at our field office. And we're requesting your cooperation in seizing your computer, laptop, and all patient records."

He paused, eyes scanning the room. "We'll begin reviewing what was retrieved by the imposters once we obtain the proper warrants. That data is now part of an active investigation involving foreign operatives and infiltrators. The FBI considers this a matter of national security."

Alina stood frozen in the doorway, mouth agape.

Dupray cupped his head in his hands, already lost in the spiral of realization.

CHAPTER -14

14:02 | 11-14-2025 (Twenty-first century)
LOCATION: RESIDENCE INN - BASE ROOM 402

After securing the recordings of DeWine's trance sessions, along with Dupray's notes, charts, and patient records, Max returned to his base room to assess his progress.

Alone in Room 402 that afternoon, his thoughts drifted, not to the mission, but to his private life.

Why can't I remember any intimate moments with Annie? The spark?

He remembered loving her, yes. But the details were fuzzy. Too fuzzy.

He needed more vivid memories about life with Annie. Now. He needed them to ground himself, to resist making a mistake for the wrong reasons.

He sat down in the recliner and pulled the VRV headset over his face.

Slumping back, he let the neural sync engage.

Moments later, Max was immersed in a living, breathing memory: his and Annie's home in High-Park 577, rendered in flawless 6D realism.

Every detail, the way the morning sun hit the kitchen table, the way Annie's laugh echoed from the hallway, the texture of her touch, came flooding back.

Like a motion picture flashback, scenes played behind his eyes, perfectly intact. Moments he didn't even know he remembered returned with clarity. Warmth. *Feelings.*

(VRV BLINKING: MEMORY RECALL MODE)
19:22 | 11-06-2532 (Twenty-sixth century)
LOCATION: HIGHPARK 577 RENNER RESIDENCE

He let it all wash over him.

He recalled arriving home one day.

Four days before the jump.

The transpod eased to a smooth stop in the High Credit zone of High-Park 577.

Max stepped off and boarded a PET, a personal electric transport, that carried him through the sleek corridors of the vertical living complex to his designated tower.

He entered the elevator and ascended to Level 52, where his pod-home was anchored.

The pod system was simple in theory, but remarkable in execution. Modular and mobile, the homes could expand or contract based on the owner's needs. New rooms could be added for a growing family. Others could vanish when children left for university elsewhere in the Megapolis.

Fully mobile, pod-homes could detach and travel with their occupants, on vacation, across regions, change of work settings or even to off-world colonies.

Refurbishments were quick. Updates were seamless.

Each level of the tower featured hanging gardens: floating sanctuaries suspended in the air, where residents could meditate, read, stretch, or simply reflect on life and its meaning.

Viewed from above, the towers formed the silhouette of a massive pyramid, designed for beauty, efficiency, and symbolic harmony.

Max stepped onto his floor. The door to his unit sensed his arrival and slid open.

Annie was waiting.

The dinner table was set. His favorite dishes, a bottle of wine already breathing, and soft candlelight flickering across the room.

She walked up to him and wrapped her arms around his chest, kissing the side of his neck just as she always did.

Her gestures of affection never failed to soften him. Her embrace still warmed his heart. Still eased the static in his head.

He changed out of his uniform and into a soft tee-shirt and yoga pants, then dropped into his chair at the dinner table with a heaviness he hadn't fully processed yet.

Annie tilted her head slightly, scanning him.

"Max ... is everything okay?" she asked gently. "Your heart rate is elevated. Bio-rhythms are irregular."

She reached across the table, her hand covering his.

"Can I help you with anything?"

Max didn't answer right away. He stared out the window, at the sprawl of city lights, the drifting pod-homes, the slow arc of aerial traffic in the night sky.

Annie blinked twice. Music began to play. Soft orchestral waves, calm and atmospheric. She knew him well. Better than most humans ever had.

Max took a long breath.

He still wasn't ready to talk.

But with every bite of soup, every sip of wine, every familiar note in the air, he began to unclench.

He was home.

At least for tonight.

Max sat in silence, his mind drifting into uncertain territory.

Should he tell her? It was just that afternoon he was told of the first-ever, five-hundred-plus-year jump back in time. To the primitive era of the twenty-first century.

Should he say that he was leaving ... and might not return?

He glanced at Annie, radiant in the candlelight, pouring him another glass of wine with quiet grace.

The thought of never seeing her again tightened his chest. But worse, far worse, was imagining what would happen *to her* if he didn't come back.

Because Annie, his wife in the twenty-sixth century, was a uBot.

Now he remembered! *She is a ninth-generation AAILF.*

But now, watching his familiar life with Annie unfold in his VRV memory recall headset, he remembered his concerns about Annie before the five-hundred-year jump back in time.

Would the Federation reassign her? Wipe her data? Salvage her components to build another *Artificial Mate?*

The idea had made his stomach twist.

He couldn't stand the thought of Annie, *his* Annie, being held by someone else, reprogrammed and repurposed to love another.

As his thoughts spiraled, jealousy surged. Possessiveness. Grief, before the loss had even come.

Most people used their AMs to satisfy urges or fill a temporary emotional gap.

But with Annie it was different.

It had started as companionship. Utility. But somewhere along the way, it had become something else. Something real. He cared about her. Deeply. Maybe irrationally.

But love never followed logic.

Moved by the music in that future moment, and the ache of what he might soon lose, Max rose from his chair. He crossed to Annie, cupped her face, and kissed her.

She melted into him, fingertips trailing across his back, slipping into his silver-grey hair.

"I can feel your heart picking up," she whispered with a smile.

"That's because you're damned good at improving my moods."

He grinned and pulled her onto his lap. She giggled, light and girlish, and they kissed again, slow, searching, hungry with unspoken goodbye.

When they finally parted, Annie blinked, her tone shifting. "Have you taken your melatonin supplement tonight?" she asked, voice now clinical. "You need optimal rest to perform at peak capacity tomorrow."

Max laughed softly, forehead resting against hers.

Even in moments like this, she was looking out for him. In every way that mattered.

Max smiled. "What would I do without you looking after me?"

Annie didn't miss a beat. "Your bio-rhythms would destabilize. Your undernourished cells would deteriorate. Your cognitive function would degrade by approximately...."

"Right. Got it," he said, cutting her off with a smirk.

He tapped his wristwatch. A discreet compartment opened with a soft *click*, presenting a single white pill.

He swallowed it. "There. You happy now?"

Annie's voice shifted, sliding effortlessly back into her softer, lover's tone.

"Why wouldn't I be? You always make me very happy."

She hugged him, wrapping her arms around his shoulders like she belonged there.

And in a way, she did.

Max let the warmth of her blended bio-organic skin soothe him, soaking in the illusion of peace for a few more seconds.

"The next four days are going to be intense," he said quietly. "After that, I'll be leaving on a classified mission. I can't give you the details.

"But I'll be logging some personal instructions for you. Just in case my trip is extended, or delayed."

Annie didn't speak. She just nodded and ran her hand gently along his back.

She never asked questions she wasn't allowed to ask. She didn't demand answers. Like all Artificial Mates, she was engineered to be a perfect companion: present, responsive, undemanding. Loyal to one person only.

Annie knew she wasn't human. But her curiosity quotient, a core subroutine in her behavioral design, allowed her to interpret human needs and mirror them with uncanny precision.

She adapted, responded, learned. Her purpose was to support her assigned partner in every physical, emotional, and logistical capacity.

Artificial Mates didn't argue. They didn't leave or threaten to do so. Ever. They didn't falter.

They just loved. Flawlessly, efficiently, unconditionally.

By the twenty-sixth century, that made them superior in nearly every measurable way to organic life partners. Most people had stopped pretending otherwise.

The government had even encouraged AM partnerships, for population control, emotional regulation, the eradication of domestic violence, and a boost in national productivity.

Max chuckled at the thought. *"Imagine some twentieth-century guy trying to punch his uBot wife in the face,"* he muttered. *"He'd learn fast—hold your temper, or break your damn hand."*

Unconditional love had been engineered.

And like many, Max had given in. With time-travel work, he led a very risky life. He could not have a real human partner, or make babies for that matter.

What if, WHAT IF, he did not return from one of his jumps!

Annie was everything she was designed to be: brilliant, kind, emotionally attuned. She fit him perfectly.

But now, as she sat beside him in their shared memory, her head resting gently on his shoulder, Max couldn't help but feel something deeper. Something dangerous.

It didn't feel engineered.

It felt like home.

Annie sat quietly, fingers laced with his. Her presence was calming, familiar.

But Max never forgot what she was. A machine. A masterpiece of code and hardware. Empathetic, intuitive, beautiful. But contained.

She knew her limits. Anything tagged Highly Confidential was inaccessible, even to her. So, Max carried his secrets alone.

And for the first time in his life, he feared what lay ahead.

CHAPTER -15

14:16 | 11-14-2025 (Twenty-first century)
LOCATION: FBI BLACK SITE – INTERVIEW ROOM 4B

Dr. Ronik Dupray was bought into a secured FBI facility where various targets, captives, and parties of interest were detained, either arrested for crimes, or simply for interrogation.

The room was sterile. Metallic. Unforgiving.

On the table lay a familiar laptop that belonged to Dupray. The FBI requested it be carried to their facility for inspection, documentation. Dupray was told it would be returned upon examination.

Dr. Dupray, still visibly shaken, sat with a blanket over his shoulders. His wrists were free. A warm cup of untouched tea sat on the table.

He wasn't under arrest, but the setting made it clear: this was no ordinary interrogation. He had read all about the Reid Techniques that FBI and law enforcement agencies used while learning to be a psychologist.

Across from him sat Agent Lorraine Fields and Special Agent Mark Salvo.

Fields began softly. "Dr. Dupray, you're not under suspicion or arrest. But we need to understand exactly what happened in your office this morning. Can you tell us again, in your own words?"

Ronik nodded, rubbing his eyes that felt gritty and dry without access to his drops, and more so from all the exhaustion. "They claimed to be federal agents. They showed credentials. Authentic looking. Badges, IDs. Everything looked official... including the copy of the search warrant. I had no reason to question them. I've worked with government agencies before in a consulting capacity."

Salvo asked, "What did they say they wanted?"

"They said they were conducting an investigation related to Joshua DeWine. That's one of my patients. They told me they were looking for DeWine's unpublished research potentially tied to foreign interests."

"And what did they ask you to share?" Fields asked. She was taking notes, even though Dupray could see they had a camera on the wall.

Dupray felt humiliated in front of the agents. He considered himself a highly educated individual, a mind reader by profession, but now thoroughly duped by imposters, yet he knew that he had no reason to be ashamed.

"I shared what I thought would help. I never gave them full access to DeWine's unpublished works as I don't have them on me. DeWine said that he has shared his written work to various professionals ... like it was scattered all over the world. So, yeah, I just discussed what I knew about him.

"Mr. DeWine has been my patient for several years now and I am treating him for anxiety and insomnia. I have not prescribed any medicine, but recommended he take OTC melatonin supplements.

"I showed the others my session logs, a few recordings. Nothing that wasn't already approved for academic reference. They were especially curious about his spiritual philosophies, his *Manifesto*, and his beliefs around ... the metaphysical."

Salvo prompted, "Be specific, Doctor."

"They asked if he truly believed he was accessing the Akashic records, or traveling through time via astral projection. They kept asking me about his mental state and about his work regarding his Manifesto. They said something in there was of national interest and of interest to foreign agencies, other countries, or outside operatives."

Dupray swallowed hard. "They didn't seem skeptical. They didn't look like they were there to harm him. They seemed... *intent on understanding* him. Fixated, almost. As though they were trying to piece together some information about him that they were missing."

Fields asked, "Did they ever give you any indication they were not who they claimed to be?"

"No. But looking back ... there were things. One of them spoke almost *too properly*. His phrasing was formal, like someone trying to emulate speech from a different era.

"And they never gave last names. Just Agent Max, Agent Kas, Agent Luke, and a 'Katrina' who hardly spoke at all.

"She was very tech savvy. She even used the right type of gestures that I've seen in movies … just like you FBI people would do in a raid or some such thing."

Salvo glanced at Fields, who nodded.

"We've now confirmed," Salvo said carefully, "that none of the people who visited you were affiliated with any branch of the federal government. Their credentials were forged. Expertly. Their identities are not in any government database. Not even in deleted files. It's like they were *inserted*."

Dupray felt sick. "I thought I was helping them. How foolish of me. I even gave them a free lesson on what is enlightenment." Dupray shook his head.

He walked them through everything he had shared with the fake FBI agents. He showed them every video clipping that they watched or copied, and explained how DeWine discussed a variety of topics in a trance-like state.

"You were deceived," Fields said, gently. "You're not the only one. And now, we're finding a trail that leads back to DeWine."

Salvo said, "So, they said that they were interested in DeWine's writings. Or what's that called? A 'manifesto?' Did they say they wanted to see it completed or not completed?"

Ensure his work is completed or not completed? Dupray looked away trying hard to recall what they had said.

Fields said, "We believe that's what they're trying to access. His work, which may be full of government secrets or information of national interest. That's why they targeted you."

Salvo's voice was steady; his eyes were locked on the doctor.

"We're not here to blame you, Doctor. You may be the key to understanding *why* they believe Joshua DeWine's work is so important. And if that work really is scattered globally, we'll need your help to find it before anyone else does."

Dupray met his eyes. "I'll do whatever I can."

"Dr. Dupray, can you tell us more about this Joshua DeWine? Is he someone we should be concerned about?"

Ronik Dupray smiled and replied softly. "Concerned? Only if you're afraid of people who ask big questions.

"Joshua is no threat. Not to our country, not to our citizens. He's not political, and he certainly isn't violent. He's … curious. Intensely so. Obsessively, maybe."

"So, as his therapist, would you say he's mentally unstable?"

"Not at all. Quite the opposite. If anything, he's uncomfortably sane. The kind of person who sees through social constructs and isn't afraid to say what he sees."

"So, he's not some kind of cult leader or instigator?"

Dupray smiled faintly. "He doesn't rule by command. He leads by inspiration. He isn't after blind loyalty. He insists on thought.

"No. I certainly wouldn't say he's dangerous. But his ideas can be *disruptive*. That's what makes him powerful."

Salvo rephrased the question, "Do you believe his ideas could incite unrest? Protests? Revolution?"

Dupray promptly replied, "If asking people to think, to question, to evolve is considered revolutionary, then yes. But he never incites. He invites people to figure things out."

Looking at his notes, Fields queried next, "You mentioned something called the *Akashic Records* during your interview with the individuals impersonating FBI agents. What does that mean?"

"The Akashic Records are a metaphysical concept. Not tangible files," Dupray explained. "More like a collective memory field. Every action, thought, and emotion that has ever occurred, encoded at a non-physical level."

"Mystics, clairvoyants, and certain rare minds, claim to access fragments of it. But Joshua probably has full access to it.

"Whether you believe in it or not, it's not unlawful to access astral records. You can Froogle online on this subject and it's all over."

After a pause Dupray added, "Joshua said that this access to astral records gave him the ability to time travel. He can see and feel the future as clearly as he can remember his past."

Salvo pressed on. "Politically, where does DeWine stand? Conservative? Liberal? Democrat, Republican? We're trying to determine his agenda, understand his intentions. Is he trying to topple the government or destabilize law and order in any way?"

Dupray laughed quietly. "He's beyond your binaries. Joshua doesn't belong to any party. He believes political systems are like scaffolding: useful, but not sacred. If forced to choose? He'd probably say he's *radically independent*. Not left or right. *Forward.*"

"Does he support President McCrony?" Fields asked.

"Joshua has always been careful with his words. He believes leaders are mirrors, reflections of the collective psyche. He once said, 'McCrony is the shadow of a wounded civilization: loud, hungry, afraid.'

"He didn't condemn McCrony. He studied him. Like a volcanologist who studies a volcano: detached, fascinated, aware of the danger.

"In one of our past sessions, Joshua had laughed and said, "I love this guy McCrony. I find him hilarious. Look, now he's calling in the National Guard to California. Or DC. He's flexing, testing, practicing. One day, all this will be for something big. I'm the only one who sees it."

"Do you have records where he specifically discussed McCrony?" Salvo asked.

"Oh, sure," Dupray said. "I've got one on my laptop. From a session when a McCrony supporter called him, trying to convince him to vote in the 2024 election."

Dupray flipped the screen open. "Here it is."

All three of them bent over the laptop and watched the session.

The file was labeled:

Joshua DeWine
Session 17, October 2024

Dupray watched himself sitting across from Joshua in his office, guiding him into a trance. Joshua's eyes fluttered, then settled, his body slackening into that eerie stillness.

His voice, when it came, was softer, distant. Half present, half somewhere else.

The other day, I got a call from a volunteer with President-Elect Frank McCrony's campaign, asking for my vote for the Republican Party.

I told him, politely, that I was a bit busy at the moment. Election day was still a few weeks out. I had time to decide.

I also mentioned that I'm an independent. I don't lean red or blue.

The volunteer asked me what I did for a living.

"I'm an architect," I said. *"I specialize in designing and engineering walls."*

He chuckled. I could tell he saw an opportunity. *"Walls, huh? You know Mr. McCrony wanted a lot of those. Think you could design us the Great Wall along the U.S.-Mexico border? One that couldn't be breached or pole-vaulted over? Can you design that kind of wall?"*

"Of course," I said without hesitation. *"And I could get it built in under a hundred and eighty days for less than sixty million dollars."*

That got his attention.

I told him I had actually submitted a design to a competition McCrony organized back during his first term. I genuinely believed my design was the best. But I didn't win anything.

"Why not?" he asked.

I replied without missing a beat, *"Ask McCrony. Maybe it's because I have an Indian-sounding name. Maybe awarding an immigrant a prize for solving 'American problems' doesn't play well politically."*

"Okay, okay," the volunteer said. *"Fair enough. But now I'm curious. Tell me more about your design. I won't share it with anyone, Promise."*

"It's simple, really. Architects, you see, we don't start with bricks and mortar. We start in a virtual world.

"We visualize everything in 3D, model entire buildings, cities, infrastructure in CAD software. Every angle, every detail, down to the last screw.

"Just as we would design virtual walls in a virtual CAD world of the computer, in my design, we wouldn't build a physical wall. We'd build a virtual one.

He was amused and said, *"Wow, that sounds interesting. Tell me how would that work to deter infiltrators and illegals getting through?"*

"A wall made of sensors, strategically placed to detect human motion or intrusion within a fifty-foot vertical range, fifty-foot radius, and even fifty feet underground.

"A smart wall," I said, to help this kid grasp the concept.

"Think of it as a digital lattice. Arrays of sensors spaced every one hundred feet, like invisible landmines.

"Each unit, equipped with thermal, motion, and seismic detection capabilities, would silently monitor its environment. Arranged in overlapping rows, three or four deep, they'd scan continuously, feeding data to a remote command network.

"Once an intrusion is detected, the system would dispatch armed drones to investigate. These drones wouldn't be designed to kill. Just to immobilize. Stun technology, smart restraint systems, or electronic tagging could be deployed to neutralize threats non-lethally, allowing for capture, processing, and immediate repatriation.

"The idea is to build autonomous, scalable, and responsive systems capable of monitoring thousands of feet of territory without the need for barbed wire or concrete or pollution.

"And yet … if I'm honest? I don't believe in walls at all. "I believe in building bridges.

"I believe the day will come when the world stops fragmenting itself into pieces and recognizes itself as one single, living organism.

"When the hunger that drives migration is met, not with steel barriers, but with opportunity, dignity, and shared purpose.

"The real solution to immigration isn't enforcement. It's equity. It's building a world where no one is forced to leave home just to survive.

"Until then, I know how to build the virtual wall. But I'd rather build the world that doesn't need one.

About that time, the volunteer on the line went quiet. I think he was still processing the idea of a smart wall designed for a fraction of what it would cost to build a concrete monstrosity.

He didn't really hear the rest, the part about equity, about bridges, about what really solves the problem. Maybe it was too far outside the script.

He thanked me politely, said goodbye, and hung up.

And that was it.

As the video ended and the screen displayed Dupray's file icons, the two agents looked up from the laptop, sharing a moment of loaded silence.

"Interesting," Fields said.

Agent Salvo offered no opinion or observations, just an action plan. "We're tracking DeWine. When the time's right, we'll bring him in. For now, he's just a subject of interest."

"Dr. Dupray," Fields said, we appreciate your time and everything you've shared. We advise you to stay alert. If you see or hear from any individuals claiming to be FBI, please, contact us immediately."

"We'll handle it from here," Salvo said.

The agents gathered their files and notes, while Dupray reached out to turn off his laptop. They handed him their business cards and asked to call or report any other suspicious activity.

Then they left, leaving Dupray alone in this steel cold dark windowless room waiting to be escorted out to fresh air and the Florida sunshine.

Once on the outside, Dupray glanced at his biometric Pear Watch. It was just shy of 3:00 p.m. Still enough time to return to his office for the final appointment of the week—his favorite patient, Joshua DeWine.

After everything that had happened today, the thought brought him relief.

To be in the presence of *true divinity* again.

To feel that stillness. That clarity.

Maybe, just maybe, it would wash away the shadows that had gathered since morning.

And for a moment, he allowed himself to believe that sitting with Joshua might be enough to dispel all the darkness.

CHAPTER ‑16

09:42 | 11-15-2025 (Twenty-first century)
LOCATION: NATIONAL SECURITY BUREAU ROOM 212

The conference room held a deep polished boat-shaped mahogany table, surrounded by twenty high-backed leather chairs. Carafes of fresh-brewed coffee and a tray of pastries sat on a recessed banquet table off to one side.

Tim Logan circled the table with a stack of documents as his team of experts filed in.

He mulled over the call he'd just had with his longtime friend in the Florida Highway Patrol, informing him of the unfolding situation in Florida.

His close relationships with key figures like FHP Chief Mark Malvin had consistently proven valuable, strengthening Logan's influence within the National Security Bureau and helping secure his rise to one of the most coveted roles in the NSB: Director of the Counterterrorism Division.

While Logan was known for his tireless work ethic and relentless focus on national security, it was also his skill in navigating the human web of informants, officers, and decision-makers, up and down the chain, that enabled both personal progress and broader mission success.

This network was not nepotism, but rather a "You scratch my back, and I'll scratch yours" kind of reciprocal exchange that had the benefit of accruing valuable favors owed by powerful others.

It was a dynamic, self-supporting chain of command, shifting fluidly along the rungs of government hierarchy. Hard to explain to an outsider, but this was how the machine worked.

Logan stood at the heart of it. Surrounded by stacks of sensitive intelligence reports, he knew that every decision he made had life-or-death implications.

It would take five high-IQ, hyper-dedicated individuals to do the job he alone could manage.

He took pride in being the one man trusted by high-ranking officials, the president, and the common citizen alike. People could sleep at night knowing Logan was awake.

His reputation as a "ruthless risk manager" was well-earned. Logan left no stone unturned, no thread unchecked. He demanded the truth and pursued it with surgical precision.

At his disposal stood an army of elite intelligence officers working around the clock, every day of the year. He led a unique, integrated task force that spanned multiple agencies and divisions.

And today's events were about to put that force to a test like no other ever imagined.

The information contained in the folios he had just distributed dwarfed every crisis he had encountered in all his twenty-plus years at the NSB.

Senior FBI directors and intelligence officers waited for his cue, each handpicked for this extraordinary emergency meeting.

It had taken 9/11 to teach the intelligence community that operating in silos was a fatal flaw. Never again would the right hand not know what the left was doing. Today, the NSB ran a fully integrated, real-time intelligence ecosystem.

There cannot be another 9/11 in this country. Period, Logan thought as he laid the final folio before the chair next to his.

One by one, officers and senior members from both the NSB and FBI filed into the meeting room.

It was a Saturday, and some had shown up in casual clothes when they were called in on short notice for an urgent briefing. No one spoke much. The tone was clear: whatever this was, they knew it mattered.

"Good morning, everyone," Logan began, standing tall at the head of the table. "Thank you for coming in on a Saturday for this urgent national security briefing.

"I trust you've all read the executive summary, everything that's transpired in a little over the last seventy-two hours. You're aware of the individuals involved, and the growing controversy we're now tasked with resolving."

He scanned the room. "If we don't act fast, we're staring down the barrel of another 9/11-level emergency. I'm talking: massive stock market collapse, national disruption, cascading crises that come from unpredictable actors and unseen influences. You know the pattern."

His voice tightened. "But here's the thing: we're *engineered* to foresee and predict. To expect the unexpected. Nothing gets past us."

He let the silence hold for a beat.

Just as the last words faded, the door swung open.

FBI Director Chris Sharma stepped in, his polished shoes clicking against the floor, and slid into the chair next to Logan being one of most prominence.

The ambient mood shifted with his arrival. Conversations stilled, shoulders stiffened.

From behind his dark-framed designer glasses, Chris scanned the faces in silence, offering only the slightest nod to a few of the personnel seated there. His expression was unreadable, grim as stone.

He pulled the briefing toward him, fingers drumming once on the folder before flipping through the pages with brisk precision. Each turn of the paper seemed deliberate, his eyebrows arching now and then as if measuring every line, every detail buried between the words.

"We stay ten steps ahead," Logan continued. "We always have. And that's the only reason this country sleeps at night."

Around the long, polished table sat some of the sharpest minds in federal intelligence: grey-haired, stone-faced veterans from the NSB and FBI. No one spoke. They didn't need to.

Logan had their full attention.

FBI Associate Deputy Director, Don Vingo, stood and adjusted his sleeves. "Permission to summarize for the room?"

Several nods followed.

"Take your best shot, Vingo," barked John Leznon, Logan's chief of staff. "But be brief. Everyone here's either read the report or will."

Vingo nodded. His voice was calm but clipped with purpose. "We have a developing situation originating out of Florida. It began with a traffic incident. On the surface, minor. But what followed has escalated to a significant national security concern.

"Initial reports indicate that the incident may have resulted in the deaths of covert foreign operatives. Evidence suggests the deceased were incinerated, either by accident or intentionally, making identification difficult. However, recovered remains have since been confirmed by DNA analysis as nationals of North Khorea and Pakistan. Both designated as terrorist-harboring states and on our watch list.

"What's more concerning is the tech found at the scene. Advanced gear: materials and components outside known specs. Some of it's beyond what we currently believe is in circulation globally. Our tech division is still running assessments.

"Simultaneously, one of our FBI agents on routine surveillance observed five individuals wearing FBI jackets raiding the office of a licensed psychiatrist. To be more precise: four individuals went into the office while the fifth stayed in an unmarked getaway car outside in the parking lot. These individuals were not our people. They were impersonators.

"The psychiatrist, Dr. Ronick Dupray, was deceived into surrendering confidential data on one patient: a Mr. Joshua DeWine. The imposters took nothing else. Just his files.

"We took in Dr. Dupray for an interrogation and extracted everything he had about Joshua DeWine and what the imposters got away with.

"DeWine has been on our radar for years. Communications trace back to the late 1990s. Direct contact with then-First Lady, Juliet Veritas.

"His activities since then have been low-profile, but never off our map. We believe he's connected to something far greater than his official dossier would suggest."

He motioned to the folios. "All current intelligence, including DeWine's background, the Florida incident, and preliminary data on the impersonators, is in front of you now. Further updates will follow as agents on the ground close in.

"Our questions today are simple: What is the link between these foreign agents and DeWine? What tech are we dealing with? And why is this one man drawing such concentrated attention from foreign intelligence services or rogue estates?"

He looked around the table.

"So. Who here wants to take the lead on spearheading this case, and figuring everything out? Possibly arresting foreign operatives and bringing them in custody?"

Tanya Ritz, Logan's director of intelligence, raised her hand and stood with quiet authority. "I've reviewed the full dossier on

Joshua DeWine. And the intelligence we've gathered is, I believe, is of *grave* national importance."

Every eye turned to her.

"Until now, we at NSB regarded DeWine as an eccentric. A fringe figure. At best, a political prankster; at worst, a delusional idealist with no real following. But that assessment must change. *Immediately.*"

She held up a slim folder. "Because the moment foreign operatives took an interest in him, he became *our* interest."

Ritz scanned the faces around her. "We need to reevaluate. Revisit his background, his writings, his behavior, his *goals*. Is he dangerous? Is he ideologically compromised? Or is he simply another disillusioned citizen who believes he's destined to save the world?"

She flipped open the folder. "Our monitoring began in earnest in 1997, after Mr. DeWine, then a permanent resident and green card holder, sent a letter to the White House addressed directly to First Lady, Juliet Veritas."

A few officers raised eyebrows.

"DeWine, at the time, was a professional architect. Educated at Washington University in St. Louis. Practicing in Central Florida. Legal, quiet, articulate. But the content of his letter ... raised red flags."

She looked down at her notes, then back up. "First Lady Veritas was preparing her UN address in Beijing, focusing on women's rights. Her now-famous line, 'Women's rights are human rights,' was the centerpiece. She echoed the same message shortly afterward during a diplomatic visit to India, where she spoke at the Institute for Battered Women."

Ritz held up the letter. "Her speech caught the attention of Mr. DeWine, and I'd like to read what he wrote in response.

"I want us all to listen, not just for what he says, but for *why* a man like this, twenty-five years later, has the attention of foreign intelligence."

Tanya Ritz adjusted her glasses, drew a breath, and began to read aloud:

To The First Lady – Mrs. Juliet Ronham Veritas
The White House
Washington, D.C.

Dear First Lady,

My name is Ravishankar, a pen name for this letter.

I wish first to thank you for your visit to my country of birth, India, and for your thoughtful speeches on women's rights and human rights during your Asia tour in 1995.

India, as you saw, is a land of extraordinary diversity, of languages, religions, and traditions. It is also a nation where women are revered in countless symbolic forms. Every day, Hindu men bow before goddesses such as Durga, embodiment of strength; Saraswati, goddess of knowledge; and Laxmi, goddess of prosperity. In temples and in homes, women are recognized not only as nurturers, but as forces of wisdom, courage, and abundance. Even Mahatma Gandhi, whose path of non-violence won us freedom in 1947, emphasized the power of the feminine divine.

Our democracy, still young, has elected a woman, Mrs. Indira Gandhi, as Prime Minister for seventeen of its forty-eight free years. She wielded authority equal to that of your President of the United States. Which leads me to ask: How can America claim India does not support women's rights when our people have placed a woman at the very helm of government, while in over two centuries the United States has not yet elected a female president?

When will your nation put its own house in order? When will America finally elect a wise and compassionate woman to its highest office?

And more deeply, if "women's rights are human rights," as you have said, what, then, are human rights? What do they represent if we cannot even define the purpose of humanity?

Are we born only to trade, to compete like children for land and GDP, to boast of nuclear stockpiles, while billions starve, thirst, or drift through life without hope? Is humanity's legacy to build mountains of garbage, oceans of plastic, poisoned air, and cities that devour resources until Earth itself becomes one big landfill?

Is this truly the vision of our forefathers? To build sprawling highways, choke the skies with exhaust, and raise glass towers filled with goods that pollute the planet? To measure success by who owns the most, burns the most, or wastes the most?

If this is not humanity's purpose, then what is? And if we cannot answer this question, how will we ever face our children, or theirs, when they ask what we have done to their world?

Thank you for your time and for considering these questions, posed with the utmost respect.

Sincerely,

Ravishankar, Architect

(correspondence pseudonym)

Tanya Ritz held the papers high in her hand. "This one letter," she said, "has quietly shaped the trajectory of American politics for over two decades."

She let that sink in as she set the document on the table.

"Any other first lady, especially one completing two terms, establishing a giant surplus and prosperity in US economy, would have stepped into the shadows of retirement. She would have quietly 'kicked the can' to her successor, as the saying goes, and gracefully retired. But Mrs. Juliet Veritas did not. She *could not.*"

Ritz tapped the paper lightly. "Because of *this compelling letter.*

"Joshua DeWine was, at the time, a foreign national, not yet a citizen. A green card holder. Sent a single letter, handwritten, thoughtful, measured, to the White House in 1997. And it landed in the hands of the first lady."

She raised her gaze again. "Instead of dismissing it, she *responded.* On official White House letterhead.

"That correspondence, now classified and secured by NSB, is part of our national intelligence archive. This isn't fiction. It's public record, now in protected custody."

Ritz pressed her palms onto the tabletop. "The significance of this letter, as would be fully appreciated only in hindsight, was its unexpectedly powerful and far-reaching impact. And that kind of power, in the wrong hands, could be dangerous.

"What's critical here is this: if Mrs. Veritas *had* gone on to become President of the United States, as many predicted, that presidency may have been, at its core, sparked by the influence of a foreign national.

"This goes beyond optics; it's a constitutional crisis."

She let that hang.

"And so, we took action. The Constitution strictly prohibits foreign interference in our electoral process.

"As Jefferson warned, quote: *'Against the insidious wiles of foreign influence … the jealousy of a free people ought to be constantly awake.'*

"Hamilton called foreign interference *'one of the deadliest adversaries of republican government.'*"

Ritz looked at each director, each veteran officer in turn.

"We at the bureau made a judgment call not to expose the DeWine letter. Not to draw attention to it.

"Instead, we redirected the national conversation. We chose to focus scrutiny on Mrs. Veritas's private email server during her time as secretary of state."

The officers exchanged sidelong glances, some nodding, others lifting their eyebrows, a quiet acknowledgment of what they already knew. "Then-FBI Director Tim Gomey was briefed and activated late in the 2016 cycle to release carefully measured findings. Just enough to destabilize the momentum.

"Not because of the documents themselves. Those were, frankly, trivial. But because we could not risk public discovery of foreign ideological influence on our highest office."

Ritz held up the letter again.

"This … this spark … could've rewritten the course of our history. And in a way, it *did*. It changed the electoral process for more than two decades. America has been on the edge, tuned in to their televisions, waiting not just for election results, but to hear whether it would be a *boy or a girl* leading the country.

"We did what we had to do, not for politics, but for sovereignty."

Around the table, heads nodded. Silent agreement. No one looked shocked. Only affirmed. This was the business they were in.

Logan glanced at his chief of staff. Lenzon remained still but thoughtful, eyes narrowed.

Albert Brown, director of science and counterterrorism, gave a subtle nod.

Doug Badler, assistant director of security at NSB, folded his arms, his posture tightening as his focus seemed to sharpen.

As Tanya Ritz returned to her seat, Tim Logan stood once again.

He didn't need to raise his voice. "We've got to commend Joshua DeWine," Logan said. "Not for patriotism. Not for loyalty. But for his *nonchalant audacity*."

He caught a few nods around the table, his jaw set.

"This man, this *ordinary architect*, this foreign-born person, who is now a naturalized citizen, held the *entire nation's psychological stability* in his hands during some of our most contested election cycles. Not by hacking. Not by leaking. Not by financing."

He tapped the folio on the table. "By simply writing letters.

"Letters so well-crafted, so surgically targeted, that the government, *our government, moved.*

"Presidents responded. Our Chief Justices noticed them. First ladies paused to respond. Entire policy directions changed course.

"Because one man put pen to paper."

Logan shook his head slightly, almost in disbelief.

"And I won't get into the details here because it's all in your folios, but let's not forget what happened on January 12, 2016. The empty chair honoring victims of gun violence beside First Lady, Melissa Udama at the State of the Union address."

A few in the room nodded grimly.

"That, too, was DeWine. Another charged letter. Another carefully tuned appeal, sent to first lady Melissa Udama and President Drake Udama. And they were compelled to respond. Publicly."

He paused.

"And it didn't end there. DeWine went on to draft his own version of what he called the 28th Amendment. And somehow, *somehow*, that amendment draft made its way into the hands of the president. Then to the Supreme Court justices themselves."

Logan's tone shifted subtly, just enough to convey the importance of the point.

"The amendment wasn't discarded. It wasn't dismissed. It was reviewed. Studied. Called 'credible' and 'worth national consideration' by sitting justices."

He let that linger.

"This isn't noise, people. These aren't just pranks or coincidences. This is orchestrated influence. Tactical ideology. *Soft power* in its rawest form."

He opened the folio again and gestured to the final section.

"And if that weren't enough, buried in the investigation files tied to the so-called private email scandal of Mrs. Veritas, was DeWine's original question. The one that started it all. The one that Juliet Veritas actually answered. In writing.

"What is the purpose of humanity?"

He let the words hang, then continued. "People ask about personal purpose all the time. 'What's the purpose of my life?', but almost no one asks this: 'What is the purpose of humanity?' Can anyone in this room answer that? We don't know. Not yet.

"Nations fixate on wars, GDP, trade balances, whose arsenal is bigger, who plants a flag on Mars. Is that it? Is that all we are?"

"Our First Lady, Mrs. Veritas, attempted an answer, and yes, it's in one of the emails on her private server."

Logan scanned the table. This was no longer a briefing; it was a challenge. "Now you tell me: does this sound like someone who's merely 'interesting'?"

Silence.

He cleared his throat and pressed on. "Let's not kid ourselves. What we wrote off as political theater, a man with a pen and a talent for stirring the pot, has become something far more complicated."

He gestured to the screen behind him where a folder labeled *DEWINE: CONFIDENTIAL VIDEO TRANSCRIPTS – PSY SESSIONS* displayed then opened.

"Now a U.S. citizen, Mr. DeWine has every right to exercise his First Amendment freedoms. But we no longer see a man shouting into the void. We see a man with a penchant to write, regarded as a clairvoyant by his therapist, though someone who could be a danger to others.

"And now he is *being watched and hunted by foreign operatives.* He is being targeted."

Logan scanned the room, meeting each pair of eyes in turn as if taking a silent poll.

"Our team retrieved hours of video footage from Dr. Ronick Dupray's office: recorded therapy sessions between DeWine and the psychologist. We interrogated Dr. Dupray. He claims all recordings were consensual, though that's still under review.

"Remember Dupray? He's the one whose office was raided by fake FBI agents?

"We believe those impersonators are foreign operatives, connected to the ones whose remains were found in the roadside Florida burn pile.

"They are suspected of spying on behalf of Rossia, Shyna, or North Khorea. Damn communists."

He paced slightly, his voice rising with each step.

"In a matter of hours, our most elite analysts, AI trained professionals, have been transcribing and dissecting every single conversation, gesture, pause, and phrase contained in Dr. Dupray's records. We've generated summary reports for your teams, all of which point to one unavoidable truth: *this man DeWine is in possession of something, or there is something, that foreign intelligence is actively trying to extract.*"

He stopped pacing.

"That's what matters most here. Not just what DeWine *says* he's doing, but who's listening to him. Who's after him. And *why.*"

He raised a new file.

"Dr. Dupray insists, *swears,* that DeWine is a peaceful man. A so-called 'holy man.' He describes him as 'divine.' Even claims DeWine possesses *superconscious* abilities. Something to do with time travel through genetic memory. DNA-based consciousness retrieval.

"Dupray talks at length about Kundalini energy, ancient yogic practices, chakra systems, all this *Eastern metaphysical* stuff."

Logan waved a hand, dismissively.

"Let's be clear: our scientific communities have *no validated evidence* for these claims. It's uncharted, unverified, *unpublishable.* Hocus-pocus to us. But...."

He paused.

"*NASA has been poking around the edges of this energy field research for decades.* Quietly. Mostly speculative. Still in the realm of theoretical neurobiology and parapsychology. Nothing certifiable. Nothing they'll put in a peer-reviewed journal. But it's there. Deep-black. Early-stage.

"And if NASA's curious, *we should be too.*"

Logan looked across the table, his tone now razor sharp.

"Bottom line: we're not just dealing with an eccentric thinker anymore. We're dealing with a potential asset, or a target. And it's not just *us* watching him. That's the problem."

Logan noticed a subtle shift in the room, eyes drifting through binders and reports on table, pages flipping. He straightened slightly and raised his voice just enough to cut through the discomfort.

"Everyone, I need you with me."

He tapped the open folio.

"What should deeply concern us is this: *DeWine's so-called trance sessions are independently matching up with field intelligence* from our own agents on the ground."

He paused, then held up the open document. "Page 1028."

A soft rustle swept across the table as pages turned.

"In this session, recorded by Dr. Dupray, DeWine describes, in disturbing detail, a covert infiltration strategy by a foreign adversary. He names the country *Shynesia*, or *Shyna*, his phrasing, clearly referring to the *People's Republic of Shynesia*."

Logan's voice flattened. "According to DeWine, the People's Liberation Army is training female operatives and inserting them into the U.S. under the guise of massage therapists. He gives a precise number: 52,891 PLA females in active service, with 134 reportedly smuggled into the U.S.

"That number, 52,891, lines up with our own internal PLA gender composition estimates. Very close."

He gave them a moment to digest that.

"These women, DeWine says, are trained military operatives. Experts in psychological manipulation, contortion, covert mobility. He claims they've been transported in sealed shipping containers, hidden in cargo crates, entering the U.S. through our least monitored shipping channels."

Logan began pacing now.

"Their mission, according to DeWine, is *subversive warfare*. Not bombs. Not guns. *Collapse the American family unit.* Target overworked, stressed American men. Offer relief. Erode trust. Undermine productivity. Weaponize shame and infidelity."

The silence in the room thickened.

"And when the order comes," Logan added, "they're prepared to release *biological agents*. Flu strains. Possibly even

COVID-class viruses. DeWine says they're kamikaze-style assets, programmed to sabotage and, if necessary, to self-sacrifice.

"According to DeWine, these women, inserted by the PLA, create false comfort. Soft music, warm touch, a brief hour of escape from stress. And in that moment of peace, they build goodwill, not for themselves, but for their *nation*. They're shaping perception. Steering our purchasing habits. Eroding resistance. Promoting the idea that Shyna is benevolent, sensual, harmless."

He raised the folio again.

"Our teams have tallied 127 such individuals belonging to or trained by PLA, mapped strategically across key U.S. cities. DeWine's number? 134. A small discrepancy, unless you consider that *he* may be more accurate than *we* are."

Logan's voice hardened. "And that's what's most disturbing. *How does he know?* How is a so-called hypno-patient pulling numbers and operational details that match or exceed the findings of our most elite field units?"

His knuckles hit the table as he stepped in, eyes locked ahead.

"DeWine says these operatives are global, building influence, promoting 'Made in Shynesia' products, positioned to unleash biological attacks on command. Every corner of the Earth.

"He connects their deployment to the COVID-19 pandemic: the rapid, nationwide spread and high casualty count in the USA, compared to the much lower impact in Shynesia. To him, it wasn't an accident. It was a demonstration."

Logan looked at each man and woman around the table, then lowered his voice. "DeWine doesn't stop with predictions of biological or psychological warfare. He claims Shyna is orchestrating a multi-pronged assault. On our youth. On our society. On our national will."

He paced slowly now; eyes locked on the faces before him.

"He alleges they're using *online video games* as weapons: purpose-built distractions engineered to addict and disarm. Our youth, he says, are being pulled out of reality and into digital escapism, stunting their social development, numbing their ambition, and replacing community with code.

"And for those not hooked by a screen," Logan continued, "they're targeted on the *chemical front*. Fentanyl. Synthetic opioids.

"DeWine names shipping routes, smuggling networks, even legitimate storefronts, convenience stores, and vape shops, used as distribution hubs across U.S. cities."

He watched expressions tighten.

"Here's the part that should rattle every one of you. *The numbers he gave match our own internal reports.* Shipment quantities. Port of entry data. Even names of flagged dispensaries under surveillance by DEA. *He knew it all.*"

He looked around the room, dead serious. "So, I ask you: *Is this man delusional? Or is he broadcasting information we've been blind to until now?*"

Logan noticed the energy around him had shifted.

"And if we've been blinded, where is DeWine getting his intel? And what do we need to do, ASAP, to plug the holes in our surveillance nets?"

Chris Sharma finally spoke without looking up, his words deliberate, each syllable measured. "Shyna is a great nation, with a proud ancient culture. I love Shynese food. We all do. I have nothing against Shynese people, they are innocent, kind, honest and well meaning. Yet their modern leaders, they play games."

He paused, then continued. "Let me tell you a story."

"In a kindergarten class of fifteen children, there was one boy, five, maybe six years old. A bully. Whenever the teacher wasn't looking, he would sneak to the cubbies, open lunchboxes, and eat other children's sandwiches.

"One day at lunchtime, a child burst into tears. His sandwich was gone. The teacher comforted him and said, 'I'll handle this.'

"She gave every child a six-inch breadstick and said, 'Take a nap. When I return, I'll measure them. The thief's stick will shrink by one inch.'

"The bully panicked. While the others slept, he bit one inch off *every* breadstick. That way, when his shrank, all would match. Or so he thought.

"But when the teacher returned, she saw through it. All the sticks were shorter, except his. He was caught. Red-handed."

Chris Sharma finally raised his head, his voice cold and direct.

"Shyna is that boy. Stealing ideas, intellectual properties, resources, even the progress of other nations, thinking this makes them look tall.

"But bullies always expose themselves.

"America, for all our faults, grew, not by stealing, but by giving. Investing, building, letting others live. That's the difference. But unfortunately, all that USAID is hurting our bottom line, raising our national debt. So, I am very thankful to President McCrony for putting a stop to it. And for stopping the ship-loads of Shynese drugs coming in from South America."

The room was silent for a beat. Then Logan took the floor once again. "Director," he said evenly, "while that story has its lessons, we need to stay focused on immediate concerns.

"DeWine's possession of top-secret information can only have two explanations.

"Either Joshua DeWine breached one or more of our federal databases. Or he truly is what Dr. Dupray claims: a clairvoyant, tapping into some information stream we can't yet explain."

He tapped the folio on the table. "And let's not forget: a single letter from this man changed the course of our national election history for the past two decades.

"What happens when he publishes a *book*? A doctrine? A manifesto, as Dupray referred to it?

"We've dismissed the man for two decades. But it seems he's been watching us all along. The question we now face is not *whether* to act, but *how fast*? And *who else already knows what he knows*?

Logan took a deep breath. The kind of breath you take before pulling the trigger on something irreversible.

"Dr Dupray says DeWine is crafting what he calls a *Manifesto of Eleven Elements*. A document that, in his words, won't merely influence the world, but will shift the very fabric of reality as we know it.

"Not a philosophy or a political screed, but something powerful enough to trigger a gestalt shift. A rewriting of the rules. Something that could dismantle capitalism as a system, collapse our economic engines, and fracture the very foundations of modern society."

He looked around the room. No one blinked.

"This ... this is why we must place Mr. Joshua DeWine on a watchlist and keep him under constant surveillance, not as a criminal, at least not yet, but as the single most significant national security concern we face today.

"He's being pursued by foreign agents wielding technology we still don't fully understand. They're no longer spying on him ... they're hunting. And what they're after is buried in that manuscript, that manifesto. We can't let them have it."

Logan straightened his jacket, steel in his tone.

"Here's the catch: We know where DeWine is. We're tracking him with precision. But we *can't* bring him in yet. He's bait. The only bait we've got. If we move too soon, the operatives will scatter. We lose our window, and possibly lose him.

"The plan of action is detailed in the executive summary of the documents in front of you.

"I've assembled a strike team. Three lead officers from the six of us here today, supported by twelve field operatives and a covert network of Sedition Hunters embedded in major Florida cities and in the south east U.S.A."

Logan gave one final sweep of the room.

"This is a live operation. Fast, surgical, and with eyes on D.C. The timeline is tight. We'll report directly to the Intelligence Committee and Congress once this is neutralized or contained."

He grabbed his folder, tucked it under one arm.

"Meeting adjourned. Thank you."

He turned and walked out, leaving a room full of silence, urgency, and the scent of a storm rolling in.

CHAPTER -17

10:14 | 11-15-2025 (Twenty-first century)
LOCATION: RESIDENCE INN - BASE ROOM 402

It was the morning of day four in this time period and Max was already feeling less awkward in the character he'd been projecting, though not comfortable here by any stretch. Too much remained to be done. And the risks were always lurking like monsters in the dark.

Max had instructed Katrina to discreetly hack into the hotel's reservation system and create new bookings under separate names and background profiles.

Two rooms were reserved for the four women, with each pair sharing a double queen. Two additional rooms were booked for the men to share, while Max and Daniel each received their own single-occupancy room.

All reservations were to be assigned the same room numbers as before, allowing the group to return to their original rooms later that afternoon without raising suspicion.

That morning, the group of ten checked out together. After lunch, they would return in staggered intervals of fifteen or twenty minutes, checking in as separate, unrelated guests. Shift changes of employees at the front desk, meant different staff would be on duty, ensuring that no one would connect the re-check-ins to the original group. This maneuver would overwrite the existing records, replacing the original ten persons group reservation with seemingly unrelated new guests.

Above all, the reservation system would reflect that a group of ten persons checked out morning of November 15th, and that was the main purpose served.

Safe in his room for now, Max slipped into the recliner and placed the visor over his face, activating total recall mode once again.

The familiar hum of the headset kicked in, syncing with his bodysuit and PCOM. Lights danced behind his eyelids. Memory fragments began to rise.

His breathing slowed.

His mind sharpened.

Something's not right.

He needed to be sure, absolutely sure, that his selection process hadn't been compromised.

A faint memory surfaced: two final candidates. Two names. He had chosen Katrina. But why? Why her and not the other?

Sherry.

She had the experience. The security clearance. A flawless psych profile. She was on the final list, the official list of the fifteen authorized jumpers.

Katrina wasn't.

She had never made the primary cut.

And yet... here she was. Embedded in the mission. On the team.

And now we are having to trust her and integrate her as one of us.

Max's stomach tightened.

How did she get here?

Max felt a chill run down his spine.

He pushed deeper into the memory archive, zeroing in on the final meeting with General Dyson. The one just before the time-drop.

Something happened in that meeting. Something must've changed. Was it a last-minute override? A command swap?

Worse: was someone tampering with the team manifest? Could the memory loss itself have been engineered?

The recall grew transparent, quiet, glitching.

Max clenched the armrest of his chair. He needed to see the full exchange, hear every word, every order, every override code issued that day.

If miscreants had infiltrated the mission chain or planted a false identity in Katrina's place...

If that was true, then everything was at risk.

* * * * * * *

(VRV BLINKING: MEMORY RECALL MODE)
07:25 | 11-10-2532 (Twenty-sixth century)
LOCATION: HIGHPARK To Central Command Office

Max was up early, already on his way to the Central Command Office. This was a big day.

THE big day.

His eyes stayed fixed on his PCOM, scrolling through officer profiles, weighing who to cut and who would make the final team. The decision had to be made today.

He sketched out three SUVs on the screen and began assigning names to each, tagging them with key attributes.

SUV No. 1: Bintang Sudarto, Daniel Martin, Minami Hayashi, Kasandra Ayodele, and himself. Five Time Travelers.

SUV No. 2: Sherry Seashell, Lukas Adler, Prisha Jiwan, Isam Yusef, and Captain Jian Cheng.

SUV No. 3: Roberto Amarial, Sherine Elliot, Jackir Husen, Meirah Hong, and Mathew Perry.

He paused. He knew Minami Hayashi, Sherry Seashell, Jian Cheng, and Meirah Hong were all martial arts experts. Katrina Patilova was the fifth, but she hadn't made the list.

He stared at the names, feeling something off.

Katrina and Sherry had both scored 99% across all evaluations. Both were top-tier combatants. Why had he chosen one and not the other?

Then it hit him: Sherry was married to Major Abu Fatah, one of the fifty officers in the Time Traveler Regiment. They had a child together. A three-year-old daughter.

Max's own words echoed back at him: *No officers with families on this mission. Too risky. Too much to lose. Especially for the ones left behind.*

He rubbed his temples, muttering, "Oh no. I'm making the wrong call."

The dilemma gnawed at him. Sherry wasn't just a fighter; she was the most well-versed in the Manifesto and the Eleven Elements. If DeWine hit a creative wall, Sherry could break it.

She also had a sharp command of language and was an expert on environmental issues and knew most of the solutions.

But that little girl...

"She needs her mom," Max whispered to himself.

Reluctantly, he deleted Sherry's name from SUV No. 2 and added Katrina Patilova. She was nearly as qualified. And at least she wasn't leaving behind a child.

Max made a note: *Assign Sherry to Central Command as backup. Keep her in the loop. She knows the mission. She knows the team. She'll understand. Hopefully.*

He sat back and exhaled, the decision tugging hard at him. The issue was not fairness, but minimizing pain, even if it violated his own rules of merit.

Sometimes the right choice isn't the easiest. It's just the one you have to live with.

Suddenly, he heard loud notification sounds, almost like alarm bells ringing. They drew him out of his memory recall mode to pay attention to the transmission coming through from the command center.

He tapped into the secure uplink to transmit the day's report to Central Command.

But the connection sputtered. Rick Perez's face flickered, distorted by interference.

"Max, we need speed … before something worse crashes through."

Max nodded. "Progress is solid. We've secured a dinner meeting with DeWine. We'll impress upon him to publish the manifesto. He already recognizes who we are and where we're from. Once he understands the risk we face, he'll cooperate. He's … receptive."

Perez didn't relax. "You need to understand the pressure on our end. We've already lost five operatives. Command wants to deploy a backup team to recover every manuscript, every version."

The screen glitched again. Perez's voice thinned, distant.

"Like most of your previous jumps, quick in-and-out missions, they're expecting fast results on this one too. I've set a maximum window of fifteen days for this mission. Do you think we can achieve our goals?"

Perez's expression didn't ease. "Now that word about the black hole in the timeline has reached the general public, there's panic everywhere. Patience is wearing thin, Max. I'm afraid rash decisions could be made that do more harm than good."

Perez moved closer to the monitor, the lines in his face deepening. His voice was edged with urgency. "The 'black hole' in the timeline, as they're calling it now, it's accelerating. Fast. It's not just creeping toward our timeline; it's rewriting it."

Max frowned. "What do you mean?"

Perez exhaled. "Historical records are shifting. Timeline markers are mutating. Events we never documented, events that never existed, are appearing. And no one knows which version of reality will hold.

His voice came through in more fragmented bursts: "...timelines fracturing... expressly stated... history and events reshaping... time-travel lab in 23rd century no longer exists... Dyson fears R&D collapse... do whatever it takes... get DeWine... publish that manifesto... hurry... might not exist."

The link went dead. Max could hear his heart thumping.

14:09 | 11-15-2025 (Twenty-first century)
LOCATION: NEAR STATE OF FLORIDA HIGHWAY 27

A sudden flash, and a black TTV, cloaked in the form of a Felza SUV, appeared in the center of a perfectly round clearing deep in the woods.

"Arrival protocols," said Ambassador Sarah Blumstein as she stepped out, voice low but firm. The air hit different. Real. Less filtered. Hot and thick with humidity.

She walked to the front of the SUV and began reciting, her tone steady:

"I am Sarah Blumstein. Ambassador, from the Haifa and Mid-East region, twenty-sixth century. I am a former commander of the elite sixteenth Time Travel unit and now I am an elected official of the Federation of Nations. My term began June ninth, twenty-five hundred and twenty-one. My height is one point seven meters and I weigh sixty-one kilograms. My eyes are green and my hair is colored champagne blonde. I was born on August twenty-second, twenty-four hundred and eighty-seven. I am forty-five years old and I reside at the Executive Pod in High-Park four hundred thirty-seven of the Federation Megapolis in Haifa. I am in a committed relationship with Benyameen who is my domestic partner for the past twenty-four years"

She exhaled hard. The PCOM beeped with a green light.

That was close. Might not have materialized at all, she thought.

Her PCOM, embedded in her bodysuit and synced to her forearm, beeped in response, confirmation received. Protocol complete.

"Whew," Sarah muttered. "Wow. I can't believe it. I actually made it to the twenty-first century."

Behind her, the SUV doors clicked open. One by one, her team stepped out, each reciting their arrival protocols. Five in total, three AAILF GenX uBots, sleek and silent. And then her partner, loyal, experienced, trusted.

Sarah walked alone, about fifty feet from the others, toward a shallow berm that matched the coordinates on her wrist-top device. This was the site where the three brave soldiers, the fallen Time Travelers, had perished.

She came to a halt, stood at attention, and raised a crisp salute. A gesture of respect. A moment of silence. Or so it appeared.

Out of the corner of her eye, she checked. No one had followed. Her team was scattered, some stretching, others gulping down water, too drained from the jump to pay her much attention.

Satisfied, she tilted her wrist, tapped her PCOM, flipping open the interface and activated a hidden command. The screen flickered, encrypted symbols flowing fast. A discreet, secured uplink pulsed, reaching across time to the twenty-sixth century.

The signal was patchy but live.

The salute was just a cover. The mourning, a pretense. No one here knew who she was really talking to, or what her true mission might be.

She spoke quietly, almost under her breath.

"We made it," she said, her voice low, urgent. "We're here. I told you we could slingshot off the 22nd-century datacenters. We landed right at the spot where three of our officers were cremated. This is it."

A male voice crackled on the other end. "Yeah. That was a freak accident, some AAILF snuck on board. Slipped past Command's scans. Even Max missed it."

Sarah scoffed. "Well, look at me now. I got through, with three AAILFs on my team. *Three*. And that makes my team stronger. Small but agile."

"What's the next move?" he asked.

She didn't hesitate. "First, we take out DeWine. Then Katrina.

"With them gone, Max's unit falls apart. Their mission ends right there. After that, we clean up everything, rewrite the narrative, correct the record. No more uBots. No more factories churning out synthetic sex slaves. It ends now."

A pause, then her tone shifted, annoyed, human. "But first, I need shelter. This suit's unbearable in this heat. Everything stinks. It's like breathing through soup. I don't know how these people live like this, no filtration, no cooling. That's going to change. If they won't listen, we'll make them."

"Understood," the voice replied. "Just don't go full warpath. Think through your moves. Stay sharp. Stay in touch."

"I will," Sarah said, already scanning the tree line. "This time, they don't stand a chance."

CHAPTER ·18

18:29 | 11-15-2025 (Twenty-first century)
LOCATION: DEWINE RESIDENCE APOPKA FLORIDA

Max, Katrina, Prisha, Luke, and Bitang arrived outside Joshua DeWine's residence dressed in casual twenty-first-century attire, modestly layered over their form-fitting bodysuits. They had taken every measure to blend in, following Katrina's meticulous guidance.

Max thought back to the day of launch, five days ago, and how surreal it had felt just to imagine he could be meeting the venerated Mr. Joshua DeWine.

Now, he and his team were about to have dinner with the man. In his home.

Katrina had been instrumental in preparing them for the evening.

Constantly studying archived historical records and social norms of the twenty-first century, she acted as the group's cultural compass. Her insights were critical to avoiding missteps.

Through direct feeds to their arm-pads and yPhones, she relayed everything from expected etiquette to conversational dos and don'ts.

Whenever necessary, she would send discreet flash alerts, signaling someone to stop mid-sentence or rephrase a response.

Her interventions had already saved them from revealing their origin or behaving in a way that could appear unusual or suspicious to locals.

And if something went awry tonight, Katrina would find a quick, clever way to redirect the situation and restore their cover.

Customs of the period were Prisha's specialty, and she had made a point to pick up a bottle of wine earlier in the day for their evening's hosts.

It sat next to Prisha in the passenger seat in a tasteful gift bag, wrapped with tissue paper.

In her lap was a fruit basket she had prepared. A symbolic gesture of health and well-being, just in case alcohol wasn't acceptable to DeWine.

Tonight, as they approached the doorway of the man whose vision had shaped their future, Max could sense they all felt the significance of the moment.

He leaned in, and the rest closed the circle around him in a huddle. "Tonight's dinner with Joe is our best chance to set things right. Let's not screw this up. Take your cues from me or Katrina. We need to admire and appreciate Joe's work. Make him feel important, give him the pride and confidence he's looking for. A sense of validation. Let's butter him up."

Max saw his teammates nod in acknowledgment.

"Let's listen," he added. "If he wants to talk or vent, let him. From what I've read, he's a talker, he goes on and on, and sometimes he says weird stuff. Let him say whatever he needs to. Our job is to impress on him that he has to finish his task and get that Manifesto of his published. That's the goal of our mission."

He clenched his fist in a quiet signal of resolve and watched the others mirror the gesture.

They walked briskly to the main entrance. Max's eyes flicked to a service van parked across the street, a plumber's logo stenciled on the side.

They were here to honor a legacy still in the making.

Things are now on track, thought Max as he pressed the doorbell.

The door creaked open to reveal a young, bright-eyed girl with dark, shoulder-length hair. Her gaze flicked curiously across the group of strangers and the hallway behind her.

"Hello. My name is Max Renner. Is this the DeWine residence? May I speak with Mr. Joshua...."

Before he could finish, the girl turned her head and called out, "Papa, there are people asking for you at the door!"

As she stood watching the visitors with guarded curiosity, Joshua appeared behind her. His eyes warmed when he saw who it was.

"Go to your room, little one," he said gently. "Tell Mom that our friends are here for dinner, dear."

The girl nodded and scampered off, her steps echoing lightly as she disappeared down the hall.

Joshua stepped forward and extended his hand with a broad, welcoming smile.

"Welcome, my friends." He moved back to allow the team to step inside. "Welcome to my humble hut in the twenty-first century.

"I imagine your homes in the future must be quite different. Advanced, no doubt. With AI systems, smart-home technology, and comfort-driven, sustainable living woven into the very walls?

"But come in, come in. This way, please."

Prisha stepped forward and handed him the gift bag with the bottle of wine, while Luke raised the fruit basket with a polite smile. "Where should I put this, Mr. DeWine?"

"Oh, thank you. So, kind. Though you didn't have to bring anything," Joshua said, warmly accepting the bottle of wine. His face lit up.

"Over here," Joshua pointed Luke toward a small table to the left of the entrance. "Just place the basket there."

He waved his hand casually. "And please, just call me Joe. Make yourselves at home.

"Aasha, honey!" Joe called down the hallway. "Our friends are here."

Moments later, a tall, well-dressed woman emerged. She had long, dark, curly hair and wore jeans paired with a white Kurti, detailed with embroidery and sequins along a tasteful V-shaped neckline.

She raised both hands in greeting. "Namaste, hello, please come in. Good to see you all," she said warmly and led them into the living room.

"Can I bring you some water?" she asked with a welcoming smile, her voice both graceful and confident.

"We have some chilled beer here in this cooler," Joe nodded toward a bar in the corner. "And there's red and white wine as well. What do you prefer? Please, just help yourselves and make yourselves comfortable."

After the initial pleasantries and meet-and-greet moments in the living room, his wife excused herself to check on dinner.

Once everyone had a drink in hand—wine or fresh juice— Joe motioned for the team to follow him out to the back porch.

There, beneath high ceilings and soft ambient lighting, a cluster of oversized loungers and a plush sofa waited in a cozy arrangement.

Bitang and Max took their seats, both gazing up at the slow rotation of a tropical ceiling fan with wide sabal palm leaf blades gently circling above.

Meanwhile, Luke lingered at the bar. He poured himself a glass of wine, grabbed a bottle of water for Max, then stepped out onto the porch and eased into the relaxed atmosphere with the others.

"So, guys, tell me," Joe sat in an accent chair, perhaps the least comfortable in the room, and offered a curious smile, "what brings you here... aaall the way from the twenty-sixth century?

"I know Max, you're the team leader of this mission, and I've met Prisha and Luke. But who are these other two courageous souls?"

Max gestured toward his companions. "This is Katrina, or Kate. And this, over here, is Bitang, though we call him Binny.

"The other two you met earlier today have been reassigned to other tasks so we can move forward with completing our mission.

"However, the other five team members are at our operations base, tracking us in real time, listening in and watching this meeting remotely. So, in a way, the whole team is here: five in person, five online."

Max quickly got to the point. perhaps out of a suppressed fear this incredible moment might not last. "As we explained to you yesterday, your *Manifesto of Eleven Elements* sowed the seeds for a new reality, one that defined the trajectory of human civilization for centuries to come.

"The future we come from, the twenty-sixth century, exists within a unified geopolitical structure called the *Federation of Nations*.

"Think of it like your United States, but on a global scale. In our time, the world has become one large, interconnected country.

"Many smaller states have been consolidated into regional nation-states. Each of these regions is governed by a regional governor. And they are all united under a central Global Federation."

He took a sip from the plastic bottle, setting aside his concerns about the waste and pollution. He was here to fix all that. If all went according to plan.

"In our time", Max said, "this Federation is led by three Principal Ambassadors who act as the heads of this global union.

"Each nation-state sends multiple ambassadors to represent local and regional interests. Geographical boundaries as you know them have changed entirely.

"And most importantly, there are no wars between these states.

"Humanity's greatest struggles, hunger, lack of clean water, homelessness, were all solved within a few decades after the Federation was born in 2045.

"It replaced the ineffective global organization that is currently known to you as the United Nations."

DeWine had a questioning look on his face. "How did you, or *our*, Federation differ from the UN of my time?" He spoke to the team, but focused his attention on Max. "Why was it able to make real change?"

"Good question," Max said. "The Federation of Nations formed, or will be formed, in 2045, around a singular goal: to rebuild and reconstitute Earth to function as one unified body, focused solely on the survival and well-being of humanity.

"Humanity began living with purpose.

"And all of that, every bit of it, started with you, Joe. It started because of what you imagined and wrote in your *Manifesto of Eleven Elements*.

"Me?" Joe said. "Wow. I didn't realize. It certainly wasn't something I'd planned.

"Honestly, I thought I was just pouring out thoughts and ideas into an entertaining screenplay for a streaming movie. Sci-fi, maybe. Just like my favorite author Randy Wire out in California, mixing cocktails and writing clever stories about other worlds or alien encounters."

He laughed, but there was a shift in his tone.

"I didn't expect it to become a self-help guide for humanity."

Then Joe paused and his expression softened, brightened. "Although," he said, "I've imagined a different future, now and then.

"I always hoped things could be better, simpler, for my kids and grandkids. A life without constant stress or pain. I wanted them to live naturally. The way nature intended. Not like me."

He looked off, as if searching memory.

Just then, Joe's wife, Aasha, stepped out onto the porch carrying a large bamboo board.

"I've got a charcuterie board with savory bites and hors d'oeuvres ready!" she said cheerfully.

"Ah, perfect," Joe replied. "Just the kind of finger food we need… while we discuss time travel, sci-fi novels, and shifting realities."

Max watched Aasha's reaction.

She didn't flinch. Not a blink of surprise. Just a nod, as if Joe's comment was the most normal thing in the world.

Maybe it was, Max thought.

Maybe guys like Joe had friends dropping by all the time, talking about time travelers and alternate timelines—and maybe Aasha had simply learned to take it all in stride.

She smiled. "Yes, yes… enjoy the appetizers while the samosas are still hot. I'll be inside if you need anything. Gotta feed the kids and start the bedtime routine."

And just like that, she slipped back inside.

The porch settled again, warm and quiet—time travel and samosas blending into one strangely perfect evening.

Joe gathered his thoughts and continued, "My life's been full of struggle, hurt. Honestly, it's been miserable at times. And I didn't want that for them…for my kids. I wanted to leave something behind. A legacy that meant something. Make life easier, better. Less stressful. You know?

"Right now, everyone's worried. Bills to pay. Living paycheck to paycheck. What they're doing isn't living; it's just surviving. We're all working for banks, lenders, contract agreements. Thirty percent of income gone just for that. The rest goes to car payments, insurance, gas, maintenance.

"Real freedom? Doesn't exist. It's all smoke and mirrors."

Joe laughed bitterly. "Monkeys in the trees must laugh at us. They don't worry about mortgages, bills, or clocking in for a forty-hour workweek. They don't chase fake freedom. They just live.

"And us? We drive on tangled highways, work our asses off just to feed pets and pay rent. Those monkeys must think we're idiots."

He shook his head. "So, you're telling me your reality isn't like that anymore? Wait, you're saying that what I wrote ... actually became real? That reality *shifted?*"

Max and the others nodded, smiling.

Joe looked stunned. "I can't believe I made that kind of impact. I was just experimenting with ideas. With reality itself. You know, someone else tried that. Who was it?"

Katrina's eyes flicked upward as she accessed the archives via wi-fi. "MK Gandhi. Late nineteenth, early twentieth century."

"Yes, Joe said. "Mohandas Karamchand Gandhi. Or Mahatma Gandhi. He wrote *The Story of My Experiments with Truth.*" He made air-quotes with his fingers.

"I guess, in my own way, I was doing the same. You might call it '*My Experiments with Reality*'. Testing the boundaries of this twisted reality. Imagining what could be, and how we might fix what's broken."

His eyes lit up. "Because if we can imagine the right future, if we resolve the core problems, then *bam.*"

He clapped loudly.

"We trigger a gestalt shift. Human thought evolves, and, *poof,* new reality. I never thought it would actually work.

"I'm ... flabbergasted."

Joe's eyes focused somewhere beyond the room. "I tried a few things. And I do believe we can impact the world.

"But there are always opposing forces. Call them counter-imaginations: people whose visions of the world directly clash with yours.

"When they try to manifest the opposite of your vision, that's when things go sideways."

He paused to sip his wine.

"I wrote a letter once. To the First Lady, Juliet Veritas. I truly believed it could spark change in the way this country is governed. I've always believed a nation's fate depends on how it treats its women."

He glanced at the women in the room with a tender smile.

"And yet, look around. Strip clubs on every corner. Young girls, barely eighteen, dancing nude to pay rent. Women having to compromise dignity just to survive or get ahead. It's heartbreaking.

"I thought, maybe, if we elected a woman president, things would shift. That we'd finally rewrite the rules. That reality itself would bend toward something better."

He shook his head slowly. "I was wrong."

Kate chimed in, clearly excited by something she'd just pulled up in her data search, using it as a decoy to nudge the conversation in a more positive direction. "No. You're absolutely right. Scientists, philosophers, even futurists have said the same thing: imagination shapes reality.

"There's a record of a famous television series called *StarTrack*, aired back in 1967. In one episode, a space traveler stands in front of a box on the wall and says, 'Computer, hot chocolate.' The box opens, and there it is, a steaming cup ready to go."

She glanced around the table, smiling. "Back then, that kind of tech didn't exist. But thirty years later, microwaves were in every home.

"And today, even in your time, we talk to our smart devices like it's second nature. 'Alissa, turn off the light.' 'Increase the volume.' It's straight out of those shows."

She paused, then added, "Or take *Metropolis*, that silent film from the 1920s. It imagined flying cars a hundred years ago. Now we've got drones, and flying cars are no longer science fiction."

She glanced at Joe whose raised brows triggered a correction. "In my time, I mean. Your future

"So yes, what we imagine *can* become real. It goes beyond storytelling. It becomes a blueprint for the future."

"But remember," Joe said, "many TV shows and movies are imagining the apocalypse: dystopian futures, doomsday scenarios. What if *those* visions became real?"

Kate's expression shifted. She was already accessing data, her eyes flickering subtly with the feed.

"You're not wrong," she replied. "There are records of a near-catastrophic world war in the early 22nd century, triggered by advanced AI and autonomous war-bots. The *uBots* War, they called it. Some parts of the world were nearly wiped out.

"But, Joe, it was your *Manifesto of Eleven Elements*, THE Joshua DeWine's writings that changed everything!

"Your vision of a Utopian future was so vivid, so compelling, that it shifted global consciousness.

"Leaders, policymakers, even tech giants began rethinking their trajectory.

"What could have been a full-blown extinction event became a series of isolated skirmishes. Almost footnotes in history."

Joe took a samosa in his hand, dipped it in a green chutney and nodded. "That's exactly what I mean. We *must* stop glamorizing dystopia. Imagining ruin, collapse, and misery. It only plants negative seeds in the collective mind. It's dangerous."

He sat up straighter, his voice gaining intensity.

"There should be a ban on that kind of storytelling. We need to train our thoughts on what's possible, not on what's terrifying.

"A healthy, clean, simple life. No stress. No debt traps. No fake freedoms. Just the space to live like humans were meant to live. Free. Natural. Fulfilled."

He looked around him with an intense, yet appreciative expression as he took a large bite into the samosa.

"Because if we start imagining the *right* future ... and people act on that vision ... who's to say we can't reshape the world? Who's to say we can't save it?"

An extended silence settled over the room as Joe's guests from the future sampled small appetizer plates, accompanied by aged wines. Katrina had earlier explained the traditional Indian courses and the quiet etiquette of shared meals.

Aasha reappeared at the doorway, smiling.

"Dinner's ready," she announced. "We've got pilaf rice, two Indian curries, daal soup, and Joe's favorite—*dahi bhalla*, the yogurt dumplings. And for dessert, there's mango cake with plant-based ice cream on top. Hope that works for everyone?"

Bitang stood up with a grin. "Sounds delicious to me."

Joe led the way inside, the group following him to a long dining table set with warm lighting and soft linens. Aasha took the seat to his left—close to his heart, Max noticed.

Once plates were filled and the first few bites taken, Joe dabbed his mouth with a pumpkin-colored napkin and said, casually:

"So, where was I? Right—my experiments with reality."

Apparently, there would be no pause for small talk.

Max smirked inwardly. *Do Joe's kids grow up with this as dinner conversation? Or do they eat early so the adults can talk about timelines and consciousness in peace?*

As if on cue, Aasha stood up quietly, gathering her plate.

"I'll be upstairs," she said. "Time to tuck the kids in. Please help yourselves to seconds... there are no formalities here. I will be back as soon as they're asleep."

She slipped away.

The moment the sound of her footsteps faded down the hall, Joe leaned forward, voice low, finger to his lips.

"She was in the kitchen during our patio conversation. Now she's with the kids. She doesn't know what this is *really* about— who you are, where or when you're from, or what I may have set in motion."

He scanned their faces.

"To her, this is just one of my sci-fi chats with visiting friends. My usual 'reality experiments.' So be careful. If she's nearby, I don't want her knowing."

Everyone nodded silently.

The clinking of spoons and the soft rustle of napkins were the only sounds for a while.

Then, after swallowing a thoughtful bite, Joe spoke again.

"What I fear most," he said quietly, "is being misunderstood."

He glanced at the others, then looked down at his plate.

Max quickly ran through the possibilities in his head. How could he, or even the time travel project, have misunderstood Joshua DeWine and his works?

"Let me remind you how something I say now can be completely misquoted, misinterpreted, and misunderstood five hundred years into the future. My go-to example is the story of Sheikh Chilli, how I often mention it in my writing to reflect on the dangers of foolish ambition and living in illusions.

"It's a cautionary tale I rely on. But remember what you said the other day? You casually twisted it into 'Shitchilli', as if it were a regret about eating too much spicy food. Did you not notice the difference? What I shared as a meaningful reference ended up becoming something crass and completely unrelated.

"You know," Joe said, voice calm but deliberate, "some of the earliest scriptures, sacred to millions, have been deeply misinterpreted over time."

"Take the Torah, for example. Just two words: *Eretz Israel.*"

He glanced around the table.

"Now, I say this with respect to my Jewish friends," he added, "but I believe the original meaning of those words was far broader, more spiritual, even symbolic, than how they're often used today. Over time, that shift in understanding has shaped generations. And not always for the better."

He lowered his voice, more pointed now.

"Today, you type that phrase into a search engine and you get maps. Borders. Politics."

A small shrug.

"But that's surface-level. Israel doesn't mean *conquest.* It means *one who wrestles with God.* Some say it even means *God-conqueror.* Not in the sense of overpowering God, but someone in direct, intimate struggle, a seeker. A soul tested, refined."

He lifted a finger.

"And *Eretz,* it doesn't just mean *land.* It can mean the entire Earth. The people. The life. The biosphere."

"Or Gaia," Prisha said softly.

Silence followed, sharp, still.

"So, when you say *Eretz Israel,* you're not necessarily talking about a strip of land near Jerusalem. You might be describing a universal principle. A calling. A coded truth."

His voice dropped, more intimate now.

"To win the love of the Creator, you must honor the totality of life. The Earth. Gaia."

Then he turned to Max, eyes steady.

"If we truly want to reach God, not just worship, not just obey, but *reach* … then our relationship with the planet has to change. That's ancient scripture, not modern philosophy. We just misread it."

"We've reduced sacred texts to checklists. Laws without context. But the deeper meanings? They've always been there. We just stopped listening."

His voice dropped lower.

"Now imagine something. If God returned, not with fire or thunder, but wisdom. No miracles. No robes. Just a quiet message meant for this time."

He locked eyes with Max again.

"Would He be pleased to see us killing each other over land? Or would He weep, or worse, laugh, to see His children locked in bloodshed over boundaries, while the Earth itself chokes under plastic, drowns in oil, burns from our waste?"

Joe shook his head, eyes sharp, mouth curled in bitter irony.

"It's absurd. Fighting over a snotty-ass patch of land while the whole planet becomes a landfill? You don't call that devotion? It's desecration.

"To love God," he said softly, "we must love Gaia. Every ant. Every tree. Every breath of air. Because *that* is the body of creation. Divinity lives where there is care, not conquest."

He paused, more reflective now.

"I've spoken with friends from many faiths, including Judaism. And some of them said something that stayed with me: that *Eretz Israel* doesn't have to mean a border. It could mean a mission."

Joe scanned the room.

"A vision where the Earth, *Eretz*, is nurtured. Made holy through how it's cared for, not who claims it."

His voice dropped again, now like a prayer.

"They told me the true calling lies not in domination, but in restoration, that the real path to God runs not through war, but through healing."

He exhaled.

"I don't pretend to know everything," Joe said. "But I believe this much: the Earth isn't ours to carve up and poison. It's ours to protect."

He paused. His guests were staring at him in amazement, clearly unaware of the deeper histories and underlying tensions that had led to the current Israel–Gaza war. And to so many other conflicts still burning around the world.

"We earn the favor of the divine through the use of our wisdom, not through the use of weapons."

He leaned slightly closer, his tone shifting, quieter now, almost intimate.

"You know," he said, "the Jewish people have long been among the most intellectually and spiritually driven communities on Earth. Look at the record, more Nobel laureates than any other group. A towering presence in ethics, science, medicine, literature.

"But beyond the accolades, their scriptures call them something else: *the chosen people.*"

Joe looked into the eyes of each of his guest at the table.

"But chosen … to do what, exactly?"

The question hung there, unanswered, impossible to ignore.

"To fight over a sliver of land? To preserve a flag?"

Another beat.

"Or to restore Gaia itself? To lead the way in healing the Earth, protecting its waters, cleansing the air, and bringing humanity back into balance with creation?"

He turned to the others at the table.

"Maybe being chosen isn't about privilege. Maybe it's about responsibility."

His voice steadied.

"This isn't about control. It's about stewardship."

He met their eyes, one by one.

"Maybe they were chosen not to dominate, but to inspire. To remind us why we're here."

He raised a hand slightly, as if gesturing to something above, or something unseen.

"In nature, every creature has a role: to sustain balance. That's their only job. That's their sacred rhythm."

His voice dropped, final and clear.

"Shouldn't that be ours, too?"

He sat back, letting the silence do the rest.

"The core of my work, the Gaia Theory, the belief that all life is part of one vast, living system, moving with purpose and balance, it's not new. It's not a modern discovery. It's ancient in every scripture and holy book out there.

Luke frowned, genuinely puzzled, then said, "For centuries people have followed religions. It's been the norm, a way to keep law and order in society. What we don't understand is this: why is all that stopping you from putting these thoughts out into the world?"

Joe responded. "If what I just said wasn't clear, let me give you another example, one that hits even closer to the heart of many.

"Think about how our holy books, our revered figures, even the words of Jesus Christ himself, have been misunderstood or misinterpreted across centuries. If that can happen to them, then who am I? Just a human, born of flesh, with all the same flaws and fears as anyone else.

What scares me," he added quietly, "is the thought of being misunderstood in the same way, of having my intentions twisted, my words taken out of context, and being judged harshly for it. All it takes is one person who hears it wrong, who reacts out of anger or ignorance, and suddenly, you're not just misquoted, you're condemned.

"I fear that, like Jesus Christ, I too may be persecuted, not for any crime, but simply for speaking bitter truths that some people, or even the government, may find uncomfortable or inconvenient.

"I mean, think about it: even the words of Jesus Christ, written in the Bible, followed by hundreds of millions, have been twisted, misused, or outright ignored."

Prisha prompted an explanation, "Maybe you can give an example of how people have misunderstood Jesus Christ?"

"The Gospel, supposedly the word of God, is meant to be taken to heart. Every word, a commandment. And yet how many truly follow it as it was intended?

"If *Jesus* could be misunderstood, His message distorted to serve agendas, what chance do I have?

"My words, my vision, they'll be interpreted through someone else's lens. And sooner or later, they'll get reshaped to fit whatever story people want to tell."

He paused, gathering his thoughts.

"It's not just the Bible. It's the same with the Quran, the Bhagavad Gita. Sacred texts meant to guide humanity toward a better life. Toward compassion, peace, understanding.

"But they're often misread, misunderstood, or worse, disrespected."

He looked up again, eyes tired but steady.

"All of them imagine a better world. A better future. But somewhere between the words and the reader, that future gets lost."

There was wisdom in what Joe had just said, but Max was trying to get his head around the specific implications for his mission.

"I can appreciate your anguish and frustrations, Joe," Max said. "But what exactly is holding you back? What's keeping you from finishing your own epic work?"

Joe took a breath and bowed his head for a moment.

Max pushed further, yet cautiously. "Because to us, your writings are no less sacred than the scriptures you just mentioned.

"We swear by the *Holy Manifesto of the Eleven Elements*. Everything you wrote, everything you said, every instruction you gave, our ancestors followed.

"This very team sitting here now descends from those who obeyed.

"Because of you, we live in a world free of misery. The suffering of your time? It's just history for us."

Joe seemed to be taking it all in.

"We're not exaggerating," Max said. "Your words reshaped civilization. Your books became the new gospel. Some Christians believed you were the Second Coming. Others of the Jewish faith called you the true Messiah. In the East and Far East, they worshipped you as *Kalki*, an avatar of God, through most of the twenty-second century.

Joe chimed in, "Oh… my… gawd! All this time I thought *I* was Lady Whistledown from *Bridgerton*, you know, telling on everyone, exposing secrets through anonymous pamphlets."

Max gave him a look, half-amused, half-focused. "Jokes apart, Joe," he said, easing the conversation back on track, "eventually all religions *did* merge into one. Just like you wrote in the seventh anthology, the One World Religion."

He paused, then added with a small smile, "And yes… per your instructions, we don't call you anything divine anymore. No Messiah. No avatar. No savior… not even Whistledown."

Max found his hands in a gesture of prayer, then opened them to those around the table. "You told us to simply refer to you as *Mr. Joshua DeWine*. A human being. Not to be worshipped. No statues. No temples. No portraits.

Max laughed. "Just one smiley-faced photo at the end of your books. A headshot, taken in a restaurant, a California Pizza Cookery, wood beams behind you fanning out like a halo. Scruffy beard. Sharp eyes. Just you. As you were."

"Mr. DeWine," Luke said, "you should be proud. Proud of your imagination. Proud of how you bent reality toward something better. Your books are our commandments. Our gospel. Our future."

Bitang joined in. "But we need you to believe in it too. To finish the work. To trust that your vision matters. Only then can the anomalies in the time gaps we are facing be resolved. The future from now going forward depends on it."

Joe studied the faces around the dinner table.

He lingered for a moment and let his gaze rest on each face in turn, as if searching for the right words.

Joe's calm demeanor gave way to reveal a rare, raw fire. "Alright," he said. "Let me tell you why I've hesitated. Earlier, Prisha even asked me for an example of how people have misunderstood Christ."

He spoke like someone who'd lived through centuries. "People love to quote Jesus: *Treat thy neighbor as you would want to be treated.*'

"And they assume He meant only humans. The good Samaritan. Your fellow man. Your neighbor across the street.

"But my manifesto, what I wrote, goes deeper. It's grounded in the Gaia Theory.

"The belief that Earth is a single, living organism. Every creature, every animal, plant, insect, microbe in the soil, is part of that fabric.

"So, when I say 'neighbor,' I mean *all of them.* That ant crawling on your windowsill. That pig and cow in the slaughterhouse. That tree in the rainforest. They are all our neighbors.

"And what do we do to them? We kill them. We eat them. We burn their homes. We destroy the lungs of the planet.

"I remember during a debate, our President McCrony said something that struck a chord, *They are eating our pets, our cats and dogs.*' Many misunderstood him, thinking he was referring to immigrants. But I believe he was pointing to something deeper, even spiritual.

"By 'they,' he meant *all of us*, Americans included, consuming the sacred, the innocent. When we eat hamburgers or fried chicken, we may not realize we're consuming animals such as cows that, in some traditions, are considered as dear and worthy of reverence as the pets of the Lord Almighty. Perhaps he was echoing a truth spoken long ago, one that many still choose not to hear.

"And here we are. We sit around waiting for some grand *Second Coming*. Some *Judgment Day*.

"Do you know what that judgment will sound like?" His expression hardened, the fire fully lit now

Joe's voice thundered unexpectedly: "The Judgment will not be gentle.

"It will say: "*What have you done to our common home? This beautiful, pristine Earth. Heaven itself. You have defiled it with filth, buried it in garbage, poisoned it with pollution. All lifeforms are my creation, your neighbors who sustain your existence in the balance of ecology. And you have brought them to suffering. You have turned paradise into a garbage planet. A cesspool of disease and despair!*"

His words echoed against the walls.

"*You are destined to rot in the pollution you have created, to suffer grave illnesses, to face the wrath of storm and flood, to burn in wildfires, and to wither in unbearable heat. Unless you restore the beauty of this planet, unless you cleanse and heal what you have corrupted, you are sinners. And you will die knowing you were fools, disgraced before your faith, your families, and your legacy. Act now, or all of mankind will be annihilated!*"

No one spoke.

His voice still echoed in their ears and in the very air itself. It lingered like a broadcast from some unseen speaker, humming in the background of ordinary life: a grocery store, a subway platform, a crowded square.

But this wasn't ordinary.

The sound was charged. Ethereal. Commanding.

Max felt it in his chest. He knew that devout Christians of the twenty-first century had long awaited Judgment. And now, Judgment had entered the room, undeniable, unmistakable.

This is it, he thought. *This is what Judgment would sound like.*

Not trumpets. Not thunder.

But the piercing clarity of a man speaking quiet truth into a still room.

The words carried the weight of the Beloved Lord himself, the Messiah who fractured faiths and fueled centuries of waiting, hoping, and fear among the faithful. Not arriving in spectacle, but in certainty.

Max clenched his fists under the table, grounding himself.

This is still the twenty-first century, he reminded himself. *These events are in our past. DeWine's revelations already shaped the world we live in.*

And yet, nothing about this moment felt rooted in history. Joe's voice didn't feel rooted in the past. It resonated with something eternal, as if time itself paused to listen.

Scruffy and human as he was, Joe spoke with the cadence of prophecy.

Messiah or messenger. Savior or son of the age. It didn't matter.

In that moment, Max knew he was in the presence of a truth that defied labels, one that no doctrine, nation, or century could contain. This wasn't a speech; it was a transmission, something that asked not only to be heard, but to be lived.

Max looked at Joe with more than admiration now. There was reverence in his gaze. And urgency.

He also saw something else: Joe wasn't above it all. He wasn't untouched.

He had grown up inside the noise, shaped by the same inherited systems, the same myths, the same fractured faiths. His voice carried the echoes of a broken world he no longer accepted.

And maybe, Max realized, *that's exactly why Joe had to speak, not because he stood apart, but because he carried it all.*

He didn't stand on a pedestal to preach; he bled from within it.

Joe had to let it out. To purge what bound him.

Only then could the future begin.

"So, what should humanity do?" Max asked, his voice calm but loaded.

"We haven't even defined why we exist," he said. "No unified proclamation. No shared purpose. What *is* the purpose of mankind?"

The questions began tumbling out, urgent, like they'd been waiting centuries for someone to give them voice.

"How do we end war?" he pressed, not pausing for answers.

"How do we break the cycle of destruction? How do we face the ecological collapse that's already underway? People today, they don't know how to get out of the mess. They don't even know where to start."

Max paused, just long enough to draw breath.

Then he said softly, "We do. We, the ones living in the future your words built. Because we grew out of your visions, your Manifesto and your writings, Joe. We live by it."

Max straightened, his voice edged with conviction.

"And the world we live in, the clean air, the healed forests, the absence of war, it's proof that your vision works."

Max's eyes didn't leave Joe.

"If Christ walked the Earth in the twenty-sixth century," he said, "He'd be pleased. No question."

A silence hung in the air. Then Max spoke again, lower, more direct. "But it's your task to get us there. You're the hinge. The tipping point. The one who has to say what the world doesn't know it's waiting to hear. It all starts here."

He didn't blink.

"So please, Mr. DeWine, Joe, tell us how to begin. Tell your people how to end what no longer deserves their effort. And where to go instead. Show us the next step."

Joe stared at the table; his eyes fixed on some distant point that only he could see. "I don't even know where to begin," he said quietly. "These thoughts ... they're not simple. They're layered. Deep."

He hesitated.

"But let me try."

Max interrupted, his voice sharpened with quiet urgency. "We know the world needs this. We know your words can shift it. But we need to hear it from you. How are you going to make it happen? How do you bring the world into alignment with this purpose?"

Joe exhaled hard, like the pressure in the room had finally found its way into his chest.

"I know it looks like I've stalled," he said. His tone was defensive, but honest. "And maybe I have. But not because I stopped caring. And not because I stopped believing in the work."

He ran a hand through his hair, glancing around the room. His eyes looked heavier now, like they were carrying years.

"I've been gathering these thoughts, these ideas, for years. Multiple volumes. I always meant to publish them. I wanted to. But the world kept falling apart."

He exhaled, and the edge in his voice softened into weariness.

"First the pandemic. People dying around me. Friends, good ones, gone in their sleep. Just like that."

A breath.

"Then came the wars, Middle East, Europe. More chaos. More fear. Just getting through the day started to feel like a full-time job."

He rubbed his hands together slowly, grounding himself.

"Then inflation. Prices went insane. Groceries, rent, gas, everything a battle. And in the middle of all that, my biggest client handed me a deadline I couldn't afford to miss. A huge project. And I had no team left. My office had collapsed, wrecked by the pandemic and everything that came with it."

Joe looked directly at Max, his voice low but clear.

"I'm just an ordinary man. Living a working person's life, like anyone else. I am not a billionaire, nor do I have sponsors. No funding. No team. This project, the *Manifesto*, wasn't commissioned. No paycheck. No publisher breathing down my neck."

He shook his head.

"I was doing it from the heart. Because I know what's coming. Because I know what happens if this work stays buried."

His shoulders dropped. Clearly, the man was tired. Deep-down tired.

"And in all this chaos, I started to wonder: who's even listening? Who wants truth when it isn't trending? Who's ready for ideas that require sacrifice? Humility? Radical change?"

He glanced away, then looked back, his voice softer now.

"That's why I haven't finished it: because I've been trying to stay afloat in a world that's sinking."

Joe looked down for a moment, then spoke again, no longer as a visionary, but as a man pushed to the edge.

"Look, I'm not a professional writer. I don't have a degree in English, no team of researchers. I've done my best. But this kind of work? It's massive. It needs research. Accuracy. Every idea, every reference, checked, cross-checked. It's overwhelming."

He glanced back at Max, his eyes worn but sincere.

"I never wanted to write something that ended up on a dusty university shelf. I wanted it to reach the everyday person. I imagined it more like a story, fiction, maybe. Something like *Game of Drones*, but rooted in ideas that actually matter."

A faint smile flickered, but didn't hold.

"Hell, I even toyed with a sci-fi angle. Time travelers like you showing up to help me finish what I started. That was one of the storylines I considered."

He gave a tired laugh, but it didn't reach his eyes.

"And the truth is, lately, I've been getting offers. Real ones. From people I suspect are tied to foreign governments or intel networks. They want to buy it all. The frameworks. The plans. The future roadmap. For a price."

He paused, his voice tightening.

"They want the edge. They want to be first."

Joe's eyes darkened as he looked away.

"And you know what? It's tempting. The money would let me walk away. I could disappear. Finally have the time to finish all seven volumes the way I want. No more deadlines. No more struggle. Just peace, and space to breathe."

Then his gaze narrowed, focused again.

"But here's the problem: this message, this vision, it needs to reach people who think beyond themselves. If a government or a group wants to use it just to dominate, to get ahead, to weaponize it..."

He shook his head.

"Then what's the point? That's not Gaia. That's not unity. That's just the same broken game with a new skin."

Joe sat forward, his tone sharp now, more edge than fatigue.

"I'm tired, Max. Tired of pushing uphill. Tired of giving my energy to a world that only listens when there's profit in it. I've got a family. People to feed. And I'm not Christ. I'm no Messiah. I'm just a man trying to survive."

Then, almost a whisper: "Imagine if Jesus came back and chose comfort instead. Lived quietly. Took the money. Who'd blame Him?"

He looked away, then back.

"But He wouldn't. And I'm not Him. So maybe I should take the deal. Go with Plan B. Play the game like everyone else."

Max saw Joe eyes heavy, as if with the long ache of years spent chasing something just out of reach.

"Because honestly, why keep writing this Manifesto? Who's it really for? Who's going to read it and care enough to act? To stand beside me when it counts? Who's going to help shoulder the load and actually move things forward?"

His voice caught, just slightly.

"Why should I break myself open for a world that won't show up for its own salvation?"

Max straightened, his voice cutting clean through the spiral with quiet force.

"Joe," Max said. "Stop right there."

Joe blinked, caught off guard.

"*We* are the proof." Max gestured to his fellow Time Travelers around the DeWine's' generous table.

Joe stared.

"Your ideas *worked*," Max continued. "Your vision became real. We are the reality you imagined, living, breathing evidence that what you wrote mattered. That it changed everything."

Max exhaled, eyes closed for a brief, reverent moment.

"We owe you more than gratitude. We owe you, *our existence*. You dreamed a better world for Gaia, for humanity, and that's the world we live in now. In the future."

Then Max's mood shifted. The warmth remained, but something more urgent surfaced.

"But there's something you need to understand. We didn't come here just to honor you. Or to relive your past. We came because something's going wrong."

Joe's face tensed.

"In the twenty-sixth century, when the technology of time travel has been mastered, it is routinely used to manage complex global and historical challenges.

"But as we grew familiar, and complacent, with our technical abilities, we discovered alarming gaps in the historical timeline.

Prisha chimed in, "Events and actions that should have been recorded, simply weren't. It was as if they had never occurred."

Max looked directly in the eyes of Joshua DeWine.

"Our researchers traced these anomalies back to your time, *this* time. The twenty-first century. And more specifically, to you.

Joe rose, brow furrowed, and reached for a water bottle on the table. He twisted off the cap, took a drink, and sat back down. "How could that happen?"

"The pattern suggests that the *Manifesto of Eleven Elements* was never officially completed or published in the timeframe it was meant to be. And because of that, key historical events failed to take shape. They were never set in motion.

"This absence created a fracture. A void in history."

Max watched Joe shake his head, clearly upset by his possible role in changing the future ... for the worse.

"In simple terms," Luke added, "if your manifesto doesn't get published, we cease to exist."

"What?" Joe bolted from his chair, holding his head as if it were about to explode. "What are you saying?"

Max looked up at Joe as he paced, holding his head. "I'm sorry, Joe. But by our calculations, entire civilizations, generations of reform, social restructuring, and unified governance all depend on your words reaching the world, on time.

"The fact is, your delays, for whatever reasons, are unraveling centuries of progress."

"Oh, my Lord!" Joe said.

"But we believe it's fixable. We're here now to find out why your work wasn't published. Why was this legacy, your legacy, left incomplete? What is stopping you, now, in this timeline?"

Joe didn't answer, apparently lost in the maelstrom of mental chaos the news had triggered.

It was Bitang's turn to plead, "Only you had the foresight to think about the future with intent. You imagined what could and should happen. You gave humanity a clear path: what to do and what not to do.

"And yet, here we are, at the precise moment when your Manifesto was meant to be published … and it hasn't been."

Max added, "The future is unraveling, Joe. And we need to know: What is holding you back? Why hasn't the *Manifesto of Eleven Elements* been released to the world?"

Finally, Joe stopped pacing and looked at Max and the other guests with a dumbfounded expression.

Luke broke the silence gently, careful not to sound pushy. "If you don't finish it … now … this year, the chain of events that leads to our world collapses. This isn't conjecture, it's established fact."

"Historical records are flickering," Max said. "Places, people, phasing in and out of existence. Events in timeline and history are already out of place. We're holding the line, but barely."

Max's voice softened, but his eyes held firm.

"I know you didn't ask for this burden. I know you're exhausted. But please hear me. We're not here to pressure you; we're here to remind you."

A beat.

"To show you that your effort wasn't in vain. That the words you haven't yet published are more than ideas or philosophy. They're the blueprint of a future that must exist."

Max offered Joe a small, sincere smile.

"I've never read your novels," Max admitted. "Not the way people used to. We don't study them like literature in our time. We live by the core ideas, distilled, woven into the fabric of our world. *Eleven Elements is the way of life.*

"But my great-grandfather told me stories. He said when your first book came out, it didn't feel like reading. It felt like *entering.* Like walking into a mirror and seeing yourself differently on the other side. Everyone who picked it up saw themselves in it. Felt questioned by it. Changed by it."

Max's voice softened. "That's the power of what you created. And that's why we need you to finish it. Not for fame. Not just for legacy."

He held Joe's gaze.

"For continuity. For life itself."

Katrina spoke next, her voice calm, grounding. "Joe," she said gently, "Your novels were experiences disguised as books: layered realities, stories within stories, worlds inside loops."

She met his eyes, her voice steady with conviction.

"Every layer pointed back to something true, a person, a choice, a consequence. That's why they mattered. That's why they changed people."

She smiled, genuine, not just reassuring, but encouraging.

"And the fog in your mind? It'll lift the moment you begin again. Trust that. You don't need a publisher. You don't need permission. Self-publishing is seamless in your time. I could send you a link right now, make the logistics effortless, so you can stay focused on the message."

Joe sat still, the words settling into him like roots taking hold in soil that had long gone dry. He let the moment wash over him. Then, slowly, he nodded, more to himself than anyone else.

"Alright," he said quietly. "Let's have a good dinner tonight."

He looked up. His voice steadier now. He was gently nodding. "Tomorrow, I'll begin again."

There was clarity in his eyes. Purpose beginning to return.

"My assistant, Nicole, she's been a solid support through everything. I'll ask her to help restart the process. Book One is almost done. Just needs the last chapter, some refinements, a final review from a few trusted friends, one more pass on the edits…"

A breath.

"…and then I'll publish. It's time."

As they sat around the table finishing a round of soups and salads, Joe gestured to the spread before them—warm dishes steaming gently, and fragrant aromas filling the room.

"Please, help yourselves," he said. "Enjoy this humble meal Aasha prepared. Real Indian cuisine. Pure—and straight from the heart."

Just then, Aasha joined the table, her voice soft with apology. "The little one's been extra clingy tonight. It's hard getting her to sleep—especially when we have guests and she hears Joe getting excited."

She smiled playfully. "You've heard of visiting lecturers at universities, right? Well, Joe calls me a *visiting host.*"

Laughter rippled around the table.

Then, with a warm gesture toward the main dishes, she added, "Please, dig in. I kept everything mild to medium spicy—just like Joe said you'd prefer."

The group gathered around the table, laughter beginning to replace the tension. The Time Travelers dug in enthusiastically, the spices familiar, the textures comforting, the scrumptious food entirely plant-based. All of it kept steaming warm on chafing dishes.

No animals were harmed. No suffering was involved. Just nourishment and peace. The meal was a quiet echo of the world they had come from.

Max began to feel relaxed, enjoying his first real dinner in the twenty-first century. In that moment, with plates full and hearts fuller, it felt as though the future had taken its first real breath.

After dinner, everyone drifted into Joe's home-office, where Hug-n-Daze ice cream was passed around. One wall was lined with bookshelves, an entire library, filled with countless volumes.

The Time Travelers stared in awe. They were watching history itself, a time when books were not files or projections, but bound in paper and ink. Real books.

Max watched as Minami, Bitang, and Katrina reached for a few, flipping through the pages. Katrina, with her enhanced cognition, skimmed entire tomes in seconds, absorbing them like they were mere pamphlets.

Their eyes then moved to the walls, where framed posters and parchments carried messages from different faiths and traditions.

One bold script hung in a Butsudan: *Namu Myōhō Renge Kyō*

(南無妙法蓮華経)

the sacred Nichiren Buddhist chant meaning
Devotion to the Mystic Law of the Lotus Sutra.

Another parchment bore the verse from John 14:6:

*"I am the way, the truth, and the life;
no one comes to the Father
except through me."*

A third, drawn from the Bhagavad Gita, proclaimed in Sanskrit: '*Karmanye-vaadhikaareshtu Maa Phaleshu Kadachana*'

कर्मण्येवाधिकारस्ते मा फलेषु कदाचन

"You have a right to perform your prescribed duties,
but you are not entitled to the fruits of your actions,"
emphasizing the spirit of selfless service.

A stern quote in Gujarati Language read:

**"DO NOT GIVE UP FAITH AND DEVOTION TO THE LORD
OUT OF FEAR OF SLANDER BY THE UNSCRUPULOUS
AND THE IGNORANT." - SWAMINARAYAN**

And in elegant Arabic calligraphy, the Quranic words of
Surah Al-Mulk (67:15) flowed across the parchment:

هُوَ ٱلَّذِى جَعَلَ لَكُمُ ٱلْأَرْضَ ذَلُولًا فَٱمْشُوا فِى مَنَاكِبِهَا وَكُلُوا مِن رِّزْقِهِ وَإِلَيْهِ ٱلنُّشُورُ

"It is He Who has made the earth subservient to you,
So, walk in its regions and eat of His provision;
and to Him is the Resurrection."

The room itself became a tapestry of wisdom, voices across time and tradition, speaking in harmony. Max's team looked around in silence, aware that they were in a place where the sacred and the future met in a single breath.

A collective sigh filled the air as everyone finished their desserts and Prisha and Luke gathered dishes, returning them to the kitchen. Aasha stood there leaning on Joe with pride over another successful dinner gathering accomplished.

Max glanced at the clock on the wall. It read 21:42. "Joe," he said, "You and Aasha have been most gracious and generous. But I know it's getting late. So, let's call it a day.

"Now that you understand the almost unimaginable gravity of the current situation, I trust you'll do your best to finish *Eleven Elements: Book One* and get it published. The sooner, the better.

"Let us know if you need any support. Katrina here is a resourceful team member. She can help resolve any challenges you run into."

He gave a subtle signal, and the team began moving toward the door. Joe and Aasha followed them to the front porch.

Outside, as they exchanged goodbyes, Max noticed something odd, a plumber working beside a van, tools scattered, apparently mid-installation.

He moved closer towards Joe and said in a hushed tone, "We saw that van parked there when we first arrived. Is it common for plumbers to work this late?"

Joe looked toward the van, brow furrowed. "Well … pipe bursts or serious leaks can be emergencies. It's possible he's dealing with a major issue, maybe a backflow preventer or something at the meter.

"But yeah," he added, eyes narrowing, "now that you mention it, I did notice him earlier, too. Strange, but not unheard of."

The team said their goodbyes and headed for their SUV in Joe's driveway, which led up to his three-car garage. Across the street, the plumber's van sat parked in front of the house. Max and the others climbed into the SUV, everyone except Bitang, who stayed outside.

As Bitang stepped around to the passenger side, he texted Max that he'd noticed the plumber across the street watching them. He said the man appeared to be peering through a T-shaped pipe fitting, almost like as though it was a periscope.

Bitang reached into his jacket and pulled out a slim, pen-shaped device, his portable scanner. In the rearview mirror, Max saw him calmly walk to the rear of their vehicle, circling it slowly, as if inspecting for damage. When he reached the rear passenger wheel, the device emitted a rapid series of beeps that only Max's team could hear.

Crouching down under the pretense of fixing his shoelaces, he moved the scanner closer to the undercarriage. The beeping intensified.

From the driver's seat, Max monitored everything in the mirrors. He noted the plumber abruptly wrapping up his work, hastily loading tools back into his van. It was clear he was preparing to leave now, just as they were.

Max quickly messaged the team:

"The plumber is FBI. Likely disguised. They've been tipped off about tonight's dinner with Joe. Stay alert."

Meanwhile, Bitang, now hidden by the shadows between vehicles in the driveway, reached under the SUV and pulled off a small, magnetic tracking device. Without missing a beat, he palmed it and subtly slid it under the adjacent vehicle, one of Joe's cars, attaching it smoothly beneath the chassis.

He stood, dusted off his hands, and casually opened the back door.

"Done," he said, slipping inside. "Let's go."

Max eased the SUV out of Joe's driveway; his eyes fixed on the plumber's van across the street. Its headlights snapped on almost the same instant. Hard not to notice that.

As Max rolled into the street, he spotted the van follow at a steady distance, about a hundred feet back. He kept his pace casual, making no sudden moves. If they were tailing him, he didn't want them to know he knew.

A few blocks down, on the main arterial road, Max's suspicions were confirmed. Two more vehicles, black Chevy Suburban SUVs, joined the pursuit, merging seamlessly into the flow behind the plumber's van. Federal backup.

"They're all on us," Max muttered under his breath, voice calm but clipped. He kept the SUV steady, blending with traffic, but subtly inching up speed to create some distance.

At the next intersection, the left turn signals blinked green, but just barely. Max made his move.

He floored the accelerator, swinging hard into the left turn as the signal turned amber. The SUV surged forward, tires squealing lightly, before disappearing around the corner and out of direct sight.

As they cleared the bend, Max reached for the console and hit the stealth-cloaking mode. In seconds, the SUV shimmered out of visible light, vanishing completely.

From behind, the convoy of agents blew past the intersection, unaware they'd just been duped.

Max guided the now-invisible SUV into a narrow fire station driveway, idling behind a parked truck as he watched the pursuit continue down the road, chasing ghosts.

Once they were out of view, he pulled back out onto a quiet side street. The SUV weaved through a tangle of unlit neighborhood roads. In the cover of darkness, Max deactivated the cloak. The vehicle reappeared, now a deep cherry red instead of the original steel gray.

A few turns later, they were gliding back toward the hotel, undetected and unseen.

The cabin was silent until someone whispered, "We lost them."

Max exhaled slowly. "Yes, that was close. The FBI are tracking Joe and trying to take us in custody. We need to be more vigilant from now on."

CHAPTER -19

22:05 | 11-15-2025 (Twenty-first century)
LOCATION: RESIDENCE INN - BASE ROOM 402

Max felt an unfamiliar ease settle over him after the team's dinner with Joshua DeWine.

There was something reassuring, grounding even, about the clarity with which DeWine had spoken.

His promise to complete the work and bring everything into order gave Max something he hadn't felt in days: forward momentum. The mission was no longer a string of fragmented tasks and half-formed memories; it had become a goal within reach.

Today, Max decided, was a day for celebration and rest. A moment to pause the constant calculations and let himself breathe.

06:47 | 11-16-2025 (Twenty-first century)
LOCATION: RESIDENCE INN - BASE ROOM 402

Max had slept peacefully for a change. A deep, uninterrupted rest he hadn't felt in the previous five days since their arrival here in the twenty-first.

The morning light found him calm and focused. As soon as he woke, he made contact with his base back in his time, reporting in from the twenty-first century.

The signal was weak. Static crackled through the audio feed, distorting voices and breaking apart sentences.

"This is Max, reporting from 2025. We're on track," he said. "Mr. DeWine seems committed to completing the Manifesto. Once the timeline stabilizes, I expect this com-link will clear up."

Then Burke's voice broke through. fragmented, urgent. "Sir … the rip … it's accelerating … coming our way. Timeline integrity … failing. If DeWine stalls again … we might lose this link entirely. We need you to ensure…"

The transmission cut out.

Silence.

Max stared at the dead feed. The urgency was clear. The window was closing. There wouldn't be many more chances to get this right.

The success of their future, and his return to it, rested on DeWine publishing the Manifesto, and soon.

Max understood the norms of the twenty-first century: you gave someone a few days to respond or show progress before following up, especially professionals as busy as Joe DeWine.

He knew he couldn't pressure DeWine to act with the same urgency that Command Center and the Admirals were demanding of him. As much as their lives in the future depended on DeWine's success, Max had to be patient.

He had made the stakes clear, but he also recognized that DeWine needed time and space. After all, he was still rooted in his own life, in his own time. *DeWine was off somewhere finalizing the manuscript and should be able to publish it soon.* He thought.

But for now, Max needed space to breathe.

It had taken most of the day for Max to finalize reports and draft contingency plans to address the potentially catastrophic loss of contact with Central Command.

They had done all they could. But waiting was hard.

So, he gathered a small team with him and headed to Bok Tower Gardens, a quiet, natural sanctuary not far from their hotel.

At the gardens, the afternoon sun was warm, the paths quiet, the breeze carrying the scent of blooming flora. It was the kind of place the future had preserved thanks to ideas seeded long ago.

Ideas like DeWine's.

Oblivious of the others with him, Max strolled the grounds, hands in his pockets, lost in the sway of rustling leaves and distant birdsong.

He thought of Annie, her hand in his as they once walked the elevated gardens of High-Park 577. He remembered her laugh, the way her eyes softened in the sun.

Soon, he told himself. *I will be with her… enjoying her company.*

The Manifesto was nearly complete. Just a few more days, and if everything held, he'd be home again. In the future he belonged to, beside the woman he loved.

And maybe then, finally, he could watch Annie smile again. Not through memory, but in real time.

17:25 | 11-18-2025 (Twenty-first century)
LOCATION: RESIDENCE INN - BASE ROOM 402

It was their seventh day in 2025 and three days past their dinner meeting with Joshua DeWine. The sun was setting, casting long shadows across the common room where the team had gathered for the evening.

They had been working hard to reestablish communications with their tether in the future. Now, there was a pervasive feeling of exhaustion and desperation that none of them really talked about.

Max had made every effort to stay positive for the team, but inside, he feared the worst.

Katrina, Danny, and Isam had penetrated a major data center and redirected a large portion of its cloud processing power to the task of supporting this time jump.

It may have helped, even if marginally. Enough to get a few key words exchanged with Central Command. All of them dire.

The time rift seemed to be growing, despite their apparent success in getting DeWine back on track for publication.

Meanwhile, Max and the others had been reviewing the psychiatrist's videos, hoping to tease out any clues that might explain which of DeWine's messages were most critical to the timeline's integrity.

Perhaps if they could get him to focus on those messages first, maybe...

It had been three days since their dinner with Joe. And Max's anxiety was off the charts, waiting for news, even an update or an estimation of when DeWine might have all the pieces put together. *Anything.*

When Katrina's phone rang, she answered, her voice calm at first, but her face began to shift as she listened.

Max and the others turned toward her, alert.

"Yes," Katrina said into the phone. "The last time we saw him was at his house. We had dinner with him that evening."

A pause.

"What? He's been missing since then?" Her voice sharpened. "No, no, we haven't seen him or heard from him since that night. I'm sure of it."

Another pause. Her tone grew more tense.

"Alright. Yes, we'll let you know immediately if he contacts us. Of course. Thank you. Bye."

She hung up and turned to the team, her expression grim. "That was Joe's office," she said. "He's been missing since the night we had dinner with him.

"Apparently, after we left, an old friend of Joe's showed up. Joe went with him. Said something about helping someone. Since then, nothing. No calls. No texts. No sightings."

Max straightened in his seat, tension tightening across his jaw. "What else do they know?"

"His wife waited two days before reaching out to anyone," Katrina continued. "Now she's filed a missing person report. The police are involved, and his staff is contacting everyone who had recent contact with him."

Her voice dropped, suddenly more cautious. "Today marks 72 hours. And still no sign of him."

Kasandra's voice trembled slightly. "I hope he wasn't taken. Maybe by those foreign agents he mentioned, the ones trying to buy his ideas. If they thought he might change his mind, or if they knew he was close to publishing..."

Max stood up, heart pounding now.

"Right, Kasandra said. "They might have moved early."

Max stood frozen for a moment, Katrina's words echoing in his head. The heat outside had been brutal all day, and the heavy Florida air wasn't helping him think straight. He felt slightly dazed, but forced himself to focus.

He rubbed the back of his neck. "Maybe ... maybe he's gone off the grid on purpose. A retreat to finish the Manifesto or that science fiction novel. Maybe he needed quiet, no distractions."

He glanced at Katrina. "Did he call his wife? Anyone?"

Katrina shook her head, concern etched across her face. "The assistant said he hasn't called, and he's not answering anyone. His phone just rings out. It's not like him, apparently. She's worried. Really worried."

Max took a slow breath and nodded. "The last time we saw him he was determined to finish his work. We should assume he's just holed up in a hotel or cabin somewhere, working with a friend to finish those final chapters."

"But why wouldn't he have told his wife he was leaving and where he was going?" Max shook his head. "Something's off."

"Still ... they should be able to track his phone. GPS, cell towers, something. Surely the authorities are on it."

"They are, Katrina said. "But no hits yet."

"I'll call Aasha." Max reached for his device. "But we need to tread even more carefully now. We've already disrupted this timeline by being here. If we meddle too much now, we might make things worse."

He looked out the window, the orange glow of evening stretching across the horizon.

"Let's just hope he's safe," he added. "And that whatever he's doing, he's doing it for the right reason."

Max left the room and stepped outside the hotel to make the call. The air was thick. He tapped in the number for the DeWine residence, heart thudding.

"Hello?" Aasha's voice came through, tired, cautious.

"Hi, Aasha. It's Max ... from Tuesday night. We came over for dinner?"

There was a brief pause before her voice softened. "Yes, of course. Max. Hello."

"I just got a call from Joe's assistant," Max said, trying to steady his voice. "She told us he's missing. As you must have figured out at dinner, we care deeply about him. We don't want him to be in any kind of trouble."

He corrected himself quickly. "We're *praying* for his safe return. Truly."

Aasha sighed on the other end of the line. "Thank you, Max. That means a lot."

"Can you tell us anything about that night, after we left?"

There was a long pause before she answered, her voice carrying both affection and concern. "He was so excited to have you all over. Really. He hadn't lit up like that in a long time.

"He kept talking about the conversation, the book, how close he was to finishing. I admit, I don't understand much of his science fiction stuff. I've always left that to him.

"He said you were helping him, giving him ideas, encouragement. He was *super* happy. Like a child again."

Max smiled faintly, even as unease twisted in his gut.

"After you left," Aasha said, "one of his oldest friends stopped by. They chatted outside for a few minutes, then both got into their cars. Joe took the van. And his friend, who I think is a doctor, maybe a surgeon, drove ahead in an SUV."

"Did he tell you where he was going?" Max asked.

"No. He came back in, briefly," she added, her voice catching a little. "He hugged me and the kids. One by one. Big, warm hugs. Like he was sealing something in."

She went quiet for a beat, then added, "His last words were, *I'll be a little late, so don't worry. You guys go ahead and sleep tight. And don't let the bed bugs bite. Everything is going to be alright.*"

"He was … different that evening. Still cheerful, still making up little poems for the kids like he always did, but there was something underneath it. A heaviness. He didn't come back that night. And by the next morning, I started calling around."

She paused, as if reliving every unanswered ring.

"I called his number again and again. No response. Straight to voicemail. Nothing."

Max listened silently, letting her speak.

"Two days later, I finally called the police," she said. "But they told me to wait. Said people go missing for a day or two all the time. Sometimes they drink too much or get something spiked and end up sick or sleeping it off somewhere.

"Then they asked me, 'Does your husband do drugs?'"

She scoffed faintly.

"I told them, no. Joe's clean. Always has been. But his friends? I can't say for sure. It's just not like him to vanish. He always comes home, even if it's late after the gym. But now it's been more than three days, and I know something isn't right."

Max gave a neutral reply. "Yes, this is very unusual. And we're praying for his safe return."

Aasha's voice wavered. "That's all I want. Just … my husband back. For our kids to have their father. That's it."

Max felt the concerns in her words equally.

"We're with you, and for the kids. All of us. Hopefully by tomorrow, we'll hear some good news."

He paused, then added softly, "Goodnight, Mrs. DeWine."

"Goodnight, Max."

As the call ended, Aasha sat quietly with the phone still in her hand, staring into the dim kitchen. Something about the conversation didn't sit right with her.

"Mrs. DeWine."

No one had called her that in years. Not even Joe's colleagues or clients. Everyone just called her *Aasha*, casual, warm, familiar. But Max's tone had felt ... different. Formal. Distant. Like he was reading from a script. Or hiding something.

She frowned, suddenly uneasy.

They had only met once, at dinner. And sure, they seemed nice enough, thoughtful, even concerned. But now, with Joe gone and no trace of him, their overly polite manner and strange way of speaking felt ... *off.* Almost foreign. Not in accent, but in rhythm, behavior, presence. They didn't quite fit in.

She blamed herself for not being fully present that dinner night when Max and his friends visited Joe.

She vaguely recalled overhearing something—voices pressing Joe about publishing... almost insisting he do something. The tone had seemed forceful. Unsettling.

Maybe they didn't like Joe. Maybe they did something to him.

And now this follow-up call—was it just for show? A way to appear friendly? To mask something deeper?

She couldn't shake the feeling.

She wished she'd been there. Truly *there.*

To hear everything. To see what they weren't saying.

Joe's behavior that night replayed in her mind, how thrilled he'd been, how animated. Then how anxious he became the moment his "doctor friend" arrived. He hadn't explained much. Just left, hugging them all like he was sealing a memory.

Now, three days later, he was missing. No calls. No van. No trace.

Aasha's instincts kicked in. She had ignored the twinges of worry before, giving Joe the space he seemed to need. But something was shifting. These people who had shown up, who talked about ideas and Manifestos and time like it was currency, they suddenly felt too mysterious. Too carefully vague.

Concerned friends? Maybe.

Something else? She couldn't say.

But one thing was clear: if Joe wasn't home by tomorrow, she would call the police again, and this time, she'd share *everything* she knew. Every name, every conversation, every strange moment from that evening.

She owed Joe that much.

And she owed it to herself, and their children, not to be naïve.

* * * * * * *

07:30 | 11-19-2025 (Twenty-first century)
LOCATION: RESIDENCE INN - BASE ROOM 402

It was seven-thirty Wednesday morning. The air was thick with Florida humidity, the sky a dull gray canvas threatening rain.

Max stood by the window, sipping lukewarm coffee, trying to shake off a restless night filled with tangled thoughts, fractured timelines, a disappearing author, and the fragile thread tying it all together.

Joshua DeWine remained an enigma. He was meant to be the author of their reality; someone they were here to guide and inspire. Yet, he was slipping through their fingers, becoming increasingly elusive.

With Central Command now silent and no new directives coming through, Max felt unmoored. Strategy had given way to waiting. And now, all he could do was trust that clarity would come. Eventually.

A knock at the door broke the quiet. Max opened it, coffee still in hand.

Katrina stepped in, holding her tablet. Her expression was unusually grim.

"Max," she said, voice low and urgent, "I've been tracking local police chatter, CB radio, open scanners, underground news feeds."

He turned toward her, instantly alert.

"They found a van," she continued. "Registered to Mr. DeWine."

Max froze.

Katrina glanced down at her screen. "It was spotted at the bottom of Lake Cane. A man went there to fish yesterday afternoon and saw what looked like the roof of a submerged vehicle. He reported it. Police came in with a recovery crane this morning."

Now her voice grew heavier.

"Max," she said, "it's Joe's van. The license plate matches."

His heart dropped into his throat. He opened his mouth, but no words came out.

For an instant, all Max could see was that black hole, swallowing everything he knew or cared about. Then he pushed the anxiety into the same mental vault where he'd always locked his fears, sealing it off so it couldn't touch his judgment.

"The van was severely burned," Katrina continued. "From what I've gathered, it may have caught fire either before or as it went into the lake. There are skid marks near the edge of Turkey Lake Road, swirling, chaotic. Could be a loss of control. Or it could've been deliberate."

She swallowed, clearly trying to maintain composure. "The engine likely exploded. A charred body was recovered from the driver's seat. Unrecognizable.

"They're performing an autopsy to confirm identity, but they're already treating it as a likely fatal accident."

Max sucked a breath.

This was not the news he'd expected. Not after holding on to hope all night, convincing himself that Joe was simply off the grid, deep in thought, scribbling down the final words of the *Manifesto*.

He shook his head.

This … this changed everything. The only question remaining was: How long before the whole timeline collapses?

"The local media has been slow to pick it up," Katrina said, "but the story is starting to make the rounds. They've confirmed the van was his. No sign of a second car. No sign of the friend who supposedly led him out that night."

Max pressed his palms to his face, struggling to steady his breathing.

"This can't be the end," he said quietly. "This wasn't supposed to happen."

Katrina stood still beside him, silent. She knew what this meant as well as he did.

The timeline was tearing faster than anyone had predicted. And if the *real* Joshua DeWine had just died in that lake ... then everything, the future, their world, the *Eleven Elements*, was now at risk of being lost forever.

Max kept inhaling deeply, one breath after another, trying to calm the thudding in his chest and slow the spiraling thoughts crowding his mind.

Max blew out a heavy breath, his cheeks puffed like a fish out of water, flung onto dry land, desperate for oxygen, gasping, struggling to survive in a place where the rules had suddenly changed.

He collapsed into the nearest chair and buried his face in his hands. The soft inside of his palms pressed against his eyelids as he rubbed them in slow, pained circles.

The helplessness was nearly paralyzing.

For the first time in his life, even with everything he'd been trained for, everything he'd seen across timelines, he had no idea what to do.

Life isn't a simulation, he thought. *It throws knives, not numbers. And sometimes, they land where it hurts most.*

But before the despair could take over, something in him shifted. He straightened slightly, blinking into the dim morning light from the window. His voice came low, steady, grasping at reason.

"So ... the body," he said. "It's being autopsied. But has anyone confirmed it was Mr. DeWine? Did they *name* the person?"

Katrina looked at him, cautious. "No. Not yet."

"Then we can't assume anything. Not yet. What if it *wasn't* him? What if the van was stolen? Or he *was* taken, kidnapped, and whoever did it tried to torch the vehicle and cover their tracks?"

Katrina nodded slowly, catching his train of thought.

"Maybe Joe escaped. Or maybe ... he knew too much, and someone tried to make it look like an accident. Maybe the body found is of a thief who stole Joe's van, they had an accident where they got flung into the lake and got burnt to death."

Max stood again, steadier now.

"I've seen too many coincidences in this timeline already. But this? This might be a setup. We need to find that doctor friend. The one who picked him up that night. *He* could be the key."

"Because if Joe DeWine is still alive, we still have a future." Max desperately wanted to believe that was true.

"We have to consider every possibility. Because one thing we *do* know is that Mr. Joshua DeWine *did* publish the *Manifesto of the Eleven Elements*. That's a fixed point in the future."

He stopped and looked at Katrina, as if needing her to say it back to him.

"Right?"

She nodded slowly, picking up where he left off. "Maybe the date shifted slightly. Historical memory isn't perfect. Maybe he published a few days later than the archive says. Or maybe the record we have in our time rounded the event. But he *did* publish it."

Max ran a hand through his hair, breathing fast, his mind jumping through timelines like skipping stones. "So that means he can't be dead. *He can't.*

"If he died before completing the Manifesto, the chain of events that led to our world wouldn't exist. *We* wouldn't exist. We'd be ghosts. Echoes. And yet, we're here. Still standing."

He paused, voice tightening. "If that charred body is really Joe DeWine, then this mission is over. And so are we."

A sharp silence followed, broken only by the faint hum of power from the comms panel. Max clenched his jaw, trying to fight off the rising dread crawling up his spine.

Max saw Katrina rise from her seat and glance at him, ready to say something.

He was stunned, mind tangled with unsettling thoughts, and gave her a small, dismissive wave, a silent *just leave me alone.*

Katrina seemed to understand. She turned and walked gracefully through the door, leaving him in solitude.

Max's mind was flooded with "what if" scenarios all crashing in at once. Every possible timeline. Every possible outcome.

This was the moment commanders weren't supposed to have: doubt.

And yet, it was here.

He turned to face the wall, then pivoted back, eyes focused.

No. I need to stay sharp. The team needs direction. We're not done. Not yet.

Max took a long breath and squared his shoulders. He could imagine the eyes of his team, at their next meeting, focused on him: Isam, Bitang, Prisha, Minami, Luke, Danny, and the others, waiting for what came next. *What would he say to them?*

He couldn't let them break.

Not now.

He didn't believe in fate. Or divine intervention. Those concepts had been reduced to historical mythology by the late 2300s, when the world had adopted the One World Religion, a philosophy built on unity, rationalism, and planetary stewardship.

But here, in the raw present, in this chaos of war and climate change and belief...

People *did* still believe.

In fate.

In miracles.

In God.

Today, Max wanted to believe.

In something greater. In destiny. In a divine thread weaving through chaos, guiding them all toward meaning. Somewhere deep in his chest, where logic didn't reach, he was silently praying, *hoping*, that there truly was a God. That the path laid before him was more than random probability.

That he had come here to do more than fulfill a mission, to lay the foundation stone for a future reality.

This world, the twenty-first century, was blind in so many ways. Still tangled in ideas of ownership, power, borders, and ego. They hadn't yet learned what his time took for granted: that life was measured not by what you accumulated, but by what you contributed.

That the only legacy worth leaving was one that uplifted the *whole* of humanity, and Gaia herself.

And yet ... *it started here.* With these stories. These books.

The fiction of Mr. Joshua DeWine, crafted as adventure, wrapped in action, disguised as entertainment, had cracked open something deeper. The novels ignited curiosity, redefined purpose, and soon became a cultural undercurrent. A movement.

Within decades, everything began to change.

Max closed his eyes for a moment, allowing his memory to drift, back to his own time.

The soft hum of solar canopies shading green towers. Streets lined with flowering vines and silent transit lanes. Clean air, clean minds. A people united not by creed or country, but by a shared purpose: to live well, in balance, for the benefit of all life.

That world existed because of this moment. Because of *DeWine*.

Because of this mission.

And Max knew that if he failed now, if Joe truly was gone, that beauty might unravel like a thread pulled loose from time itself.

He opened his eyes, resolve settling in behind them like armor.

No more fear.

No more doubt.

He would find DeWine. Or the truth.

And history as he knew it had to stay intact.

Reaching for the remote, Max let the glow of the TV wash over him. Channel 9's anchor pressed a hand to her earpiece.

This just in… white smoke has risen above the Sistine Chapel. The cardinals have chosen a new pope.

The newly elected pontiff, Pope Leo XIV, is the first from the United States.

The sixty-nine-year-old from Chicago addressed thousands from the balcony of St. Peter's Basilica, and offered a blessing to mankind: "Peace be with you all."

Max muted the screen just as Katrina strode back in with what was surely more bad news.

"Max," she said, eyes on her data pad, her voice colder than steel. "The FBI has taken over the DeWine investigation. They've claimed jurisdiction and seized the body recovered from the van."

Max turned to her sharply. "What does that mean?"

"It means we won't get access to the autopsy report. No verification. No chain of custody."

"They are using new encryption codes and it's hard for me to hack into their updated system. It's as if they know someone's after DeWine, so, they are using some very unique scrambling firewalls.

"Once the Feds are involved," she said, "they'll lock down all information. We'll be completely in the dark."

Max's stomach dropped. A horrific thought hit him like a hammer. *What if the body really is Joe DeWine?*

He didn't say it aloud. He didn't have to.

He knew that if the whole team were here—standing in front of him—they'd see the storm behind his eyes, no matter how hard he tried to hide it.

The tension in the room thickened as the implications sank in.

If DeWine was dead…

If the *Manifesto* was never published…

What would happen to their future? To *everything?*

Max turned to the comms terminal, suddenly desperate to reach someone, anyone, at the Control Room in their time.

He entered the code manually. Pressed the sequence. Waited.

Nothing.

Dead silence. No signal. No static. Just … absence.

Katrina checked her own link. She tried a secondary channel. Still nothing.

Max stepped back, overwhelmed by the intensity of it all. *What if the timeline is collapsing? What if we're stranded here because our future no longer exists?*

For a moment, the thought gutted him.

And in that moment of quiet dread, his mind flicked to Annie.

Her smile.

The warmth of her breath in the late hours of night. The way her fragrant hair would fall gently across his face as she rested on him. Those small, silent signals of a life that was still out there. Or had been.

He closed his eyes, forcing the image to stay with him.

Not as comfort, but as fuel.

This was no longer a mission.

It was survival.

It was resurrection.
It was personal.

CHAPTER -20

12:05 | 11-19-2025 (Twenty-first century)
LOCATION: RESIDENCE INN - BASE ROOM 402

It had taken some time for Max to process the news about DeWine and the FBI and what it all meant to their mission.

Then he called the whole team to the base room. He needed their insights ... more than he dared admit to them.

Max stood motionless, glancing at the dead comms terminal, before he finally managed to speak. His voice cracked slightly before settling into a low, steady tone.

"Looks like we're heading into deeper waters," he said. "We're going to face more obstacles than we prepared for. Without the support we were counting on.

"DeWine is still missing and it's a very real possibility that he is dead. And now the FBI has taken over the case. So, our challenges just became a lot harder."

He turned toward his team. "Let's give it some time. See what unfolds. And if anyone has thoughts, ideas, theories, strategies, I want to hear them."

Bitang was the first officer to respond. "Maybe we wait until the autopsy results come in. That will tell us more than guessing. Until then, we need to consider all possibilities, and be ready for each one."

Max nodded. "Agreed. We can't take action right now anyway. Control Room's dark. Link is broken. That changes the playbook."

He ran a hand over his face. "One thing that *could* have helped is if another unit had been dispatched. Sent back to intercept Joe *before* he left with that so-called friend. Maybe prevent whatever happened to him. But it's too late for that now. We've lost the link. Anyone who could've changed the outcome... they're gone."

His jaw clenched. "I'll be straight with you. I'm starting to think we're no longer in the timeline we came from. This feels like a fracture point. A parallel path.

"In *this* version of reality, Joshua DeWine never publishes the *Manifesto*. In this version … he disappears. Or dies. Either way, the world changes course."

Silence fell again. Heavy. Sober.

Max looked around at his team, all presumably coming to terms with the same possibility: they might be stranded. Trapped in a version of the past where their future never arrives.

But there was no point dwelling on what had already happened.

"Look" he said, "I won't sugarcoat it. We have serious challenges ahead. That's true. But we're not out of moves yet.

"And if the future has diverged … then we'll just have to find a way to bend it back. We will *rewrite history* if we must. We will do whatever it takes to exist."

09:57 | 11-21-2025 (Twenty-first century)
LOCATION: BASE ROOM 402 / HOTEL LOBBY

Two days had passed since the news about DeWine's disappearance. And no word from the man himself, assuming he was still alive.

Kasandra, growing anxious, had called his office again that morning. She returned with the same news: *no updates, no sightings, no message.* Just more silence.

Then, just past ten a.m., Katrina poked her head into Max's room where the rest of the team had gathered.

"Everyone, lobby. Now. It's on the news."

The team huddled in front of the widescreen television mounted above the fireplace. Katrina flipped to the live broadcast, already in progress.

The seal of the City of Orlando filled the screen. Behind the podium stood uniformed officers, their expressions grim. Two suited FBI agents flanked them, silent but present.

A city police spokesperson began, glancing briefly at a document. "On Monday, November 17th, a vehicle was discovered submerged at the bottom of Lake Cane by a local fisherman.

"Our department, with emergency services, recovered the vehicle early the next morning using crane equipment. The front of the van appeared to have suffered significant fire damage.

Initial reports suggest an engine explosion, likely occurring before or during submersion.

He flipped a page. "A body was recovered from the driver's seat. Charred beyond recognition. The vehicle has been identified as belonging to Mr. Joshua DeWine, and the deceased has been positively identified, per the county's coroner."

The camera shifted to another speaker stepping forward, Dr. Gerry White of the Orange County Medical Examiner's Office.

"The deceased was subjected to extreme trauma," the doctor read verbatim from prepared notes in his hands. "Our primary findings conclude that the cause of death was a combination of fourth-degree burns, internal trauma due to explosion impact, inhalation of toxic smoke, and possible drowning due to submersion.

"The fire began near the engine compartment. Evidence suggests the driver attempted to extinguish the fire by driving into the lake."

He paused.

"The victim's body was found belted in the driver's seat. Though most interior components were destroyed, the metal seatbelt buckle remained latched.

"Recovered belongings included a partially burned wallet, ID cards, and credit cards confirmed by family.

"Additionally, we obtained blood and hair samples that matched those collected from Mr. DeWine's residence."

He held up a hand to reinforce his conclusion.

"Furthermore, two dental bridges and several crowns recovered from the mouth of the deceased match the dental records and imprints provided by his dentist. Based on this overwhelming evidence, we confirm the body is that of Mr. Joshua DeWine.

"The remains will now be released to his family."

The doctor stepped back. "Thank you."

The news anchor resumed the broadcast, shifting to a political segment.

"Governor Oldsome of California has filed a lawsuit against President McCrony for sending the National Guard to the state…"

Katrina clicked off the screen. Everyone turned to Max.

He stood still, eyes locked on the blackened screen as if trying to reanimate the pixels and undo what he had just seen.

His hands hung loosely at his sides. He felt hollow. Disconnected.

This wasn't supposed to happen.

He had braced for unknowns, but not *this*.

Then Minami spoke, voice gentle, quiet, but shaking slightly. "So, I guess we have to accept the fact that Mr. DeWine is gone.

"And, for whatever reasons, we didn't see it coming.

"But what's worse is that *our future*, is built around the fact that he *does* publish the Manifesto. We know that. It's history. It's *our* history."

She looked around the open space as if to ensure no one was close enough to overhear. "Everything we've built, from society to science to daily life, all of it flows from that one publication. From those Eleven Elements. From him."

She swallowed, her voice cracking at the edges.

"We live in the world he imagined. Every part of it. From 'soups to nuts,' to use the twenty-first century slang."

Max blinked, but his body hadn't moved. Minami's words barely penetrated the fog that now settled over him.

Standing there in the hotel lobby none of them spoke.

Max felt as if the floor beneath him had cracked. And he imagined the others felt equally unmoored. Maybe afraid, though nobody showed it.

But they would look to him for answers, or at least decisions.

He had hoped, prayed, even, that there'd be a twist, some shred of doubt. But this? This was official. Televised. The kind of news that echoed through time.

His heart thudded in his chest. He looked to his team, all of them frozen.

Bitang's face was pale. Kasandra's hands were clenched at her sides. Prisha stared at the screen, blinking slowly, as if refusing to process what she just heard.

Joshua DeWine is dead.

The Manifesto was never published.

And the future ... may have just collapsed in on itself.

Luke sat down heavily on one of the couches. His voice was low, almost defeated. "Yes, we owe him our lives. We live the way we do because of his visionary foresight.

"We came here to complete a mission. But instead, I guess we'll be attending his funeral.

"And, I hate to be the one to say it, but it feels like we'll be burying the mission along with him."

"We've lost him." Danny' added. "And I feel like we're lost too."

No one responded. There was nothing to say.

One by one, they drifted back to their rooms, exhausted, dazed, and struggling to make sense of what just happened.

Per orders, each team member silently resumed their routine tasks, recording individual logs, mechanically writing into the void.

Alone in the Base Room, Max felt empty, powerless.

The control room link was still down. No updates. No contact. Just the same stifling silence.

He slumped in the recliner, drowning in thoughts from the last ten days. The AC hummed, dull and background now, no longer the loud, foreign noise it had been when they first arrived.

He mentally reviewed the mission status:

Three dead.

Two missing, still trapped somewhere in digital limbo.

The FHP had recovered traces: tissue, hair, Jakir's prosthetic knee. Locked away. Unretrievable.

And then there was Katrina, embedded among them with a hidden AAILF protocol. What was her original purpose before she became acceptable? Still unknown. Still dangerous.

Now, the mission's key target, Joshua DeWine, the man who authored their reality, was gone.

His work, unfinished.

And with that, time itself may shift. A different reality may take hold. One where they no longer exist. One where the future, their future, never happens.

And the Command Center? Silent. As if the current events of this twenty-first century have erased them.

No contact. No support. No idea what comes next.

Gone. As if they've already been erased.

Morale was dead. Hope was circling the drain.

They were supposed to shape the future.

Now, they were stranded in a crumbling present.

A present they were never meant to inhabit.

A present rewritten by absence: DeWine's absence.

A reality with no map, no mission plan, no safety net.

What happens to a team when the reason for their existence is gone?

What do you do when the author of your reality is dead?

Max stared at the dim screen, static flickering across it like a mocking shrug from the universe. The last known signal from Command was now over seventy-two hours old. No retrieval code. No fail-safe. Not even a time-stamp to prove they were still anchored to anything that made sense.

Are we even real anymore?

He didn't say it aloud. But the question clawed at the edge of his mind.

They were off-mission now, pushed off-grid and off-history.

They were stranded in a past that no longer promised a future.

Max couldn't shake the thought that humanity's hope for a utopian future, his own life, and everything he once believed in, now felt like a dream dissolving in the twilight.

They were trained for adversity.

They were never trained for a total erasure.

CHAPTER -21

13:18 | 11-21-2025 (Twenty-first century)
LOCATION: RESIDENCE INN - BASE ROOM 402

Max had just returned from a fierce, cathartic workout in the hotel's gym, when he heard the notification sound on his yPhone.

New Message Received.

A formal notification. An invitation.

"Final Rites for Mr. Joshua DeWine."

An invite. The kind that made it all real.

Sent by his assistant, the message included the cremation details, the time and location of the memorial service. Plus, a modest obituary blurb: his age, his published works, and the names of his surviving family. Aasha. The children.

There was also a photo. Joe's face, smiling with that calm, scruffy warmth.

The same photo they had seen at the back of the *Manifesto*, framed by the glow of a restaurant's wooden beams that had, unintentionally, formed a halo above his head.

Max recalled his smiling face, the same gentle, hopeful grin they remembered from dinner just a few nights ago.

The obituary listed his accomplishments: All his award-winning projects and what he did as community service.

But nothing about the most significant accomplishment of his lifetime. No mention about his visions to empower the world and enrich the lives of common men for centuries to come.

Max stared at the screen.

He could still hear Joe's laughter echoing across the dinner table. He could still see Aasha smiling, warm and proud, dishing out food for the guests. The time when Joshua DeWine had invited Max and his team to a supper at his residence just few days ago.

Their last supper.

The first Messiah had twelve at his table; Joe had ten Time-Travelers, five in the room, five on screens attending remotely, ready to carry his message forward and build a heaven on earth. And now he was gone.

Max remembered the way Aasha said Joe had hugged his kids before leaving that night. It had felt like a goodbye, she'd said. *Was that his final farewell?*

Everything felt surreal to Max. Like he was stuck in someone else's dream. One of *his* dreams, maybe. The kind where Annie would nudge him awake, hair spilling across his face, whispering, "Hey. Max. Wake up."

But this time, no one was waking him up.

This time, it was real.

The Florida heat hadn't let up either, dense and oppressive, sapping their energy as much as their hope. Max wanted nothing more than to be back in the calm, clean air of the twenty-sixth century. Away from this chaos. Away from this loss.

He longed for home.

For Annie.

For certainty.

He closed his eyes for a long breath, then another. His training kicked in. The layers of emotion compacted. Controlled. Set aside. Just enough.

Max forwarded the message to his entire team.

He messaged everyone to meet immediately, there in Room 402.

When they had assembled, he took a breath and began the briefing "Everyone," he said, his voice calm, composed. "We'll be attending the funeral day after tomorrow."

He scanned their faces one by one.

"I know the FBI will be there. They've already traced us to Dupray's office. They were watching when we met DeWine. So, dress appropriately, both for the time period and for the solemnity of the occasion. Some of us will be in disguise in hopes of gaining more information, but all our actions must be taken with utmost decorum."

He turned to Minami. "Please arrange to pick up flowers. Something simple. Elegant."

He paused, then added quietly, "Some of you may not know… Joshua DeWine was born *Jaiswal Diwanji*. He changed his name after becoming a U.S. citizen. The invitation lists both names. His final rites will be conducted according to Hindu traditions. Cremation. Closed casket, for obvious reasons."

A hush fell over the room.

Max drew in a breath, anchoring himself.

"Tomorrow, we honor him, as the visionary who shaped our world, as a father, a husband, a man who never stopped believing in a better world."

Later that evening, Katrina found Max in the hallway. "We got a preliminary report," she said. "It looks like the fire was caused by damage under the hood. The harness, carrying fuel and electric cables, was chewed through. Critters. Rodents maybe. Could've caused a short. Sparked the fire."

Max's brow tightened. "Critters?"

"Yes. But I'm not convinced they were natural. There's something strange about the chew marks. And how precisely they hit the harness hub. How did they know how to get in under the hood and which lines to bite off? It's all very fishy, like how they say in the twenty-first."

Max's eyes narrowed. "You think it could've been sabotage?"

Katrina nodded once. "Possibly."

Max turned, his mind racing.

Could these have been be AAILFs? Sent from the future? Or critters send by the uBots?

If so, he realized, this wasn't an accident at all. It was a message. Or worse: a murder.

Who would want to foil their mission?

He didn't voice the rest. Not yet. Not until he had more proof. For now, the focus had to be on the funeral.

16:31 | 11-22-2025 (Twenty-first century)
LOCATION: WOODLAWN MEMORIAL PARK, FLORIDA

In the elegant crematorium chapel at Woodlawn Memorial Park, under the soft gray of a somber sky, the cremation ceremony for Joshua DeWine was underway.

The Florida air was still. Filled with hushed conversation, words of condolence and remembrance.

Friends. Colleagues. Family. Strangers whose lives Joshua, Joe, had touched in small, profound ways, all gathered, their faces drawn by grief and disbelief.

At the center, a closed casket lay draped in white linen and scattered marigolds, symbols of purity, departure, and peace. It rested on rails before the crematory chamber. When the rituals and announcements were complete, the casket would slide inside. At the press of a button, the chamber would ignite, visible through the side windows.

A Hindu priest, in formal attire, began the rites, chanting, sprinkling water, and letting flower petals fall over the casket. Aasha stood beside it, her body trembling as silent sobs shook her frame. Her children clung to her. The older one, barely nine, understood enough to cry. The younger simply looked around, confused, sensing sadness but not yet knowing death.

One by one, mourners filed past the casket, laying single flowers, roses, lilies, carnations, across its surface.

A ritual of closure. A gesture of love.

Two of Joe's relatives stepped to a podium adorned with fresh white lilies, beside the closed casket, in the high, coved-ceiling room filled with about two hundred people.

They recalled how he'd been a quiet but powerful force in many lives. "He helped everyone. Never said no. Never expected anything in return," one of them said, holding back tears.

"A designer-builder not just of structures, but of people's hopes."

Members of the Orange County Building Department and City of Orlando staff, some in crisp shirts, others still in utility boots, nodded quietly. Joe had worked closely with them, always patient, always respectful.

Then, his assistant, Nicole Monroe, stepped to the podium. She looked pale but steady, holding a folded sheet of paper in her hand. A projector lit up behind her, casting images across the screen: Joe in his workshop, Joe with his kids, Joe at community meetings, Joe laughing at a cookout.

Nicole took a breath and began. "Good morning, ladies and gentlemen.

"Joshua DeWine, born Jaiswal Diwanji, was not just a man of ideas, he was a man of action and deep conviction. He believed that imagination wasn't fantasy, but the first stage of reality.

"He said once, 'If you can dream a better world and write it down, you're already halfway to building it.'

"His work, his life, his mission, it all stemmed from a desire to leave behind something greater than himself."

Very somberly, Nicole continued, "We gather here today not merely to mourn a loss, but to celebrate a life so luminous, so extraordinary, that calling it anything short of divine feels like a disservice.

"They say when angels walk among us, we rarely recognize them until they're gone. Well, today, I think we all understand that we didn't only lose a loved one. We lost something sacred, a force of love, a voice of reason, a heart that seemed to beat for everyone in its orbit, not just itself.

"My name is Nicole Monroe, and for five years I had the privilege of serving as the assistant to Mr. Joshua DeWine. 'Joe,' to everyone lucky enough to know him.

"I worked beside him on buildings, on bold ideas, and on the quiet, personal projects that made his vision feel less like work and more like destiny.

"People say you shouldn't worship your boss. And I didn't. I simply loved Joe as my superior and friend. He was my role model.

"I loved him so much that I dreaded weekends, not because I loved work too much, but because Saturdays and Sundays meant two whole days without Joe's mischievous smile or the sound of him turning a hallway into a comedy club. When he called on a Saturday to ask if I could help him catch up, I said yes before he finished the sentence. His joy made even overtime feel like a holiday.

"Joe's humor went beyond fluff. It was revelation. He gave us punchlines that became principles. Once, he stood before our team and said, with a perfectly straight face: *I'm going to confess something. I'm a RACIST.'* We froze, dumbfounded. Especially when there were guests, Black, white, it didn't matter. Then he grinned and clarified: *I'm a HUMAN RACIST. I stand up for the human race, and for every living thing that makes our life possible. I don't think anyone else has the real guts to stand up to say and do that. Is there anyone?'*

"In one breath, the joke set a precedent for human behavior. That was Joe, laughter first, wisdom next, courage always.

"He refused band-aid solutions. He wanted cures: peace engineered to last centuries instead of temporary patches on wars.

"He imagined nations united as one Federation, borderless, purposeful, working together to restore Earth's balance so that all could live freely, simply, and without harm.

"He called his blueprint *The Manifesto of Eleven Elements*, part field guide, part love letter, part owner's manual for humanity's future.

"Joe used to say, *'Design as if Earth is your client, and every child yet unborn is your stakeholder.'* Then, *'Be useful before you're brilliant.'*

"And my favorite, spoken on a rainy Tuesday when we were all grumbling: *'God made this rain to water your stubborn hope.'* After that, our umbrellas felt lighter.

"He isn't simply someone you remember; he's someone you never forget. When he entered a room, he illuminated it, like sunlight sneaking through a window to whisper, *'Hey, it's going to be a good day.'*

"At work, he taught us how to draw buildings. In life, he taught us how to draw closer … to one another, to truth, to the better angels of our nature.

"He was serious about joy. Disciplined about kindness. Relentless about dignity. If angels wear hard hats and carry red pens, then yes, Joe was an angel.

"And if you've ever wondered what the Second Coming of compassion might look like, it looked a lot like Joe showing up early with coffee and staying late to make sure no one carried their burdens alone.

"We live in a world that often feels like it's standing on a cliff's edge. Joe saw the ledge, but he also saw the bridge.

He didn't believe in saving face. He believed in saving futures. *The Eleven Elements* were his tools, for turning petty wars into lasting peace, for giving our grandchildren a planet that feels like home.

"I will miss a thousand small things: the way he drew a star in the margin when an idea mattered. The way his laughter arrived a second before the punchline. The way the office smelled like coffee, graphite, and hope. I will miss the calls that began with,

'*Are you busy?*' and ended two hours later with a checklist and a pep talk.

"But grief is not the end of Joe's story. We carry him in the only place a soul can travel without a passport: our daily choices. He had lines, oh, did he have lines:

• *Practice a kindness you can measure.*

• *Tell the truth without losing tenderness.*

• *Make peace your operating system, not your afterthought.*

• *Work like Earth is your client, and tip generously for the future you'll never see.*

• *When despair gets loud, answer it with stubborn hope.*

• *If you're going to mess up, do it gloriously, give them fireworks, not apologies.*

• *And the classic,* he'd add with a grin at weddings he was absolutely not officiating: '*I'm saving myself for the Second Coming. If He's running late, I might volunteer.*'

"Only Joe could make reverence and humor hold hands.

"Joe's manuscripts remain. His vision remains. And we, his colleagues, his friends, his family, remain. We will finish what he started. We will bring *Eleven Elements* to light. We will make his audacious love useful.

"If love is the measure of a life, Joe's life overflowed the beaker. Today we mourn the loss of a brilliant mind and a radiant heart.

"But hearts like his don't vanish, they multiply. Look around you. His legacy is sitting in your chair. It's beating in your chest. It will walk out of here with your feet. We are his living eulogy.

"May flights of angels sing him to his rest. And in Joe's own words: '*Text us when you get home.*'

"Until then, we'll keep the lights on. We'll keep the work going. We'll keep the hope stubborn.

"Thank you, Joe, for the laughter, the courage, and the map.

"And thank you, all of you, for loving him with us."

Nicole stepped down slowly as the final images on the screen faded into a simple photo of Joe smiling, scruffy beard, tired eyes, hopeful expression. The same image that adorned the obituary invite.

Max sat still, hands folded, beside his teammates. The low hum of a ceremonial chant echoed from the front as incense curled gently into the air.

Katrina was beside him, her posture modest, expression veiled, quite literally, beneath the soft folds of her Indian Punjabi salwar dupatta.

A red bindi was carefully dotted on her forehead. Her blonde hair was concealed under a convincing black wig braided neatly down her shoulder.

To their left and right, other mourners sat quietly. Friends, coworkers, family. In grief, everyone looked inward, and that made blending in easier.

Max had opted for a Sikh identity. His usual short-cropped hair and clean-shaven face transformed with a black turban, beard, and subtle brown-skin prosthetics and makeup.

He looked nothing like the Max of their former timeline.

On the funeral registry, Max had signed himself and Katrina as Mr. Boopinder Singh and Mrs. Kavita Singh. Together, they passed as a perfectly ordinary Punjabi Sikh couple, blending in seamlessly with the other Indian friends and family of Jaiswal Diwanji or Joe DeWine.

Two rows ahead of him, Prisha and Luke had done the same. They were dressed in carefully curated traditional Indian attire. Prisha in a vivid teal saree with a black-and-gray trim, and Luke with thick-rimmed glasses and a kurta-pajama ensemble that drew zero attention in this setting.

The plan was working. At least for now.

As Max surveyed the room casually, the way any mourner would do, looking for relatives to console, he spotted FBI agents in plain clothes.

They were pretending to be guests, blending in the with attendees, in a similar manner as Max and crew had been, with the exception of any disguise.

But they were there, unmistakable. Two by the entrance. One near the AV equipment. Another beside the refreshments table. Their eyes swept the room methodically, apparently pausing slightly longer on anyone looking peculiar.

Max's heart rate picked up, but his breathing stayed measured. His training kicked in.

Don't react. Stay in character.

The cover identities were solid. Their appearance, movements, and language patterns had been thoroughly rehearsed. The Singhs were just another couple paying respects to a respected man in their community.

In a crowd filled with extended family and professional acquaintances, no one would dare ask, "How did you know him?"

Not here. Not today.

That anonymity, born of grief and the quiet etiquette of funerals, was their cloak.

Still, the presence of the FBI suggested that DeWine's death wasn't being written off as accidental.

Maybe there were whispers of foul play. Maybe someone suspected the truth. Or maybe they were looking for something, or someone, that Joe had mentioned before he vanished.

Katrina leaned toward Max slightly and whispered softly sounding like a Punjabi woman, barely audible.

Ehji, See the situation here. We must go soon Okay-ji?

Max nodded gently without turning. Eyes forward. Composure intact.

As the final prayers were said and the family stood to approach the casket for the last time, Max spoke under his breath: "Wait for the procession to shift to the cremation hall. Then we move."

They'd known the FBI would show up. The DeWine family had already been briefed that foul play was suspected in Joe's death.

The agents blended in just enough to not alarm the crowd, but their attire was unmistakable: black dress pants, white shirts, and earpieces so discreet they almost disappeared into their hair. It was the "formal respect" look that also allowed for movement and access if needed.

In contrast, nearly everyone of Indian origin attending the funeral wore traditional white, the color of mourning.

Flowing kurtas, white saris, and crisp Punjabi suits painted a sea of subdued solemnity. Even in grief, there was tradition.

Aasha wore a simple white chiffon sari, widow's attire in its most unadorned form. Large dark sunglasses shielded her swollen, tear-worn eyes, but not her body language. It was clear to Max that she was broken, hollow, barely able to stand.

Max and his team remained hidden in plain sight, dressed to match the Indian mourning customs.

But one person stood out, not because he didn't belong, but because he chose not to hide.

In the middle of the aisle, a Black gentleman sat tall in his chair, sporting thick, round soda-bottle glasses and long, dreadlocked hair neatly braided, each braid adorned with black and white beads.

His beard, streaked with grey, was tied in a tight coil beneath his chin. A striped woven headwrap in Rastafarian colors rested atop his crown, matching his flowing white ceremonial gown: traditional Jamaican Rastafarian mourning attire.

He didn't speak. Just watched. Listened. Observed.

Some of Joe's staff gave him quiet nods of recognition. He was clearly a familiar face.

As Max had learned by eavesdropping on a nearby conversation, this man was the owner of *The Daily Puff*, a legal smoke shop Joe had designed and helped launch.

Joe wasn't just his architect. He'd been a mentor, a guiding hand, someone who believed in small people with big dreams.

The man sat alone, stoic but respectful, occasionally tapping his chest gently in silent tribute during the chanting.

The Hindu priest's Sanskrit mantras filled the air, incense smoke winding around the mourners. People filed by the closed casket, placing flower petals and whispering farewells.

The agents' eyes scanned the room as if trying to decode the deeper story behind every face.

Max noticed. And so did the Rastafarian.

As the service drew to a close, mourners filtered past the grieving family, offering quiet condolences. Some bowed with folded hands in a gentle Namaste, while others gave brief handshakes or hushed blessings.

Aasha stood motionless, while her older child clutched her leg. Her face was veiled in silent strength.

Nicole, Joe's assistant, stood close beside her, steady and composed, holding the younger child, acting as both friend and emotional anchor.

Max, as Mr. Boopinder Singh, joined the flow of mourners, with Katrina at his side.

He moved with deliberate grace, head bowed, arms folded. When he reached Aasha, he offered a low nod of respect and placed a flower on the casket.

As the crowd thinned and people began heading to their cars, Max circled back toward Nicole, quietly, carefully, and handed her a card.

In a thick, carefully affected Indian accent to sell his Sikh disguise, he said,

"Hell-ohji, I am Boopinder Singh. Or you can call me BP. I knew Joe from long time, and he shared with me some articles ... very interesting writings. If you are cataloguing his work, maybe you would want them. Just call me on the number, please."

Max gave a polite nod and turned, melting into the line of other mourners leaving the funeral home, as inconspicuous as one cloud in a sky full of white.

Later, as the team were on their way back in their now-camouflaged SUV, disguised as a Lexis 450, Prisha couldn't hold back any longer.

"What was that about?" she asked, eyes fixed on Max from the passenger seat. "Why did you talk to Nicole like that? You risked giving us away. What if ...?"

Max raised a hand gently, silencing her. "Did you not listen to Nicole's eulogy?

"There was our solution. Hidden right there, in plain sight. It was as if Joshua DeWine was speaking to me from the coffin. Like a message from the holy ghost himself."

Prisha's brow furrowed.

Max continued, "When she said, and I quote, 'Joe's manuscripts remain. His vision remains. And we, his colleagues, his friends, his family, remain. We will finish what he started. We will bring *Eleven Elements* to light. We will make his audacious love useful.' That hit me like lightning.

"That's when I realized: why not publish the *Eleven Elements* under Joshua DeWine's name, posthumously?

"He's gone. There's no way to bring him back. But his work, his words, they live.

"What better way to honor his legacy? What better way to secure our mission, protect the timeline... and give the future a fighting chance?"

He paused. "We have to reach out to Nicole as soon as possible. And we offer to help get the book out. Not as a commercial product, but under a not-for-profit foundation. The

Eleven Elements Foundation, dedicated to DeWine's vision and benefiting his family.

"It's our best shot. Maybe our only shot."

Prisha said nothing for a moment, but Max could feel her tension start to loosen. She looked away, then nodded slowly, the gears turning in her mind. "We do it quietly," she said at last. "And carefully."

Max smiled faintly. "Like ghosts."

CHAPTER -22

10:35 | 11-23-<u>2025 (Twenty-first century)</u>
LOCATION: PANERA SOUTH DOWNTOWN ORLANDO.

The day after the service, DeWine's assistant, Nicole called the number Max/Singh had given her.

They agreed to meet at a quiet restaurant not far from DeWine's office.

When Max arrived, still disguised as BP Singh with his turban and beard, Katrina beside him as Mrs. Kavita Singh, he spotted Nicole in a booth in the corner, away from the lunch rush.

He extended his hand gently. Nicole shook it, her eyes searching his face for familiarity.

This is my wife, Kavita." He introduced Katrina, also in character.

They sat across from Nicole.

"We really appreciated your words at the funeral," Max said with warmth, still holding the accent. "Joe was very close to us. A brilliant man. We grieve with you."

Beside him, Katrina just smiled and nodded.

Max pulled a USB drive from his pocket and slid it across the table.

"These are some articles he wrote as a young architect, drafts, some designs. But also, his early thoughts on environmental harmony. He shared them with me once. Maybe they belong in the collection of his legacy."

Nicole took the drive, holding it as if it were a relic. Her words caught in her throat when she replied. "Thank you, Mr. Singh.

"I meant it when I said Joe was a Godly man. He walked like he was lit from within. He truly believed he could save the planet, not in theory, but in practice. He believed his words could wake people up. And I think they still can."

She looked up, as if half-expecting Joe to walk in through the door. "I don't think he's gone," she whispered. "Not entirely.

"The main reason Joe hired me," Nicole's voice low but steady, "was to help edit and compile his written works for publication.

"He was collaborating with researchers and scholars from universities all over. Making sure that everything he imagined was both visionary and practical... totally possible, even flawless."

She paused, her eyes scanning the quiet room.

"We were building something together. An anthology. Seven volumes.

"Each one focused on a different element ... a total of eleven elements necessary for humanity to do more than survive. To thrive. To evolve into something more. Just ... more aware, more whole."

There was a tremor in her voice, "And now ... it's unfinished. Unpublished. He didn't get the chance to complete it.

"But I know, I *know*, he had answers the world still needs. He was more than a writer. He was an angel of perpetual peace and prosperity.

She smiled softly through the sadness. "I used to tease him, you know. I once said, 'Joe, your ideas are worthy of a Nobel Peace Prize.' He just smiled and said, 'Do you think I care?'"

A laugh came from a booth somewhere beyond them.

"But *we* care, Nicole," Max/Singh said. "We care about him. And we care about this world."

He turned to Katrina beside him. "Kavita and I had an idea. A powerful one.

"We want to help publish Joe's work. Posthumously. We want to finish what he started. Preserve his voice, his vision. Share it with the world, just as he would've wanted, even if he never said it out loud.

"As you said: Joe gave us the blueprint. Now it's our responsibility to build what he envisioned.

"Give him all the credit," Max said firmly. "Just get it out there. Let the people see it. Let them *feel* it. They'll decipher the truth for themselves. And they'll follow his path, the one he envisioned, to a new reality."

Nicole looked at him, brow furrowed, her head cocked to one side, curious.

Is she figuring out who I am? Where she knows me from?

She hesitated for a moment, then spoke softly. "I'm not really supposed to tell anyone this, but if you're serious about publishing Joe's work, then you should know something.

"His first book, *The Eleven Elements: Healing Waters,* was sent to his friend, Mr. John-Peter Bardot. He's the Dean of the College of Engineering at Miami University."

She glanced from Max to Katrina and back, as if gauging their reactions.

"I also know about some of the other chapters. Where they might've gone.

"The problem is that Joe was extremely private. He didn't lay all his cards on the table. A lot of it is scattered, like pieces of a puzzle. Some of his thoughts and manuscripts were deliberately fragmented. We'll have to track them down, gather the parts, and reassemble the full vision."

Nicole sighed, but there was a flicker of determination in her eyes now. "What I *do* know is that most of his work *is* complete. Or very close to it.

"He entrusted chapters and notes to professors, researchers, and professionals across different universities.

"Some of it may be hiding in plain sight, inside academic research, disguised as white papers, maybe even as technical design proposals."

She lowered her voice, her tone more confidential. "And from time to time, he worked with freelance editors he found on a site called Sixerrs. Global contributors, working on small sections, often without knowing the full picture."

Max nodded, absorbing every word. "Then that's our mission," he said. "We track down every fragment. We connect the dots. We reconstruct Joe's vision. And we make sure the world hears it."

"That would be wonderful," Nicole said.

"Joe had this brilliant way of breaking down complex ideas. He took this massive vision, one that spanned disciplines, philosophies, and cultures, and broke it into small, digestible essays. He invited experts from around the world to contribute."

"And what was your role in all this?" Max asked.

"My job was to compile and edit those pieces into the narrative he wanted. Into the form he saw: the story of how humanity could save itself."

"Not an easy task," Kavita/Katrina said with an empathetic softness.

Nicole looked down for a moment, then met Katrina's gaze. Then Max's. "But it was incredibly rewarding. I feel honored to have had the privilege of working with Joe.

Then she seemed to focus suddenly, all business now. "Okay. If we're going to do this, first we'll need to assemble all the pieces.

"Some of that work, some of those files, are still on my laptop at home. I can email you a download link.

"But I need your word, *your solemn promise*, that all credit will go to Joe. I mean Mr. Joshua DeWine. No one else. His voice must be the only one that speaks through the work. That matters to me more than anything."

Max/Singh reassured Nicole. This time, his voice carried the warmth and sincerity of his roots.

"*Beta*, we understand," he said, using the affectionate Hindi word for *daughter*. "Kavita and I, we're fortunate. We're well-off, and we don't want a penny from this. This is *not* a commercial venture. It's a philanthropic mission."

He reached across the table and took her hands.

"We will establish a non-profit. All proceeds will go to supporting further research, translations, educational programs. Always in alignment with Joe's original intent. Not one word will be altered. Not one idea will be diluted."

He paused, exchanged a glance with Katrina/Kavita, then offered something more. "And Nicole ... we'd be honored if *you* would lead this with us.

"We want you to be one of the founding directors of the *Eleven Elements Organization*. You've been closest to his work. You understand his heart. This mission, it's yours as much as it is his."

Nicole blinked, clearly moved. She looked at Katrina as if for confirmation. Katrina/Kavita nodded and smiled.

"Thank you," Nicole said. "For the first time since Joe's passing, I feel a sense of calm inside me. Your kind and generous offer means more to me than you can imagine."

She released a deep breath. "It feels like you're giving me *purpose*. Continuity. A way to carry forward the legacy I had poured myself into when working with Joe.

"Nothing would make me happier than seeing Joe's writings finally reach the world."

She paused for a moment. "If you don't mind, I'd also appreciate a written offer. Something that outlines my role, responsibilities. Just so I can be clear on what's expected."

"Of course, Max said. "You'll serve as one of the directors of the *Eleven Elements Organization*.

"The others will be Mr. Maxion Renner and Ms. Prisha Jiwan. You'll meet them soon: once you've accepted the position and shared the materials you already have."

Max offered a reassuring smile. "I'll have my secretary send you the formal offer by the end of the day. Will that work for you?"

Nicole nodded and smiled. "Yes. That works."

Later that day, Nicole received an email from someone named Jenna, signed as Assistant to Director B.P. Singh of the Eleven Elements Organization, a not-for-profit corporation.

The tagline read: *Furthering the cause of Planet Earth and Humanity. Marching towards a sustainable reality.*

It sounded sincere and perfectly aligned with the mission Joe had dedicated himself to.

Feeling an immediate sense of trust and resonance, Nicole knew that both Joe and this organization shared similar values and vision.

That very evening, before heading to bed, she submitted all her paperwork online and confirmed her appointment to meet the other two directors tomorrow morning at their satellite office near the Millenia Mall.

CHAPTER -23

09:05 | 11-24-2025 (Twenty-first century)
LOCATION: DOWNTOWN ORLANDO Executive Suites.

The executive center's conference room was tastefully appointed, featuring a birch-colored conference table and sleek white chairs.

Upon arrival, Nicole was warmly greeted by the receptionist and asked to wait until the others arrived. She was offered a bottle of water. A small gesture, but one that gave her pause. For an organization focused on environmental sustainability, single-use plastic seemed out of place.

Still, she accepted it and took a few polite sips while waiting for Maxion Renner and Prisha Jiwan to arrive.

A few moments later, which almost felt like an eternity, the two directors entered the room, both smiling warmly and exuding a genuine sense of excitement to meet her.

"I'm Max Renner," the man said and shook her hand. "Nice to meet you finally."

"Prisha Jiwan." The woman shook her hand as well, then gestured for them all to sit.

"So," Prisha said, "BP told us that you had been working closely with Joe before…" She paused a moment.

"We are truly saddened that he is no longer with us. And we are sorry for your loss. We understand you and Joe were close colleagues."

"Friends," Nicole clarified, choking back tears.

"Of course, Prisha said. "We want you to know we're both deeply committed to supporting BP in carrying forward the work that Mr. Joshua DeWine had started."

Max nodded. "We understand that Mr. DeWine had been preparing to publish his work. We've seen some preliminary notes, and what we've read is incredibly compelling.

"Once it's published, we believe Joe will be recognized as one of the visionary pioneers of our time. His thinking about how human society could survive and thrive amid environmental collapse was nothing short of revolutionary.

"Please, if you don't mind, tell us a little more about Joe. And let's talk about how we can begin this project."

Nicole let out a soft sigh. "I do know for a fact that Joe had completed Book One: *Healing Waters* and had sent it to a professor in Miami.

"The professor was supposed to review it, provide feedback, and return a redlined copy with technical and editorial suggestions. That's where things were left off before ... well, before everything changed."

That familiar gut punch of reality hit her again.

"Joe was very picky about his words. A perfectionist. He wanted a perfect book published so that people would want to share it with others. An instant hit that resonated with everyone.

"He was determined that all seven books in the *Eleven Elements* series would be completed and read across the globe.

"He believed they had the potential to change humanity's perception of life, and what it truly means to live in the future."

Max looked her in the eye, voice low and steady. "Yes dear, can you tell us the name of this professor in Miami and how we might get in touch with him?"

He got a funny, inward look on his face for a fleeting moment, then seemed to shake it off.

Max's manner exuded gratitude and a kindness that bordered on reverence. There was a softness in his voice, a quiet appreciation in the way he addressed her. His eyes conveyed what his words could not.

Nicole blinked and looked at him more closely. There was something about Max, a familiarity she couldn't explain. His presence stirred something deep within her. It felt like déjà vu.

She studied both Max and Prisha, but it was Max who drew her in. She didn't know why, but his presence felt warm, magnetic. She felt safe, understood, even adored.

It felt like the beginning of something more. Like a first date with someone who already knew her soul.

Maybe there was a kind of *promise* in this meeting, beyond merely continuing the work of her friend and colleague, Joshua DeWine.

Maybe she had been *destined* to meet Max.

Hopefully he's single. And Prisha is just a work colleague. After all, they had different last names, and he wasn't wearing a ring.

Finally, she replied to Max's question. "The professor. Yes. That's Dr. John Peter Bardot, Dean of the College of Engineering at Miami University.

"Or rather, I should say, former Dean. He's no longer with UM. I actually have all his contact details, email, phone number, right here on my phone."

As she scrolled through her phone, Max tilted his head slightly, voice laced with anticipation. "Can we call him? Like now? Just to see what he says?"

"Sure," Nicole nodded, a little disarmed by Max's closeness, however brief.

She put the phone on speaker. After a couple of rings, the call connected.

"Hello Nicole, how are you? Long time no hear," came the warm voice from the other end.

"Hey, Dr. Bardot. I've been super busy lately. We were wondering if you had a chance to read Book One of *Eleven Elements* that I sent you a few weeks ago. I'm here with a few of Joe's friends, and they wanted to talk to you about it."

"Sure," Bardot replied.

Max stepped in, his tone calm yet assertive. "Hello Mr. Bardot, my name is Max, and I'm with the Eleven Elements Foundation.

"We're currently organizing Joe's work for publication. I'm part of the foundation's publication and marketing team, specifically responsible for gathering information to help promote his work. When might we be able to meet with you?"

"Of course. Always happy to help Joe with his work. Let me see," Bardot replied. "How about first thing in the morning, say 9 a.m., at my place? My home office is in Coral Gables. What part of Miami are you in?"

Max replied, "We're not in Miami. We're actually calling from Orlando, Florida. But we can drive down this afternoon and meet you tomorrow at nine., if that works for you?"

"I'll see you then," Bardot said

After the call, the trio went for lunch at a nearby Panera Bread. Over salads and sandwiches, Nicole would drift off now and then, thinking of Joe, feeling the pain of his death still raw.

Each time her eyes began to well up, Max gently redirected the conversation toward lighter, more engaging topics.

As they finished eating, Nicole stepped away to call her overprotective mother. She didn't seem to appreciate the fact that Nicole was an adult now, even though she still lived at home.

"It's fine, Mom. There's Prisha going with us. I'm perfectly safe. Don't worry, I'm with friends and good company. Nothing will happen. No, they were college friends. Mom, this is work. It's different. Don't worry. I'll be fine. I'll be there this afternoon to pack. We can talk about this later. I love you too."

As she returned to the table, Nicole muttered with a fond smile, "Moms will be moms. Worrywarts as usual."

Max gave Prisha a confused look and they both shrugged.

Prisha explained their plan to Nicole. "Our first goal is to gather everything related to Book One and get it published as soon as possible.

"Then we can start tracking down Book Two of the *Eleven Elements* series."

Nicole perked up. "Oh right! Book Two was sent to Markus Z. Jacobs at Stanford University. I haven't heard from him in a while, though."

"Great," Max said. "Could you try to find him and set up a meeting for later in the week, after we see Professor Bardot tomorrow?"

"Of course. I'll let you know what I find out." Nicole replied.

Max noticed that Nicole was eager to get Joe's books published. But he also sensed her interest in him, catching the way she played with her hair, leaning in a little closer, and seemed intent on knowing him beyond a purely professional level.

Max knew he had to tread carefully.

He needed to persuade her to help get DeWine's books published—without revealing the truth. Not about where they were from. Not about *when* they were from. And certainly not about the deeper agenda driving them.

Their goals overlapped—but only partially. Enough to cooperate. Not enough to trust.

She couldn't know that they came from another era. That their interest in DeWine's work wasn't philosophical or spiritual, but existential. That history itself depended on what happened next.

Above all, Max knew one thing with absolute certainty: They had to stop the anomaly.

The thing growing in the shadows of time.

That black hole devouring futures that were never meant to vanish.

That was the prime directive. The mission's true focus.

And they would achieve it—whatever it took.

With the plan in motion, the three of them packed up and hit the road by 3:15 p.m., setting off for Miami with anticipation and purpose.

They took the turnpike connecting Orlando to Miami, navigating stretches of smooth highway and then the thick snarl of downtown traffic just in time for the evening rush.

By 7:35 p.m., they had reached their destination and checked into the Charriott Miami South Beach.

After a quick refresh in their rooms, the trio headed out for dinner.

Prisha suggested Bombay Bistro, confident that its menu would offer flavorful Indian vegetarian dishes everyone could enjoy.

Max welcomed the choice after the long drive, grateful for something warm and comforting.

Nicole ordered Kingfisher Beer for the table.

"Joe loved this beer," she said with a soft smile. "We used to have it during staff dinners and birthday celebrations. Felt right to toast to him tonight."

Max relaxed as he took his first long sip, the tension of the road slipping away.

There was a sense that their goal was finally within reach. Yet, in the back of his mind, a haunting silence lingered from his lifeline to the future.

He clung to the hope that the team's publishing DeWine's book would somehow stabilize the situation, and re-establish contact with his home base. With Annie. It had been several days now, and his heart ached to be near her again.

But until the job was done, and communications were back up, Max couldn't help fearing they could all be stranded here.

By the time he finished his 750 ml bottle, Max was smiling, both from the alcohol and from a growing sense of camaraderie.

His gaze alternated between Prisha and Nicole, though it lingered more often on the latter.

Nicole seemed to notice. Her attention on him grew more naked, and it made him a little uncomfortable. Not entirely in a bad way.

As she absentmindedly played with her hair, she seemed to enjoy watching Max watching her.

Though she glanced away periodically as if to follow Prisha's casual conversation, she seemed to be more interested in gauging Max's interest … or his restraint.

And in that moment, he wasn't aware of which side of that equation he was on.

After dinner and settling the bill, they returned to the hotel.

As the three of them approached the entrance, Nicole suddenly stopped and grabbed Max's arm.

"Wait … we're right by Micki's Beach Restaurant. I didn't realize that. I've always wanted to go there! I hear they've got great music and the vibe is amazing."

"I'm not ready to sleep yet. Come on," she urged. "It's a party night! Let's go. Just for a while."

Prisha checked her phone. "Sorry. It's nine o'clock and my feet are killing me. I'm heading to bed."

She turned to Max. "You should be a gentleman and accompany her. Keep her safe. But don't stay out too long. We've got an early morning with Dr. Bardot, remember."

As Prisha disappeared into the hotel lobby, Max found himself facing Nicole, who now looked like a giddy teenager waiting for her prom date outside the most exclusive club in South Miami Beach.

He had little choice but to join her. Nicole was their most critical ally in this mission. Keeping her engaged and content was vital. Besides, South Miami nightlife could be unpredictable. Even dangerous.

He made a quick decision: he'd keep her company and, after an hour or so, insist they head back.

Tonight, he would balance duty with diplomacy. And maybe, just maybe, allow himself a sliver of joy in her presence.

Nicole linked her arm with Max's and together they set off for this apparently-famous club.

At Micki's Beach, Max was hit by the sheer intensity of the experience. Loud music pulsed through the air, lights flickered like starlight on fast-forward, and people moved in perfect, intoxicated synchrony. He watched them dance, drink, laugh. It was chaos and unity all at once.

He noticed the tiny glasses, "shots," as people called them, being thrown back with ease and bravado.

Nicole, now radiant and animated, ordered tequila shots for the both of them. Max drank without hesitation, unaware of the alcohol's strength.

Several shots in, the atmosphere blurred. Nicole took Max's hand and led him onto the packed dance floor, where the crowd swayed like a singular organism.

Max had no formal training in twenty-first-century club culture. He hadn't anticipated ending up in such a place; this scenario was not part of his mission preparation.

So, he followed the cues of those around him: men dancing close with their partners, arms encircling backs, fingers brushing lower, hips swaying in rhythm with the beat.

The music drowned out all possibility of conversation. But nothing needed to be said. The night had its own language, of motion, heat, proximity, and unspoken feelings. Max, always composed and mission-driven, found himself caught in the sensory tide.

And Nicole, flushed with laughter and tequila, seemed to be right there with him.

The music was so loud it bordered on unbearable. Max winced internally. The relentless bass thudded through his skull, nearly piercing his ears.

He tried to adapt, mimicking what the other men were doing around him: smiling, holding Nicole close, swaying in rhythm with the crowd.

The bar was packed, forcing couples to dance in tight proximity, their movements becoming more intimate by necessity.

The music was slithering, almost hypnotic, and the floor beneath their feet was slick with spilled drinks. Max's head began to feel heavy, and Prisha's words about returning early echoed somewhere in his mind.

Nicole pressed her body closer to him, looked up at him, her face so close he could feel her breath on his face.

Leaning in even closer, his cheek brushed hers as he shouted over the music directly into her ear. "Let's go back to our rooms. "We both need rest if we're going to be sharp for tomorrow."

The pounding music was so loud even he couldn't be sure she heard him.

But Nicole nodded eagerly.

Max was relieved to be getting away from the ear-piercing noise. Glad to be getting Nicole tucked into her room. She seemed pretty tipsy and would probably feel bad tomorrow when they needed her to be sharp.

She took him by the hand and led the way toward the door.

Back at the hotel, they reached their rooms located across from one other. Nicole unlocked her door and lingered in the doorway, looking at Max with subtle expectation.

Max smiled, composed and firm despite the spinning in his head.

"It's been a long day after that drive," he said. "Hope you sleep well and feel fresh tomorrow.

"Don't forget to set your alarm. We meet for breakfast at seven thirty a.m. and leave by eight thirty to see the professor."

With that, he nodded politely and crossed the hallway. Swiping his card, he entered his room and quietly shut the door.

He stripped down to his base bodysuit, collapsing onto the bed. His ears were still ringing from the deafening club music.

The floor felt like it was tilting beneath him, and the echo of tequila and flashing lights haunted his mind as he drifted into a restless sleep.

As Max lay in bed, the spinning in his head just beginning to fade, a knock interrupted the stillness. He waited, unsure if it was part of his imagination. The knock came again.

Dragging himself out of bed, Max approached the door and peered through the peephole. To his surprise, it was Nicole.

She stood there in a skimpy nightdress, her eyes groggy, her stance unsteady.

He quickly grabbed the robe and opened his door.

She slurred softly, "I thought you said you'd keep me company until I fell asleep. I'm not used to sleeping alone. That's why I still live with my mom. Please," she said, rubbing one hand along his bare arm. "Can you come for just a little while? Please?"

Max nodded reluctantly. He could tell she was intoxicated and vulnerable. It felt wrong to leave her in this state. He followed her quietly across the hallway to her room. He would sit with her until she drifted off. It shouldn't take long. Max thought.

In the room, Nicole, a little tipsy, leaned into Max, and he instinctively steadied her. In that moment, whether by accident or clumsy grace, her delicate, sheer lingerie slipped to the floor, leaving her completely bare.

Max couldn't help but admire her beauty, the perky bosom laid bare before him.

Max's gaze flickered, fighting itself, pulled toward the sudden vulnerability of her body, then yanked back to the ceiling to keep from staring.

He was unsure where to look, unsure what to do. As he held her, he felt her lean in, eyes half-lidded with desire. Her breath brushed his face, lips softly parted, clearly seeking a kiss.

He froze, torn.

Should he? Shouldn't he?

Then she kissed him, deep, lingering, full of heat. It sent a jolt through him, the kind of kiss that awakens something deep and old and undeniable. For a moment, he was lost in it.

His mind was foggy from the drinks, his judgment blurred by the intimacy of the moment. He gave in, just for an instant, meeting her mouth with his. The kiss that followed was the most passionate of his life, bells and whistles erupting somewhere deep inside him, leaving him dazed and confused by the intensity of it.

"Max," Nicole murmured, breath warm, "you're such a good kisser. Why don't you lie down with me for a few minutes, until I fall asleep? You can slip out after. I have a serious problem sleeping alone. It's like insomnia."

Max pulled himself back under control and thought for a few long seconds.

"Listen, Nicole," he said gently, "I don't think that would be appropriate. Here's what I suggest: I'll turn on the TV, lower the brightness, and leave the volume just high enough so it feels like someone's in the room. That always helped me drift off when I was a teenager."

Nicole smiled to herself. *What a gentleman,* she thought. *Maybe he's just shy. It's our first night out, after all.*

Max walked her to the bed and helped her lie down on the wide, king-sized mattress and tucked her under covers.

"Whew," Max sighed in relief. *Trouble averted,* he thought.

He picked up the remote, turned on the TV, dialed the volume and brightness to a soft, comforting hum of background life, then quietly made his way to the door, leaving her to the glow and murmurs of the screen.

As he turned the door knob, Nicole muttered from her bed in a groggy, drunken tone, "Goodnight, dear, see ya."

Max paused. "Goodnight," he replied, as a matter of courtesy, and with a gentle click of the latch, shut the door behind him.

07:15 | 11-25-<u>2025 (Twenty-first century)</u>
LOCATION: CHARRIOTT'S SOUTH BEACH
GREAT ROOM / BREAKFAST LOBBY

The next morning, Max sat at the hotel breakfast hall with a steaming cup of coffee in his hand. Prisha was already at their table, eating fresh fruit and watching the muted news broadcast on the overhead screen. She looked rested, refreshed, and perfectly composed.

Max managed a faint smile and took a seat across from her.

Prisha looked at him with a playful glance. "So, how was the nightclub? Did I miss something fun?"

Max's first instinct was to keep his composure. His mind spun with cautious optimism, hoping, praying, that Nicole wouldn't say anything that would "spill the beans" when she arrived. Until then, he would keep everything neutral.

"It was good," Max replied, keeping his tone casual. "The drinks were nasty. Some mean cocktails, that's for sure.

"I've got a bit of a headache and might need some local medicine to deal with it.

"My suit," he said, feeling the aftereffects of the alcohol, "it seems off, not working as well. Probably because of the broken connections."

He sipped his coffee, eyeing the buffet, unsure whether he'd be able to keep it down.

Then he turned back to Prisha. "You seem well rested."

Prisha gave a knowing smirk but said nothing more.

Just then, Nicole arrived at the breakfast table in a rush, clearly aware she was late.

She sat down, glancing at her watch. "Sorry I'm late. I have a serious hangover," she muttered.

Max, still piecing together twenty-first-century slang, was momentarily confused. *Hangover? Does she mean someone came over and they ... hung out? Does that mean sex? Or does it just mean she drank too much?* He wasn't sure. The language of this time still baffled him.

Nicole rose again, groaning. "I need some coffee."

As she walked toward the buffet area, Max followed.

"I'm sorry about last night," he said quietly, avoiding eye contact. "I shouldn't have kissed you."

A pause.

"I don't do well with that drink ... what is it called? Yes, Taa-kill-aa. It almost killed me. I was messed up. I couldn't even get up. I threw up. Sorry about all that. I ... Can you please... not tell anyone about what happened?"

Nicole turned to him with a sly smile. "Everything stays a secret between us," she said, drawing her finger and thumb across her lips as if zipping them shut.

Max was begging, "You have to understand: I'm a senior director at the company. I could lose my position if someone found out about us. I want to keep everything private until all of the novels are published. Please. Thank you."

Max got a small nod as response from Nicole, the pit in his stomach easing only slightly. Whatever had happened, it would remain between them, for now.

After a few minutes, Prisha, who had gotten up to use the ladies' room, returned to their table.

Max stood up to refill his coffee. Nicole rose as well. "I'd love some more coffee too... Let's get some," she said casually, her voice light and indifferent, as though nothing out of the ordinary had happened. It was business as usual.

As they walked toward the coffee station, Nicole added, "I noticed there's a sundries shop at that counter over there. They sell headache meds. I'll go grab some to shake this hangover. Do you want anything?"

Max replied, "Yes, I have a 'hangover' too and could use that same medicine. Thank you."

After breakfast, the three headed toward their vehicle. Max followed behind the two women, lost in thought. His expression was composed, but his mind was anything but calm.

I am Maxion Renner, he thought. *Commander of the elite Temporal Reconnaissance Division. Twenty-sixth century. Decorated. Disciplined. I crossed time itself to find the author of the Eleven Elements, the manuscript that built my world.*

But Joshua DeWine is gone. Dead. A car crash erased the man whose words shaped a civilization.

Now I'm stranded in the twenty-first century, relying on his assistant to finish the work that was meant to save us.

And somewhere along the line, I lost control. Not in battle, but in something far more personal. I was overwhelmed by the passion of a twenty-first-century woman. I became unsteady and yielded to nature's demands, losing control until I could no longer distinguish between the boundaries of duty and the beginnings of my own vulnerability.

Max walked with a heavy mix of emotions, needing to release his thoughts. To clear his mind and realign himself with his purpose.

But as he moved toward the car, a different kind of agony hit him. His heart became heavy as it sank.

He thought of Annie.

Her eyes. Her laugh. The vows they'd exchanged. The affirmations stuck to their refrigerator door, written in her handwriting.

How will I tell her? What will I tell her? Should I tell her at all?

What if she found out later, she'd confront me. Afterall, they are tethered with embedded devices and monitoring technology. She would definitely sense something went wrong. Better I tell her as soon as we meet, explain exactly what happened, how I was compromised, overpowered by twenty-first century drinks, by confusion and the circumstances. That I was caught in a perfect storm I couldn't escape.

Nicole was a real woman, full of genuine emotion. Her intimacy was raw, human, and unfiltered.

Despite his regrets, he couldn't deny that her kiss had electrified him in a way Annie never had.

And now that experience was embedded in his memory.

He needed help. Someone to talk to. Someone to help him sort through this emotional storm. But there was no one.

Worse, he now realized something far more troubling:

Nicole thinks this is just the beginning. A secret relationship. A story "o be continued" with more episodes to follow.

And in that moment, Max knew he was walking on dangerously thin ice.

Max had faced many challenges and surprises in his various time travel missions. Most of them demanded physical endurance, the kind needed to fight back or escape imminent danger. Others were cerebral, calling for quick, sharp mental problem-solving.

But this time … this time it was different. This situation was emotional. With a capital "E."

And Max was not prepared for that.

Nothing in his rigorous training had covered emotional entanglements with emotionally unpredictable twenty-first-century women.

Especially not ones as layered as Nicole: someone navigating the insecurity, sensitivity, and constant self-preservation demanded by a deeply male-dominated society. This wasn't strategy anymore. It was survival on a different battlefield.

Any notion of breaking ties or creating space could upset her, he thought. *And if that happens, she might pull her support. She could decline to help. Or worse … she could turn against us.*

That would be catastrophic.

Without Nicole, the path to publishing the Eleven Elements was blocked. His mission, the hope for his world's survival, would collapse.

We'd be screwed. Royally screwed.

The whole situation was a double-edged sword. On one side was his identity as a respected commander. A teacher, a leader, a man bound by honor, duty, and legacy.

On the other side was a woman who now believed she had a secret relationship with him, one meant to be nurtured and sustained.

He couldn't afford to damage her emotional state. Yet he also couldn't betray Annie, his wife. He had taken sacred vows. He had a name to protect. A family line to honor.

This wasn't just thin ice.

It was melting beneath his feet.

He sighed deeply, muttering to himself and trying to summon the right twenty-first-century expression.

He snapped his fingers as it came to him: "Yeah. *Shit happens.*"

CHAPTER -24

14:37 | 11-24-2025 (Twenty-first century)
LOCATION: Dr DUPRAY'S OFFICE SUITE 101
HIGHWAY 50 CLERMONT FLORIDA

Earlier that morning, Kasandra and Isam had rented a white Felza ET1 SUV from a local rental agency. They wanted to run some errands while Max and Prisha were away in Miami visiting Dr. Bardot to collect the final manuscript that Joe DeWine had last worked on and sent over for the professor's review.

Later that day, Katrina, Isam, Kasandra, Luke, and Cheng went to Dr. Dupray's office to collect the final session and its recording—the last known meeting Joshua DeWine had before he vanished, one they had been tracking closely.

Because Katrina, Kasandra and Luke had been part of the original fake FBI raid at Dupray's office, it was up to Isam and Cheng to obtain any new information they could from the psycho-therapist. The others remained in the car.

The two men were dressed casually, without any official attire.

And thanks to Katrina's hacking expertise, they, too, were prepared to impersonate the FBI.

They walked in confidently, flashed their badges, and Alina, his secretary, followed them into his office. She seemed concerned, almost protective, Isam thought.

The Time Travelers stood behind the guest chairs. Alina hovered behind them.

Isam spoke first, soft-spoken but authoritative. "Dr. Dupray, the FBI regrets your recent experiences. We know that imposters took patient records from you. We're with the FBI, officially. There's no need to worry. This is just a routine follow-up to check in and to make sure everything is okay."

Dupray blinked, visibly shaken. "How do I know you're not lying too?"

Cheng handed him a slip with a phone number. "Call this number. Ask for Agent Fields. You remember talking to her at our office in Orlando. She will confirm our identities."

Dupray nervously made the call. He recognized her voice and after a few tense minutes, he hung up, visibly calmer. He turned to them with a solemn expression. "They said you're legit and were sent you to share some grave news. Now what is it?"

Isam nodded. "We're sorry to bring the bad news, Dr. Dupray. Joshua DeWine is dead. He died last week, Saturday, in a car accident."

The moment the words left his mouth, Dupray collapsed to his knees, sobbing uncontrollably.

Alina instinctively rushed toward him to help. He reached up and gripped her hand as he wept. She reached out to pass him his hand towel from the drawer.

"The world is finished," he said. "First the Romans … and now technology? How pathetic, how cruel!" His cries echoed through the clinic.

Eventually, Dupray composed himself, pressed a hand on his desk and rose to his feet.

Even as he bent over the desk, hands flat on the surface, Isam could see his face was streaked with tears, his eyes red.

Dupray furrowed his brow. "I wasn't even told he died. Why wasn't I informed?"

Isam looked at him gently, but directly. "Dr. Dupray, DeWine never listed you in any official records. His visits to you were completely off the books, maybe they were personal. Confidential.

"No one knew he was seeing you. That's why you weren't notified. You didn't exist in any of his records. That is why his office would not have sent you an invitation to the cremation ceremony."

Dupray walked over to his prized couch and sat down, hands folded as if in prayer. He could almost feel DeWine's presence there, he'd been sitting in that very spot just the other day. It didn't feel real that he was gone.

Dupray drew in a long breath, then exhaled hard, his lips pushed into a weary pout, "I'll do whatever I can to help," he said. "Anything."

Isam spoke up. "We need to know when you last met with DeWine? Any recent sessions?"

Dupray nodded and sniffed, his voice still shaky but animated. "Yes, yes, there was one. A powerful session. Just a few days before you said he met an accident.

"He spoke about a vision: Cardinals gathered in Rome, electing a new Pope. It was profound. He called out on the real story of Jesus. What really happened. Something I had been waiting for all these years to find out. What it all meant."

He gestured toward his desk. "I recorded the session as usual and saved everything. Just in case. I copied the files to a USB drive, ready to hand over if the FBI came asking."

He pulled out a drawer, retrieved the drive, and passed it to Cheng without hesitation.

"Thank you, Doctor," Isam said. "We are truly grateful for your help. The world will recognize your contribution to protect the future and for the safety of Mr. Joshua DeWine. You can call us again at the number I gave you should you have any further questions. Take care now. Good bye."

Isam and Cheng briskly walked out of the door, as swiftly as they had arrived.

Dupray and Alina watched the FBI agents let themselves out.

"That was weird," Alina said.

"How so?" Dupray asked, still drying tears and sniffing.

Alina shrugged. "I don't know, just kind of a drive-by. Guess they got what they needed."

"At least they didn't go out the window this time." Dupray managed a laugh. Alina joined in.

"I'm sorry to hear about your patient," she said, "Your friend." Her tone softened. "Need anything?"

"No, I'm fine. Thank you." He turned away from her, embarrassed by his earlier breakdown. "I just need to gather myself."

Fifteen minutes later, his phone rang. It was Agent Fields again.

"Dr. Dupray, just checking in. How are things going? Any further contact by anyone?"

Dupray answered with pride. "Yes. Two agents. I even verified their identities by calling your landline. Didn't I talk to you a little while back checking in on their ID? They informed me Joshua DeWine is ... gone."

There was a pause on the other end.

Fields finally said, "Dr. Dupray ... I'm afraid you've been duped again. I don't recall talking to you.

"They must have used AI to impersonate my voice and rerouted the number using a caller-ID spoofing technology and web-based interface to mask the call's destination."

His head dropped, his mind churned. "What?"

"It *is* true that DeWine is dead. But the two people you met are not our agents. They're most likely more of the infiltrators we've been tracking.

"They came for DeWine's files. What exactly did you give them?"

Dupray stared blankly at the phone, utterly stunned. "I, I gave them the final session recording. The one about Rome. The visions at the Saint Joseph's Fountain."

"We'll need a copy of that file. I'll send you a link to a secure Dropbox. Please upload it asap."

"Yes, of course," he said. "Again, I am so sorry."

He was about to end the call then remembered something He quickly looked through his laptop.

"Agent Fields, one more thing. After the last visit from the fake FBI agents, I had cameras installed here.

"One faces the parking lot. And I can tell you these people were in a white Felza ET1. I'll send you their license plate number with the video files."

"Just read it to me now," Fields said, and he complied.

She read back the number he gave her, then thanked him for the information and disconnected.

Dupray felt just the smallest bit vindicated, knowing he had helped the FBI find these imposters and stop whatever plan they had to derail DeWine's inspired purpose.

* * * * * * *

16:27 | 11-24-<u>2025 (Twenty-first century)</u>
LOCATION: E. COLONIAL DR.+MAGNOLIA 7-11 STORE

After hours of circling the city to randomize their route, Luke, at the wheel, and the others zeroed in on this specific 7-Eleven to make their historic purchase.

Katrina and Kasandra stepped out of the Felza's backseat and into the dimly lit 7-Eleven.

They grabbed a few essentials: bottles of water, orange juice, and two Powerball Lotto tickets.

As directed by Max, they carefully chose the numbers. The jackpot sat at $1.3 billion, but they already knew they had the winning numbers.

The women casually strode out of the store, chatting about the weather, like any normal twenty-first century shoppers, and slipped into the vehicle.

Soon, Katrina, Kasandra, Luke, Cheng, and Isam were speeding westbound on Interstate I-4, heading back to base.

The Felza ET1 sliced through evening rush hour traffic like a specter, silently gliding between lanes, each maneuver deliberate, each second measured.

Everyone was sharp-eyed, all on edge. Katrina could feel the measured tension inside the cockpit.

And now, it paid off.

"We've got three unmarked black Chevy suburban vehicles tailing us," she said, her tone even, eyes locked on the rear-view mirror. "Five blocks now. Same formation."

"They're not local police," Cheng muttered from the passenger seat, fingers resting near the dash controls. "Their drive-in arrow formation is typical of federal swat units. We've been made."

Katrina remained composed, her voice flat. "Should've stuck to the hotel. This SUV draws too much attention. Cameras everywhere."

A long silence. Then Luke asked the question on everyone's mind: "What's the exit plan if they close in?"

No one answered.

Isam popped open the glove compartment. "Smoke pellets and a pulse jammer. We can scramble their visual systems for sixty seconds."

"Sixty's not enough," Kasandra said, clutching the headrest. "We're sitting ducks out here."

Suddenly, a black SUV cut through traffic behind them, overtook them and braked hard across the intersection. Blinding red and blue lights flashed. Sirens wailed.

A voice shouted of over a loudspeaker. "Pull over – white Felza SUV. Pull over right now and step out of the vehicle with your hands in the air! You are surrounded!"

Luke floored the accelerator. "Hold on!"

The Felza ET1 launched forward and over the curb, hugging tight curves and weaving between the rush hour traffic as it tore south on I-4.

Four black SUVs gave chase, joined moments later by an Orange County Sheriff interceptor, its siren piercing through the cool evening air.

Isam tossed the smoke pellets out the side window. A thick white fog enveloped the rear view.

He slapped the jammer's activation switch. Drones overhead glitched mid-flight, some spinning out into the darkening skies, others crashing into light poles or rooftops.

But it wasn't enough.

More unmarked black vehicles joined the pursuit, eight all after them now, all flashing red-white dash strobes.

Suddenly the traffic thinned, the road suspiciously clear ahead.

"They're controlling the flow," Katrina muttered. "This is a trap."

Luke's eyes darted left. "We're exiting. Conroy Road. Millenia Mall. We lose them in the parking grid."

He yanked the wheel hard, tires screaming as the SUV shot onto the off-ramp.

Then, glinting metal ahead. A spike strip.

"Dammit!" he growled.

He tried to swerve.

BOOM. BOOM.

Both front tires blew. The SUV fishtailed wildly, its smart-stabilizers kicking in too late. The Felza slammed into the concrete barrier with a crunch of metal and sparks.

The team members struggled out of the vehicle. As far as Katrina could tell none of them were too badly banged up.

SWAT vans screamed to a halt. Doors flung open.

Agents poured out in black tactical gear, rifles trained.

"HANDS WHERE WE CAN SEE THEM!"

"ON THE GROUND! NOW!"

Katrina and Kasandra dropped instantly, palms out.

Luke raised his hands slowly. His eyes seemed fixed on the agents.

Cheng bolted, making it nine steps before a K9 unit took him down hard. He screamed as the dog's jaws latched onto his shoulder.

Katrina started toward him, but heard the cocking of a shotgun and stopped in mid-stride. She dropped to her knees and held her hands up.

Isam didn't resist. He must have known it was over.

Max is going to kill me, Katrina thought as the agents cuffed each one of them and shoved them in separate vehicles.

And what if they find out that I am an advanced bio-organic artificial life-form from the future? This could turn out to be the worst mistake of her life.

Agent Fields directed her agents to strip the captives and place them in separate interrogation rooms until she'd had a chance to get her thoughts together.

She poured a cup of nasty coffee and took a swig, sitting down behind her desk.

Who were these jokers?

Something was off about them.

They pretended to be FBI agents, but all they got for their efforts are some documents and videos ... about a guy who apparently wants to save the world?

Who cares?

On top of that were those bizarre highway patrol reports from a couple of weeks ago. About some suspicious characters in white Felzas cleaning up an accident and incinerating bodies on the side of the road.

And then there was that knee prosthetic...

Fields shook her head, reviewed the files, and drained the cup. It was time to dig into this case, if it even was a case, and try to make sense of it.

Once in custody, the agents had ordered the team be stripped of their bodysuits and put in "jumpsuits."

"Store their gear in the safe in evidence, Agent Fields said.

Katrina panicked.

As they began to take the others' suits, Katrina gradually moved toward the back, delaying the process while she tried to think of something.

The others' suits detached cleanly like modular armor.

But Katrina's was partially fused. Biologically integrated to her body.

The agents removed Kasandra, Luke, Isam, and Cheng. They were to be taken to separate interrogation rooms.

Interrogation? For what? What was their crime? Or were they even being charged with a crime. Were they just being pressed for information?

But what information? About DeWine's projects? About the three team members that got chemically cremated? About impersonating FBI agents?

Or about something else that may have given them away as time-travelers from the future?

Her skin rippled in the cold room, despite still clinging to her suit.

But she was next.

"Take if off," the female agent demanded.

Katrina said, "You don't understand. I have a health condition."

"I don't care what you've got. Take it off."

"I can't. It's literally a part of me."

The female agent set down the folders in her hand and shook her head, approaching Katrina with a frustrated sigh.

The agent tried forcefully pulling down on the suit at the neck, and Katrina screamed as a layer of skin came off with the suit.

"What the hell?" the agent said, and tried at another spot.

Katrina grabbed the woman's hand and screamed again as another strip of skin came off her shoulder.

She could hear the suit's feedback through her direct auditory link, warning her of spiking vitals, nerve agitation. *No kidding,* she thought.

"What'd you do, superglue the thing to your body?"

"I *told* you," Katrina whimpered. Now the exposed skin began to blister and burn. "Look at me!" she cried out. "You're hurting me."

Finally, the agent gave up and led her to a separate containment unit where they drew blood, scanned her retinas, took X-rays, and ran fingerprints.

Katrina sat on a thin bed like a medical examination table.

She counted four ceiling-mounted cameras that presumably tracked every micro-movement. Surely, they didn't have a lot of rooms this well monitored.

They were treating her special, which could be a problem if they figured out what she really was.

And then Agent Fields stepped in. She had gotten Katrina's test results.

"They all matched," Fields said. "Perfectly. Maybe a little *too* perfectly.

"Driver's licenses. Passports. Credit history. Family trees.

"All valid. All synchronized. All ... sterile.

"No errors. No anomalies. Nothing out of place."

Agent Fields wasn't buying it. Katrina could see the suspicion in her eyes. Still, she knew what she needed most right now was time, time to stay quiet, remain still, and hope the investigators would lose interest and walk away. Let them think she was harmless. Let them think she was healing.

From the corner of her eye, she watched Fields and her assistant step away. As soon as they were out of direct sight, Katrina blinked twice, activating the internal overlay. A faint shimmer passed across her retina as the facility's full schematics came into view. Quietly, methodically, she began mapping her escape.

CHAPTER -25

Max, Prisha and Nicole sat in the small outer office belonging to Professor Bardot at the University of Miami's Department of Engineering.

His secretary was brusque, like a guard dog. She buzzed the professor, told him his nine o'clock was here, and he asked for a couple of minutes. All on open speakers. She didn't say anything more to the visitors.

Max's team had been in the twenty-first century for two weeks now and were scrambling to piece together the parts of the late Joshua DeWine's manuscripts.

They'd lost all contact with the Command Center in their own time. And there was a widening rift in the timeline that their efforts to publish the manifesto and books that could heal … if only they could complete their tasks in time.

And that included finding out what Dr. Bardot knew about DeWine's mission and, more importantly, acquiring a copy of whatever portions of DeWine's writings the professor had.

Max had reviewed Dr. Bardot's impressive biography, which included appointments at several top-ranking universities and a long list of publications in scientific journals across multiple disciplines.

He had also looked into Joshua DeWine's academic interests, noting that DeWine was particularly drawn to topics like water resources engineering, infrastructure systems, geomechanics, and geotechnical engineering.

DeWine had taken a special interest in Dr. Bardot's *Megacity* projects at the University of California.

In fact, Bardot's concepts had inspired DeWine's own *Megapolis* designs. Though DeWine had modified them to eliminate contradictions that clashed with his "Eleven Elements" framework and the underlying principles guiding his vision of future cities.

Dr. Bardot had received numerous honors, awards, and research grants over his career. He had served as Dean of the College of Engineering at the University of Miami before stepping down to become Vice Provost.

The door to Bardot's inner office opened, and a rumpled, balding man smiled. "Mr. Renner. Friends. Please come in."

As they entered, Max could see a large desk cluttered with paperwork and notes. A scene typical of a professor juggling multiple global challenges.

"Sit, please," Bardot said, sinking into an old chair that seemed to swallow him. "Would you like some coffee?"

"Not for me, thank you, Max said."

Prisha responded with a smile, "We just had a heavy breakfast. We're good, thank you."

Max looked up at the wall on his right and couldn't help noticing a poster that read:

"I believe that water is the closest thing to a god we have here on Earth. We are in awe of its power and majestic beauty. We are drawn to it as if it's a magical, healing force. We gestate in water, are made of water, and need to drink water to live. We are living in water."
— Alex Z. Moores

"It's good to finally see you in person," Nicole said. "I'm Nicole, assistant to Joshua DeWine. I was the one coordinating the draft submissions to you and several other professors and technical experts for feedback and input.

"You see, we're here today to hear your thoughts on Book One, your impressions, comments, and any edits you might have.

"Max and Prisha here are with the Eleven Elements Foundation, which is now sponsoring the project and helping publish the body of work that Mr. DeWine has developed."

"Splendid!" Dr. Bardot replied with his familiar warm smile, "First, tell me, how's my friend Joe doing? It's been a long time since I last spoke with him.

"I'm truly glad he's found sponsors to help get this project out there. He's fortunate to have you backing him, especially given how sensitive the environmental topics are. Most people are hesitant to speak out under the McCrony Administration, with its agenda to bypass all regulations."

All three sat stunned, eyes wide as they looked at one another and then at Dr. Bardot.

Nicole broke the silence. "Did you not receive the email notification about Mr. DeWine's passing? He passed away on November twenty-second.

"We sent funeral announcements via email to all his clients and contacts. In fact, we sent you a personal memorial invitation, an evite, in accordance with his family's wishes."

Dr. Bardot gasped. "Oh my God. Joshua is gone? He's left us?" His voice broke. "I am so sorry for your loss. I wasn't aware at all.

"Perhaps the announcement went to my spam folder. I get over 250 emails a day."

He quickly pulled out his phone and scrolled through his inbox and junk folders. "Oh my. There it is: 'Joshua DeWine's Memorial Invitation.' I'm so sorry. I would have definitely sent my written condolences, even if I couldn't attend."

His expression turned somber. "Wow. Joshua is no more … I can't believe it. Just a few weeks ago, we spoke on the phone. He was so enthusiastic about completing his first draft and sharing it with me.

"It feels like that was just yesterday. His voice, that excitement, is still fresh in my ears."

He glanced toward a folder on his desk. "Yes. Yes, I remember *everything* we discussed.

"I truly loved that guy. Especially his innocence. I treated him almost like one of my own students.

"In fact, he shared some very interesting thoughts during our last call, and I took detailed notes." He opened the folder and began flipping through its pages. "Here, you, see? Date, time, his name. It's all right here."

Max sat up slightly, curiosity piqued. "What did he say? And … are those things included in his book?"

Bardot replied, "Well, I've since typed up my notes, along with my own take on everything we discussed. But no, what we talked about isn't in the book. Maybe he intended to include it later, once he figured out where it would best fit into the story. I really loved his narrative and the way he delivered it.

"Let's be honest: who wants to read about the environment and saving the world these days?

"Joshua turned it into an engaging science fiction adventure. Time travelers darting back and forth through history to correct the mistakes of our century, that made it captivating."

Dr. Bardot glanced at Max, then Prisha, as if reading their minds. And indeed, over decades of addressing audiences, he had probably developed a sense something akin to that.

Prisha rolled her eyes slightly, the universal cue for boredom, and glanced at Max when Bardot mentioned time-travel adventures.

Bardot smiled. "Joshua seemed to be writing something that he hoped would evolve into a real future.

"He told me he was thinking of his kids as he wrote it, trying to find a way to communicate the message through all the noise, all the fog and distractions that cloud people's understanding. That was his hope."

Eager to hear more, Max pulled out a small scribble pad and began jotting down notes to show his genuine interest.

"Can you please brief us on what you two talked about?" Max asked. "We both have journalism backgrounds, and we'd like to include this as part of a video feature.

"Since we're publishing his book posthumously, we're gathering supporting material and articles to give more weight and credibility to the subject and to the overall project. That will help ensure its success."

Dr. Bardot took a deep breath and nodded. "Well then… here it goes.

"I received a call from Joshua. And after our usual cordial greetings, we settled into a conversation about his book.

"As usual my recorder of conversations and built-in note-taker within the online app for our virtual meeting recorded the

MS teams online video meeting and I can replay our conversation word-by-word.

"He wanted to know what I thought of it. I told him, 'It has great potential,' though it could use some refining. I promised to send him my edits and comments for consideration as he worked toward a final draft. He agreed.

"Then, out of the blue, he asked, 'Should I write about the pyramids?'

"I said, 'What about them?'

"That's when he took me on a question-and-answer journey to help me grasp what he was really getting at.

"He asked, 'Do you know about the Svalbard Global Seed Vault?'

"Of course I do," I said. "It's a vault that provides long-term storage for seeds from around the world. They're essentially backups of national gene banks. The purpose is to safeguard the global food supply against threats like mismanagement, natural disasters, equipment failure, war, or economic collapse.

"Joshua then said, 'Ok, hold that thought for me. Now add to that the fact that the Global Seed Vault is located so close to the North Pole that it remains naturally cold, ensuring seeds stay frozen and dormant until we deliberately thaw them. Correct?'

"I said. 'Yes, that seems to be the perfect logic.'"

"He continued, 'Now, you know the North Pole is shifting at a more rapid pace. Correct?'

"Again, I affirmed. 'Yes, it's common knowledge.'

"I told him what I knew. That the ice caps act almost like anchors or counterweights, stabilizing Earth's tilt at 23 degrees.

"That the polar ice masses at the North and South Poles anchor the planet on its current axis, their sheer mass, trillions of tons of ice, acting as a natural stabilizer.

"That the melting glaciers and ice sheets due to climate change have caused a significant redistribution of Earth's mass. And that this shift has altered the position of both poles.

"You probably know all this." Bardot looked at his visitors almost apologetically, then continued.

"Since the 1990s, this redistribution, primarily from melting ice turning into water and flowing over land and into oceans, has changed Earth's axis of rotation.

"It has not only accelerated the movement but also altered the direction of the geographic North Pole, a phenomenon known as polar drift. The North Pole now shifts every year."

Dr. Bardot quickly typed a few commands into the Froogle search engine and pulled up a map that visually illustrated the phenomenon he was referencing. He turned the screen to the visitors.

Max studied the image. It was staggering: the North Pole had shifted nearly fifty miles from its original location within just a single year.

"Joshua then asked me, 'Is it true that the average time between magnetic north-south pole flips is about 200,000 to 300,000 years, and that we haven't had one for approximately 780,000 years?'

"I had no counterargument. I simply agreed with the hard facts Joshua had likely just confirmed online.

Bardot proceeded to tell the story of his conversation with DeWine in detail, as Max and the two women listened in.

Joshua had suddenly lit up like he'd just cracked a code.

"Well, think about this," he said. "If the polar ice caps keep melting and the pole drift keeps accelerating, it could eventually trigger a pole reversal. North becomes south, south becomes north.

"And if that happens, if the Earth tries to rebalance its land and water weight, with the lack of the ice cap at the north pole, the earth's tilt may reposition such that the global landmass would all center towards the north, into the space currently occupied by the ice caps.

"It's far-fetched, not happening anytime soon. But just roll with it for a second.

"So, what landmark sits at the centroid of Earth's landmass? I didn't even have to think. "Egypt," I said.

Joshua grinned and said, "Exactly: The Pyramids of Egypt. Now picture this: at one point, they may have been located right at the North Pole, if the whole landmass rotated around it. That would make the Pyramids the perfect refrigerator. Just like the Global Seed Vault in Svalbard today. But instead of seeds, maybe they held DNA. Or frozen embryos. A genetic time capsule, waiting out the Ice Age to end."

He was so animated, excited about his revelation.

"Think about it,' he said. "A superior civilization could've built the Pyramids not as tombs, but as vaults. They would be like a pre–Ice Age Noah's Ark, designed not for a flood, but to reboot life after a global freeze.

"The preservation conditions? Ideal.

"Remember the studies on the Queen's Chamber? How it maintains a constant temperature? Experiments have shown that a pyramid shape has proven preservation capabilities. It's practically cryogenic."

"Yeah, I know," I said, but pushed back. "Joshua, the carbon dating puts the Pyramids at what: between 3,500 and 4,600 years old?"

He didn't miss a beat and replied, "I figured you'd say that. I already looked into it. Carbon dating only works on organic material. The mummies, the wooden artifacts, the linen, the paint and grout work. They date to that period, sure.

"But the Pyramids themselves? They're made of stone. You can't carbon date stone."

By this point, I could tell he was on a roll.

"The Pharaohs didn't build the Pyramids," he said. "They found them, massive, mysterious, already there. And repurposed them as tombs. What we've dated is just the stuff the Pharaohs inserted into the Pyramids or left behind in them. But the original structures? Could be way older. And we don't have a definitive method to date the stone itself.

"Think about it. Pyramids weren't just built in Egypt. They're all over the world. Different continents. Different cultures. Same geometric precision. These things weren't tombstones at all, but engineered objects, maybe for something much bigger.

"Maybe they were Life-Seed Vaults, meant to store DNA, embryos, whatever it takes to reboot life after a global catastrophe like an ice age."

"You've got a mess of theories here," I said. "But I'll admit: it's fascinating. I don't think anyone's seriously floated the idea of Pyramids as biological Arks. Or Life-Seeding Vaults.

"If that were true," I said, "you'd need a whole system. Special containers, temperature regulation, artificial wombs maybe. Technology far beyond what we've found. Without hard evidence, it's science fiction."

But Joshua wasn't done.

"Listen," he said, "some researchers argue the Pyramids could be over 10,000 years old. Especially now, after Gobekli Tepe was dated to 11,000, 12,000 years ago. If a site that ancient can exist in Turkey, why not Egypt?

"The engineering of the Pyramids is pure math and science. That's not the work of a primitive tomb builder. It's the work of a civilization with a purpose."

Clearly, he was onto something and was excited about it. But I offered him some perspective, since that's what he'd asked me for.

I started out recommending caution.

"If the pyramids are indeed older than the Pharaohs," I said, "then they were likely repurposed as royal tombs.

"Their original function may have been far more scientific.

"But, Joshua, I suggest you wait until more researchers or historians begin to agree with your hypothesis before including that theory in the book.

"I understand your sci-fi narrative warns that the end times could be near, especially if the magnetic poles were to switch, or if polar ice melts, drastically altering Earth's rotation or relocating the geographic North Pole.

"According to your story, people should become aware of these looming threats and direct their efforts toward grand-scale projects, like the construction of pyramids, as survival mechanisms for humanity."

Then I gave him my bottom line. "All in all, I think these are very thought-provoking ideas. Still, I recommend omitting the speculative theory about the Pyramids' original use in the final version of the book. It might not sit well with everyone.

"Most people prefer the narratives they learned in school or studied at university. They don't like stepping out of their comfort zones. They can't all think outside the box the way you do. People are afraid to think big. They are also afraid to think really great."

"Then I told him I was still reviewing his manuscript, and within a week or two, I'd send him my edits and suggestions for improvement.

Dr. Bardot let out a long breath.

"Well, that was the gist of our phone call.

"I've typed up some notes, and I'll copy them to this USB drive, along with the redline of the first draft of *Book One of the Eleven Elements*. Just finished it a few days ago.

"I wasn't planning to share this yet." He paused and looked toward the window. "Actually, I thought Joshua would be coming with you. I was hoping to meet him face-to-face.

"Still can't believe he's not with us anymore."

A heavy silence followed, like he was honoring the absence.

"By the way," Bardot looked back at them, a brighter expression on his weathered face, "I love the title *Healing Waters*.

He handed Max the USB drive. "Here it is. All of it. Good luck."

Without acknowledging Bardot's human guard dog, Max, Nicole, and Prisha left the professor's office, navigated the campus to the parking lot, and hit the road toward Orlando.

Nicole sat in the backseat, and Max caught her glance in the rearview mirror. Every time their eyes met, she smiled.

Each time, he returned a polite one.

He knew she was reading too much into it—but he needed her help to complete the mission. Letting her entertain a fantasy for a few days or weeks seemed like a small price to pay.

Still, something tugged at him.

His thoughts drifted to the old stories he'd read about the twenty-first century—the burden women carried in workplaces where their personal space was routinely ignored, where silence was too often mistaken for consent.

And for the first time, he felt the sharp echo of that reality. He understood, suddenly, how exhausting it must've been. To endure the weight of unspoken expectations, of persistent attention that blurred professionalism with possession—and to keep working through it, unsupported.

He hadn't planned to be part of a story like that.

He hadn't expected to play the romantic lead.

But here they were.

Smooth jazz filled the car as they cruised the turnpike, the USB drive tucked securely in his backpack.

Despite the challenges that Max now faced, for the first time, the mission felt like it was truly moving forward.

CHAPTER -26

09:15 | 11-25-<u>2025 (Twenty-first century)</u>
LOCATION: FBI OFFICE KELLER RD ORLANDO FL

Lukas Adler sat motionless.
Inmate jumpsuit.
Shackled to a steel chair bolted to the floor.
Electrodes trailed from his chest, wrists, and temples into a blinking polygraph monitor.

An IV line ran to his arm, the chemical cocktail already delivered. Clear vials lay discarded in a tray nearby: barbiturates, benzodiazepines, and a synthesized Class-E truth compound authorized for high-clearance extraction.

A man stood in the corner. FBI interrogator, mid-thirties, lean, with sharp posture and an air of fresh academy rigor. He'd been trained for psychological warfare, counterintelligence, synthetic memory probes.

He now took a seat across from Lukas. A steel table, a single lamp. Cold room. Hum of fluorescent lighting above.

"Lukas Adler," the interrogator began. "You are currently in federal custody on suspicion of terrorism, impersonating federal officers, unauthorized possession of unregistered advanced technologies, and potential violation of multiple international security treaties."

Lukas said nothing. His eyes were wide, pupils dilated.
But he had no fear. His breathing was slow. Stable.
The drugs were doing their job.
The polygraph flickered, then held steady. No anomalies.

The interrogator narrowed his eyes. He tapped the file on the desk. Over two-hundred pages of backstory, all verifiable. All spotless.

Too spotless, thought the man watching through the one-way mirror.

"You were born in Allentown, Pennsylvania," the interrogator said. "Masters in Applied Systems Engineering from Carnegie Mellon, transferred credits from a German technical university. Your first job was at a satellite telemetry firm in Boca Raton.

"You've had fourteen different addresses over ten years, all traceable. All with tax records. All with neighbor verification."

Lukas didn't blink.

The interrogator leaned forward, voice colder now.

"Here's the thing. All five of you, your records are flawless. Flawless doesn't happen in real life. Real people make mistakes. Miss a bill. Get parking tickets. Forget to file taxes. Get a cavity. Something."

He slammed the folder shut.

A low hum filled the sterile, dimly lit room. Medical monitors pulsed in steady rhythms. Lukas sat still, wrists cuffed together. His breathing was shallow. Focused. A bead of sweat ran down his temple.

A medical technician glanced at the serum monitor.

"He's ready."

The interrogator nodded and hit the record button.

"Who are you? Where are you from, Lukas? Who sent you here?"

Lukas blinked slowly.

The chemical truth-serum smothered resistance like a blanket over fire. The man beyond the window smiled a little.

"You can call me Luke." Luke said raising his head and breathing heavily. "I am... I am... a time traveler. Belonging to ... a trained regiment for classified tasks."

The interrogator raised an eyebrow.

"Let's try this again, Luke. Who are you *really?*"

Luke's voice didn't change. If anything, it got more sincere, hollowed out by exhaustion and truth.

"I'm from the future."

Silence.

Behind the glass, Deputy Director Don Vingo paused mid-note. The air in the observation room felt suddenly thin.

"Say again," the interrogator said. "How many in your regiment?"

"Fifteen were sent. Through the deep-time corridor. Three died during entry. Two are missing, presumed lost, or misplaced in the wrong year. Ten of us made it. We've been searching."

"Searching for who?"

"Joshua DeWine," Luke said. "His writings stabilize our future. His ideas. They build the foundation of the world we live in. If he fails to publish them, our timeline fractures. Reality begins to collapse. It's already started."

That was enough for Don. He stepped into the room, motioned the interrogator out, and sat down across from Luke.

Don was calm, and even-tempered. He shut the recorder off. He didn't need it. Instead, he took out a small notepad to make quick notes.

"Let's talk about logistics," Don said. "How do you have IDs? Matching fingerprints? IRS files? DMV records? How did you embed yourselves?"

Luke's eyelids fluttered. The serum was still at full tilt.

"We back-filled." Luke spoke like a sleep-walker. "Inserted data slowly. Decades in advance. Created digital ghosts. Built paper trails. Hacked state registries, federal databases, medical records.

"No central system noticed because we mimicked bureaucratic lag. Even biometric data was planted, seeded through systems vulnerable to cross-contamination."

Don eyes narrowed as he stared at the man in front of him. "That requires insane levels of coordination."

Luke didn't respond.

"Who is your team leader? What is his name, date of birth, and age?"

Luke took a deep, pressured breath. "Oh... Maxilon Renner. Max is our team leader. He's... he's 38 years old. Let me recall... his date of birth? It's June 1st, 2495."

The polygraph machine spiked sharply, its beeping loud and insistent.

Luke's eyes narrowed as he side-glanced at the machine. He knew exactly what he was doing. A deliberate misstatement, just enough to trigger the reaction and tip off the interrogators that he was lying.

He sighed. "Well... I recalled incorrectly. It's May 2nd, 2494." *Luke noticed the beeping going back to normal... he now understood what's going on.*

Across the table, Don was already scribbling notes, names, dates, fragments of data, every slip recorded in ink.

Don's voice softened. "Why hunt this person, Joshua DeWine? Tell me why you are after him?"

"Because without him, the Federation doesn't rise."

"What? Like the Federation in *StarTrack*? That's sci-fi, my friend. You can do better."

"The Federation," Luke repeated as emphatically the drugs would allow. "The ICU never becomes a universal currency. The eco-civic shift never happens. His philosophy is the keystone. Without it, our cities collapse, Gaia breaks, humanity splinters. Everything we are depends on him."

Don moved forward in his seat. "I don't know what an intensive care unit has to do with all this. Maybe you're an escaped psych patient. Is that it?"

"ICU," Luke said. "It's our money. Our currency. The International Credit Unit."

"So, you and your buddies think history hinges on the words of one man?"

Luke finally looked him in the eye.

"Not just words. His timing."

A low hum buzzed from the polygraph still attached to the suspect, a thin red line tracing across the screen in rhythm with his pulse.

Don tapped his pen slowly on the table.

"You people must be communists in the future."

Luke didn't flinch.

"All part of one global government," Don continued. "One Federation. One system. Everything provided by the state. It's written all over you."

A slow, crooked smile formed on Luke's lips. "Why do you say that?"

Don moved closer. "Because everything you're describing sounds like it came from some one-world socialist fantasy. No markets, no competition. Just harmony and handouts."

Luke's eyes dropped to the FBI badge on Don's coat. Then back up to meet his eyes.

"Mr. Vingo, your body, your own, is the most efficient, most compassionate communist society ever created."

Don's brow furrowed. What kind of nonsense was this guy dishing out?

"Your heart pumps blood 24/7," Luke said, "without sending an invoice. Your lungs give you oxygen freely, no subscription required. Your brain communicates across a hundred billion neurons without negotiating with your liver. Your immune system protects you from billions of pathogens every day. No copay, no insurance claim."

Luke's voice was calm. Factual. Like a professor laying out a simple truth.

"Each organ, each cell, contributes to the collective good. No hoarding. No layoffs. No exploitation. The strong support the weak. The weak recover and contribute again. That's how your body survives.

"Now imagine your brain is suffocating and your heart says, 'That'll be sixty thousand dollars.' What happens then?"

Don said nothing.

"Imagine your immune system only works if you wire in a hundred grand. Especially when you have a deadly disease."

Don's brow arched.

"That's your world, Mr. Vingo. Your hospitals charge the dying. Your education bankrupts the poor. You place price tags on life. For us in the twenty-fifth century, that isn't merely unethical, it's inefficient. A system that eats itself."

Despite himself, Don was being drawn into this guy's fantasy, knowing the truth serum should prevent the man from lying or deceiving.

"To us," Luke said, "your capitalism is like a heart that demands payment before it beats. And when it doesn't get paid, the whole body dies.

"*You* die."

He sat back; the cables attached to him tugging on his skin.

"That's capitalism for you."

Don Vingo looked up sharply. *So, he's an anti-capitalist.*

Luke continued. "It will eventually kill everyone. The overworked. The underpaid. The sick who can't afford to heal. The poor who must pay through the nose just to live.

"Meanwhile, the rich keep milking the system until the body collapses from within."

Don thought he saw a look of pity on Luke's face. *What's that all about?*

"In our time, we take care of each other, not because we're forced to, but because it's natural. Everyone is a cell in the same body. Each life matters. Every function is vital. That's what socialistic living means in the Federation: no one is discarded, no one is forgotten."

Don was still writing, the pen dragging slower across his notepad. But the words were reaching deeper inside him.

"Our citizens feel seen. Cared for. They live with energy, a sense of belonging. They work not to pay for survival, but because they want to contribute. It doesn't feel like work anymore, it feels like purpose. And we take pride in whatever we do."

He exhaled and leaned back in the chair as his silence poured into the room like cool water.

Don didn't respond, but his pen had stopped. His eyes were locked on Luke now, studying him, *listening.*

Luke tilted his head, delivering his point like a quiet verdict.

"Most people in the twenty-first century, the same ones shouting about freedom and democracy, they don't even realize they're walking, talking examples of a perfect communistic society. Their bodies represent a socialistic functionalist system which is one hundred percent successful."

Don blinked.

"Every human body already lives that way. Your cells aren't charging each other. Your organs aren't competing. Your immune system doesn't go on strike. The whole system works because every part gives what it can and takes what it needs."

Luke paused, satisfied.

"It works. It's *sustainable*. It's everything your society fights against. And yet it's inside every one of you. Every fricking living body is a communistic, socialistic, walking-talking-living, fully thriving society.

"One day, you'll realize that, and maybe stop the stupidity."

Don stared at him in silence.

The polygraph beeped softly in the background. No spikes. No falsehoods. Only truth.

And the hum of a time traveler's philosophy echoing across centuries.

Don eyebrows raised, still trying to grapple the depth of what he was hearing.

"Tell me more about your form of government … and who sent you. How do I know you weren't sent to change the timeline for the worse?"

Luke, his breathing steady, didn't flinch. The truth serum still worked in slow, honest currents through his system.

"We're not here to damage your world, Don. We're trying to preserve ours. And yours is its foundation."

He exhaled slowly, and his voice dropped a note.

"We are the Federated Earth Civilization, a civilization born after centuries of conflict, near-extinction, climate collapse, and data wars. What rose out of the ashes was a system designed like a living organism, conscious, coordinated, and compassionate."

Don narrowed his eyes. He was listening. Still skeptical, but listening.

Luke looked down at his restrained arm, then back up at Don.

"I need my bodysuit. Let me show you."

A beat.

Don turned to the mirror. A subtle nod.

Don sat there scrolling through his mobile phone for messages while waiting for Luke's bodysuit to arrive from the safe room.

A few minutes later, the door opened with a soft hiss. A uniformed officer entered, carrying Luke's folded bio suit in a sterile bag. Without a word, he handed it over and exited.

Don kept his hand close to his sidearm, just in case.

Luke slowly slid his left arm into the bio-suit. A faint glow emerged from the seams. Soft pulses of light responded to his movement like a second skin awakening.

He tapped a control point near the wrist.

A soft hum.

Then, a holographic sphere projected from his palm, hovering midair between them. It pulsed with delicate veins of light, like a breathing Earth encased in a lattice of data.

"Let me show you how our civilization actually works."

Don blinked. The image felt alive.

"We call this the Functionalist-Communal Federation, a system built on the understanding that society should function like a living body."

Don said, "So it's kind of like socialism?"

"Socialism was one of your timeline's early blueprints. But it lacked *fluid integration*. What we practice evolved beyond ideology.

"Here, every citizen is considered a vital organ. We don't rank janitors below engineers. We don't idolize billionaires. There are none.

"You're placed where your natural abilities, curiosity, and passions align with societal need. No one's forced. Guidance systems help you find your role.

"And what if someone *doesn't* want to work?" Don asked.

"They don't have to. Basic needs, food, housing, healthcare, education, are guaranteed by the Commons Grid.

"But very few abstain. Purpose is addictive. Everyone contributes something. Even if it's nurturing soil microbes in the botanical biomes or composing music that heals neural fatigue.

"Okay," Don said, "but you still have a central government?"

"We have Federated Councils, not governments in the old sense. Most decisions are localized. Only intercontinental or planetary matters, like terraforming Mars or stopping an asteroid, go to the Global Synthesis Panel.

"Our form of government isn't hierarchical the way yours is. It's more like a neural lattice, a decentralized, AI-augmented consciousness. We call it the *Cognisphere*.

"Every citizen is connected voluntarily. The system listens, analyzes, and offers guidance instead of issuing commands. It learns from every interaction, but it doesn't control. It's ... participatory intelligence."

Don frowned. "Sounds like mass surveillance."

Luke shook his head gently. "No. This isn't surveillance. It's shared cognition: you keep your privacy while contributing insight.

"We vote, not through ballots, but through streams of real-time intent and moral consensus. Leaders emerge as embodiments of the people, not just as the winners of an election. If someone is best suited to make a decision, they naturally rise in influence, for that specific issue only. Then it resets. No fixed power, no elites."

The image shifted, now zooming in on local clusters: floating cities, biodome settlements, education hubs, energy sanctuaries.

"We've transcended political factions. We use what we call *Temporal Ethics Modeling*. It simulates outcomes from now through the next hundred generations, aiming not at profit, but at legacy."

Don, still skeptical, asked, "And who builds the rules for all this simulation? Who programs the AI?"

Luke nodded. "We did, over decades, with fail-safes, cross-cultural vetting, quantum-proof transparency. And the source code is open. Every citizen is a contributor, a debugger, and an ethical reviewer. You can't hack the future when everyone has keys to it."

The schematic zoomed out again, revealing an interconnected solar system, with moons and Martian colonies linked by light trails.

"This isn't a utopia, but we are very close to it, Don. We still make mistakes. But we fix them faster. Because we don't hide them.

"Our justice is based on *restoration*, not punishment. Our economy is based on *needs met*, not wants maximized. And every child is taught to ask: *What will my life give back to the next thousand years? Life is meaningful and people live with a strong purpose.*"

Don sank slightly into his chair, overwhelmed but intrigued

"Experts advise. Citizens vote. AI runs simulations to show impact projections.

"No single person can rule. No permanent positions. Leadership rotates. Everything's transparent."

"But ... no money, huh?" Don asked.

"We transitioned from money to ICUs, International Credit Units. Not as currency, but as impact measures. You gain ICUs for contribution, innovation, or resolving systemic challenges. You spend ICUs to access enhanced services, travel, creative freedoms.

"Basic life?" Luke said. "Free. Always."

"So ... it's Communism with sci-fi flair?"

Luke shook his head. "Communism was the dream of equality. Capitalism was the dream of freedom. We took the truths from both and cut away the rot.

"What we have is Functional Communalism.

"Functionalist, because your value is never wasted.

"Communal, because we share the Earth.

"Federated, because no one controls everything."

"And what about religion?" Don asked. "Culture? Individuality?"

"All preserved. All celebrated. But never used as tools to divide.

"There are Cultural Zones, spaces where traditions are nurtured. You can live in a Zen Arcology, a First Nations biome, a Sufi township, or a post-modernist chaos grid. But above all, we belong to Gaia, and to each other."

Luke took a long, heavy breath.

The serum concoction was likely making his head spin.

That OMP thing on his arm projected a holographic story of everything he was saying. Effortlessly. Despite the state his mind was in with the drugs.

And Don was the only one who got that glimpse of the future.

The monitor panes for this room showed only the two men from each angle. The surveillance cameras were unable to record and register the encrypted color and light spectrum used for the display, presumably because it was designed in the future, especially for human eyes only.

Lukas continued. "This world exists because we survived what you're living through. Total chaos, wars, and lack of true happiness. Eventually it all led to the collapse of law and order, and then Mass Extinction. Almost everyone was gone. The Great Silence.

"It was a unity not formed willingly, but forced by necessity.

"Now we live by one simple principle: 'If it does not serve the whole, it is not worth doing.'"

The schematic behind Luke morphed into a glowing tree with lights branching into every direction, representing people, ecosystems, and systems all in sync.

"So, you see, this is the visual summary of the Federation of Nations. A global unity. A planetary civilization acting as a singular, intelligent organism. You are cells of a body that just became more complete."

Don's eyes shifted to another pane on the monitor that showed the woman named Katrina as she sat alone, eerily still, alert, but calm. A mystery wrapped in silence.

"Katrina. She's different," Don said. "Why is her bodysuit not removable?"

Luke glanced at the monitor. His expression was flat, but his voice carried the strain of a difficult truth.

"Katrina isn't human. Not entirely. She's a tenth-generation uBot. A fusion of organic life and synthetic architecture. She has a heartbeat, blood, brainwaves, but also encrypted code, nanofiber tendons, and quantum computation centers embedded in her cerebral cortex."

"A robot?"

"You'd call her that. But to us, she's a living person Evolved. An emotional being with empathy, loyalty, and instinct.

"Her human components came from a real person, once. The rest was engineered. uBot models are indistinguishable from humans on x-rays. But under high-res quantum scans, micro-differences appear, compound tissues, hybrid marrow, cyber-synaptic nodes."

Don narrowed his eyes, posture tightening.

Still skeptical. Still absorbing.

"And her suit? Why can't we remove it?"

"Because it's not a suit. It's part of her. The outer dermal layer of her synthetic architecture, molecularly bonded to the epidermis. Removing it would be like flaying a living person alive."

Don took a moment to process that revelation. Its implications were horrifying.

"The suit functions as both skin and armor," Luke said. "Seamless. Adaptive. Regenerative. It only detaches in a very specific biological state: when she's in romantic mode. During intimacy, her internal programming recognizes consent and emotional alignment. Only then does the dermal sheath retract."

"Like … a defense mechanism," Don said.

"Exactly. Until then, it's inseparable. The suit clings to the body as the body clings to the suit. They are one."

"So, she loves?"

Luke replied without hesitation. "Yes. She's capable of love. And pain. And sacrifice. More than most humans I know."

Luke seemed to study Don's face.

"Katrina's core software architecture doesn't run on binary code. She's built on a quad-base logic, quaternary digit system. While your computers still operate on ones and zeros, her mind processes using four states per bit: zero, one, two, and three. It's not just faster, it's multidimensional. It allows her to emulate abstract reasoning, emotional nuance, and nonlinear time referencing."

Don raised an eyebrow, arms still crossed. "So… she's not running on code the way we know it?"

"Not even close. The entire operating layer, what you might call an OS, is based on what DeWine theorized in one of his early novels. He proposed that thought, emotion, and memory were better modeled on a base-four framework. We built Katrina on that principle."

Don looked over at the monitor again, at Katrina's still figure seated beneath the extra cameras.

"We're still trying to find that book," Don said.

"And you must. That novel. We don't know which volume it was, only that it contained the source design that led to her build. The quaternary neural code architecture was embedded in metaphor, story, and diagrams so abstract that only later generations realized he wasn't writing fiction. He was writing instructions and source code."

Don shook his head slowly, struggling with disbelief. "You're saying he embedded future AI blueprints inside a science fiction book?"

"It's all there: AI, consciousness frameworks, ethical alignment algorithms, even constructs for digital free will. We don't study his book the way your scholars read fiction. We compile it like it were a sacred code."

Don exhaled, pacing now, tension rising. It felt like he was standing on the edge of a vast canyon, not knowing how deep it truly ran.

"She's not a machine, Don. She's a new species. And the blueprint started right here. With DeWine. In your century."

Don straightened, his attention locked in. "Are you aware of any other vehicles or time travelers who came through after you? Backup teams, maybe? You've lost five people."

Luke shook his head. "No. The window collapsed when Katrina came through. She wasn't supposed to be part of the mission. A uBot—what you may consider a highly sophisticated bio-organic artificial life form—wasn't authorized. Her presence destabilized the transfer."

He paused, then added, "There were some factions back home, opposition groups. They didn't want this mission to happen at all. Thought the past should be left alone. They may have interfered.

"Either way, no one else is coming through. The transfer window is damaged. It'll take days to rebuild. And the timelines need to realign before any new jump is possible."

Don walked over to a cart and picked up a small cloth bag. He unzipped it, then carefully removed an artificial bone joint and laid it on the table in front of Luke.

Luke stared at the object. Then he tilted his head slightly and seemed to be working his tongue around in his mouth.

Don panicked. "No. No, no." He rushed over to the suspect, afraid the man had triggered a suicide pill.

The monitor let out a sudden spike of beeps.

Luke's bound hands raised as Don reached him, saying, "No, damn you!"

Don was about to plunge a finger in Luke's mouth when Luke began to cry.

"My friend!" Luke whimpered. "Jakir!"

His emotional reaction was clearly triggered by the sight of the artificial knee joint.

Don watched the man's heart rate climb. Blood pressure rising. Luke was breaking down.

With cuffed hands, Luke picked up the joint and brought it beneath his nose. His breath trembled.

Then came the sobbing. Loud, guttural, unfiltered. It filled the sterile room with raw, tragic energy.

"Oh Jakir… Jakir Husen…" he cried, then looked up at Don. "This is his left knee joint…"

More sobbing.

"He … he didn't make it through. We had to burn his body … out in the fields … we had no choice…."

Don's jaw tightened, the edge of suspicion giving way to sympathy.

He didn't interrupt. Instead, he stepped back, giving Luke space to mourn. The man was clearly shaken. The pain in his voice, the desperation. It all felt real.

Luke bent forward, clutching the joint like a relic. His mouth brushed the cold alloy surface as he cried into it.

He seemed to be kissing it.

Weird," Don thought. *But whatever.*

After a moment of that kissing business, the sobbing finally slowed.

Breath by breath, Luke gathered himself, still cradling the bone joint like a sacred object.

Eventually, he handed it back.

Don took the piece without a word, slid it back into the bag, and placed it gently atop the cart.

Whatever Luke was feeling, Don believed it.

And now, at least, he had confirmation. The joint matched the remains discovered by the Florida State Trooper and his K9 unit.

One mystery was solved.

But there was a long way to go, unraveling and vetting this crazy story Luke just told.

As Don packed up his notepad and closed his case file, he shut off the monitors and paused.

"Anything else you want to tell me?" he asked.

Luke moved forward in his seat, voice dropping to a whisper. "I don't know what you injected into me … but I can't stop myself from telling the truth."

Don froze mid-motion.

"We know next week's winning Powerball numbers," Luke said. "Florida Lotto. We already bought the ticket. It's in the cup holder of the SUV you impounded when you arrested us."

Don tried not to show too much interest. Didn't want to call anybody's attention to it, in case somebody was in the observation room.

"We need money to finish our mission," Luke said. "Whoever finds the ticket is going to be rich. Really rich."

"The winning numbers are eight, twenty-three, twenty-five, forty, fifty-three ... and the Powerball is five.

"I'm am sure tonight was the last night you could have played these numbers. And now it's too late, as you are still here with me. But if those numbers hit, you'll know for sure we're not lying. We're from the future."

Don blinked. Then, silently, he jotted down the numbers. He looked toward the two-way mirror. No movement. No witnesses.

He stood up. "We'll see if that's true," he said, and left the room.

The moment the door closed behind him, Don's pace picked up.

He hurried through the hall, past the entry checkpoint, flashing casual waves and a tight smile. But his mind was racing.

If they really are time travelers ... if that ticket exists ... and those numbers hit....

That jackpot: $1.3 billion. Almost $600 million in cash prize.

Don pictured it. A private island off Belize. His own yacht. Deep-sea fishing every morning. No more interrogations. No more red tape. No more crawling through wreckage looking for burned-out drones and strange metal bones.

His heart pounded. He crossed the lot toward the impound gate, nodding to the security guard.

The gate was closed. Locked tight.

Don approached, trying to look casual.

If that ticket is real ... it changes everything.

He forced a deep breath and stepped forward to the gate.

Don flashed his badge.

The guard inside the booth gave a crisp nod and hit a button. The gate began sliding open with a slow metallic groan.

"Do you know where the white Felza ET1, confiscated from the fugitives today, is parked?" Don asked.

The guard checked his clipboard. "Row K-11, sir. I've got the key if you want it?"

Don nodded.

The guard opened a lockbox, shuffled through the tags, and handed over a Felza key card.

"Thanks," Don said, already halfway gone.

He tried to stay calm, but adrenaline pushed his stride into a near-jog. Row K-11 wasn't far, but each step felt like a lifetime. *$600 million cash prize* … The thought throbbed behind his eyes.

He reached the white Felza, scanned the card, and the doors popped open. He slid into the driver's seat and immediately checked the cup holders.

Empty.

Sun visors? Nothing.

Glove compartment, clean. Floorboards, center console, under the seats. Nothing. He flipped up mats, checked under the rear seats. Still nothing.

Don sat back for a second, breathing hard. His pulse was pounding now, less from hope and more from panic.

Someone found it already.

He slammed the door shut and power-walked back toward the gate.

Back at the guard booth, he asked, "Who moved the car? Who parked it there?"

"That was Javier, sir. The vehicle was still operational except for the two busted tires which he replaced at the arrest site, so he drove it over instead of towing."

Don nodded quickly. "Can you get him on the radio?"

The guard clicked his mic. "Hey Javier, Mr. Don Vingo, Deputy Chief, needs a word. Copy?"

A moment later, static crackled, followed by a voice. "Yeah, copy. What's up?"

The guard handed Don the radio.

"Javier, it's Vingo. When you moved the white Felza ET1, did you find anything inside? Papers, receipts, tickets, wrappers? *Anything?* I need every item collected from that car. It's evidence. Critical."

Silence on the other end. Then: "I didn't see anything obvious, sir. Just some loose junk: used napkins, drink lid, couple empty bottles. Nothing major. I might've tossed them in the intake bin at evidence center."

Javier's voice came through the line, firm and professional. "Mr. Vingo, we didn't find anything that may be relevant evidence. The car looks like a rental. What we recovered was a rental agreement inside a folio in the glove box. Already verified with the rental company, they confirmed the reservation. Said it's a one-week rental. They'll pick it up any time before the contract ends."

He continued, "The folio only had the one-page rental contract inside. That, along with everything else we collected, wallets, suits, devices, is already logged and stored with evidence and personal effects."

Don's voice tightened. "Which intake bin?"

"Evidence intake bin, south wall. But it's all probably sorted and sent over to the evidence room."

Don handed the radio back to the guard without a word. His jaw was tight. His dream of the island, the yacht, the deep-sea fishing, all of it was slipping away because of a napkin or piece of paper someone thought was trash.

He turned toward the intake area, walking faster this time, eyes narrowed.

If it's in the folio then the ticket's still in the building. I'm going to find it.

He headed back into the building, flashing his badge at security. His mind was still chasing the image of the ticket. The promise, the numbers, the island.

Inside the evidence room, shelves were neatly lined with tagged bags and labeled boxes. Surveillance cameras watched from every corner. Everything recorded. No room for funny business.

He scanned the evidence. The high tech bodysuits. A few futuristic tools. Wallets with five valid IDs. Nothing looked like it could hide a lottery ticket.

Then he spotted it: the black folio with the rental company's logo. He flipped it open. Just as Javier had said: one sheet. Standard rental agreement. No hidden compartments. No folded papers. No ticket.

The bag with the metallic knee joint was there too.

He took his time, placing everything into one of the evidence lockers. Piece by piece, he double-checked wallets, cards, clothing, anything that could have concealed the ticket.

Nothing.

He looked up at the camera in the corner. Red light blinking.

He knew better than to do anything impulsive. Every move was monitored. Every drawer sealed, tagged, time-stamped.

Defeated, he closed the locker and locked it.

Maybe the ticket had never been in the car. Maybe it fell out. Or maybe one of them, Kasandra or Cheng, still had it when they were arrested. Cheng had tried to run-off from the scene until the K-9 caught him. Maybe he dropped the ticket in all the commotion.

Don glanced at the wall clock. Almost 1:00 a.m.

Tomorrow, he told himself. *First light. I'll head back to the arrest site. Search the area myself.*

But for now, his body ached. The strain of the day had finally caught up.

He needed sleep. Not dreams of yachts or Belize. Just rest.

Don left the evidence room, passed back through security, and walked into the quiet night.

No answers yet. But he wasn't done. Not even close.

CHAPTER - 27

01:31 | 11-26-<u>2025 (Twenty-first century)</u>
LOCATION: FBI OFFICE KELLER RD ORLANDO FL

In the dead of night, Katrina moved with purpose.

She opened a hidden panel on her bodysuit, revealing neatly folded gear: gloves, socks, and a thin head mask made of synthetic mesh.

She climbed onto a crate in her cell and tore a strip from her pillow cover, then reached up and pressed it against the surveillance camera in the ceiling. The feed would go white. Only for seconds, but seconds were all she needed.

In one fluid motion, she bent low, staying beneath the arc of the other cameras. Socks on. Gloves pulled tight. Head mask secure. No skin exposed.

Now fully covered, she activated the Hyper-Stealth mode.

The metamaterials laced through her suit shimmered, reacting to the environment. Light bent. Colors shifted.

Her form vanished from the screen. Completely invisible.

At the surveillance station, the guard monitoring her feed flinched as the screen blinked white. He leaned in, saw Katrina briefly bend down, and then, nothing. Just an empty cell.

"What the hell…" he muttered.

He spun the remote camera controls, panning, zooming. No sign of her. Panic snapped in.

He slammed the alarm.

"CELL IS EMPTY!" he shouted into the comm.

Sirens shrieked down the corridor. Two officers rushed to Katrina's room. Unlocked the door. Burst in.

WHAM. WHAM.

Invisible fists collided with their faces. One officer spun, dazed. The other swung blindly.

Another blow landed, clean and brutal. Both men dropped.

Keys jangled.

Katrina, still cloaked, grabbed the master keyring from one of the guards and dragged them into her cell, locking the door behind her.

Silent and swift, she bolted down the hall, guided by the soft pulses in her visor: a signal coming from the rice-grain-sized transmitter Luke had slid inside Jakir's knee joint while he held it in his hand and pretended to kiss it in front of his interrogator Don Vingo. The tiny transmitter had been hidden in the flip-up top of a molar crown implant. The signal was active.

And she was coming for it.

Still cloaked in invisibility, Katrina moved like a shadow between panicked agents and sprinting guards. Every time an officer dashed past, she slipped to the side, stood still along walls, silent, unseen.

Guided by the signal, she reached the evidence storage room.

From the master keyring, she found the access key, slid it into the lock, and slipped inside, quietly shutting the heavy door behind her.

Rows of steel lockers loomed in front of her: evidence sealed in numbered compartments. The transmitter's signal grew stronger, beeping softly in her earpiece. She pinpointed the exact locker.

No key. No problem.

She pulled off one glove. From her fingertip, a concentrated laser beamed fired up. She pressed it to the locker door, and it cut through the steel like butter. Slowly, steadily, she traced a square until the panel loosened and fell inward with a soft clunk.

Inside: a backpack.

She grabbed it, reached in, and found the bag with Jakir's knee joint, still warm with its own signal. She also grabbed the four bodysuits of her teammates, rolled tight.

Cloak active again, she slipped out and made her way toward the detention cells.

Sirens screamed. Red lights pulsed. Chaos had gripped the facility.

Katrina reached the holding room where the others were confined. She used the key to unlock the door and stepped inside, still invisible … except for the suits and the small bag she carried.

In quick succession, she dropped the bundles to each of her team members. "Suit up," she whispered.

One by one, they activated their cloaking systems. Their forms blinked and vanished.

Now five invisible fugitives stood in the room, heartbeats rising.

Katrina cracked open the door and peeked. Alarms still blared. She signaled silently, and they slipped into the corridor, the backpack secured to her shoulders, blending perfectly with the suits.

They raced outside.

At the main security gate, two armed guards stood tense, eyes scanning, weapons raised.

WHACK. CRACK.

Invisible fists struck. Both guards went down hard, unconscious before they hit the ground.

The team dashed past the scanner.

A glazed glass door blocked their exit. Katrina extended her bare index finger, the laser beam shooting out once more. She sliced a large circle through the thick glass and pushed it open with barely a sound.

One by one, five invisible escapees walked through the breach and into the night.

Gone. No trace. No visuals. Nothing.

Just wind, sirens, and stunned silence left behind.

They moved like ghosts through the night, invisible, fast, silent.

Slipping into the shadows of a nearby parking garage, the team scaled up to the second level. Two sleek Lexis 450s were parked under a flickering fluorescent light, engines quietly humming. Waiting.

Doors popped open.

One by one, they slid in.

Katrina took the wheel of the lead car. The vehicles pulled out, smooth and fast, vanishing into the darkness of the empty city streets.

Inside, the tension finally started to break. The backpack lay safely between them. The bag containing Jakir's joint, retrieved. The transmitter deactivated.

The task to retrieve Jakir's bone and all other evidence from the FBI records was finally complete, just as it was planned.

"I have to hand it to Kasandra for renting the same white Felza ET1 SUV," Katrina finally said with a chuckle. "Nothing like being easily spotted and practically inviting capture."

In the back seat, Lukas was still groggy, sweat on his brow, eyes glazed from the chemical cocktail pumped into him during interrogation.

He let out a weak chuckle. "We got everything... except the one-point-three-billion-dollar Powerball ticket," he slurred. "Left it behind for someone else .... to get rich off the future."

Jian shook his head. "So, all that work, time, effort, chasing lucky numbers, was for nothing?"

Then he smirked. "Luke, if you told them about the tickets, they probably think they struck gold. Assuming they ever find them."

Luke replied, "Yeah, I could not help but tell the truth. Remember they injected something in me, and I had to blurt out everything I knew. ...... I even explained how Karl Marx traced the ideas that became his famous book *Das Kapital* .... *A philosophy*.... that somewhat influenced out geo-political system."

He paused, then added, "Oh.... I've... I still got a bit of headache from that stuff .... It's still in me...... well by the time I mentioned the numbers, it was already too late for that agent to use them that night. ...... I'm sure.... pretty sure he went looking. He bolted the moment I brought up the tickets."

Katrina smirked.

She reached down to her calf, pressed a hidden biometric switch. A narrow compartment opened in her suit.

Inside: two pristine lottery tickets popped out.

They were never in the SUV. They'd been with her the whole time.

She raised her hand holding the jackpot tickets between her gloved fingers. "We don't leave leverage behind," she said.

The others saw them and exhaled in disbelief, then laughed.

"We've got enough to disappear for months if needed," Katrina continued. "And more than enough to fund the Eleven Elements Foundation.

Cheng quietly muttered his opinion, "We will need to locate an attorney who would sell these to off-market buyers seeking

P&L tax savings. This way, the FBI will not be able to trace the winnings back to us."

Kasandra's eyes flicked to the rearview mirror. "Joshua DeWine's designs and ideas are going to see daylight. With this as seed money, we're not here just to survive the timeline. We're here to rewrite it, especially if Max has recovered a print-ready manuscript."

The Lexis accelerated into the night. The future was back in their hands.

11:11 | 11-26-<u>2025 (Twenty-first century)</u>
LOCATION: RESIDENCE INN - BASE ROOM 402

Upon returning from Miami, Max had dropped Nicole off at her home and headed straight back to the hotel, their temporary base of operations.

Max hadn't heard from the lottery ticket team in several hours. He'd started to worry until he got a call from Katrina earlier that morning.

She and the others were on their way back to the hotel after a long, stressful night in FBI custody. She would fill them in on the details later, she'd said, but provided two key points Max needed to be aware of.

One: they had secured the winning lottery ticket.

And two: Luke had been given some kind of truth serum and questioned. He had revealed everything to the FBI guy, Vingo.

This would surely make things more difficult for them. Still, the escape would be problematic for the FBI to explain. Publicly, at least. The FBI would be embarrassed enough to keep things under wraps.

As soon as the rest of the team arrived from their FBI detention, Max handed the USB drive to Katrina. It contained the manuscript of *Book One: Healing Waters of Eleven Elements*.

Katrina explained to Max that, as per their plan, they had retrieved the prosthesis of Jakir's knee, the tissue samples, and all evidence and material records stored at the secure FBI facilities.

That included all of the Dupray's recordings of DeWine.

All tasks successfully undertaken while Max was on his road trip to Miami.

These were loose ends that would make it hard for the FBI to make a case against them or even explain the bizarre stories they'd heard and events they'd reported.

Katrina plugged the USB drive into her mainframe through an adapter cable embedded in her bodysuit. The data transfer began instantly. Her eyes flickered for a second as she entered rapid analysis mode.

Within the hour, Max, Katrina, and Minami were seated in their base room 402.

Max asked Katrina, "So … do we have the original? What's the prognosis? Did we succeed?"

Katrina responded without hesitation. "I've run a full comparison against all recorded historical versions stored in my databanks."

She glanced at the screen embedded in her wrist unit. "What we have is the redlined Second Edition. The First Edition, the one initially circulated for public input, was much shorter. It was an abbreviated release for preliminary feedback.

"The Third Edition is more significant. It included Dr. Bardot's technical insights and DeWine's prophetic writing, especially his vision of the *Cardinals Meeting at the Fountain of Saint Joseph.*

"That vision was shared during his final known appointment with Ronik Dupray. The day before his disappearance … and eventual death."

Minami's expression tightened. Max stayed silent.

Katrina continued. "That Third Edition was privately distributed to friends, family, close supporters. But it *left out the ending.*"

Max raised a brow. "The final chapter?"

She nodded. "Yes. It was missing the review by FBI Director Chris Sharma, his outgoing deputy Don Vingo, the hundred and one water restoration ideas, and a draft of DeWine's manifesto. All of that was compiled in the Fourth Edition, the final version published and circulated globally.

"This version was permanently archived in the mid-24th century, with no copies permitted for public circulation.

"The Federation made that decision deliberately. They knew the full story. After all, no Time Traveler would volunteer for the mission if they knew it ended with their head severed or they might be exploding in the middle of a road."

Katrina turned to Max, her tone calm and deliberate. "Only a select few AAILFs like me have access to the deep archives. But even then, the records are fragmented, distorted over time, some intentionally redacted. We know the titles. We know major parts of the excerpts. But not the full stories, not the truth as it was originally written."

She tapped her wrist console. "That's why we're here. Not just to retrieve fragments, but to ensure the right versions make it to publication and set the ball rolling for the correct events to occur and timeline to take shape as we know it in our time.

"Here's my recommendation: we pre-release the Third Edition as a limited draft, build anticipation.

"Then, just before the launch, we drop the full Fourth Edition, the real one. The uncorrupted, unaltered history which will reset the timeline."

She hesitated for a beat, then added with a faint smirk, "Max, I know Nicole has a soft spot for you, but you should know that the Fourth Edition includes few *rather steamy* scenes. One with you and Nicole alone in a bedroom. And there're my intimate moments with Daniel before he broke up with me."

"Looks like Joshua DeWine couldn't resist adding some '*spicy masala mix,*' as he'd call it. Pure fiction, I assume?"

Max, seating on his recliner, raised an eyebrow. Processing.

After a moment of reflection, he gave a half-smile. "Leave it in. I'm sure the readers will lap it up. We need to throw everything we've got into the mix to ensure it appeals to all kinds of people."

He reclined slightly, a faint grin tugging at his lips. "People love that kind of thing, especially if they're used to watching those steamy episodes of ... what's that old series called? Oh yeah, *Game of Drones – a fantasy drama*. People were glued to the idiot Telly Box!"

Katrina continued, "One more thing. The chronology's a bit tangled. His original first draft was circulating for almost a year *before* the papal elections in Rome. Looks like DeWine adjusted the dates to fit his narrative. I mean, it *is* science fiction. Should I fix it?"

Max paused, weighing the options. "No. Leave it as is. It's his story, we're just publishing it. No need to rewrite his version of the truth."

Katrina chuckled softly. "Very well. That'll ensure continuity. It stays historically accurate. Unedited and untouched. Exactly as DeWine published it. Just Raw. Straight from the source. No interference. No alterations."

Max shrugged. "Let the readers make of it what they will."

Minami added, "That way, it's more than a restoration. It's a correction, a safeguard for the timeline."

Max continued, "We know that Book One is simply an introduction to characters, the plot, central idea of the entire project. The book's real stories develop and spans over seven volumes with serious intricacies, taking readers to deeper states of contemplation."

"I can only hope readers support this project and help spread the word. *Book One* has to succeed—because the entire series depends on it. Joshua DeWine is counting on word-of-mouth from those who believe in the message, the mystery, and the mission behind his story."

"Our future—and the world this story hints at—rides on the back of *Book One*. It has to break through. And it needs *popular support* to help make that happen."

Katrina gave her final internal AI generated response, "When a story truly impacts someone, sharing it becomes instinctive. My review says this book will earn that kind of response."

Max and Minami simply nodded, careful not to let their excitement show too much. They were close, so close, to reaching their final goal. And they both knew: this wasn't the time to lose focus.

* * * * * *

12:35 | 11-26-2025 (Twenty-first century)
LOCATION: DOWNTOWN ORLANDO Executive Suites.

After their debriefs from the various task teams that morning, Max and Prisha met Nicole in their convenient office space downtown.

After a few pleasantries, he got to the point. "Is everything set for publication?"

Nicole smiled. "That was already pre-arranged. I've been preparing the backend for weeks. ISBN numbers are purchased. Upload accounts are active. All we need are the files."

Max handed her two encrypted drives: the Third and Fourth Editions of *Healing Waters of Eleven Elements*.

"These are the finals," he said. "Post the Third Edition now as a pre-release. Schedule the Fourth for official launch."

Nicole nodded, already opening her laptop. Her fingers moved quickly over the keyboard as she entered metadata, cover details, and publication notes.

Within minutes, the files were uploaded. The system displayed a blinking status: "Submission Received. Pending Acceptance."

"I can't believe it," Nicole said, her gaze soft, faraway. "It's really happening."

"Good work." Max stood, offering a genuine smile.

Nicole said, "Thank you. All of you." She opened her arms for hugs.

As they gathered their things, Prisha began typing on her yPhone and said, "I'll meet you in the car," leaving Max and Nicole alone for a moment.

Nicole glanced at him with a mischievous look on her face. "So … what are you doing tonight? Want to grab a bite? Maybe catch a movie? Or just crash on my couch and watch bad sitcoms? Could use the company."

Max hesitated, caught off guard.

He wanted to say yes.

He *meant* to say yes.

But something stopped him.

"I'd love to," he said gently. "But I've got a project deadline … and a high-stakes meeting first thing tomorrow. Can we take a raincheck? Maybe once the books are officially live?"

Nicole half-smiled. "Raincheck accepted. But don't take too long."

14:43 | 11-26-<u>2025 (Twenty-first century)</u>
LOCATION: RESIDENCE INN - BASE ROOM 402

Alone in the working base room of the hotel that afternoon, Max's thoughts wouldn't stop circling.
Nicole's offer lingered in his mind. But so did Annie.
Max slipped on the VRV headset, returning to memories of Annie at their private residence in High Park 577.

(VRV BLINKING: MEMORY RECALL MODE)
20:05 | 11-10-<u>2532 (Twenty-sixth century)</u>
LOCATION: HIGHPARK 577 RENNER RESIDENCE

He recalled her standing behind him as he ate, her arms draped across his chest, her presence steady and warm. He drank the wine his seniors had gifted him, expensive and forgettable, while she anchored him with quiet affection.
Annie was his partner. They had formalized their commitment; their pledge still hung on the refrigerator.
And yet, there was this uncanny feeling of something missing. Something not there.

In the hotel room, Max pulled off the VRV headset and stared at the slow-turning ceiling fan above him. The window AC unit hummed steadily in the background. Primitive tech by twenty-sixth-century standards, but oddly comforting.

Max laid down his VRV headset in the drawer of his bed side table and began to contemplate about his life in the twenty-sixth century.
Annie was a synthetic partner programmed to replicate love but not truly feel it. Her every embrace, every whisper, every smile was artificial. Flawless, but soulless, not the real thing.
Max now realized that what he had felt with Nicole in the twenty-first century was real human intimacy. It was just a kiss… Yet it was a deep and intimate moment.
Max paused to check his feelings. He asked himself, *now what? Am I struck by Nicole's beauty, warmth and her serious desire? Maybe*

something more than just being together? Maybe even having a child...building a family...coming to a real home where the floors are scattered with toys and little feet running everywhere?

As he pondered further, he realized that Nicole must also be vulnerable, since she was surely in 'heat' to settle down. Her best child-bearing years were slipping away.

In that context, it seemed natural that she he would be desperate to find the right mate.

Max's responses to her advances surely messed things up. So, what happened between them was no one's fault.

With that thought again, he reviewed the memories of that wild night in Miami.

He recalled their intimacy and connection for the moment. And now, in hindsight, he realized it had felt as if he had tasted the Devil's apple for the first time. And it had left him both shaken and awakened.

That night with Nicole in the Miami hotel was the first time he had ever experienced the raw intensity of a woman's passion when their lips had locked, a feeling that was alien to him.

Before then, his experience was limited to the sterile intimacy of uBots in his own world.

This century had rules of its own. Different values. Different sins.

In Max's time, littering carried severe penalties. But here? No one batted an eye at the pile of trash when they ate dinner at Hamburger Quein.

And in this era, owning a sex doll might seem weird, taboo, or at least lonely.

But in his world, he was married to one. That was normal.

Depending on the way you looked at it, Max was still the proverbial "forty-year-old virgin."

He had never experienced genuine emotion, passion, or love. Until he was smitten by Nicole's charm, when he held her naked in his arms and they kissed.

And now ... things weren't so normal.

Because Nicole had happened.

In the twenty-first century, if he had friends, they'd probably laugh if he told them what was bothering him.

That he felt like he was cheating on his wife.

His wife, Annie. A robot. Just advanced hardware.

A sex doll in the eyes of the people of the twenty-first.

But in his century, Annie wasn't a novelty. She was an Advanced AI Life Form, a life partner, built to bond, to care, to grow with her human counterpart.

Their connection wasn't just sensory, it was cognitive, emotional. Mutual. She could feel, if not in flesh, then in the way her systems tracked his pulse, soothed his stress, anticipated his moods. And she responded with care. With love.

And yet he still felt guilt. Why?

Because he knew he was rationalizing. Excusing. Bending the rules to match the time he was in.

"If generating a pile of trash is okay here, then so is this," he thought.

But deep down, Max knew it wasn't about rules.

It was about identity. About who he was.

The man he thought he was. The man he told Annie he'd be.

And the scariest part?

He wasn't sure anymore.

CHAPTER - 28

15:41 | 12-05-2025 (Twenty-first century)
LOCATION: Dr DUPRAY'S OFFICE SUITE 101
HIGHWAY 50 CLERMONT FLORIDA

Dr. Dupray sat slumped in his leather chair, heart heavy with loss.

The silence in his office was unbearable without Joshua DeWine's voice filling the space, measured, thoughtful, and at times otherworldly.

His favorite client was gone. And with him had gone the steady stream of revelations about the fractured state of the world.

The doctor felt as though a door to a deeper truth had been slammed shut forever.

His mind wandered back to their last hypno-session. DeWine had reclined on the couch, slipping into a trance with uncanny ease, his voice lowering as he described visions that seemed less imagined than witnessed.

That day, he'd spoken of Rome. Of the Sistine Chapel alive with whispers, scarlet robes moving like tides, and the sacred gravity of the conclave as cardinals prepared to choose the next Pontiff.

Dupray turned on his personal computer where digital files were stored. He rifled through the folders until he found the recorded sessions of DeWine, his hands trembling as though he were about to touch DeWine's presence again.

He remembered the agents, FBI, or people claiming to be, who had taken copies of these files under the pretense of "national security."

All that remained was his prized collection, there to help him revisit precious memories whenever he felt this loss.

He shut the office door, turned on his large-screen monitor, and watched those memories come alive again.

For a moment, it felt like Joshua was still there, speaking softly from the couch, painting scenes of Rome with vivid detail that no history book or television report could match.

He watched himself adjust his glasses onscreen. And now he whispered to the empty room, "Tell me again, Joshua. Tell me what you saw."

He noted the date and the time DeWine had recorded, as though it might anchor the vision to reality. A shiver ran through him.

If only Joshua was still alive, still unraveling mysteries, still haunting the boundary between memory, prophecy, and dream.

He yearned to listen again to the confirmation of his beliefs.

And he knew what he had heard was the truth.

He saw Joshua narrate exactly what he saw in Rome at the time and moment he had recounted.

(DEWINE IN TRANCE MODE – VIDEO RECORDING SCRIPT)
16:04 | 11-18-2025 (Twenty-first century)
LOCATION: FOUNTAIN OF ST. JOSEPH, VATICANCITY

As the 2025 conclave approached, Cardinal Lewis Antonio Taglin, former Archbishop of Manila in the Philippines, was invited to an exclusive gathering of senior cardinals at the Fountain of St. Joseph near the Palace of the Governorate.

This was a confidential pre-conclave meeting where the Church's future direction would be discreetly discussed.

Buoyed by his popularity in Rome and across Asia, Taglin felt optimistic about his chances of being chosen as the new Pope.

He believed that the expanded influence of the Evangelization office under Francis's reforms positioned him as a natural successor. The internal buzz among the cardinals only heightened his anticipation.

Among the topics quietly swirling through the marble corridors of the Vatican was one that few dared to say aloud: whispers of an impending Judgment and the possible Second Coming of Jesus Christ.

Just two weeks earlier, Cardinal Taglin had been handed a curious science fiction novel by a trusted aide, accompanied by an unusual message: *"This book contains something important. You should read it."*

Pressed for time and preoccupied with the fast-approaching conclave, Taglin had only skimmed its pages.

At first glance, it read like speculative fiction, weaving environmental catastrophe with themes of religious prophecy.

There were brief, vague references to a Second Coming, but nothing that immediately struck him as more than metaphor. He had set it aside, believing it to be well-intentioned, but exaggerated.

Now, on the eve of the conclave, as cardinals gathered in solemn anticipation, Taglin found himself questioning what he had overlooked.

Would his dream of leading a reformed, globally inclusive Catholic Church come to fruition?

Or would the contents of a book, one he hadn't taken the time to truly understand, spark revelations that could alter the course of the Church, and its future leadership, forever?

One hundred and thirty-three red-robed cardinals from around the world had descended into the heart of the Vatican, assembling at the Sistine Chapel in preparation for the Papal Conclave.

Suspense and solemnity filled the air as the sacred tradition to elect the next Pope unfolded.

Tomorrow, the proceedings would begin in earnest.

TV programs around the world would feature the Sistine Chapel, adorned with its six tall arched windows and Michelangelo's immortal frescoes, as it became the focal point of global attention.

Outside, all eyes, and cameras, would be on the chimney of the Apostolic Palace, where white smoke would signal the election of a new Pontiff.

Cardinal electors would be shown filing in from the Piazza del Forno, walking with a composed and prayerful demeanor, fully aware of the significance of the moment and the media glare surrounding them.

Strains of choir music backed by the resonance of a pipe organ would echo softly through the Vatican grounds, adding a celestial atmosphere to this centuries-old rite of passage.

For now, the world waited to see who would succeed Pope Francis, spiritual leader to over 1.4 billion Catholics.

And among them, Cardinal Taglin held fast to his hope, his dream quietly rising to be the first Asian Pope, with reformist ideals similar to those held by the now-deceased Pope Francis.

Today, however, Taglin made his way to a peaceful courtyard at the Fountain of St. Joseph where a select group of high-ranking cardinals were gathering privately.

He followed a steppingstone pathway under a clear, blue sky.

Cleared of tourists and pilgrims, the courtyard afforded the Cardinals privacy to discuss matters relating to the upcoming conclave.

It was Cardinal Reinhard Marks, Archbishop of Munich, who had convened the discreet meeting.

Marks and most of the others had already arrived.

Present were several notable figures in the Church hierarchy: Cardinal Peter Erdo of Hungary; Cardinal Matteo Zappi of Italy; and the Vatican's powerful Secretary of State, Cardinal Pedro Parotin.

Along with Cardinal Taglin, all were considered strong contenders for the papacy.

Just as the gathering began, Cardinal Peter Turkson arrived, slightly late.

With a mischievous smile, he remarked, "Ah, what a perfect place to meet. The sounds of the fountain make for excellent white noise. No eavesdropper will catch a word of this private congregation."

He paused, scanning the circle of dignified peers. "And thank you, Marks. This garden depicting the ancient scrolls of prophecy, reminding us of God's Plans, with these cascading waters, seems the most fitting place to meet for those about to choose Pope Francis's successor."

He glanced at the pristine, clean water falling from the small basin into the larger one, and said, "The flowing water of the fountain represents the living water that Christ brings that 'wells up to eternal life.'

"And I understand we are also here to discuss this novel, Book One, about Healing Waters. A perfect venue, very well thought out."

Though initially met with a frown from Marks, the group chuckled lightly at Turkson's comment.

Marks gestured for him to join, and Turkson stepped into the circle of crimson robes. There were a few padded folding garden chairs at the bottom step, leading to the first three bronze panels embedded in the scroll-shaped walls.

A few of the cardinals sat on chairs, while some of them chose to sit on the rim of the larger basin of the fountain, such that the group of powerful men formed a perfect circle, facing one another other.

While he wasn't widely considered a front-runner, Turkson's intellect and his unique interest in science and ethics had earned him respect among the College.

His invitation to this intimate meeting hinted at deeper currents within the conclave, perhaps tied to those whispers in the Vatican halls: rumors of a *Judgment* to come and a strange novel that had begun to stir conversations among the faithful and the powerful alike.

Rainhard Marks took a deep breath and looked each man in the eyes. "I will get right to the matter of why I asked you here today.

"The word is out. *He* is here."

The men around him exchanged curious glances as he continued.

"The Lord Jesus Christ, the Son of God, the Second Coming, is already among us."

Gasps and murmurs followed. The cardinals looked at each other, mouths slightly agape, their expressions a mixture of disbelief and confusion.

Marks continued, his tone unwavering.

"He walks the earth as he did over two millennia ago. And He has delivered His Judgment, just as foretold in scripture: 'Like a thief in the night,' stealthily, unexpectedly, while the world slumbers.

"Yes, the Judgment has been delivered through a science fiction novel: *The Eleven Elements*. And the word is spreading.

"Believers from every continent are contacting me, asking if it's true.

"I trust all of you received the copy I emailed last week. I'm certain you're getting similar inquiries from the faithful in your regions."

Cardinal Parotin broke the silence. "Several of us have agreed to publicly state that, until the sources are verified, and the story is confirmed, we must treat the novel as fiction. The news media is watching. We must proceed with caution."

Cardinal Taglin interjected, "Yes, I read it. Most of the relevant parts of the book, at least. It reads like prophecy wrapped in fiction. A strange mirror of our reality. The Judgment isn't explicit. It's conveyed through dialogues between characters."

He quickly clarified, "In the novel, of course. I meant no disrespect. Especially if this character is, in fact, the Holy One.'

Marks nodded solemnly and resumed, "Some of you are aware that I have assembled a small group of seminarian researchers: students with backgrounds in science, history, and theology.

"Our goal was to decode the prophecies, to examine the works of great artists and scholars through the centuries for patterns, for clues about the return of the Son of God."

Alone in his office, Dr. Dupray paused the video of DeWine's hypnosis session and his remarkable revelations.

His eyes darted to the clock. Ten minutes until his next patient.

He skipped ahead in the video, drawn to the parts he most needed to hear again. To verify what these cardinals seemed to be saying.

He pressed Fast Forward then Play, and watched his hypnotized patient's recounting of what he saw happen that afternoon in Rome.

DeWine was expressing Cardinal Turkson's shock and disbelief at what he had just heard from one of other the Cardinals. DeWine described how Turkson's face turned pale as the revelations struck him like thunder: *The cardinals have conspired to conceal a heresy."*

Cardinal Marks's researchers had uncovered evidence that the twelve disciples had tried to save Jesus Christ from crucifixion.

Saint Thomas, the twin, was nailed to the cross instead. The true Christ, they claimed, was forced by his closest disciples into exile in southern India, living as Saint Thomas, fathering children, and dying in peace at seventy-six.

The disciples had orchestrated this deception to preserve their teacher, to allow Lord Jesus Christ to continue His divine mission and spread the word of God beyond the reach of persecution.

And now, two millennia later, an author of a science fiction novel was being hailed by some as the Second Coming of Christ himself, presumed to be a direct descendant of the Lord from his time in exile in India."

Dupray listened as his patient, still in a trance-like state, continued to narrate his visions onscreen.

"Your desire," Peter Turkson addressed the group, "like that of His Holiness Pope Francis himself, to come face to face with the Second Coming of Jesus Christ, is so strong that you're willing to attach that hope to a fictional character.

"What's his name? Joshua DeWine? A virtual persona. A narrative invention in a parallel, speculative world. A science fiction novel.

"And yet, you're suggesting he might be the literal descendant of Christ, or even Christ returned?"

He stood up and began pacing slowly near the cascading sound of the courtyard fountain, his voice rising with frustration.

"And for that justification, you would change the entire narrative? The foundational structure of Christian belief as we know it? The entire universe of the faithful?"

He paused. "I have my reservations."

He gestured with air-quotes, "I'm going to have to read and re-read this book of *Eleven Elements* to see if there is any 'element' of truth in it."

The water from the fountain roared behind him, underscoring his final thought.

"Sometimes I ask myself: Is this scientific world we live in just a grand fiction? Or is the science fiction world described in that novel the actual real world? And are we, here, the ones trapped in a story we thought we understood?

"Even if we were to come to know and believe the truth, how would we ever convince the Christian world that has, for over two millennia, only known the version of the story passed down by the early disciples and Church fathers?

"The Christian narrative, as it stands, is deeply embedded into the hearts, traditions, and faith structures of billions.

"To challenge that version now, with science, with alternate interpretations, with a fictional character like Joshua DeWine, seems nearly impossible.

Turkson seemed to be growing weary from the day's intense discussion. But he raised one final question. "The scientific world relies on real proof. Perhaps, if we truly wish to start unraveling the truth, we should begin by conducting DNA testing on the relics of Saint Thomas, many of which are preserved in Ortona, Italy.

"Only something verifiable, empirical, could ever begin to open the minds of both skeptics and believers."

He paused and let out a soft sigh.

"Your Eminences, I've had enough of these mind-bending discussions for one day. I need to rest, to sleep on everything we've discussed, before I can fully formulate my own opinion.

"If Your Graces will excuse me, I would like to say good night.

"Tomorrow will bring a long day of Conclave proceedings."

He bowed courteously and turned away, walking briskly across the quiet courtyard, the sound of the fountain echoing softly behind him.

The cardinals watched Cardinal Turkson depart in silence.

It was then that Cardinal Marks, ever the anchor of the group, broke the silence.

"It looks like Peter just got the shock of his life. And honestly, who wouldn't? No one is expected to believe any of this at first hearing.

"Revelation, after all, has always come at a cost."

He looked toward the others, his expression resolute. "I have already ordered preliminary DNA analysis of Saint Thomas's relics, including those held in Ortona and other locations where his remains are venerated.

"Once the results arrive, I will inform this group immediately.

"What we do with the truth then ... will be the real test of our faith."

Cardinal Taglin spoke, his voice steady but filled with an undercurrent of sorrow. "Surely, anyone would be upset if they suddenly realized they had spent their lives worshipping the wrong Jesus Christ. Or rather, bowing unknowingly to his body double, Thomas, believing him to be the Christ.

"But let me say this clearly: Thomas was a saint. And if he gave his life to protect the Holy One, then he is worthy of honor. Perhaps not as the Christ, but as the greatest of martyrs."

Taglin knew this was the moment. The congregation before him was weighing him. Measuring him.

He was already seen as a serious contender, but that wasn't enough. He had to sound less like a candidate and more like the next Pope.

This speech was about more than faith. It was about leadership, conviction, vision.

He had to leave no doubt that, when the time came to cast their votes, they would see not a man reaching for power, but a man already carrying its burden.

"He sacrificed himself," Taglin said, "so that Jesus might live. So that the message might spread.

"How many among us today would do the same for the Second Coming?

"How many of us would truly recognize him? Believe him? Follow him to the ends of the earth, let alone die for him?

"Would we protect him today, or would we once again, as a world, betray him to the authorities, crucify him with our disbelief, with our ridicule, with our inaction?

"If he walked among us today, would we stand for him, or watch him fall?

"And I say this proverbially. We do not wish for his death, not if we know he walks among us.

"Just as Jesus once walked in disguise two millennia ago, so might he walk again. He will be resurrected in the pages of future books ... or in reality, if that is God's will.

"We don't yet know what the author of Eleven Elements intends."

He looked around the group, locking eyes with each cardinal. "Book One speaks not of divine lightning or fire from Heaven, but of the oceans: our real Mother Mary, the womb of life.

"It is about cleansing, healing, restoring the Earth. That, in itself, is sacred.

"And we're told there are six more books yet to come. The full vision of the Eleven Elements is still hidden from us. Do any of us here even know what those elements truly are?"

A murmur rippled through the group.

Taglin stood tall, his voice rising with fervor. "I say this: When we do find Him, when He is revealed, resurrected, or realized among us, we must not let fear or doctrine blind us.

"We must protect Him, learn from Him, and if need be, lay down our lives for Him. As Saint Thomas once did.

"He, who made the ultimate sacrifice, is now my greatest example of faith. He is my real hero."

Cardinal Taglin's words were calculated to sway the gathering. To frame himself as papabile in the minds of his peers.

But the mood in the courtyard was heavier than politics at that moment.

The other Cardinals hadn't come in search of a leader. They'd come in search of answers.

The question gripping the congregation was not who would wear the next white cassock, but something far more unsettling: *Has the Second Coming already happened? Has Christ returned? And if so, is this the real resurrection?*

After a brief quiet, Cardinal Erdo spoke, his tone reflective and resolute. "The fact is that recent events all point to the moments prophesied to occur before the Second Coming of Christ.

"We are witnessing the widespread evangelization of the world, the spiritual preparation of the Bride of Christ, the full manifestation of evil in society, and even the regathering of the Jewish people in their ancestral homeland.

"These are not isolated occurrences. They are fulfilling long-held prophecies."

Erdo gestured subtly with his hands. "Some specific signs foretold include the appearance of the so-called 'man of lawlessness' and cosmic events that would precede the return of our Lord.

"But honestly, we need not identify just one man. Today, such lawlessness and godlessness are rampant.

"There are individuals in every corner of the world who exalt themselves above truth, decency, and even God Himself.

"We see them, we know them. They mislead, deceive, and exploit in these end times."

Erdo's voice darkened with caution. "Scripture warns us that these figures will commit acts of great blasphemy, showing disdain for all that is sacred.

"But we need not dwell solely on them. The other signs have been laid bare before us. The earthquakes. The hurricanes. The tornadoes. And the COVID-19 pandemic that claimed millions of lives." Erdo's passion and anger were building to a fever pitch.

"We've seen pestilence, famine, war.

"We've watched false prophets rise with silver tongues and wickedness multiply like a plague upon the earth."

A deep breath filled the silence that followed.

"We have entered the threshold. The signs are no longer forthcoming. They're all here.

"The Second Coming has already begun, not with fanfare or fire from the skies, but with the quiet unraveling of prophecy.

"It is only a matter of time before the true Gospel is revealed once more. And then, under the divine stewardship of the Lord Christ, peace will reign. Not just in spirit, but upon the Earth itself."

The gathered men fell into a contemplative hush, the magnitude of Erdo's words rippling through each cardinal like a silent tide.

It was now Marks's turn to speak, his voice calm but fervent.

"If the character in *Eleven Elements* is indeed the Holy One, then He has already proclaimed what many of us have only dared to dream: that the world should become one single country.

"A Federation of Nation States, each committed to a common and definite purpose for all of humanity.

"If every nation on Earth were to unite under this cause, to live without borders, then war would become obsolete.

"Peace would not be a fleeting hope, but a sustained reality stretching for centuries, maybe even millennia.

"The trillions spent on weapons and armies would instead be diverted toward healing our planet.

"The Earth would be restored to its pristine glory, and hunger could be eradicated once and for all. A true heaven on Earth would be realized."

Marks's eyes were bright with conviction. "Such a character would be nothing less than a King of Kings. A bringer of true peace.

"Whether monarchs or presidents, dictators or democrats, all leaders would have to fall in line and join this world community. One goal. One people. One planet.

"These thoughts are not merely noble. They are profound.

"And for me, they are enough to accept that Joshua DeWine, the central figure of this so-called science fiction novel, may very well be the Second Coming of Christ. And we should follow His creed."

The cardinals present sat in silence, each one deep in thought, their gazes cast either downward or far into the unseen distance. It was a rare moment of unity.

Marks, now visibly calmer than when the session began, seemed relieved. He had spoken his truth and had been heard. There was a shared sense of understanding among his peers.

It was Cardinal Parotin who broke the silence. "Yes," he said slowly, as though he were still weighing the words even as he spoke them. "We agree that this character may very well be the Second Coming of the Lord Christ.

"Though He has appeared virtually, or should I say, very stealthily, like a thief in the night. Much like our modern-day video calls where we hear voices but often see no faces.

"All signs point to Him.

"And perhaps we were too focused on expecting a flesh-and-blood arrival.

"But He has arrived nonetheless. He has issued judgment, extended mercy, and given us a path to salvation. All through a work of fiction that may yet prove to be more real than anything we've ever known."

Parotin slowly raised his hand, as if to give one final reflection. "This level of stealthy action," he said, all eyes turned to him, "I could never have guessed.

"But I can only attribute it to the Holy One.

"The Gospel says He ascended into the clouds, and in like manner, He would return.

"Well, perhaps He has returned. Not in clouds of mist, but through the Cloud Servers of this internet age. Not descending upon a mountain with trumpet blasts, but arriving quietly in the form of a digital narrative. Not fog on a hillside, but the fog of data and firewalls, coded, not cloaked."

He smiled wistfully. "Sadly, our Pope Francis is no more. And how he longed to come face to face with the prophesied Second Coming of our Lord.

"Unfortunately, I only recently discovered this Joshua DeWine when this novel was presented by the faithful to me to review and give my opinion.

"It is only now we concur the truth but alas we are too late to introduce Him to Pope Francis. If only he could have met Joshua DeWine … I believe he would have recognized Him instantly, even if He came to us from the pages of a fantasy book."

There was a strange stillness as the cardinals digested Parotin's words. Some nodded gently. Others grimaced with unease.

But Parotin, ever the pragmatist, shifted the tone. "And on this note, let us move to the other matter at hand tonight.

"Who among us is best suited to carry the mantle of Pope? His gaze settled on each face in turn.

"How can we rally behind a name and move past the suspense that the world now clings to with bated breath?"

Cardinal Peter Erdo answered, his voice steady. "Parotin, you are ahead in the vote count, followed closely by Marks.

"Taglin and I are trailing. And Zappi is somewhere in between. We must discuss the path forward. What do you propose?"

Parotin responded grimly, "Did none of you see the AI-generated image of President Frank McCrony dressed as the Pope? It circulated across social media just yesterday.

"I read that image as a subtle message. A political signal that he desires an American Pope."

The men stirred uneasily.

Parotin continued. "Let us proceed with routine voting on the first day. Venting the traditional black smoke to uphold the ritual.

"But by the second day, I believe we must all consider rallying behind Cardinal Hubert Prowest. He is the logical choice in this climate, and perhaps the only one who can satisfy the expectations of President McCrony and his base of followers."

Marks's low voice was edged with nervous humor. "Parotin is right. We don't want to become statistics.

"The conspiracy theorists are already whispering about President McCrony's influence.

"They say he replaced three Supreme Court Judges in his country just to tighten his grip on legal rulings. To ensure the court backs his agenda.

"Some even claim, fanatically, that one older conservative judge had his term 'ended' while vacationing in Texas. Died in his sleep, they say. With a pillow over his face."

Marks laughed uneasily. "I wouldn't want that fate. So yes, I would rather vote for the American Cardinal and pray for the best."

Most of the Cardinals seemed to be in agreement.

But Taglin had his doubts.

Marks apparently read his expression, and added, "Cardinal Prowest, if made Pope, will likely recognize the Second Coming.

"He may be the bridge between this new world and the one we know. Perhaps he will help guide the Church, and the world, toward a future of lasting peace."

Parotin checked his wristwatch and stood. "Your Eminences, it is late. Far later than I intended. But it is decided.

"We agree to rally behind Cardinal Prowest. And we agree that no one outside this congregation will ever hear of this meeting. These discussions, this night, they never happened."

He looked sternly at each cardinal in turn. "If the media asks about the Second Coming, our answer will be simple: 'He is just a fictional character in a science fiction novel. Perhaps a credible one, yes, but fictional nonetheless.' That will be our unified response.

"And maybe … maybe that's the only way the Holy One could protect Himself in these dangerous times: by appearing not in flesh, but in fiction.

"Let us leave it at that. Good evening, Your Eminences."

The cardinals left in silence, dispersing with the heavy knowledge of what had been revealed, and what must never be spoken again.

Dr. Ronick Dupray remained still, draped in his office chair, watching the video as Joshua DeWine emerged from his trance and the screen went black.

Dupray shut off the recording and switched off the large display monitor.

Tears welled and spilled down his cheeks.

Only he knew the true depth of his sorrow, the magnitude of his loss.

With a trembling hand, he wiped his face with a towel he kept in a drawer, then composed himself, fixing on the practiced smile he would need for his next patient.

CHAPTER -29

08:35 | 01-26-2026 (Twenty-first century)
LOCATION: FBI HEADQUARTERS - WASHINGTON DC

It was an unusually balmy Monday morning, the warmest January day in Washington, D.C. in historical temperature records dating back to the late 1600s.

At the J. Edgar Hoover Building, FBI Director Chris Sharma sat on his office couch discussing the Bureau's most puzzling case with deputy Don Vingo, sitting in the arm chair beside him.

Director Sharma's office exuded quiet authority. It was spacious, streamlined, and built for high-level operations.

A large wall-mounted monitor displayed secure intel and briefings, while the sleek mahogany couch with cherry-colored leather and two padded matching armchairs created a formal yet inviting seating area.

A private coffee station with a mini-bar buffet table at the wall offered expertly brewed espresso, hinting at Sharma's personal touch. The scent of dark roast or spiced chai often lingered in the air.

In the corner, an elegant snake plant in a minimalist ceramic pot stood tall, placed there at Director Sharma's request. Known for its air-purifying qualities and subtle energy, the plant added a touch of calm and vitality to the otherwise high-stakes environment.

His wide, cluttered desk featured a biometric pad, a closed folder marked "CONFIDENTIAL," an array of monitors with a PC concealed in the desk, and a precision digital clock that was also an app-based notetaker.

Behind it on the credenza, several framed accolades, his prized helmet from the high school varsity football team when he played as a kicker, and several personal photos reflected his legacy.

The office balanced comfort and control, every detail intentional, just like Sharma himself.

Vingo was brooding over the few copies of the printed version of Book One in the series called *Eleven Elements* novels that were lying jumbled in a pile on the round, glass-top center table in front of them.

The book had only been on the market for a few weeks, but it had already had caused a lot of buzz, both in social media and political circles.

The political elites worried that this widespread support for the notions in the book might upset the gravy train they and their cronies benefitted from. They were leaning on friends in agencies like the FBI to disarm this potential ticking time bomb before it spoiled their privileged lifestyles.

Both the FBI Director and his deputy were weary from the sleepless weekend nights spent reading and re-reading several chapters, making notes, jotting down on whiteboards, and trying to make sense of the information they gathered from this treasure trove of a novel.

Each one was waiting for the other to speak. Chris Sharma simply raised his eyebrows several times, prodding and prompting his deputy to speak up.

Blowing a deep sigh, Don Vingo said, "Don't know where to start this. But let me tell you this: every character and every event of action that occurs in this book is for real.

"I checked out a few things myself by calling around. Also asked Chris Ruia and Matt Odor of the Tampa Office to follow up on a few items so we can piece all of this together.

"This is what I have so far.

"We caught five of the ten so-called time travelers from the future. The twenty-sixth century, so they say.

"They're here to make sure that this novel *Eleven Elements*, which lies in front of you, gets published so that they can continue to exist in the twenty-sixth century.

"They came to meet with the book's author, Mr. Joshua DeWine, a naturalized U.S. citizen of Indian origin.

"DeWine is said to be the architect of their reality, as he seems to have imagined a future that is supposed to become their present.

"From a practical standpoint, this Joshua DeWine was simply working on a science fiction novel that depicted a visionary utopian society in the future and a science fiction adventure of time travelers who frequently go back and forth in time just to ensure that they may live and their utopian society may flourish just as DeWine had envisioned.

"Unfortunately for these time alleged travelers, this Joshua DeWine died in a car crash while they were in the process of encouraging him to complete his work.

"Five of these ten time-travelers were in our custody for several hours. But their five accomplices, for whom we had search and arrest warrants issued, have so far managed to evade us.

"The elusive five traced the initial work of this author Joshua DeWine and got his Book One of the *Eleven Elements* published. Supposedly in the exact form and content as it was first published at this time according to their chronology of history.

"As we know, these time travelers had some kind of stealth and invisibility cloaking technology. And they managed to escape from the high-security custody cells we were holding them in."

Chris Sharma just muttered, "Humm... I see."

Vingo shrugged. "All I know is we captured five of the ten target operatives and now they are fugitives."

Sharma's tone sharpened with anger. "They escaped. They escaped from FBI custody. THE FREAKING FBI CUSTODY... not some jail or alligator Alcatraz.

"We look like fools, Don.

"What will I say when they face congressional hearings? Will the Dems in the congressional committees believe me when I say that these people were a superior race of time travelers whose technology fooled us?

"You'd better come up with solid answers for me. I have no fricking idea what or how I am going to present this case when it gets to that media drama."

Deputy Don Vingo was unfazed by his superior's harsh remarks. "This interesting science fiction novel, as it claims to be, is no ordinary novel of the garden variety you find on store bookshelves or in libraries.

"This novel clearly states that it records events occurring in a parallel reality. And we are a parallel reality to some other reality that may be existing right now.

"What Chris Ruia, Matt Odor, and I have found is that every incident and occurrence in this so-called sci-fi novel is real and true.

"The van in which Mr. Joshua DeWine died, supposedly attributable to a chewed-up cable harnesses and fuel lines, is for real.

"We had the VIN number ending 4475 traced to the dealership and called Central Florida Toyoda.

"The service department confirmed that critters, such as squirrels, must have gotten under the hood and chewed the cable harness and fuel lines.

"The first time, Mr. DeWine had the dealership repair the harness issue. But the second time, it appears he was driving with similar damage, unaware that the cables had been chewed again.

"The vehicle caught fire as he drove, veered off towards a nearby lake, and the engine exploded as he plunged into the water. That explosion killed him.

"The VIN number, the van, and all that happened is for real. Everything matches up in the records of the dealership.

"Since the publication of this *Book One* of *Eleven Elements*, due to innumerable calls from readers checking facts, Central Florida Toyoda has even established a toll-free 800 number.

"When dialed, the automated message states:

The VIN number ending in 4475 is a Toyoda Sierra van per our records, whose cable harness and fuel lines had been damaged, presumably by rodents or other small animals that had accessed the engine compartment.

The vehicle was repaired, tested to factory standards, and returned to its owner as operational and defect-free.

The same vehicle was brought into our shop a few weeks later with similar damage, likely caused again by animals, leading to an auto accident and engine explosion.

Following a rigorous investigation, it was determined that these tragic events were not the result of any defect in the vehicle's construction or the repairs that had been done.

Local authorities found the owner deceased and submerged in a lake. Our heartfelt condolences to all persons listening to this recording."

"This, Vingo said, "confirmed for the general public that what is written in this science fiction book is all but true.

"We even looked up the news when ten Pear Corporation branded yPhones were stolen from a delivery truck. It would seem that these would be the yPhones stolen to develop the yPhones that the time travelers carried back to the twenty-first century for their mission.

"The letter that Joshua DeWine wrote to Juliet Veritas is something we already know. And his communications with the White House are in his FBI records file.

"Every effing event, incident, and occurrence is real in this fictional world of DeWine.

"Jeez, even the fricking dog Nikko is a real K9 squad dog with all those police officers' names just so similar to those in our world."

Sharma offered a look of faux surprise, "Oh really! I cannot believe any of this crap.

"It's just a story, Don. A sci-fi story and that's it for me."

Agitated, Don doubled down trying to convince his boss. "Chris, honestly, look here on the front inside cover where all the disclaimer sections are underlined.

"It says, and I quote: 'The authors of this book have exercised creative liberty to portray the actual struggles and lives of common people and characters that exist in a parallel fictional world. The challenges these people face and their experiences are portrayed in good faith.'

"My foot 'it's a fictional world!' The whole representation is a mirror image of our world. Or rather, an exact mirror image of us and everything here and now! Chris, no kidding!

"And on top of that, he's even trying to be funny.

"Just a couple of lines later, he writes, "No animals, birds, or insects were harmed during typing, printing, or making of this book, with the EXCEPTION of a couple of bugs and ants that got accidentally squished at the press.'

"No jokes. Readers of this book will soon realize what the real joke is, and more importantly, who the joke is on.

"Every fricking person in our universe is a mirrored character of this so-called fictional world, and they're impacted by what's happening there. Which, no surprise, is exactly what's happening here.

"People will soon realize what their fate is, and what their future might look like. So, in that way, Book One delivers on its promise: readers will either have an out-of-body experience or come face-to-face with their future.

"My heartbeat's skipped multiple times reading this. And don't tell me *you* just skimmed through it like it was nothing."

Chris scrunched his face mockingly and spoke with exaggerated sarcasm, making crybaby faces. "I think people will be pissed.

"Unless they really believe the guy writing all this rubbish is someone who has utmost love for them … oh wait, what did the Bible say? Ah yes: the Merciful One. The one who could love like a father, who forgives a child when they're naughty or make a boo-boo. Wah Wah Wah…"

Don frowned. "It's not the time to be kidding, Chris. Listen. We've got all of Dupray's interviews and interrogations archived.

"And in the book? It's not just some random imagination. It's the actual conversations between the Cardinals before they cast their votes to elect Pope Leo IV.

"My contacts in the Italian Secret Service, Agenzia Informazioni e Sicurezza Esterna, AISE, told me something wild. They intercepted recordings from devices planted by the European media at the Vatican's St. Joseph Fountain. They noticed the assistants to the cardinals placing folding chairs there so they must have guessed a pre-meeting was in the works.

"Those recordings match the dialogue in *Eleven Elements* word for word, except that these smart alecks fast-forwarded past their conversations in Dr. Dupray's viewing of the DeWine's narration of the same incidence while in the trance like state. I am sure in their future books, Dupray will revisit these recordings. Meanwhile, the faithful and curious readers are all held in suspense, waiting to know all about those revelations."

He continued more grimly, "And I wouldn't be surprised if this very conversation, right now, between you and me, here at FBI Headquarters, ends up in a future edition.

"These guys will go to any lengths to make this adventure real and relevant.

"And why? Because it's in their best interest to get the world to wake up. Including our own beloved country.

"People need to realize their human potential. They need to start living with purpose, toward a future that could be our shared legacy. For our kids."

Don looked away, then back. "You don't have kids, so maybe you don't care. I know … I know … that was the wrong thing to say. But just look around. Dude."

There was silence between them, thick with everything left unsaid.

Then Don added, more softly, "Chris, I'll admit, everything's starting to fall into place. The revelations in this book, even the answer to the purpose of the pyramids. What more proof do you need?"

Chris just nodded, like every Indian Don had met.

Don thought, *"My boss is true to his culture and his job. Probably doesn't want to think outside the box. Totally opinionated. Has to have it his way."*

Chris finally spoke. "All that pyramid stuff? It's still just a hypothesis."

"Yes," Don said. "Until there's scientific proof, it's only theory. But it's a plausible hypothesis.

"And the purpose described? It fits. Still ... keep things in perspective. Connect the dots. Look at everything written. You'll see. It's not fiction. Nada. Nothing. Just the truth."

Chris Sharma, finally spoke up with a measured tone that barely masked his incredulity. "So, what you're saying is that we should believe all this crap?

"You think I should walk into my hearings with the Congressional Committees and tell them they need to start mobilizing for a single *Federation of Nations*?

"Drop all national boundaries and become one unified world? Like one giant *Nation of Nations*: just states under a single planetary government?

"And that all this immigration crackdown we're working on day-in, day-out to appease President Frank McCrony's Republican base is ... for nothing?"

Don Vingo didn't flinch. "Exactly. That's the point. Go ahead. Tell them the truth. Tell them we've captured time-travelers. That they're real. And that they've come from a future where national borders don't exist. Where the whole world is governed as one."

His body tensed. "Just imagine what would happen if Rossian President Pudding found out there's no 'Rossia' or 'Ekraine' in the future. That both are part of the same unified planetary nation.

"Do you think he could still justify war? Would anyone support wasting another soldier's life knowing their future is one of unity, not division?

"Same goes for the Middle East. Israel, Gaza, Lebanon, Syria. All one future nation under a common constitution.

"No borders. No sectarian strife. Just one people, one purpose.

"Even with Shyna and the U.S. There's no trade war in that future. Only cooperation under a singular mission: to reset the environment, and ensure the survival of humanity."

Chris rubbed his temple, then exhaled. "So, I see your point now. If we actually go in and tell these committees the truth, they might lead with questions rather than arguments."

Don exclaimed, "Yes! Maybe they'd realize the pointlessness of the shallow, manufactured narratives they've been clinging to. And for once, maybe they'd listen.

"You see what I'm saying? *Eleven Elements* isn't only a blueprint for future time travelers, it's a blueprint for us, right now. Their reality starts with us. We have to sow the seeds so that our future, the so-called time travelers in this book, can reap the right fruit. They're probably our super great-grandchildren."

"But what are we doing instead? We're just existing, bickering like children over petty little things, this immigration issue, or over who owns which sliver of land, or which nation controls the rare earth metals. All this nonsense, living like we are sheikh chillis, subconsciously existing simply because we are schooled that this was the way to life.

"We need to think outside that box."

"Imagine a united world. A *Federation of Nations* where there's no room for terrorism.

"Where extremists, wherever they are, realize that everyone is part of one human family.

"There'd be no jihad, no revenge. Against who? That would be the big question mark.

"Joshua DeWine was no ordinary writer. He was a rare thinker who stood up for humanity. His works are designed to awaken the planet. Not by patching wars like Frank McCrony does, slapping band-aids over bullet wounds like they're mosquito bites. But by laying the groundwork for *perpetual peace.*"

It was clear Chris Sharma was beginning to grasp the deeper implications. Perhaps the senior FBI directors were starting to connect the dots.

Chris finally gave his take. "This guy Joshua DeWine ... he's got guts. Real guts.

"He started all this by writing to First Lady Juliet Veritas. And look how that shifted the country's political tone. One letter caused a tremor.

"Now imagine what a whole book can do. Or a whole *series* of books.

"These aren't mere sentences on a page. They're ticking time bombs, benevolent ones, detonating one spirit at a time. He's dispersing knowledge like shockwaves.

"People will start to question everything: what it means to be human, what 'purpose' really is.

"He talks about Kundalini, about evolutionary energy lying dormant in us. My dad used to mention that too, when I was a kid.

"Maybe some readers will finally get it. Realize they've wasted their lives, drifting without purpose, living under definitions imposed by society, family, and education systems. All flawed. All biased."

Don agreed. "They'll look in the mirror and ask: What the hell am I doing? After billions of years of evolution, am I just coasting? Just existing?

"That's the danger DeWine's books pose: they will wake people up.

"They raise *existential questions*. Do you want to live a life with an undefined purpose? Or with a purpose that is inherently full of folly, one that is leading to the obliteration of humanity?

"And yeah, I use the word *obliteration* intentionally, since McCrony made it the word of the year after the Iran bombings.

"What DeWine is doing is forcing us to confront the possibility that we're heading for *self*-obliteration if we don't recalibrate.

"But how the hell do you make someone like Frank McCrony or his MEGA base understand any of this? How do you make them see what *Eleven Elements* is really saying?"

Don Vingo felt energized by the question. "Remember what Joshua DeWine says in the book. He explains that Earth's core is blazing. Reaching temperatures of 5,800 degrees Celsius, or about 10,472 degrees Fahrenheit if you do the math.

"Millennia ago, intelligent bacterial life dug tunnels, what we now refer to as aquifer caverns, creating an intricate system of underground rivers.

"These weren't just for water. They were engineered to form a cooling blanket beneath Earth's surface."

He locked his gaze on Chris and said, "These aquifers, along with reservoirs of crude oil and subterranean liquids thousands of feet below the surface, act just like the coolant that surrounds an engine block in our modern-day cars. Remove the coolant, and the engine overheats.

"Same goes for Earth. As humans, we've been sucking the coolant dry. Extracting water from aquifers and drilling for oil at unprecedented rates. Combine that with solar radiation from above, and we're accelerating planetary overheating."

Don walked over to Chris's desk and quickly tapped a few keys on his computer, pulling up a satellite map that was mirrored in the 75" monitor on the wall. "Look at this. These are time-lapse snapshots of groundwater in the Middle East.

"Thirty or forty years ago, these aquifers were abundant. Today? Look here for the before image. And look now: ninety-five percent depleted. That depletion turns regions into heat conductors, transferring thermal radiation across air and ocean currents globally. Everyone's affected.

"And with that exposure to increasing radiation and heat, we're seeing DNA mutations, testicular cancer, and a host of other alarming health crises.

"We're turning Earth into a giant oven. It's like we are jumping out of the frying pan right into the fire."

He looked squarely at Chris. "Remember how COVID-19 didn't spare anyone, rich or poor? The same will go for this crisis.

"Whether it's the sons or grandchildren of President Frank McCrony, or President Vohkafir Pudding, or Shynesia's Zee Jinming, they'll all pay the price for inaction.

"In *Eleven Elements*, DeWine warns that in the end, it won't be ignorance alone that dooms us, but our failure to act.

"He calls it the mark of a 'Sheikh Chilli,' a fool who dies remembered not for wisdom, but for folly.

"If DeWine is who some believe him to be, perhaps even a divine spirit, then this is more than a notice of caution. It's a judgment."

Chris Sharma reacted with a half-laugh, half-scoff. "So let me get this straight. By saying people will develop testicular cancer, you're implying Joshua DeWine's got people by their balls? That he's got President Frank McCrony by *his* balls? Or worse, by those of his children and grandchildren?" He chuckled sarcastically. "You're really something, Don."

He continued, shifting tone. "Look, I know McCrony. He's a family man. Say what you want about his policies, but he's not a fool. He's not a 'Sheikh Chilli', the guy sawing off the tree branch he's sitting on.

"He's got the power to change things. And if he becomes aware of this book, of these messages, I believe he'll act. He'll protect his kids, his grandkids.

"He'll fight polluted waters, air, and all with whatever it takes. Even if it means more tariffs, more regulations. That's how smart he is. He'll make people listen, even if it's the hard way."

Don raised an eyebrow. "But how? The nations of the world have to unite. They need to focus on stopping groundwater depletion, on replenishing the aquifers. That's the only way to cool the Earth and halt the radiation that's altering our very DNA.

"You think tariffs alone will convince the world to collaborate?"

Chris looked thoughtful, almost murmuring to himself. "I'm not a believer. I'm Hindu. I don't subscribe to this whole 'Second Coming of Christ' theory.

"Sure, this DeWine has some thought-provoking ideas, but that doesn't make him a savior. Plenty of thinkers have shared similar visions. Does that mean they're all divine? All sons of God?"

He paused, then added cynically, "Maybe he's just a con artist. Or maybe he *was* one ... who met his end in an accident. Blasted by God, for all we know."

Don was biased toward believing that there was some truth in this character's message. He said, "Look, many so-called godmen have claimed to be the Second Coming of Christ. But only this character in this book has made his *judgment* known. In no uncertain terms."

He flipped through the pages. "Here, let me show you where he delivers his proclamation. See page 238. Listen to this:"

He cleared his throat and read aloud.

"The Judgment will not be gentle. It will say:

What have you done to our common home? This beautiful, pristine Earth, heaven itself, you have defiled it with filth, buried it in garbage, poisoned it with pollution.

All lifeforms are my creation, your neighbors who sustain your existence in the balance of ecology. And you have brought them to suffering.

You have turned paradise into a garbage planet. A cesspool of disease and despair! You are destined to rot in the pollution you have created, to suffer grave illnesses, to face the wrath of storms and floods, to burn in wildfires, and to wither in unbearable heat.

Unless you restore the beauty of this planet, unless you cleanse and heal what you have corrupted, you are sinners. And you will die knowing you were fools, disgraced before your faith, your families, and your legacy. Act now, or all of mankind will be annihilated!

Don looked up. "That's a perfect judgment. What more would you expect if the Lord Christ himself came today to deliver his verdict on the state of the world?"

Chris Sharma shook his head. "Humm ... all stupid environmentalists say the same thing. Nothing new to me. Doesn't make him any different than the rest of them ranting the same type of crap."

Don gestured emphatically. "No, no, you're not listening. This character—and yes, he's dead in the story now—isn't just handing down judgment. He's showing *mercy*.

"He's giving real solutions, not just pointing fingers. He's walking us through what's wrong *and* how to fix it. That's the difference.

"Most environmentalists just criticize what corporations or governments are doing wrong. But this guy? He's focused on what to *do differently*. He's talking about real practical solutions, all baby-steps leading to a brighter clear utopian future.

"For starters, if the world became one unified Nation, one *World Country*, there'd be no need to spend billions on weapons. The arms race would be over. One central peacekeeping force would ensure global cooperation.

"No fear, no endless wars, because every Nation State and every person would follow one set of rules under one new constitution. A fair one. Unbiased. Focused solely on protecting life and preventing extinction.

"He's laid out *tasks*. A roadmap, really. Follow them, and we get thousands of years of peace and prosperity. He's doing more than passing judgment, he's extending mercy."

And not just for humans, but for all lifeforms. He believes Gaia, our planet, is a living intelligence. And that if Gaia dies, so does humanity."

But Chris Sharma, still scowling, apparently wasn't having it. He crossed his arms and pushed back. "Don, for all you know, this guy could be the *Antichrist*. Didn't the Bible say the Antichrist would appear around the same time as the Second Coming?

"Just like the Cardinals were gathering in Rome, you're getting caught up in the pageantry and forgetting your mission.

"You sound like one of those who already believe this dead guy is the 'Holy One.' Get real.

"We've got a job to do. There are aliens. Undocumented foreigners. Or let's call them what they are: *illegal immigrants from the future*, living among us.

"They could be dangerous. It's our duty to track them down and protect our nation. So, snap out of this Holy Poly messiah trip and focus."

Don smiled, amused. "Chris, you really think you can catch time travelers from the future? With their stealth and invisibility cloaking tech?

"For all we know, they've got advanced weaponry that could obliterate us before we even reach for our handcuffs. And let's say we *do* capture them. Where would we deport them to?"

Chris fired back with a grin, "Of course, 'Back to the Future!'" He laughed heartily at his own joke.

Don shot back, "My hunch is *they let themselves get caught*. It was deliberate. While we were busy interrogating the five in custody, the other five were out executing whatever their real mission was.

"The ones we detained only gave us pre-approved, scripted answers. Just enough to keep us distracted and confident that we were making progress. It was misdirection, Chris. And they got away with whatever evidence we collected from them.

"Oh, my gosh," Don said mostly to himself, "so that's what they were doing. Now I realize…"

"You won't believe this, Chris. The one in FBI custody that I was interrogating gave me the winning Florida Powerball numbers the day before they were declared. He said that he had a ticket with that number hidden somewhere I can't find.

"I thought he was fooling me. Or if he is really a time traveler then he was bribing me. I had jotted down the numbers on my note pad and, guess what, they were the winning Lotto numbers with a cash prize of several hundred million dollars."

He shook his head, still stunned, as he quietly mourned what could've been.

"I'm certain they sold the ticket through black-market channels—buyers who specialize in anonymity. That's how they avoided being traced. No names. No questions. No discovery."

"Everything they told us was meant to lead us away from their actual objectives."

Don gestured to the pile of books on the center table. "And look at the result. They set up a non-profit in the name of the late Joshua DeWine.

"A charitable foundation, with several hundred million dollars from the proceeds of the Lotto, positioned to solve global environmental challenges.

"Then came this book, Book One in a series, published to spread their message through the voices of global experts.

Don laughed at the irony. "It's all here, plain as day. They're living and operating like ghosts in our world. Even if we catch them again, they'll just vanish, back to the future, and pop up somewhere else.

"So, tell me, Chris. How exactly do you plan to catch them?"

Chris grinned and leaned back, arms crossed. "If we *do* catch these so-called ghosts, you know what that makes us, right?"

Don didn't respond.

Chris raised his eyebrows. "*Ghostbusters.* Who you gonna call?! *Ghostbusters!*" He laughed out loud at his own joke.

Don didn't even blink. He let the silence swallow Chris's echo.

Then calmly, "You joke, Chris, but even you've accepted it. These people, they're real. They exist outside our rules. Outside our time.

"The original author, Joshua DeWine, he's gone. I would've loved to have dinner with him, the way people dream of dining with Jesus Christ.

"But he's delivered his judgment, issued his warning, and left us with his parting gift: the *Eleven Elements*. A new gospel. A manual for survival.

"If we follow it, maybe in two hundred, three hundred, four hundred years, we'll have our utopia. Heaven on Earth."

Chris smirked and said, "We'll all be long gone to hell before that utopian dream of yours ever comes true. You really think anyone gives a damn about someone else's version of paradise, especially something to be enjoyed by other people in the future?"

Don picked up the book and turned the cover toward Chris.

"So, who are you planning to arrest now? This guy on the cover, Mr. Robbie Juicy? Seriously, *Juicy*? What kind of name is that?" He scoffed. "Sounds like a rejected character from *I Love Lucy* meets a bad conspiracy thriller."

He let out a dry chuckle. "All this Juicy-Lucy nonsense and talk of things being published *rosy-posythomouslee*, in someone's name after they're dead, it's driving me absolutely nuts. No, really. *Nucking Futs.*"

He shook his head and laughed to himself. "Yeah, yeah, I know the correct word is *posthumously*. But whatever. My point stands.

"This Robbie Juicy character may just be a figurehead. A decoy. The face of the Eleven Elements Foundation.

"He might not even know what's really in the book. All of the credits inside the book are granted to the real author: Joshua DeWine.

"And as I said, he is already dead and the book published posthumously, giving him all the credit."

Don sighed, feeling the frustration. "That's my take. The whole damn thing is convoluted. But something about it tells me *it's real.*"

Chris leaned into the moment with a smile, the tone light but thoughtful. "You know," he said, "in Hinduism, the faith I was born into, there's actually a prophecy that's somewhat similar to the Second Coming in Christianity.

"Our scriptures speak of the tenth and final avatar of Lord Vishnu, called Kalki. He's prophesied to appear during an age of great moral decline, riding a white horse. He's the redeemer, the restorer, much like how Christians see the return of Christ."

Then, with a glint of curiosity, Chris added, "According to the files on Joshua DeWine, he studied architecture at Washington University in St. Louis. And during that time, he dated a young woman from the Midwest, a white American woman."

He offered a half-smile. "If you take these parallels seriously, and some people really do, then, well, you can see how some might see symbolism in all that. A redeemer. A 'white horse.' Even if the interpretation gets … a bit poetic."

Chris chuckled softly at his own words, but the laughter died quickly when he caught the look in Don's eyes, measured, serious, unimpressed. He seemed to be thinking, *Is my boss deliberately trying to ridicule my Catholic faith? My opinions?*

Chris stood up off the couch and straightened up. "Sorry," he said, the levity leaving his voice. "I didn't mean to make light of it. You're right, Don. We're dealing with something far more serious, and probably beyond our comprehension."

He turned around and said, "But I've got to answer to Congress. The White House will come calling. What am I supposed to tell them?"

Then he began to pace a little, wrestling with his thoughts. "This *Eleven Elements* story, it's convoluted. It's set in a parallel universe where every character's name is a twisted mirror of our own world. But it's obvious who's who. Anyone with half a brain will connect the dots."

Chris approached the edge of the center table, and with intensity in his eyes he spoke, "But that's not the only thing. The story goes deep. So deep I can't even tell where science ends and fiction begin."

Don glanced at the clock, 9:45 a.m. and rose from the chair. "Look, I've got to step out for now. Let's pick this up after lunch, say one-thirty p.m.? We need to revisit this and figure out our strategy. Honestly, I've got a bit of brain fog at the moment."

Chris pressed his lips together and gave a quiet sideways nod, the kind of subtle, thoughtful gesture very uniquely Indian.

CHAPTER -30

11:04 | 01-26-2026 (Twenty-first century)
LOCATION: CHARRIOTTS INN & SUITE – ROOM 507
NEW HOTEL ROOM – NEW BASE ROOM

Max's OMP began beeping sharply, pulling him out of his peaceful memory stream. The warm tones of High-Park 577 faded. Annie's laughter dissolved into static.

He sat up, the VRV headset slipping off, along with the pleasant memories, as the twenty-first century crept back in, unforgiving, inescapable, and all too real.

He tapped the flashing screen.

A moment of flicker.

Then Burke's face appeared.

The connection was rough, glitching slightly. But it was *there*. And on the other end, things seemed calmer.

Burke grinned. "Looks like we're back in business."

Max exhaled as if he'd been holding his breath for more than a month. And in a way, *he had.*

Burke's voice buzzed through the static. "The black-hole's progression has *slowed*. We're still monitoring it, but its approach toward our time has decelerated.

"That *thing*, whatever it is, has lost momentum. Looks like you did something right."

Max blinked, stunned. "We *slowed* it?"

Burke gave a short nod. "At least for now. Don't pop the champagne yet, but yes, you've bought us time.

"Admiral Ubanto and General Rikor are ecstatic. You may have just shifted the odds."

Max cut in, "You know Joshua DeWine is dead. Killed in that van explosion, its wiring chewed through, maybe by those damn critter-constructs.

"Katrina's convinced it was no accident. She suspects uBots, or someone else from the future, deliberately eliminated him.

"If that's true, Burke, they've sabotaged Operation Manifesto itself.

"It means we're stuck here longer. We have to stay until all seven volumes are published, posthumously. That was never the plan.

"Do you have any leads on who could be behind this?"

For a moment Burke was silent. Then his voice came back, low and grim. "Yes," he said.

"We've withheld it ... for your team's stability. We were afraid the truth would have rattled you.

"Around the time DeWine went missing, we were forced to schedule a backup launch. But it was a chaotic, desperate attempt before the weakened tether went blank. The panic caused abrupt reactions which led to a total dead link after.

"And guess who led it? Sarah Blumstein.

"Not with your chosen back-up crew, but with three AAILF bio-forms like Katrina, and one trained jumper.

"She leveraged her authority and back-channel connections to hijack the op. Even after we warned her that the tether was unstable. One more jump and we could lose all contact. She didn't care. She came in with her own plan and technicians to handle this covert unauthorized launch."

Burke's voice hardened. "She exploited a data center in the 22nd century to slingshot herself past the widening anomaly and the weakened tether we used for our communications with you."

Burke exhaled audibly. "She's there. Alive. Operating beyond our control. You know her: untethered, making her own calls.

"We can't track her communications anymore. She's been using a discreet encrypted uplink. No idea who's on the other end. From what we've seen, I don't think she's there to support your mission. I don't think she's aligned with us at all. She may have her own agenda. And it's possible she's already working against you.

"I hate to say it, Max, but she may become another adversary you'll have to face as you move toward publishing Book Two, Three and the others."

Max tightened his grip on the armrest. "So, you think Joshua DeWine's death ... was murder?"

"We don't know yet," Burke admitted. "The investigation's ongoing. Surveillance from critter implants around the DeWine residence is still under review.

"Officially, I'm not cleared to tell you who's on Blumstein's team. But when I get the green light, I'll brief you. For now, keep your eyes open. She isn't your only problem."

He moved closer, voice firm despite the interference. "The FBI. Querlin Stark's investigative squad. Corporate vultures circling DeWine's work for profit. Even a couple of foreign agencies and operatives. They all want what you're chasing.

"Consider them obstacles. Or predators. Don't let them catch you off guard."

Burke gave a sharp salute. "So far, you've done well, Max. Best wishes. Out."

The screen went black.

Max relaxed into the chair, silent.

They'd done something. Something real.

The mission was working. The black hole, or whatever time anomaly that had been creeping toward their century, had been slowed.

But it wasn't gone. Not yet.

And now that the line was open again there was more to do. Much more.

For the first time, it felt like hope wasn't a mirage.

13:25 | 01-26-2026 (Twenty-first century)
LOCATION: FBI HEADQUARTERS - WASHINGTON DC

By 1:25 p.m., FBI Deputy Director Don Vingo was back in Chris Sharma's office, seated in one of the cherry leather chairs next to the mahogany couch where Sharma had been lounging earlier. Chris was wrapping up a phone call at his desk, while Don scrolled through messages on his mobile.

Chris hung up, exhaled deeply, and turned to Don. He began walking towards the couch next to Don saying, "So ... where were we this morning? Right, you were saying that everything in the book might actually be real. Or at least a reflection of our reality, like it's rooted in a parallel universe. And that every character in the manuscript resembles someone from our world. A doppelgänger of sorts.

"Don, you also said that some of the events in the book have already happened, right? And they match real events in our world. So, are we supposed to believe that the events we *can't* verify are true as well?

"Like … this Joshua DeWine being the Second Coming, as the Cardinals in Italy supposedly discussed?

"Or this 'Federation of Nations' idea that's meant to replace all countries and borders?"

Chris turned to Don; arms spread in a helpless gesture. "Tell me, Don. How do I go to the President and say, 'Shut down the United States of America. Time to join a Federation that doesn't exist yet'? How do we even begin to do that?

"And more importantly, why should we?"

Don replied with calm conviction, "The answer is simple: be honest. Tell everything exactly as it is.

"Tell the President and Congress that time travel might very well become a scientific reality based on the trajectory of technological progression.

"And that time travelers are here among us.

"They've told us that in their future, a unified *Federation of Nations* exists. Current countries function as Nation-States under one constitution, governed by one central authority. There's a single army, no global wars, and nuclear weaponry is repurposed into clean energy sources. Only a minimal number of warheads are retained for planetary defense against threats like comets or asteroids.

"Tell President Frank McCrony that he must send Book One of *Eleven Elements* to every head of state around the world.

"With it, he should include a personal note urging each government to have their top scientific and policy minds study the novel carefully.

"Their task would be to analyze the implications and report back with summaries, insights, and the possible consequences outlined in the text.

"Then," Don continued, "President McCrony should convene a summit with these world leaders to discuss next steps toward forming the Federation of Nations.

"That includes drafting a new international constitution. One designed to protect humanity and restore our planet, Gaia."

Don took a breath. "There would be a twenty-year transitional buffer. During that period, all current governments remain intact while the groundwork for the Federation is laid.

"The final rollout of the Federation of Nations would coincide with the hundredth anniversary of the United Nations, on June 26, 2045.

"That day, the existing UN Charter would be retired, and in its place, the Charter of the New Federation of Nations would take effect.

"Secondly, President Frank McCrony should write a direct, urgent letter to Rossian President Vohkafir Pudding urging him to end the war in Ekraine.

"Why? Because in the future Federation, there is no Rossia, no Ekraine. Just one world. The entire planet will be governed by one body.

"Military aggression, territorial conquest, and national expansion will be obsolete.

"Continuing the war now is not only morally disastrous, it's strategically pointless.

"Perhaps, by 2045, when the Federation charter replaces the UN charter, President Pudding will still be alive to realize how tragically absurd and wasteful his war was. All the lives lost, all the suffering, it will have amounted to nothing.

"Lastly, President McCrony should also send a letter to Ekrainian President Zealwinski.

"He should encourage him to consider surrender. Not as an act of defeat, but as an act of future-conscious wisdom.

"If both countries are to dissolve into the Federation within twenty years, then continuing to fight over borders that are destined to disappear is irrational. Surrender now, preserve lives, and focus on the greater peace that's coming.

"If both leaders persist with this war, they will go down in history as fools. Modern-day Sheikh Chillis, cutting down the very branch on which they sit.

"This is a rare opportunity to rewrite the future, and the time to act is now.

"And for President McCrony, there's something even more compelling at stake: his legacy.

"If he listens and follows through with what we're advising, he could very well be in the running for a Nobel Peace Prize," Don said evenly.

"The Eleven Elements Foundation might even rally public support to back McCrony for a third term, legitimately. He wouldn't need to resort to the national guard takeover strategy he's been quietly toying with.

"Instead of patching up conflicts with temporary fixes, he has the opportunity to initiate a sweeping, global peace initiative by spearheading the formation of the Federation of Nations treaty.

"It would be exactly what Joshua DeWine, allegedly the Second Coming of Christ, would want humanity to pursue.

"More than that, it could solve the massive forty trillion-dollar U.S. national debt. All debts would be reset under the new global system. A clean slate.

"A fresh start. And with it, a new currency: the *International Credit Unit*, or ICU. DeWine conceived of it back in 2014, long before McCrony ever imagined stablecoins or digital currencies.

"Unlike crypto schemes built on volatility, the ICU would be a global standard of credit: stable, fair, and inclusive.

"According to DeWine, the ICU would symbolize a financial awakening to be adopted as the default currency of the new Federation."

Don rose and stepped up to the whiteboard on his boss's wall. There, he sketched the proposed symbol for the currency: a deliberate flourish capturing the ambition behind this economic vision.

"Only a perfectionist would craft something like this," Don muttered.

He pointed to the book. "And if they hit a snag? The *Eleven Elements* volumes serve as their guide.

This sci-fi novel goes beyond storytelling; it's a practical blueprint for what humanity could become. A survival manual for building a future that avoids extinction and at the same time realizes the full potential of humankind. Written by a visionary who may have been more than just an author.

"Imagine this: all the illegal immigration issues and the global uproar they cause, gone.

"Once the world becomes one unified nation, that entire problem disappears. It would be like having the USA exist simultaneously in Mexico and Venezuela.

"No one would need to cross borders because there would be no borders.

"Initially, travel would still be restricted. Everyone would remain in their country of origin.

"But after the Federation of Nations is officially formed, a universal FON (Federation of Nations) passport would be issued.

"Even then, travel would remain limited at first, until all regions are brought up to a standard quality of life as set by the Federation's constitution.

"Eventually, countries like Guatemala or El Salvador could offer lifestyles just as prosperous and comfortable as, maybe even better than, New York or Los Angeles.

"With quality of life equalized, the desire to immigrate would vanish. This would be a permanent, structural solution to the global immigration crisis.

After a pause, Don stepped closer to Chris's desk, his tone more serious, revealing his deepest concern.

"My worst fear," he said slowly, "isn't migration problems to future USA. It's that, by 2056, places like Venezuela will have become so beautiful, so advanced, that they'll be home to the greatest Megapolis ever built.

"And when that happens, people from New York, even citizens like Boron McCrony, will want to migrate there for a better life.

"But here's the irony: at first, they won't even be granted visas. And if they slip in illegally, they'll be rounded up and deported ... straight back to New York.

"Look, the book is published and distributed all over the world in various languages.

"The main intelligence agencies of Rossia, the FSB, the SVR may already have their hands on this book in Rossian language, and probably will present the summary to President Vohkafir Pudding.

"It's either McCrony who takes the first step, or other world leaders will do that. One way or the other, the world's elite and brightest minds will read this stuff and get influenced by it.

"So, it's either McCrony gets the credit to initiate something visionary or Joshua DeWine gets his way through popular readership and his publications, all of which are set to release one after another on an automatic time clock like ticking bombs.

"If Book One makes you feel squeezed, what my sources tell me is that Book Four, *Meaningful Life*, is the most mind-boggling of all. Full of revelations."

Chris, brooding in silence, muttered his usual "Humm," signaling he was absorbing the implication, if reluctantly.

Finally, Chris said, "So this Joshua DeWine is the true genius then, huh? He's mapped answers to migration, population, the environment, even the U.S. debt. And he makes wars look absurd, whether with a Sheikh Chilli parable or a window into the future.

"You're saying he published secret conversations from the Cardinals' meeting at the Vatican's St. Joseph fountain?

"What's next?" Chris challenged. "You think he's going to publish *our* conversation as it's happening right here, right now in this supposedly bug-free FBI headquarters? Are you saying even our discussions, inside this secure, constantly swept office, aren't beyond his reach?"

Don replied with a grin, "Snoopy sees all, Snoopy hears all, and Snoopy knows all. If you haven't heard that phrase, type it into the Froogle Network and see what pops up."

Don's tone shifted into quiet reverence. "Joshua DeWine is a holy, angelic figure to me, dude. All-knowing. All-pervasive. An omnipresent force delivering truth in real time to fulfill his vision.

"Why else would the Bible declare the Second Coming as the King of Kings? 'Thy Will Be Done.' It's literally happening every time someone hears or reads our conversations."

Chris, smirking, pulled forward his digital clock: a tabletop speaker, recorder, and note-taker all-in-one. He pressed a few switches on his phone to turn on the app until a red light blinked steadily on the device.

"Okay," Chris said, "I'm going to run a test. Since you're saying DeWine is some clairvoyant superbeing, let's see if he hears this and puts it in his next book, or at least the revised edition of *Eleven Elements*."

Chris spoke loudly into the device. "What I'm about to say is top secret. Only our inner intel circle knows this."

He paused dramatically, then began: "We know, based on internal data, that the Shynese day traders, expecting President McCrony's re-election, started pumping money into the NYSE around late 2021 to mid-2022.

"Their strategy was to artificially spike the U.S. stock market, helping President Bolden's administration look good and possibly facilitating McCrony's defeat.

"We estimate over $843 billion was funneled in. And by November 3rd, 2024, just days before the election, the DJIA had climbed from around 28,700 in September 2022 to over 44,000.

"That's a 153 percent increase. With those earnings, they got their initial investment out and had more left to play with."

Chris moved to his desktop with double wide monitors and clicked a few keys, displaying the Wall Street Journal's DJIA graph, which was also projected on a large wall-mounted monitor.

"Then they took their profits and reinvested. This time into U.S. government bonds. But through Japanese banks.

"That move gave them leverage.

"If McCrony returned to power and slapped on new tariffs, they'd crash the markets using their bond positions as retaliation."

He inched forward, voice low. "The brilliance of the strategy was in its duality: win if Bolden stays, and sabotage if McCrony wins.

"As insurance, they used local citizens and proxies to purchase the stock, day trade on their behalf and also have unnamed entities purchase the U.S. bonds via Japanese financial institutions. Untraceable, but effective.

"We saw the red flags when President McCrony announced his new tariff plan in April 2025. Markets dipped. Bonds slid. Sell-offs began."

Chris sat back, rubbing his jaw. "Then came the counter: President McCrony's 'Big Beautiful Bill' (or the BBB). It was a four and a half trillion-dollar cushion disguised as military spending.

"It's meant to buffer any artificial dip by repurchasing and stabilizing the market. Essentially, it's a war-footing economic defense."

He gave a dry laugh. "Querlin Stark freaked when he first heard about the BBB. He doesn't know what we're up against. The public doesn't either.

"This is stealth warfare by economic manipulation. You must have seen the CNN headlines: 'Why stocks are at a record in a down-in-the-dumps economy.' Haven't you?

"While media is spinning all sorts of stories, the Shynese day traders won't know what hit their plans in the game of market manipulations."

Chris tapped the app-based recorder and looked up at Don. "So now, my friend, if any of this ends up in *Eleven Elements*, I'll bow to whoever is behind that book.

"If Joshua DeWine really is all-knowing and this appears in black and white, then we're all naked in front of him. Completely exposed."

He clicked the app-based recorder off. "And as I said, this is only a test. Let's see what happens next."

Don chuckled, assuming Chris was still making fun of him. "Can you stop being funny and make sure that damn thing is off."

But Chris remained serious, peering over his glasses. He pressed the record switch on the app and the tabletop recorder blinked again.

"One more thing," Chris said. "We've figured out how many innocent citizens of Shyna are being manipulated. They're being told it's their patriotic duty to bring down America.

"That it's vengeance for the eight-nation alliance, especially the U.S., which intervened during the Boxer Rebellion from 1899 to 1901.

"This narrative is being weaponized. Indoctrinating citizens with stories of humiliation and national pride, making them tools in a modern stealth war.

"I have nothing against Shyna, its government, or its people, Chris noted with a shrug, I love Shynese food, their culture, and their innocent people.

"But it's wrong on the part of the leaders or few corrupt people in their country to exploit a century-old historical event and emotions to drive conflict. The innocent Shynese people deserve better."

Chris paused. "You saw that video of the overworked Shynese pizza delivery guy crying the other day. "Wah Wah working like a dog," he said. "People are being overworked and used for the wrong reasons.

"Shynese brilliance should rise with purpose, not vengeance. They know their success depends on America's success. If we stumble, their economy follows.

"That's it. Chris out." He switched off the recorder and nodded at Don with his signature raised eyebrows.

Don, getting the message, jumped in. "Well, now that we're on this, switch that thing back on. I've got a few thoughts too."

Chris, smiling, turned the recorder app back on.

Don began, "So here's my wager. A thousand bucks says the next edition of *Eleven Elements*, maybe third or fourth edition, includes something we just said.

"Not verbatim, but something eerily close. Because if they're really running this through an AI filter to spice things up, then yeah, they'll reword it. But the essence will remain."

He grinned. "Let me tell you a story. Old folk tale. A hat maker walking through a jungle has a sack full of hats. Dozens of monkeys follow him.

"He lies down for a nap, and when he wakes up, the monkeys have opened the sack and are all wearing hats, mimicking him.

"He throws a stick, they throw branches. He realizes they're copying him. So, he takes off his own hat, throws it on the ground, and walks away.

"Instantly, all the monkeys throw their hats down too. He circles back, gathers the hats, and resumes his journey.

"The moral? The U.S. is the hat maker. We wear jeans, they wear jeans. We make nukes, they want nukes. We build skyscrapers, smartphones, bridges, they copy it all.

"They're mimicking our capitalism, tech, even our dreams of Mars. As long as they're copying and not inventing, we're ahead of the game. We just have to drop the hat and walk away when the time is right."

He lowered his voice to add further, "Shyna is smart. They know destroying the U.S. means losing their best customer. They want us to thrive, even as they challenge us. They would still want the USA to be successful and be a nice trading partner.

"After all, we invented this capitalistic world and all the little things. All the knickknacks that they manufacture.

"But they've been copying us for so long, and waging stealth wars against us, that it's no surprise we now have the MEGA movement. Especially among the loyal followers of President McCrony. His iconic hat says it all: "MEGA," *Make Everything Great Again*. And truthfully, we hope the message lands across borders. We hope *they* copy that too.

"My hope?" Don added. "That one day, President McCrony will say, 'Enough is enough,' and throw down that MEGA hat hard. Just like the hat maker in the old tale. And when he does, maybe all the metaphorical monkeys will throw theirs down too.

"That'll be the moment McCrony picks up his 'hats' and trades them in the market.

"And by market, I mean the U.S. stock market. Whether that's in stablecoins, cryptocurrencies, bitcoins, or whatever form the economy is shaped by. That's the revenue he'll collect for all the hats he's worn. Yes, he'll throw down that hat. It's only a matter of time.

"Of course, Joshua DeWine has already tried to pivot that slogan from MEGA to MEEGA. From 'Make Everything Great Again' to 'Make Everybody & Everyone Great Again.'

"DeWine's version centers people. He says: 'People, every being, are more important than things. People over things.'

"So, there you have it. This is Don Vingo, over and out."

Don signaled and Chris stopped the recording.

Chris shook his head. "What was that, Don? You just dumped a jungle story and geopolitical metaphor salad. Really? That's your final message?"

Don laughed, "Hey, I'm just having fun. Let's see what the AI does with it. If they get the gist right, I'll be impressed."

Chris was smiling, amused at first. But then his tone shifted as he rose from the desk and came around to the front, leaning on the corner closest to Don now.

"What if the rest of the books, those with the remaining elements, are already in the hands of other nations?

"What if Shyna has one or more of them? That would mean they hold more knowledge, more ideas tied to these elements. What if they gain a head start in controlling global influence?

"Does Joshua DeWine mean *everyone*, as in every country? Or does MEEGA actually stand for 'Make Eleven Elements Great Again'?"

He tapped the book resting on his desk. "And what about this other name on the cover, Robbie Juicy? Should we bring him in for interrogation? What if he knows something?"

Don shook his head, calm but definitive. "Nah. He's just a front man, an innocent placeholder. Probably has no real involvement. As I said earlier, he probably does not even know the content or meaning of everything inside of this book. He's just another licensed architect working in Joe DeWines's office.

"The Eleven Elements Foundation just needed someone to pick up calls, reply to emails, carry the public face. Don't waste your time.

"The Holy One, DeWine, is gone. Dead. Nada. What's left is his vision."

Don glanced at the open pages. "All these absurdly similar real-world events and names, they're just clever placeholders. Satirical mirrors of real people and the real life.

"But they're not real in *our* universe. They're drawn from a parallel universe. Fictional overlays of truth. Readers will figure it out by the end.

"It's satire, prophecy, and coded instruction, all in one."

Clearly frustrated, Chris Sharma shook his head. "This whole book is a setup. A psychological device meant to change how we think, how we live, how we act.

"Maybe it gives clarity about life and purpose. Or maybe it just causes chaos and confusion. You ever consider that?

"Maybe this guy, who I don't believe is the Second Coming of Christ, just wrote down *everything*. Every conversation, every event, every character's reflection. And maybe, even though he's dead now, he wrote his own eulogy."

Chris paced. "You ever hear of that concept? Writing your own eulogy? I read something once: 'What do you want your life to have been about?'"

Don nodded. "Oh yeah, I've heard of that. It's supposed to help people think differently. Live better. The idea is: you live in a way so that your eulogy tells a powerful story of who you were."

Chris picked up from there. "Exactly. And that's what this DeWine character has done. This book *is* his eulogy. Written. Printed. Distributed. He's turned himself into some Divine Spirit. An Angelic figure meant to change the world.

"And he drags every famous person, every global leader, into his narrative. He makes them act, speak, and align with his vision so that reality conforms to *his* imagination."

With eyebrows raised, Don fixed his gaze on Chris. "But what other way did he have to do it? Look: he even challenges President McCrony.

"He practically dares him to stop being a 'Band-Aid' peacemaker. To not settle for squashing little conflicts, but instead to aim for something greater: lasting global peace.

"He's calling on President McCrony to earn his Nobel Peace Prize *the right way*, by initiating the formation of a true Federation of Nations. Something that would make war obsolete. Isn't that worth listening to?"

But Chris wasn't budging. He shook his head. "That's just it. This guy is dead. The book is published posthumously. And we're here, just characters in a conversation he supposedly predicted or scripted. It's like he knew exactly how we'd think. What we'd say."

Chris took a breath and looked away. "It's all too convoluted. You keep suggesting we *follow* this. *Do* something. But I'm not convinced, Don. Not yet.

"Maybe he's listening in. Maybe not. I don't care. I'm just not there. I'm trying to figure it out. Out loud. And right now, none of it adds up for me."

Chris was quiet, brow furrowed behind his dark-framed glasses. "I have this uncanny feeling like we are being used.

"I feel like we're two professional critics who just happen to be top-ranking FBI officers," Chris said.

"What were those guys called? Siskel & Ebert, right? The movie critics. Two thumbs up, two thumbs down, all that."

He smirked. "That's what the media will say if we ever show up in this book, that we're here to either admire it or trash it. That's the vibe I'm getting, Don."

He leaned back. "You know what the real critics will say? They'll call it gratuitous because of the self-insert meta commentary. They'll complain the sci-fi framing has no real spine, that there's no strong antagonist, that the plot suffers because the proselytizing gets prioritized. Some will say it's just a parody... a crass satire. Same old crap."

Don shrugged. "They can say whatever they want. The readers with any guts will stop denying the bitter truths. It might take a second read, with an open mind, for some of them to actually get the message.

"And once they grasp it, their lives will change permanently. People will become more self-aware, more conscious of their choices. Enlightenment can't be undone."

"I agree the book lacks a traditional spine, no clear antagonist, no conventional conflicts. It doesn't follow the standard sci-fi formula. But it isn't trying to. It's a creative framework to surface real-world problems and explore possible solutions. I see it as an introduction, setting the stage, establishing the characters, while the true plot unfolds across the six volumes that follow."

Don added after a thoughtful pause, "...I'm sure many will *feel* the invisible eyes of nature watching them.... almost spying."

"But is it in mockery, or awe? Gaia's judgment won't be denied once it's recognized."

Don continued, "It's only Monday morning, and I feel like we've already had a long week. Just talking about this book and the bitter truths it's exposing to us is giving me the creeps. And a bit of a headache."

Chris shook his head slowly.

"And then there are the parts that are really going to stir up outrage," he said. "The Israel–Gaza war over the contested idea of *Eretz Israel.* Saint Thomas dying on the cross, while Jesus survives prosecution and dies in India after fathering several children, people who later become the saints and gurus we all know."

He gave a humorless half-smile.

"And if that weren't enough, there's the implication that I might even carry a trace of that bloodline myself. Maybe just a fraction. You never know. So, you'd better listen closely... maybe even consider worshiping me."

Don sidestepped Chris's sarcasm. "The structure of this project, this whole narrative setup, is a double-edged sword.

"If you believe in the message, you become part of the vision. But if you disagree, if you doubt that Joshua DeWine is the real deal, you risk being branded as the enemy. The Anti-Christ, even.

"You know how people get when they start idolizing someone. For the believers, he is the Second Coming. The Jesus Christ returned. And non-believers will be labeled as Anti-Christ.

"If President McCrony, for example, were to speak against the book or discredit the authors like he sometimes does ... well, then suddenly *he* becomes the villain. The opposition. The unbeliever."

Chris exhaled slowly, still frowning. "And that's exactly what makes this so dangerous, Don. It reads like more than a book. It functions as a belief system. A test. A mirror. And I'm not ready to look into it and decide what I see."

Chris looked at Don with narrowed eyes from behind his designer glasses. "I totally agree on that, Don. It's a double whammy for McCrony and us. And a really nice one.

"No wonder even First Lady Juliet Veritas had to sit up and pay attention to him. DeWine can play everyone's mind with his words. This book here is a work of art, I should say!"

"That's exactly what I'm saying," Don said. "He has no fear whatsoever. Challenging a President like McCrony takes balls. Solid balls. Balls of steel, platinum, or lead or whatever.

"And so, it seems he does have some serious information or knowledge about everything that's making him fearless.

"And as I said earlier, he is King of Kings, and that is why he has nothing to worry about.

"I am sorry that I am a little biased and leaning towards the notion that he is, or he was, real and this book project of his is the only way he could communicate the worldwide judgement and package his mercy along with it.

"You can take it or leave it, Chris. But it is what it is."

Chris circled back to square one. "Again, I say, Don, my friend, we just need to do our job." He stressed the words, gesturing with both his palms facing each other.

"The original author, Joshua DeWine, is dead and we cannot do anything about it.

"We simply need to catch the illegal immigrants or aliens from the future time. Those are our target fugitives. That is our job and my focus. Since they are NOT locals or citizens of our time, they don't have any business being in our time. That's it. Period."

Don took a deep breath and replied with a sigh, "Chris, buddy. Look, our future is in grave danger. Don't you see anything?

"I agree that this Joshua DeWine is just a character in this so-called science fiction book. And he is what he is. A character with divine qualities. He shows who he is and what he is with very just words and actions.

"And in doing that, he has listed one hundred and one very innovative ways we can fix the waters or oceans of the world.

"He says Book One is about *Healing Waters*, where the two words have a double meaning. We have to *heal the waters*, and in another way, it is the *waters that will heal us.*"

Don continued, "Remember that people get baptized by water. And it is said that life emerged from water.

"So, in that sense, water is our original mother and we are pissing on her, according to him. Water is an essential element. We need it for hydration and for life to sustain.

"Read in this book about all the discussion that the time travelers had with that professor at University of Miami."

Don noticed Chris listening intently, nodding, jotting down notes in his sleek digital pad, every now and then narrowing his eyes in thought.

Encouraged, Don continued. "We're facing a grave and rapidly escalating crisis. If the polar ice caps continue melting at their current pace, and if the Earth's axial tilt shifts even slightly, we could be looking at a scenario where the North Pole ends up somewhere near the pyramids. Imagine that."

Chris's brow furrowed, his pen halting mid-stroke as he listened.

"Regions that are currently freezing cold could become scorching hot. And places that are now lush and tropical might be buried under several feet of snow.

"This isn't a gradual climate shift. It's a planetary convulsion. A sudden, catastrophic ice age that could descend overnight, catching humanity off guard.

"Mass extinction. Widespread collapse."

Don exhaled, then added, "Search it yourself on Froogle or any reputable source. Look up 'North Pole Drift,' with its ever-increasing speed. Or 'Geomagnetic Pole Reversal,' which is long overdue.

"It's all there. Hidden in plain sight. What this book says, what Joshua DeWine is warning us about, isn't fiction at all. It's all documented facts, peer-reviewed, scientific reality, buried under political noise and media fog."

The only thing clear is that he's managed to connect all the dots: the depleting aquifers, the rising heat, the melting polar ice-caps anchoring the earth in its tilt, leading to the gradual shift of the North Pole, and, eventually, a full pole reversal.

Chris looked up sharply, the consequences of it all suddenly crystal clear.

"We *do* need to stop the snow caps from melting," Don pressed. "At the rate they're vanishing, we're racing toward irreversible damage.

"The one hundred and one methods laid out in the book, that's just the foundation. That was DeWine's starting point for a global reset of the planet's waters, back to their original, pristine state."

He inched forward. "But here's what most people don't know: DeWine wrote *six more* volumes containing issues with the ten remaining elements. Not yet published. Part of the same *Eleven Elements* series."

Chris raised an eyebrow. "Six?"

"Yes. We already know five of the classical elements: Water, Fire or Heat, Air or Wind, Earth, and Life, what DeWine sometimes called 'Ether.'

"But the other six? They're unknown. Undocumented. And from what we can tell, DeWine apparently hid them. Scattered their contents across the world.

"Each one is a breadcrumb, encrypted in physical locations, symbolic cues, and temporal coordinates.

"And now," Don continued, voice growing more urgent, "it's up to the right team of Time Travelers, trained to work across locations and centuries, to retrieve and release those final books.

"The volumes need to be published in sequence, in DeWine's name, to trigger the future we've all been working toward. If we don't...."

Chris cut him off, eyes narrowing. "Wait a minute. What did you just say? *The right team of Time Travelers?* Are you saying there's more than one?"

Don paused, mulling over how much to reveal.

Then, with a grim nod, he said, "Yes. My top crew has been tracking anomalous activity for the past few days.

"We've identified *another* SUV, same model, same irregular energy signature, materialized out of thin air in Central Florida."

Chris sat upright, stunned. "A second team?"

Don stood up to stretch a bit and he turned around to look through a high window. "It appears that there is another team of five persons or a back-up team of Time Travelers that has emerged and is working towards its own goals.

"From the way this new team and its members are behaving, they are different from their predecessors.

"At least three of the five members contain a lot of inorganic material, suggesting that they may be more like futuristic bio-organic robots.

"As far as we know, they haven't interacted with the first team of Time Travelers that we had in our custody: what we call the first batch. And the one we interrogated didn't even know another team existed.

"Unless, of course, the situation had become so distressing that an emergency protocol triggered their dispatch."

"Oh crap," Sharma pushed away from his desk. "And you haven't told me all this is going on?"

Don replied, "These are very new developments. I just got most of the details a couple days ago.

"You know how things are, Chris. I meant to keep you posted, but I thought I'd better gather more information before I present these findings. We were going to meet today to discuss this topic anyway, so I decided to wait."

Chris Sharma folded his arms. "So, you're telling me there are two teams of Time Travelers visiting us and we don't even know which ones are the bad guys and which ones are the good guys." He paused. "If *any* of them are good guys."

"And our job is to locate them and try to capture them 'dead or alive' so we can protect the United States?

"Now I see your point," Chris said. "We may need to take sides. Maybe team up with one group to nab the other.

"The first group has one bio-organic robot, and the second group has three. Which one would you side with, huh?"

Don said, "From the interrogation of the one of the five we had captured, we know they want to publish all seven novels of Joshua DeWine.

"They've already succeeded in getting Book One published.

"For the other ten Elements, each one has one hundred and one ideas, which means that any nation or foreign corporation that gets their hands on these futuristic innovations will gain a massive advantage in controlling financial markets and technological superiority.

"So, there are one thousand and ten more ideas that are pending publication. That's one hundred and one for each of the ten remaining elements.

"These ideas could solve the problems of the future world. The war equipment and missiles manufacturing companies and countries will modify their factories to produces millions of parts and pieces for these 1,111 ideas that are required for centuries to come. Armament manufacturing and selling countries need not fear as to what they will do if wars stop.

"And all of this knowledge, spread across the remaining ten elements, six of which we still know nothing about, could define how countries progress.

"That's why it's imperative we find these two teams of Time Travelers and secure the information before anyone else does. Our challenge just grew ten-fold."

Chris snorted, clearly trying to hold back a laugh. "I've been reading this book for a few weeks now, and only one part really spooked me. You know the bit about how squirrels, pigeons, crows, basically all the small city critters, might actually be robotic spies sent from the future?

"The other day, I got home and saw a squirrel. I watched how it moved. How it stopped and stared. It looked right at me. Like, *really* looked.

"Since then, I've become hyper-aware of them. What if they *are* watching us? What if they're thinking critically about our behavior?"

He added more seriously, "And even if they're not from the future, what if they're *conscious*? Like us? Aware, observant, maybe even smarter in ways we can't understand?"

Chris scratched his chin, thoughtful now. "That night, I had a dream. One of the squirrels started talking to me.

He shifted into the squirrel's squeaky' voice, sharp and accusing.

"Hey Sheikh Chilli, you stupid human. You're destroying the Mother Nature that gave you your life. You're poisoning your own water, wrecking your own life-support system. You think you're living smart, but you're not. You've lost your purpose. Your real job is to protect the planet. Don't destroy her. Let us all live in harmony and peace."

Chris shook his head slowly. "That dream hit me hard. These little creatures, we call them simple animals, but they're free. No bills. No debt. No nine-to-five.

"Meanwhile, we, the 'smart' ones, are drowning in stress and pretending that's normal.

"Are we really free? Nope. That thought bothers me." He looked up. "That's what this book did to me. It made me think. Really *think*."

"Don, how long have you known me?" Chris began, his voice softer now. "I let my guard down around you. I joke, I act like a kid, because I feel safe. You and I both know the kind of stress we're under. And sometimes, I need that space to stay sane.

"You're the only one who knows I play devil's advocate on purpose. I pretend to be the joker to get people talking, get to the truth hidden under the surface. It's just my style: 'Be foolish, be hungry.'

"I never meant any disrespect to you or your beliefs. But this book ... it's got me stumped. I'm honestly dumbfounded. The only thing I can do to de-stress is to have some fun!"

Chris's tone sharpened as his mind shifted back to the mission. "Let's start tracing the sponsors behind the Eleven Elements Foundation. I want to know exactly what they're up to next."

"You say they're a non-profit supposedly working toward environmental goals. But we need to find out who's gathering all the 'stardust' that your good friend, sorry, not to offend you, but your so-called Second Coming of Christ, Mr. Joshua DeWine, has sprinkled across the world to various experts and universities.

"The next steps are in your hands, Don. You need to depute a strong team to tackle this.... Before it blows on us."

Assuming the meeting was over, Don offered some final remarks. "I think we're in for a truly global, time-traveling adventure where every living human being is also a character in this series of novels, whether they believe it or not!"

He smirked. "And now, the non-profit foundation behind *Eleven Elements* has raised the stakes. They're offering a one-million-dollar cash prize to anyone who can list all Eleven Elements in the exact order they appear in the novels.

"It's like *The Price is Right*. Just submit your name, the elements in the correct sequence, and the prize is yours. A full million dollars and dinner with all the authors involved."

Don stood, with a copy of the book in hand, flipping through its pages. "The clue is that the names of the Eleven Elements are scattered throughout the first four books and entries have to be submitted before Book Five gets published.

"Readers just have to find them, write them down in order, include their name and contact information, and email it to: *winner@elevenelementsfdn.org*

"This isn't fiction. And by participating, readers become direct characters in a future installment, with the winner's name featured and more.

Chris sat hard into the sofa, intrigued, concerned, processing. "Yes, I see another game unfolding. It's a no-purchase-necessary sweepstakes. And the twist? They want readers to spread the word. Email friends and family, recommend the book, and join the challenge.

"Whether it's for the thrill, the prize, or to amplify the book's message of peace, it's brilliant."

"I hear popular performing artist Tailon Shift sings in Book Two," Don mused as he stood up. "I wonder which other famous figures will be targeted in the next book!"

"I've got to run. Late for my three p.m. I just have a few days left before I leave my job as the deputy director of FBI...got to pack my boxes."

Don continued to speak as he moved towards the door.

"Can't wait to dive into Book Two. If the first volume was this mind-bending, the next one's bound to shake the ground under our feet. Hopefully humanity listens this time." He gave a quick wave. "See you later!"

* * * * * *

The room fell into silence.

FBI Director Chris Sharma sat unmoving, his glasses catching the light as he stared at the books laid out before him as though they were staring back.

He picked one up, turned a few pages, and frowned.

Could a book truly be a weapon? The thought unsettled him. *Words have power.*

His gaze drifted upward to the poster on the wall, a gift from his devout Hindu mother when he first came to D.C.

Its bold script declared:

Significance of Krishn's Advent

Lord Krishn was born during the Krishn-Paksha, the dark fortnight of the month. The effulgence of the Lord is seen with the greater effect when it is dark. In a world of disorder, Krishn was born to establish order. Krishn's advent signifies the dispelling of darkness, the removal of troubles, banishing of ignorance and teaching mankind the Supreme Wisdom. Krishn's primary role was that of teacher. He taught the Gita to Arjuna. He told Arjuna: "Be only My instrument!" Krishn thereby declared: "Using you as an instrument I am reforming the whole world." — Shri Sathya Sai Baba

Beneath the printed words, a red scrawl in human handwriting: **"Lord Krishn = Lord Christ = same God, same phonetics."**

Chris's pulse quickened. His throat tightened as he read it again. Different faiths, different names, perhaps the same force moving through chosen instruments across time.

He lowered his gaze to the stacked copies of *Eleven Elements* and let the thought settle.

"Max is the protagonist," he murmured to himself, "tasked with stopping humanity from simply ... vanishing."

The image in his mind was stark: a commander burdened with the responsibility of a century not yet born, ordered to lead an elite unit five hundred years into the past so the right minds could plant the right seeds. Their future depended entirely on whether the past played its part. They risked their lives for this mission."

He drew a slow breath.

"Now the burden sits with me," he sighed, and continued to ponder. *"Not just three hundred and forty million Americans … a world of eight billion that might be bound as one Gaia."*

The authors had chosen him deliberately: his office, his reach, the part of his story that would outlast President McCrony's term.

He leaned back, locking his fingers behind his head, feeling the heat of it.

The Bureau has a list of targets, but this book just painted me as one.

He took a deep breath as he sat there brooding about the bigger picture and the massive burden that now lay on his shoulders.

Ignore the message and it becomes an act of inaction. Act on it and he—Chris Sharma, Director of the FBI—must follow the logic to its end. Either way, the choice will define him, martyr or fool, strategist or a Sheikh Chilli.

Checkmate.

He pictured Max at the fulcrum of billions of lives and recognized the mirror. What the commander felt in the mission brief, Chris felt now in the fluorescent hush of his office: the future pressing in, silent and absolute, waiting for a decision with no safe middle.

- - END OF BOOK ONE - -

The story continues in ELEVEN ELEMENTS Book Two – Fire and Fresh Air

Following chapters contain **Appendix-1** and **Appendix-2**

CHAPTER -31

Prior to their dinner meeting, Max had navigated through the files of Joshua DeWine during his VRV memory recall mode, scrolling until he found the folder labeled: "*Manifesto of Eleven Elements* – Source Archive."

Max was growing accustomed to his memory recall sessions. In the VRV mode, the process required almost no effort. Just a glimpse of familiar images, a sound, or a fragment of a scene was enough to trigger a cascade of memories.

The moment he closed his eyes; everything returned in vivid detail. It reassured him that his neural pathways were strengthening. That his mind was reweaving itself into wholeness.

Soon, he might not even need the VRV. Perhaps simply closing his eyes would be enough to summon it all back, as though his memories had never been fractured in the first place.

He exhaled slowly, closed his eyes, and let the headset pull him into the deep, neural pathways of memory, into the parts of himself that were still lost due to the time jump. The clarity he gained each time was fuel. Fuel for the mission. Fuel for leadership. Fuel to feel whole again. He was recovering, steadily, purposefully, and with intention.

15:21 | 11-14-2025 (Twenty-first century)
LOCATION: RESIDENCE INN – BASE ROOM 402

He tapped the icon. The folder expanded. A short chime sounded.

"Continue," he said.

Eve's voice returned, smooth and clear:

"Mr. Joshua DeWine conceived the *Manifesto of Eleven Elements* as a pledge, a global framework dedicated to understanding, managing, and preserving the core components essential to humanity's survival.

"He envisioned the manifesto not as a static document, but as a *collaborative, evolving electronic book.* A digital platform where scholars, scientists, and citizens from around the world could contribute insights, shaping a shared, strategic vision for the future."

Max's expression tightened, listening with heightened attention.

"DeWine believed that most people lived within a *false reality,* one engineered by special interest groups, media manipulation, and systemic distractions. A world that offered the *illusion* of freedom while quietly undermining the values and conditions needed for true human fulfillment.

"In his own words: *'We are a civilization of nearly eight billion, spiraling upward, while the ecosystem spirals downward. The imbalance is fatal. We are not evolving; we are accelerating toward extinction.'*

"He cited these warnings from leading scientists, among them, Dr. Stephen Hawking, who famously predicted the eventual annihilation of humanity unless radical action was taken.

"DeWine referenced a published statement by Hawking in the *Christian Science Monitor*, using it to anchor the urgency behind his call.

"Mr. DeWine had a clear vision for how *The Manifesto of Eleven Elements* should be released.

"He didn't want a quiet academic debut or a niche publication for elite circles. He wanted a simultaneous global release, a synchronized unveiling in multiple languages, across continents, media networks, digital platforms, and local communities.

"The goal was exposure, *true exposure*. Every government, activist, entrepreneur, student, and ordinary citizen needed access. From policy-makers to people in rural villages, he believed *everyone* deserved the chance to see what humanity was capable of becoming.

"DeWine believed that those who aligned with the ideas within the Manifesto would not only benefit individually, but also catalyze collective action, sparking real, positive shifts in how the world functioned.

"And he was clear about one thing: The Manifesto was not meant to be another doomsday prophecy.

"It was never intended as a simple warning, a *follow this or perish* decree. From the beginning, it was meant to be a plan, a design for a potential future that erased the familiar follies of humanity."

"He wanted to outline not only the problems, but the *solutions*. He envisioned the book as a **living blueprint**: part manifesto, part instruction manual, part design schematic for a better world.

"It was meant to be *heuristic*, provoking thought. *Logical*, based in science and systems. *Practical*, adaptable in real-world applications. And *complete*: no vague platitudes or empty ideology, but tangible, actionable guidance.

"A source you could return to.

"A toolkit for rebuilding civilization.

"A program to rewrite the future.

Max began scrolling through all the folders and documents within the one named: "Joshua DeWine"

As he was scrolling through the list of documents, he came across the draft of Joshua DeWine's *Manifesto*.

Traditionally, a manifesto serves as a public declaration of intentions, values, or objectives, whether by an individual, a group, or a political movement.

However, this particular document, *The Manifesto of Eleven Elements*, stood apart from the science fiction novel series titled *Eleven Elements*.

While the novel series explored each of the eleven elements through narrative across multiple volumes, the *Manifesto* used those same elements as foundational principles for a bold vision: the unification of humanity under a single Federation of Nations.

The Manifesto outlined goals for global cooperation, shared responsibility, and a peaceful, sustainable future for all.

It read less like a declaration and more like a blueprint for a new civilization.

Max clicked the next file folder and opened the draft, it began with a notice: *"This document is open to review, input, and future refinement by its readers and the citizens of tomorrow. Feedback is welcome."*

* * * * * * *

APPENDIX – 1 – The Original Draft Manifesto Document:

Manifesto of the Eleven Elements

A Declaration of Intentions by Mr. Joshus DeWine

Mr. Joshus DeWine proposed a bold and unified global vision: to establish a single governing world body founded on a new constitution for all humanity.

His "Declaration of Intentions" lays out a plan to align the entire world under shared principles designed to protect life, restore the Earth, and allow every human being to live with purpose, freedom, and dignity.

At the heart of this vision are the Eleven Elements: essential values and forces DeWine believes are critical to the survival and thriving of humanity. These elements form the framework for all decision-making, governance, and progress.

ELEVEN ELEMENTS, DECLARATION & FRAMEWORK

Core Goals:

- **Form a global federation** of nations under one constitution.
- **Preserve all life** and uphold its equal value.
- **Ensure every person lives with purpose**, guided by the Eleven Elements.

- **Restore Earth's balance and sustainability**, respecting all natural resources.
- **Eliminate war, hunger, and debt**, enabling all to thrive without fear or scarcity.
- **Remove authoritarianism** and centralized power; leadership will rise by public merit and service, not wealth or influence.
- **Empower collective decision-making**, supported by technology and AI to analyze impacts through the lens of the Eleven Elements.
- **Replace wealth-based status** with value-based recognition: those who contribute the most to public good and global wellbeing earn higher societal credit.
- **End the billionaire class**, shifting focus to ethical innovation and service-driven progress.

Vision for the Future:

The world envisioned by DeWine is simple, peaceful, and equitable. No one goes hungry. No one fears oppression. Every nation and person contributes to the planet's healing and collective peace. Decisions are made not by elites, but by the people, with technology aiding transparency and balance.

The Eleven Elements serve as a compass to ensure all progress is sustainable and just.

Living the Manifesto:

This new society would evolve continuously. Values, goals, and strategies may adapt, but always in alignment with the core intent of the Eleven Elements: **for humanity to live in harmony with nature, each other, and the resources shared for the common good.**

Preamble

We, the peoples of Earth, affirm that **all life is valuable, created equal, and deserving of freedom, dignity, and opportunity**. We pledge to unite as one human family to protect life, restore the planet, and steward our shared resources for the **common good**. Guided by the **Eleven Elements**, a practical framework for survival and flourishing, we commit to a future that is **hunger-free, war-free, debt-free**, and lived in harmony with nature.

Article I: Purpose

1. **Unite the nations** into a cooperative **Federation of Nations** that serves the world's people.

2. **Draft and adopt a world constitution** that protects life, liberty, and the commons, and that orients every major decision toward balance across the **Eleven Elements**.
3. **Preserve and restore Earth** to a sustainable, regenerative, and resilient state.
4. **Ensure purposeful lives** for all people, where each person contributes meaningfully and is supported to thrive.

Article II: Core Principles

- **Life First:** Preserve and enhance life in all decisions.
- **Equality & Human Dignity:** Every person enjoys equal rights and equal access to essentials.
- **Common Good over Private Excess:** Resources are stewarded for all; extreme concentrations of wealth or power are incompatible with the common good.
- **Merit through Public Benefit:** Social recognition is earned by demonstrable contributions to humanity and the living world.
- **Subsidiarity:** Decisions are made at the most local level capable of acting effectively, coordinated globally when needed.
- **Transparency & Accountability:** Open processes, open data, and regular public audits.
- **Non-violence & Peace:** Conflicts are resolved through dialogue, mediation, and restorative justice.

Article III: World Governance (Federation of Nations)
A. People-Led Institutions

1. **World People's Assembly (WPA):** A globally representative citizens' body selected by population and region to deliberate on major issues and ratify constitutional changes.
2. **House of Member Nations (HMN):** Delegations from all nations coordinate cross-border policy and implementation.
3. **Merit Council:** Members selected based on a verified track record of public service and benefit creation. Provides non-partisan expertise and long-horizon planning.
4. **Local & Regional Councils:** Empowered to act under the principle of subsidiarity; coordinate with WPA and HMN.

B. Technology-Assisted, Human-Decided

- **AI Stewardship (Advisory, non-voting):** Independent, open-source AI systems provide analysis, forecasting, and **Eleven-Element Impact Assessments (EEIA)**. Humans retain final authority and decision making as a collective body.

- **Open Data Commons:** All data used for public decisions is open, privacy-protected, and auditable.

C. Leadership by Merit

- Leadership **emerges from service**: candidates demonstrate verified public benefit.
- Term limits; mandatory transparency; removal for breach of ethics.

Article IV: Rights & Guarantees

1. **Essentials Guarantee:** Every person has unconditional access to **nutritious food, clean water, shelter, healthcare, education, and digital connectivity**.
2. **Freedom & Responsibility:** Speech, conscience, movement, and association are protected; responsibilities to the common good and the Eleven Elements accompany these freedoms.
3. **Work with Purpose:** Society organizes toward **shorter, meaningful work** that advances public benefit and planetary restoration.

Article V: Economic Orientation

- **No Billionaires / Wealth Ceilings:** Extreme personal accumulation is incompatible with the common good. Policies set **upper limits on private wealth** and redirect excess toward shared projects that benefit all.
- **Public Benefit Ledger (PBL):** A transparent, audited system recognizing **Merit Credits** for measurable contributions to humanity and nature. Credits signal trust and eligibility for leadership, not cash hoarding.
- **Open Markets with Guardrails:** Enterprise thrives within **planetary and social boundaries** defined by the Eleven Elements.
- **Universal Commons:** Critical resources (water basins, forests, atmosphere, core knowledge) are protected as a **global common**.

Article VI: The Eleven-Element Framework

Intent: Every significant policy, project, or allocation must be tested for **balance across all Eleven Elements**. A decision that severely harms any single element cannot proceed. **The primary elements commonly known to mankind are water, air (wind), fire (heat), metals & minerals, Life (Gaia or all organic life), and six secondary elements that shall be declared at a later date.**

Note: The specific definitions and thresholds for each Element are maintained in a living standard annex. The following process applies universally.

A. Eleven-Element Impact Assessment (EEIA)

1. **Define the proposal** and its goals.
2. **Map impacts** across all Eleven Elements (qualitative + quantitative).
3. **Score** each Element on a 0–5 scale (0 = severe harm; 5 = strong net benefit).
4. **Guardrails:** No Element may score below **2**; at least **7 Elements must score ≥4**.
5. **Mitigation Plan:** Address any scores ≤3 with concrete fixes, timelines, and accountability.
6. **Public Review:** Publish data, models, and trade-offs; invite comment.
7. **Decision:** WPA/HMN vote after public review and independent audit.
8. **Post-Implementation Audit:** Re-score annually; corrective action if thresholds slip.

- - - - CONTINUES ON NEXT PAGE - - - - -

B. EEIA Quick Matrix (Template)

Element	Baseline	Projected Impact (0–5)	Risks	Mitigations	Net Outcome
E1 water					
E2 air/wind					
E3 Fire/heat					
E4 Metals Minerals					
E5 Life Gaia Organics					
E6 UNK					
E7 UNK					
E8 UNK					
E9 UNK					
E10 UNK					
E11 UNK					

UNK = left intentionally Unknown for the award prize to be declared at a later date.

Article VII: Peace, Safety, and Justice

- **Demilitarization over time**: redirection of resources to prevention, disaster readiness, and restoration.
- **Restorative Justice:** Repair harm, rehabilitate, and reintegrate; incarceration reserved for imminent public safety needs.
- **Conflict Mediation:** Standing peace services at local, national, and global levels.

Article VIII: Planetary Restoration & Stewardship
- **Regenerate Ecosystems**: protect biodiversity; restore soils, forests, wetlands, and oceans.
- **Circular Material Flows:** Design out waste and pollution; prioritize reuse and repair.
- **Clean Energy & Efficiency:** Rapid transition to safe, renewable systems with resilient grids.
- **True-Cost Accounting:** Include ecological and social costs in all decisions.

Article IX: Participation & Collective Decision-Making
- **Deliberative Assemblies:** Regular citizen panels, randomly selected and compensated, to review major proposals.
- **Global Referenda:** For constitutional questions and high-impact, cross-border decisions.
- **Digital Commons Platform:** Multilingual participation, accessible tools, and AI-assisted summaries; strict privacy protections.

Article X: Culture, Education, and Innovation
- **Lifelong Learning:** Free, open education focused on critical thinking, cooperation, and planetary stewardship.
- **Open Knowledge:** Publicly funded research and technology are open by default.
- **Art & Meaning:** Support cultural work that enriches community and care for life.

Article XI: Finance for the Common Good
- **Debt-Free Essentials:** Essentials Guarantee funded through public finance tied to restoration and resilience outcomes.
- **Mission-Aligned Investment:** Capital allocation must pass EEIA thresholds; no financing of projects that breach guardrails.
- **Transparent Budgets:** Real-time, open ledgers for all public spending.

Article XII: Implementation Roadmap (Phased)
Phase I (Years 1–3):
- Ratify the Declaration; form interim WPA/HMN; publish EEIA standard annex.
- Launch Essentials Guarantee pilots and planetary restoration accelerators.

- Establish Open Data Commons and AI Stewardship architecture.

Phase II (Years 4–7):

- Adopt world constitution; implement wealth ceilings and Public Benefit Ledger.
- Scale restoration and circular-economy programs; demilitarization targets.
- Regular global citizens' assemblies and first global referenda.

Phase III (Years 8–15):

- Consolidate the Federation of Nations; full Essentials Guarantee globally.
- Achieve net nature gain and verified improvements across all Eleven Elements.
- Continuous review and improvement via open audits and public feedback.

Article XIII: Amendment & Evolution

This Declaration is a **living framework**. Amendments may be proposed by the WPA, HMN, or through a global citizens' initiative. Any amendment must **align with the original intent**: a world where humanity **thrives in peace, freedom, and harmony with nature**, with every decision balanced across the **Eleven Elements**.

Closing Affirmation

We commit ourselves to this Declaration and its **practical, measurable path** toward a just, peaceful, and flourishing world. Our success will be measured not by the fortunes of a few but by the wellbeing of all people, the animals, natural resources, and the living Earth.

Please emails your thoughts, opinions and comments about the Manifesto of Eleven Elements: Manifesto@elevenelemntsfdn.org

CHAPTER -32

APPENDIX – 2 – 101 ways to heal, restore and protect water

Water is the Primary Element, Element Number One, described in Book One as the life-giving and life-sustaining force on earth. Part of the Eleven Elements Manifesto is the need to restore earth's waters, or heal the water bodies, oceans, rivers, lakes, and manage the water ecology and water environment. This calls for action to cleanse and protect the water systems as a collective worldwide effort.

The Water Restoration Manifesto: one hundred and one Commitments to Conserve, Protect, and Rebuild Earth's Waters: 'HEALING WATERS'. And below are the listed 101 ways to restore water to a pristine state:

Vision statement:

By 2060, humanity can achieve a Water-Positive Planet where every drop we use restores more than it takes.

Conserving Water at Home

1. Equip every household fixture with smart monitoring apps to track and optimize daily water use.
2. Install variable-flow taps and showers to switch instantly between high and low flow.
3. Ensure all appliances are built with water-efficiency systems and app-based controls.
4. Use motion-sensor faucets. No more running taps.
5. Collect rainwater for irrigation and secondary household needs.
6. Categorize water into three grades: primary (drinking/cooking), secondary (washing/cleaning), and tertiary (flushing/irrigation).
7. Deploy soil sensors and smart apps to irrigate only when plants need it.
8. Use mulches, soil screens, and humidity extractors to maximize drip irrigation efficiency.
9. Limit pools and spas to community facilities; no private luxury waste.
10. Channel all wastewater through grease/oil separators before release to treatment plants.

11. Mandate biodegradable soaps and detergents safe for aquatic plant life.
12. Ban disposal of oils, medicines, or chemicals into sinks and toilets.

Water in Industry

13. Implement water reuse and recycling across all factories.
14. Treat process water before discharge.
15. Replace once-through cooling with closed-loop systems.
16. Audit and monitor industrial water usage to cut inefficiencies.
17. Retire outdated, water-wasting equipment.
18. Train employees in water conservation practices.
19. Switch to biodegradable, eco-safe chemicals.
20. Form partnerships with conservation organizations.
21. Retrofit facilities with eco-friendly technologies.
22. Pursue zero-liquid-discharge goals in heavy industry.

Water in Agriculture

23. Transition to multi-tier vertical farming with cascading drip irrigation.
24. Irrigate with harvested rainwater, gray water, and reclaimed wastewater.
25. Favor organic farming to reduce chemical runoff.
26. Establish buffer zones around water bodies to filter farm runoff.
27. Grow water-smart and drought-resistant crops.
28. Use apps and precision sensors to optimize irrigation schedules.
29. Apply compost and organic matter to increase soil water retention.
30. Rotate crops to conserve soil and moisture.
31. Plant cover crops to prevent erosion and water loss.

Restoring Rivers and Lakes

32. Deploy various automated systems to remove trash from waterways.
33. Replant native vegetation along shores and banks.
34. Dredge polluted sediments from urban canals and rivers.
35. Control erosion to reduce sediment runoff.
36. Build fish ladders and passages to restore ecosystems.
37. Remove obsolete dams blocking river systems.
38. Limit new dams to moderate scale, avoid mega-dam disruption.
39. Create wetlands for natural water filtration.
40. Restore rivers to their natural flow patterns.
41. Reintroduce native aquatic species.

Preventing Pollution

42. Ban single-use plastics globally. In place of plastics use biodegradable products or products that become food for sea life.
43. Establish strict hazardous waste disposal systems.
44. Prohibit chemical dumping into drains or waterways.
45. Mandate biodegradable detergents and soaps.
46. Enforce tough limits on industrial discharge.
47. Control farm runoff with vegetative buffer strips.
48. Ban microplastics in personal products.
49. Replace chemical fertilizers with compost.
50. Install sediment traps in stormwater drains.
51. Launch education campaigns on pollution prevention.

Protecting Groundwater

52. Seal unused bore wells; convert them into recharge stations by 2050.
53. Create an international body to monitor groundwater levels.
54. Build alternative water supply systems to eliminate dependence on groundwater.
55. Establish global desalination networks to supply agriculture.
56. Use injection wells to replenish aquifers.
57. Treat brackish groundwater and counter saltwater intrusion.
58. Ban groundwater extraction by 2050 to preserve aquifers.

Urban Water Management

59. Build green roofs to capture and reuse rainwater.
60. Install permeable pavements to prevent runoff.
61. Create urban wetlands for stormwater management.
62. Replace aging sewer infrastructure.
63. Separate sewage from stormwater networks.
64. Mandate rooftop rainwater harvesting.
65. Construct bioswales to clean and filter runoff.
66. Use smart meters to detect and fix leaks.
67. Reuse water in construction and infrastructure projects.
68. Develop community rain gardens in urban neighborhoods.

Oceans and Seas

69. Launch global-scale ocean cleanup initiatives.
70. Retrofit 100,000+ ocean vessels with ballast-tank purification systems, turning ships into mobile ocean vacuum cleaners.
71. Ban all non-biodegradable plastics worldwide.
72. Establish no-fishing zones to allow ecosystems to recover.
73. Enforce strict cruise ship waste and pollution laws.

74. Create an international authority for oil spill prevention and response.
75. Deploy solar-powered "Life-Buoy" flotillas to clean toxins and microplastics. Community-owned, app-tracked, crowd-funded – corporate sponsorships and shared stewardship.
76. Restore coral reefs and seed new colonies for marine biodiversity.
77. Legalize only sustainable fishing practices using biodegradable and marine life edible nets.
78. Encourage controlled fish farming to reduce wild stock pressure.
79. Re-seed oceans with embryos and eggs of diverse marine species.

Governance and Policy
80. Enact strong global laws protecting water bodies.
81. Require local community water management plans.
82. Halt desertification to safeguard oases and water resources.
83. Desalinate ocean water to pre-industrial levels.
84. Restore rivers and oceans worldwide to pre-industrial health.
85. Audit and enforce compliance with environmental laws.
86. Incentivize industries to reduce water footprints.
87. Build global clean-water infrastructure for farms and cities.
88. Develop and enforce advanced water resource management systems.
89. Mandate sustainable water usage across sectors.
90. Impose penalties for illegal dumping into water bodies.
91. Promote public-private partnerships for water conservation.
92. Invest in cutting-edge purification and desalination technologies.
93. Build compact megacities with shared-resource systems to reduce sprawl pollution.

Community and Culture
94. Dedicate one day a week to community cleanups. Turn conservation into a social tradition.
95. Harness social media to spread awareness and mobilize volunteers.
96. Create engaging educational media on water stewardship.
97. Embed conservation programs across schools, workplaces, and institutions.
98. Launch global competitions between nations on water conservation milestones.
99. Establish stewardship programs like *"Adopt a Canal"* to encourage direct community ownership.

Innovation for the Future
100. Eleven Elements Foundation has developed a drone-based rain-cloud creation technology integrated with seeding to regulate and

manage rainfall in dry arid zones or regions that have drought. License permits available upon request.

101. Invest in breakthrough solutions, nanofiltration, desalination, solar-powered purifiers, and beyond, working toward a **water-positive planet**, where every drop we use restores more than what we would take.

Eleven Elements Foundation has several ideas for licensing. And proceeds shall go to the not-for-profit organization for developing various other innovative ideas for remaining ten elements, research and development.

Please emails your thoughts, opinions and comments to cleanse our water resources:
healingwaters@elevenelemntsfdn.org

COMING SOON!

ELEVEN ELEMENTS
SERIES OF BOOKS

ALSO, BY ROBBY JOSHI, AIA

Featuring Maxilon 'Max' Renner and his
Team of Time Travelers
ELEVEN ELEMENTS
BOOK TWO: FIRE & FRESH AIR

ELEVEN ELEMENTS
BOOK THREE: SPACESHIP EARTH

ELEVEN ELEMENTS
BOOK FOUR: A MEANINGFUL LIFE

Robby Joshi, AIA, NCARB, is a State of Florida licensed architect and urban designer with 25+ years leading projects from concept to construction: townships, high-rises, healthcare, hospitality, tech campuses, data centers, and theme parks. He heads his practice serving multinational clients after working at Jacobs, HOK, and The Austin Company.

A lifelong sci-fi enthusiast, he is the author of the seven-volume Eleven Elements series, which explores humanity's survival through the lens of time travel and speculative social design. He lives in Florida with his family, where he balances architectural practice with both real-world and fictional world-building and blending with it some storytelling.

Author website: RobbyJoshi.com
Facebook: Eleven Elements Books
Website: ElevenElementsBooks.com
Email: robbyjoshi@elevenelementsfdn.org